The Water Man Legacy

TIDES OF TIME, Volume 1

GERARD DUNMOORE

Published by Green Man Books, 2023.

The Water Man Legacy is a work of fiction inspired by real historical events. All dialogue in this story as well as all the characters, excepting certain real historical figures, are products of the author's imagination and should not be construed as anything more than that. Any events or dialogue involving such historical figures are fictional and are in no way intended to depict real incidents. Any resemblance to actual persons is entirely coincidental.

1
Water Takes Many Lives

The woman's drenched body lay limp on the grass, her lips an ashen-blue. Sweeping strands of viscid black hair half-covered her pallid face. The burst of a siren announced the arrival of an ambulance.

Her life had meant everything to him, all his promises, all his regrets, and she had only come here today because he had asked her to. They lifted her onto the stretcher and into the ambulance.

'C'est vous qui avez appelé les urgences, monsieur?'

'Oué … oui,' said Declan, lips trembling, tears welling.

Another man's voice, a walkie-talkie, Velcro and zippers and clicking metal tubes. The siren again and blue lights. He watched the ambulance disappear along the road and felt a deep ache in his heart – that agonizing grief associated with only the most devastating of traumas – the loss of a loved one.

And as abruptly as that, she was gone.

2
Olivier Declan O'Leary: 2015

The combination of rural Brittany's clear roads with her endless panoramic delights can sometimes tempt the less cautious driver to lower his guard. Without so much as a glance over his shoulder, the driver of a tractor pulled out in front of the white, mark 1 Audi TT. The brake-pedal juddered violently the instant tyres touched turf. The rear end veered uncontrollably across the verge, and as the car began to spin, Declan stiffened his grip on the wheel and began to pray.

Sat at his desk just two months earlier in mid-June – he couldn't even remember the date, but at 8:15 it had been, going through his mail he was, on a Friday. His phone had rung. The boss, something about:

Sorry you weren't told in person – it came from head office – just following orders – cuts had to be made – will write you a great reference – stay in touch – if there are any other openings, you'll be the first to know – blah, blah, blah.

So it was for real. Twelve years Declan had been with O'Dell–IT Inc.

A dark-haired young woman, basket in arm, had been tracing her way along a narrow track, picking blackberries, when Declan finally skidded to a halt. Hearing the noise, she ran out to see what had happened. He felt a total jerk, and as he slowly steered the car from the grass verge back towards the road, he looked over at her and their eyes met. Some call it fate, others simply put it down to coincidence, but Declan, unbeknown to him, had just set eyes on the face of the woman who would influence the next seventy-two hours of his life in a way that nobody could ever have predicted.

There had been three letters in his mailbox – all bad news. There were his redundancy notice and two others concerning personal matters: another refusal from the record producer for his band's latest recording, and a letter from a solicitor's office in Dublin. The solicitor had forwarded an envelope from a French notary based in a town called Carhaix in Brittany, France.

Declan was his middle name and the one he used in Ireland. Brought up in the heart of Brittany until the age of five, he was the son of an Irish trawlerman. His Breton mother was the only child of a miller. He never referred to himself as Olivier at home in Ireland: not since that scurrilous first day at school, aged just five – the *posh* little French kid.

For now he was back in Brittany and Olivier would suit him just fine. At nineteen, on stage at Trinity College, Dublin, a silent guitar caused by a faulty jack-lead, had made his whole life seem to collapse around him. And then there had been that time when, aged just twenty-four, his parents failed to return home from a New Year's Eve party. That night his whole life really had collapsed and if his career had ever taken a blip, it was during those short weeks that followed; he had started using cocaine. That couldn't be the reason for being *let go* now surely? His boss was the one who'd offered him his first line:

'You look shattered, Declan – dead on your feet, man. Have you prepared for this presentation? It's a big client.'

'I've barely slept since the funeral. I've done the homework and the PowerPoint's good. I know exactly what I have to say; I just can't keep my eyes open.'

'You should try snorting some of this angel dust; it'll pick you up and give you the edge. Really, Declan, trust me – it can be tough at the top.'

It was a time in his life when he could have seriously derailed, and it was only the meeting with the surgeon in the hospital that made him come to his senses that day. If he would agree to take care of his little sister, paralysed from the waist down from the car accident on that fateful night, then assuming her physiotherapy programme progressed well, she could leave the hospital in a matter of weeks. He had agreed to sign, but the surgeon had taken him to one side and asked him about his drug problem. Declan denied it instantly, but then broke down.

His sister, Isabelle Sinead O'Leary, just fourteen at the time, would have to go into care if he didn't agree to look after her. The surgeon, Dr Flaherty, would have none of it if Declan didn't also agree to participate in a detox program in a clinic just outside Limerick. It was in the second he saw his sister's smiling face look up from her wheelchair, he realised he had to react. He accepted the detox program and happily agreed to take care of Isabelle. After a walk in the gardens pushing her chair, after they'd both cried a lot together, he walked back to the car park alone. He picked up the contents of his dust-bag and emptied everything he had collected from his dealer that morning into the top of the privet hedge that bordered the newly tarmacked square.

The detox centre, run by a Sister O'Donnell, was set in an old mansion house just outside Limerick. Declan dutifully followed the six week program, but he already knew when he left Isabelle and drove away from the hospital that day, he would never, ever touch the bloody stuff again; he had too much to live for.

3
Déjà Vu

Declan's French grandmother's death certificate had been sent with the letter from the notary. Françoise Le Dour or Soazig, the Breton for Françoise, had died in the spring of the previous year. It had taken the authorities fourteen months to find him. The last time he had seen her had been almost ten years ago; he and Isabelle had been over for a week to celebrate her seventieth. Isabelle had talked of moving over there to live, and suggested they apply for their French id cards. Declan had gone along with it, but had never even bothered to return to the mairie in Langonnet to collect his. He had vowed to visit his grandmother again, though never had, and over time he just stopped thinking about her. *God, what an arse he was.*

He had contacted the notary's office to inform them he was in France and had spoken to a lovely woman on the phone, but when he went in to collect the door key, a prick in a suit hadn't even bothered to return the customary "bonjour".

Today, with the key in his pocket, he was off to visit his grandmother's mill and maybe even to stay there for a while, after all, he no longer had a job to go back to, he wasn't motivated to re-record, and Isabelle, who was very independent, also had her boyfriend Carl. Declan didn't like him much but Isabelle loved him and she seemed happy enough.

As he approached the village of La Trinité-Langonnet, he could see the spire of the old church and out of the blue, he decided to park up and have a reminiscent look inside. The ornate wooden carvings were beautifully painted and it astonished him just how well they had weathered the five centuries since their construction. Quietly and alone, he knelt down at a pew at the back of the church and said a prayer for his late grandmother, both his parents and finished

7

by asking God to watch out for Isabelle should anything happen to him. He opened his eyes, let them readjust to the light and stood up slowly, looking up as he did so, to the enormous and dominating carving of the Green Man's foliate face watching over his assembly.

He walked out of the entrance and back into the gardens where the cemetery had once been. He was looking at an illegible, lichen-covered, carved slab lying in the grass when the rain started. It only lasted five minutes but by God it poured. It fell in drops so big, they splatted noisily, stinging his skin as they obliterated under their own weight. As he ran for cover in the entrance to the church, he saw that he wasn't alone; linking arms with an older man, was the dark-haired woman. She looked at Declan and he smiled, but she didn't smile back. The man she was with was holding a white stick. There were a number of other cars in the car park now and Declan guessed that one of the cars must have belonged to her.

Returning to his car, he saw a rivulet of coloured oil pooling on top of a puddle, before it flowed away towards the drain. Someone had had an oil leak and Declan had parked just there over it. He had intended to stop for a coffee at the local bar opposite the church, but the woman's reaction and the look on her face had taken the wind right out of his sails. Instead, he set off up the road, not completely sure of where he was heading. Mindful of his earlier near-miss at the wheel, he pulled away gently, imagining she was with him, that she had smiled back and had accepted his offer of a lift. He drove sedately for the three-mile-run just before the turn-off to the town of Carhaix. As he approached the junction, he touched the breaks gently so as not to cause any discomfort to his imaginary passenger, but nothing happened. He pressed the pedal again and again and still nothing. He changed down a gear as fast as he could, and then pulled on the handbrake as he steered towards the verge. The car spun a half-turn and mud flew up around him. Gravel showered the bodywork and he could hear scraping. The car stopped, the engine stalled and Declan just sat there listening to his own breathing.

There were some scratches along the bodywork on the passenger side, but no dents. He was barely a hundred metres from where he had first seen the dark haired woman earlier that day, and he thought to himself what a good thing it was she had not been in the car beside him.

4
An Old Friend

The engine fired up first time, but he didn't plan going anywhere like that. Pulling out his iPhone, he checked the directory for the number of the garage in the village of La Trinité-Langonnet, where Albert, his late mother's best friend's son had his workshop. Albert took a second to recollect who Declan was, but turned up in his old, blue and white Renault Estafette breakdown truck within fifteen minutes of the call. Declan walked towards the driver's door, pressed the chrome button on the handle to open up for Albert, when suddenly the window shot down like a retracting guillotine.

'Don't touch anything,' said Albert. 'She's fragile.'

'Still running around in that old wreck, Albert?'

'My *old wreck* still drives, which is more than you can say for yours.'

Albert, now almost forty, hadn't aged much in the last ten years – flecks of grey here and there, but that was all. He stepped down from his truck and turned towards Declan.

'Ça va, mon ami?' he asked, reaching out for Declan's hand.

'Very well, Albert,' he lied, 'and you?'

It had been a decade since they had last seen each other. Despite the age gap of nearly six years and the fact that Declan had left Brittany aged only five, he and Albert had become good friends. For the fifteen years or so that followed the move to Ireland, he and Albert had met up every summer while Declan had spent the holidays at his grandmother's. Declan would catch up on local gossip, but he never talked about Ireland and Albert never asked.

Dipping down low over the bonnet, as if about to play a difficult snooker shot, Albert ran his fingers over the damaged paintwork and said,

'You were lucky, there's no depth to these scratches. What happened then?'

'That's a relief,' said Declan.

'So? What happened?'

'The brakes just failed,'

'Well, let's get her back to the garage and we'll see what went wrong.'

Albert reversed the Estafette onto the verge to line up with the Audi. He then lifted the ramps one by one and lowered them onto the grass. As he walked up one of the ramps onto the recovery platform, he said to Declan, without even looking back at him:

'It's sad that you never came back to see Soazig before she died.'

Declan felt a dry lump form in his throat and, unsure of what his voice would sound like, didn't even dare to reply. Albert put on thick suede gloves before unhooking a snatch block from the electric winch and pressing on the steel cable release-button. As the cable reeled off, he pulled it free to make sure it didn't get wrapped around itself.

'Here,' he said to Declan waving the snatch block in his hand, 'pull this out would you?'

Declan hopped onto the recovery platform, stepped towards Albert, and holding it firmly in one hand, he began to walk back down the platform towards the ramps. He hesitated for a second to see where to attach it.

'Keep pulling,' yelled Albert over the noise of the engine and winch.

A gloved hand touched his shoulder and Declan looked up from his reverie.

'We'll run her back to my garage and then we'll go and have a cold beer at the bar – catch up on old times,' suggested Albert smiling.

'That sounds like an excellent idea.'

For the next five minutes, Albert performed his role of vehicle recovery mechanic, while Declan stood there in silence just watching. The front wheels rolled up the ramps and a combination of the cable idling its way across the winch and the back end of the Estafette shifting under the strain, all contributed to a perfect landing.

Despite his second *near death experience* on the same road, Declan was mildly amused. As he had walked around to the passenger side of the Estafette, he saw that Albert had slipped around from the front and was already holding the door open for him. To watch Albert fall so comfortably into his roll of a professional with his client brought a smile to his face.

The car loaded up, they drove back to La Trinité. The high-revving engine and the rattlings – an unimaginable number of them – prevented any conversation.

Albert wasn't in the slightest hurry to look at Declan's car; he drove straight into his hangar, jumped quickly out of the recovery truck and almost as quickly out of his overalls.

'Let's go and celebrate your return shall we?' said Albert, his head barely visible above the roof of an old Peugeot 405 – one of many dodgy-looking run-arounds that littered his forecourt. 'Tu viens?'

The bar hadn't changed. Ever. Still the same décor, or lack of it. Worn formica tables with old wooden benches that creaked and groaned through years of misuse and abuse. It didn't seem to matter so long as the beer was good. A tractor rumbled past. Everybody waved. The tractor rumbled back. Everybody waved. Hay time, wheat harvest time, potato time, then firewood time and cider-apple time – here, people lived their seasons.

'Qui veut des patates? J'en ai trop,' announced Amédée, pulling up outside the bar – his Renault 4 weighted down so much, he worried that if nobody would take any potatoes from him, the tyres, already hot from rubbing on the undersides of the wheelarches, would catch fire, and he didn't know if he would make it home.

They sat there, the two of them, ordering round after round of cold beer and Declan began to feel that he was supposed to be doing something else.

Jean-Yves, a local butcher, walked into the bar. Not impressed, he said to Albert:

'C'est l'heure de l'apéro et tu bois de la bière?' *Aperitif time and you're drinking beer?*

Albert ordered three whiskies, but Jean-Yves said he couldn't end his working day without at least a quick half of Coreff – the local ale.

'Phew, that's better,' he said and sat down to join them.

Declan woke up in a dim room. He wasn't alone for he could hear people talking.

'Il se lève. Je t'avais dit qu'il n'est pas mort.' Declan heard Albert laughing in the room and a woman's voice saying that she knew he wasn't dead because dead people don't snore.

He sat up slowly, his head pounding. He began remembering bits of the previous afternoon and not so many bits of the evening. He recognised the voice of a man called Philippe who was explaining that when he was an assistant *croque mort*, he had personally heard a dead guy snore. Albert's wife, Monique, was a nurse and she reckoned it was nonsense. She claimed it must have been all the gases coming out. Croque mort in French is the colloquial name given to an undertaker. The name means literally, *bite dead* and allegedly comes from an old trick of the trade, namely, that before any preparation of the body began, somebody would bite down on a big toe of the dead person to make sure they really were dead. Declan, feeling as he did, couldn't cope with any more of this conversation so he stood up from Albert's sofa and quickly headed for the toilet. Philippe said his goodbyes and after Monique had served him his second cup of fresh-ground coffee, Declan started to feel a little better.

'I should have stayed on the beer; I'd feel a whole lot better this morning if I hadn't touched the whisky.'

'What I have to show you, Olivier, won't make you feel any better. I had a look at your car. I put her up on the ramps this morning: bad news I'm afraid.'

'Why? Is there some serious damage?'

'Best you come and see for yourself,' said Albert, ominously.

As they left the living room to go and look at his car, Albert stopped by the front door to kick off his slippers and put on his steel toecaps; Monique was a stickler for tidiness and Albert was a well-trained husband. They walked across the garage forecourt, past a whole peck of more or less abandoned-looking vehicles, before arriving at the enormous sliding corrugated metal doors of Albert's oily-smelling, diesel-soaked workshop.

Declan looked around at what seemed to him to be total chaos and he could understand why Monique was so insistent on the changing of footwear. Down one side of the garage was a sprawling workbench: a wheel hub in a vice, angle iron clamped ready for welding, silhouette tool-boards showing most things out of place, an old oil drum marked ELF, and a pile of old car batteries. This was not his first visit and not much had changed. Albert had his way, always able to lay his hands on a spring, a spare filter, a gasket, a windscreen wiper in better condition than the one that it was replacing, or fan belt that no other garage would stock. Albert would be able to lay his hands on parts in an instant; things he hadn't seen in years. Declan often marvelled at the capacity of the human brain compared to the computers he worked with. Order out of chaos was Albert's system, and a system it certainly was.

'Tu viens voir ou quoi, Olivier?' asked Albert from the other side of the garage. *You coming to look or what?* Joining Albert under the car ramp, he followed the light of an inspection lamp. Albert cleared his throat:

'The problem here, Olivier, is far worse than I thought,' he said, and shining the lamp up under the car's chassis behind the front offside wheel, he pointed a finger to a metal conduit. 'Someone has cut through your hydraulic brake line. Probably with something like this.' Albert held up a pair of bolt croppers for Declan to see. 'This was an act of sabotage. Somebody might as well have been trying to kill you, Olivier.'

'I think I need a drink,' said Declan. 'You know, hair of the dog and all that.'

'Bloody good idea,' agreed Albert. 'Listen here though,' he whispered, 'I think it would be wise to keep this to ourselves until you've spoken to the police. We're Sunday today. I'd go in to make a formal complaint at the gendarmerie tomorrow if I were you; they'll not appreciate being disturbed on a Sunday.'

Back in the kitchen, Monique watched as Albert poured two whiskies. She said nothing at all and Declan guessed that she knew full well what Albert had discovered.

As Declan recalled the events of the previous day, he remembered seeing the dark-haired woman at the church and pretending she was with him in the car. And then he remembered the rivulet of oil in the car park before he drove off after the rain had stopped. That's where they'd done it. When he was parked up by the church; that's where they had sabotaged his brakes. He had seen no one else except the woman with the blind man.

'Here's that drink you ordered,' said Albert, handing over a large whisky. 'Who could have done this?' Declan wished it was a cold beer rather than a whisky, but chose to say nothing.

'I've thought about that,' he replied, struggling to hold down the mouthful he had just swallowed. 'There were two people in the car park who arrived after me: a man and a woman. They were together and she must have been driving, because the man was blind. But there was also another car there.' He polished off the remains of his glass and said to Albert, trying to make light of the situation, as he slid his glass across the table:

'Same again, squire, if you would be so kind.'

Albert moved the single malt bottle an inch or two in Declan's direction and gestured to him to help himself.

'The question that really gets me, my friend, is not, who *could* have done this, rather, who *would* have done this?' said Declan, frowning. 'I wouldn't have the faintest idea.' Albert looked very glum.

'You can stay here of course. You know that,' he said, helpfully.

'Thanks. That's very kind, but I think I'm going to wander down to Grandma's mill and have a little look around. I think it'll be safe there; the place is empty and I've been thinking of staying on here for a bit anyway. I've got a couple of bottles of red wine, some bread and some pâté in the boot of the car: they won't keep forever. Why don't you come down with me and we can have a bit of a light lunch together?'

'I can't today,' said Albert. 'I've promised to fix Marcel's tractor and later I'm going round to Philippe's to try and sort out his sit-on mower. Labour Zul, labour nul,' added Albert quickly to see if Declan would be able to understand the Breton phrase.

'Sunday work, worthless work,' Declan said proudly.

'If you're sure you want to stay on at the mill,' said Albert, 'I'll come round and see you mid-morning tomorrow and we'll go to the police together – some moral support, eh?'

5
The Abduction

Declan heard a noise. What it was he wasn't quite sure but it sounded like birds singing. His head was thumping and he struggled to open his eyes. Where the hell was he? Oh God, his head hurt and his whole body felt stiff and sore. There were two empty bottles of red wine on the table and only one glass. He awoke with a blinding hang-over to find himself at the table in Mamie Le Dour's old kitchen in the mill; he was on his own. Dehydrated and desperate for a drink of water, he slowly unfolded himself from the old bench with its long chestnut-plank table, and headed for the brass tap above the sink of the scullery. The little light there was, came through the gap between the faded-blue shutters and the granite surround of the window, but it seemed blinding to Declan who had to cover his face with his hands to allow only the thinnest cracks of light through his closed fingers to view the room.

Having retrieved a large soup bowl from the cupboard on the wall, left of the sink, he stood leaning all his weight onto the kitchen unit. Carefully and slowly he lowered the bowl under the tap and filled it with water. Putting the bowl to his lips he took a sip and then gripping it tightly to his mouth, he drained it. God that felt good. Leaning forward and placing the bowl on the draining board, he turned the tap to half-throttle and bent right down to drink from his cupped hands as they filled from the crystal clear column of falling water.

Shortly afterwards, settled once again on the bench at the kitchen table, he crossed his arms on the planked tabletop and nestled his face into the crook of his elbow, wishing he could lay his hands on some paracetamol. Mamie Le Dour used to mix up some strange pain-killer drink using the bark from "haleg" or "saule"

– willow trees in English. She'd given him some once when he had banged his knee falling out of the hole in the wall. His mother and father had sworn by this potion, claiming that it was better than any pills. He had been playing hide-and-seek and climbed into the niche in the wall where Mamie used to bake her bread. The morning after her bread-baking days, the stone oven was still warm and he used to sit on a stool with his back tight up against the granite and wonder how far back the little cave-like opening went beyond the wall. On the day when he had fallen out of the hole, his grandmother had seen him hiding in there and ordered him out at once – "tout de suite", she had said. He had tried to come out shoulders first, had seen the black soot all over his hands and arms and then suddenly slipped from the entrance of the bread oven, banging his knee on the hearth on the way down. As Declan sat there reminiscing, he began to drift off to sleep and images of his grandmother came back to him. Her aprons, sometimes flowery, sometimes a checkered pattern, were always clean. She was forever storing things away in jars, high up on shelves or in pots under the sink. Sometimes it was food, jams or pickles, sometimes seeds or roots or useful little bits of thread or, well anything really. Once she had scolded him when he watched her from behind the washstand. She hadn't seen him standing there, although he wasn't really hiding. He had been imagining his escape from a sort of maze made of curtain-lined walls; his curtains, in reality, being tea towels that Mamie had draped over the clotheshorse to dry. As he stood there in silence and watched, Mamie had locked the kitchen door behind her and reached deep into the bread oven with what looked like a giant wooden lollipop, which she withdrew making a reverse hand-over-hand action along the wooden pole-like shank. As the pole came out towards the entrance of the oven, Declan had seen a wooden chest appear in the opening in the wall.

'Il y a du trésor là dedans, Mamie?' he'd asked. She spun around so fast with a look of terror in her eyes that he had never seen in anyone before or since.

'Il n'y a absolument rien dedans,' she had screamed at him, 'et de toute façon, ça te regarde pas.' *Not treasure, nothing at all and none of your business.* And then she'd sent him off to bed.

A short while later, Mamie had come up to his room to give him a great big hug and say she was sorry to have shouted. Then she gave him a huge chunk of gooey Breton cake with prunes in it and asked if he wanted to walk to the fountain with her. He had taken the cake and agreed to the walk.

He loved that fountain. It was odd in a way, but he had always felt drawn to it. The old granite wall, built centuries earlier, surrounded a natural spring. The granite ledge surrounding it also served as seating, and it was rumoured to be a mystical fountain which had hosted many pagan ceremonies. Whatever the case, what was magnificent about it was its form; it was in the shape of a keyhole. Similar old fountains could be found all over Brittany, but this one was special, and as Declan drifted off even deeper into his dream, he was walking along with Mamie, holding her hand and looking up at the hedgerows as she pointed out different wild flowers and herbs. He could smell the wild honeysuckle and Mamie pinched a flower off the climber and handed it to him. He placed the tip into his mouth and sucked out the honey-like dew that was always inside. Some of the berries she pointed out to him tasted bitter, but once served up on one of Mamie's crêpes as a dessert, they all tasted so rich and wonderful. "That's fit for a pagan prince," she would say, with a gleam of satisfaction in her eyes. Then, as they sat down together on a part of the stone-bench surround, Mamie began to tell him about the fountain, why it had been hidden for centuries and why it was still a secret.

Declan was awakened abruptly and violently. His cheekbone smashed against the chestnut table as he felt his hands being wrenched behind his back so fast and firmly that he had no time to react. His instinct was to lift his head up and hold his face in his hands, but both wrists had been bound tightly behind him with horrifying speed. As he looked up, Declan saw the masked face of a man in front of him and he suddenly felt the cold terror of death enter his entire body. He began to whimper and moan, unable to form any proper words. A sack was pulled down over his head and as Mamie's kitchen went dark, he screamed out as loudly as he could. As he screamed he felt what seemed like a hammer blow to the side of his head, sending a deafening thud penetrating straight through his skull and blackness followed instantly.

He was reawakened into his nightmare by the jerking and bumping as he lay across the corrugated metal floor of a vehicle travelling at low speed on what must have been a very rough track. His head thumped ten times worse than any hangover and his first reaction was to lie there and try to wriggle in such a way as to align his body with the ridges on the vehicle's metal floor. He did this partly to stop the metal floor digging into his ribs and partly to support his head to prevent it from swaying as it followed the action of the vehicle on the bumpy track. He tried to move and found that his hands were still bound and that now his ankles were too. As he remembered the attack that awoke him in Mamie's kitchen, he thought of the seconds before his head had been covered. He couldn't work out if his head still had a sack over it and decided finally that it must have, not just because his eyes would not adjust at all to the darkness, but also because he could hear only very muffled voices over tyres on gravel and the engine noise. Declan had always prided himself on his hearing and as a boy, he used to pretend to have a bionic ear. His music teacher told him he had the gift of perfect pitch. He was sure he could hear his sister's hamster's breathing at

night when it stopped running in its wheel and nobody, even at
school, could whisper quietly enough to stop Declan from hearing
everything they said if he cared to listen. Sometimes they tested him
and he was always right, and in the end his school mates gave in. In
his early teens, some of the older boys would even give him money
to tell them what two girls were whispering about to each other, but
sometimes Declan had had to lie to avoid being thumped. Right now
he could hear so little of this conversation that he couldn't even work
out if they were both men or if one was a woman.

After what must have been about four or five minutes the vehicle
stopped, and now he could hear the voices clearly. There were three
of them, all men and all talking in French.

'Get him out, take him around the back and get him tied up in
a chair,' said one of the men very matter-of-factly. 'He will talk first,
then you two can have him.'

It's a very strange thing fear, thought Declan to himself. Still
absolutely terrified, but not facing instant death anymore. He now
overheard three, no four things that meant he could, just maybe,
work out some deal or even escape his captors. Though he feared
them immensely, these were not IRA. Declan who had had no
dealings whatsoever with the Republican Army nor ever even heard a
bomb go off in his life, though Christ knows he'd read enough about
them, was at first, unable to understand why he felt a deep, gut-feel
relief about what he had just overheard. At school everybody knew
from the papers and television, that bombing was a non-negotiable
attack and that even James Bond would never have been able to
worm his way out of a knee-capping. But these guys had just let
him know that there were three of them; he could understand their
language; two of them were going to get him out of this vehicle and
not kill him immediately and all because the one whose voice he had
heard most, needed something that Declan supposedly knew about.
That part very much baffled him.

First, the two front doors of the vehicle were slammed shut almost simultaneously, then another vehicle door opened and closed and a car drove away. There must have been more than one approach to this place, because the vehicle, an electric engine and therefore probably a small car, went off in a direction opposite to the one in which they had arrived. Another door opened, then another and Declan felt the corrugated floor on which he was lying, sway to one side as if someone had climbed in. Someone grabbed his ankles and jerked him onto his back as they pulled him towards the rear of the vehicle. He knew it was daylight because he could make out part of the tight black weave of the cloth sack they had put over his head. He tried to act as best he could to be a man asleep, but these guys were no fools.

'Is the bastard still unconscious?' asked one man. Declan thought he was acting pretty well, but suddenly he was pulled to his feet and shoved.

'When you see the fuckers brace themselves for the fall, you know they're conscious, Big Boy,' replied the other man.

Declan hit the floor hard and heard the air wheeze out of his lungs. He had braced himself against banging his head, yet instead had hit the gravel with his entire flank.

'Qu'est-ce que tu veux, connard?' Declan yelled. *What do you want, asshole?*

He felt a boot straight to his stomach and he was winded instantly. Again somebody grabbed his ankles and started dragging him across the gravel and suddenly his bottom hit a step. It jarred his whole body.

'Give me a hand lifting the fucker up the steps then. Come on.' Declan heard one of the men say and by the voice, this one was Big Boy.

Declan was lifted up what seemed to be four quite long steps before being put down abruptly or rather dropped to the floor by both men at the same time. He felt bruised all over, but somehow he knew this was just the beginning.

'Give me the fucking keys before anyone sees us, you dick!'

Declan heard keys being tossed over and a door being opened rapidly. The handle had been levered down, but not quite enough so that the catch on the lock just caught the metal plate into which it fitted. This caused a noise that was instantly familiar to Declan: that short-lived, almost unperceivable vibrating of plate glass all across a shop front.

'Give me back the keys then, Big Boy.'

'We're gonna get him in and lock the fucking door first, you tosser.'

'Give me the keys; the Boss doesn't want you fucking up again.'

Declan was dragged through the door, but as he was dragged, he tried to shuffle his body to catch the glass with his shoes so as to cause the glass to vibrate and maybe even crack – that would attract attention to the outside world – these men were obviously on their guard and didn't want to be seen. The glass shop-front vibrated loudly and, for an instant, Declan was quite pleased with himself.

'He did that deliberately. He's being difficult, just club him again. Do you want to be tyin' him to a chair with him squirmin' around like that? I fucking sure as hell don't.'

Declan felt that hammer-hit again and didn't quite complete his thoughts of regret. Blackness.

He awoke again, still in darkness and could feel he was sat in a chair. His head was so sore, he was surprised he could think at all. It was not so much a throbbing anymore for the pain was constant, and he began to worry about possible brain damage. He could feel his hands strapped to the back of the chair legs and his ankles too were bound to the legs at the front. He sat in silence and listened.

In a sudden but purposeful rush, a door was flung open and Declan heard the men walk into the room. Again they were speaking in French; these were the same guys.

'Vous avez demandé s'il veut boire quelque chose, les gars?' asked the boss man. *Have you asked him if he wants a drink, guys?*

Declan heard the button of an electric kettle being switched on and then, a short time later, the telltale brushes-on-a-symbol sound that water makes when it is just beginning to boil.

'Would you like a coffee, Olivier?' asked the boss man, directly.

Declan couldn't quite believe what he was hearing. This was a normal question for a normal situation, but here, like this, the man was mad. Declan, totally unsure how to answer, lifted his head slightly so as to show a sign of life, to acknowledge the question at least, so as not to provoke, to gain some time, something, anything. But in that flash of thought, Declan felt the kettle of scalding water being poured over the upper part of his right leg and he screamed out in agonizing pain. It was so unbearable that all Declan wanted to do was to pour cold water over the burn. In this sheer frenzy of torture, he had an image for a second of sitting in the fountain to cool off his leg. He screamed out but was punched hard in the face on the already sore cheekbone. He cried out again and was thumped again, this time on the jaw and he felt himself bite deep into his tongue.

Some forms of pain dissipate: not burns, they get worse before they get better. Declan gritted his teeth in an attempt to control his hyperventilating and moaned as quietly as possible; rocking the upper part of his body backwards and forwards on his seat in excruciating pain. He was going to be quiet for these men – keep them calm, but he could still hear his own whimpering. Through his trembling lips, he could feel himself dribbling a thick salty mix of blood and saliva. A moment later his hood was ripped from his head and Declan felt older wounds open up again as the clotted blood still joined to the cloth was torn away from his face and scalp. In front of him were three men in black balaclavas with eye and mouth holes. The middle one of the three men spoke up:

'If you talk, you will live. Do you understand me, Olivier?' the boss man asked. Declan tried to say yes but couldn't form the word quickly enough.

'Bag him,' ordered the boss.

Declan hadn't been paying enough attention. The man on the right had slipped around behind him. Out of the blue, the third man, the tallest, the one on the left, punched Declan hard in the chest and he exhaled through the impact of the shock. At the same instant, the man who had moved behind him, thrust a plastic bag straight over the top of his head. As he tried hurriedly to breathe in, the plastic, now stretched tightly over his wide-open mouth, sunk in like the seals on Mamie's cooled down jars of homemade confiture. Declan's chest heaved up and down but to no avail. He had no idea how long this lasted, for he began to see red in front of his eyes and then just brightness and then stillness and ...

Ahh, suck, intake, AIR, and bright light.

'Jesus,' screamed Declan and he breathed in again. And again, and again.

Finally, his heaving chest and panting began to calm and the pain returned sharply to his leg.

'If you talk you'll live,' the boss man repeated, this time in an almost friendly tone. 'Do you understand French, Olivier?

'Ou ... ou ... oui,' he replied.

'You have some information which you are going to give me, Olivier,' stated the boss. 'You're okay with that?'

'Yes,' said Declan, having absolutely no idea what the man was talking about.

'Where is it kept, this family secret of yours?' probed the boss.

'Which one?' replied Declan, who wanted to add that there were lots, but very quickly thought better of it.

'Don't be fucking funny,' said the plastic bag man, raising a black rubbery-looking cosh to his shoulder.

'Not now,' said the boss to the bag-balaclava, raising his hand up in a calm, but authoritative protest.

In that instant, Declan saw something that caught his eye. He had seen it somewhere before, but where? The cosh-balaclava man was wearing a watch, a Smiths Deluxe watch on the wrist of his right arm. The watch was silver and had an ivory face. *What was a Frenchman doing wearing an English antique watch?* Somewhat out of place. Declan could not recall this déjà-vu clearly enough to remember where exactly it had been that he had seen the watch, or one like it, but he knew that he had thought it out of place there too.

'Your parents must have told you, Olivier, at least your mother. You know exactly what I'm talking about,' said Boss Balaclava.

'Both my parents are dead,' said Declan.

'We know that, Olivier,' said the boss man and Declan began to wonder who the, "we" was referring to.

'I just mean, monsieur,' said Declan, as politely as he could manage, 'that my parents told me nothing of a family secret, sir. Nothing that strikes me as important. Really, truly, monsieur.' The boss man's voice rose suddenly and he shouted at Declan waving a warning fist:

'If you think playing games is going to work with me, boy, let me explain again, talk and you will live, don't, and you *will* die. How do you want to die, Olivier, have you thought about that? You can burn to death,' he screamed, close up in Declan's face, pointing a finger vaguely in the direction of the very tall balaclava on Declan's left who had momentarily walked away to fetch the electric kettle, 'or you can suffocate.' And with this, Boss Balaclava gave a sign with his hand to Smiths Watch Cosh Balaclava, who rustled his plastic bag and grinned through his mouth hole. 'Dry-drowning they tell me it's called,' said Boss Balaclava, quietly and calmly now, as if Declan might have a genuine interest in such chit-chat. 'It can last for hours. My colleague here loves playing that, drowning then reanimating. And when he gets bored, he finishes off his victims using one of those polyurethane expansive foam cans by sticking the nozzle up a nostril. Then they sure as hell don't fucking talk no more,' his voice reaching a screaming crescendo at the end.

'Honestly, they told me nothing like that, monsieur, or I would just tell you, I swear.'

'Somebody must have done,' yelled Boss Balaclava. 'Grandparents? Is that it? Was the old cow right? He knows something and I'll get it out of him or he's of no use to us alive, guys!' concluded Boss Balaclava. As he signalled them all to leave the room, he motioned to the other men to hood Declan and once again, the room went black. The door slammed shut and a deadbolt was slid in place.

He listened carefully trying to make sure he was on his own. The burning pain on the top of his right leg was numbing slowly, but the burning was starting underneath by the seat now, and once again he could do nothing about it. He gritted his teeth together and tried to concentrate on his situation.

The boss man had said, "If you talk you'll live". What if he couldn't talk, what if he knew nothing. "He knows something or he's no use to us alive," he'd said. Was that to scare him? No. There was no need for that; they all knew he was scared witless already. Wondering what all this meant, he couldn't seem to rationalise properly. Then he remembered what had been said outside, while he was still tied up in the van. The boss man had said, "Get him out, take him around the back and get him tied up in a chair". And then Boss Balaclava had added, "He will talk first, and then you two can have him." Declan realised then, these men had never had any intentions of letting him out of here alive. He had to think.

Where was he? All he knew was that he was a prisoner in a room which he had been able to see just briefly. There seemed to have been a kitchen area in the corner behind and to the left of Boss Balaclava. Looking from there to the left and following the wall around, he had seen a table, no chairs other than the one he himself was sat on. Declan was now certain he had seen a fridge in the corner – maybe there was a freezer and he could somehow get some ice on his leg. He had also seen what might have been a sofa or a mattress to his right and Smiths Watch Cosh Balaclava had had to manoeuvre carefully around Declan's right side to get behind him with the plastic bag. There had been a single light bulb, but it had not been switched on so therefore there must have been at least one window and it must still be daylight. He had no idea how long he had been unconscious this last time. Although still chair-bound he tried to stand up on his tiptoes. As he did so, he thought he felt some of the skin on his upper right leg tear and peel away with his trousers. He screamed out and collapsed to the floor in a contorted pile, unable to move.

He desperately tried to calm down his breathing so as to listen for any noise. He feared he had made so much noise that the men would return and hurt him some more. As he listened, Declan heard a voice. It was Boss Balaclava:

'One of you go and see what he's doing, would you? Not you; I don't want him knocked unconscious again – not now.'

The door opened and footsteps walked towards him. This man had been on his left – this man was big and he lifted Declan and his chair back upright with virtually no effort at all. As he sat upright again, he noticed that his hood was not completely over his face anymore and he could see into his own lap, a metre, say, to the left and nearly two metres to the right. The big balaclava grabbed at his hood and yanked it down hard, foiling any plans that he could have made for an escape. The feet walked away, the door was closed, the deadbolt slid across and once again there was silence, nearly. Declan heard the voices again – one man saying:

'He'd fallen over in his chair.'

'Go in every twenty minutes from now on if you have to, I don't want him getting any sleep. I'll be back in about four hours, it'll be dark and we'll deal with him then. And you, don't you bloody hit him anymore, you got that? You'll have your fun and games tonight.'

Declan had seen cable ties round his wrists. He would never be able to snap those. He'd also seen that it was a mattress on the floor and not a sofa. That must be why they had tied him to the chair, so he couldn't sleep on the mattress. He assumed that sleep deprivation was just another part of their torture. He had also seen a small but chunky-looking, cast-iron wall-mounted radiator next to the mattress. So this building was pretty old if the central heating still used those old cast-iron rads. He wondered where they could have taken him.

As he sat and winced through the pain, Declan began to analyse what he could do. He could probably manage to edge his chair around the room instead of trying to stand up and walk, but how that could help him he couldn't really fathom. There was no way he could tear through the cable ties, no he'd have to cut through them and for that he'd need a knife and free hands. Then out of the blue he had an idea. He visualised the chair to which he was bound and thought that although he could never snap the cable ties, he may be able to break the wooden rungs on the chair. The cable ties round his ankles had been tied to the chair legs above the cross rungs preventing him from simply tilting the chair backwards and sliding the ties under the chair legs. But to Declan, the weak spot seemed to be this rung, this wooden dowel halfway down, which held the two legs together. He pictured himself trying to snap it through with a good karate kick and he could easily imagine it giving in to that amount of physical force. The problem was that he would need a leg free already in order to be able to deliver such a powerful, wood-snapping kick.

Declan thought of using his weight to land on something, maybe a couple of house bricks, with the wooden dowel straddling the bricks so that his weight would split the spindle of wood. And then he remembered the radiator. He had not in fact even seen the radiator clearly; it was only the feed pipe from the bottom end of the cast iron block that he had seen – just before it disappeared into the wall. Now if the radiator fitting was higher than the dowel joining the two legs, then he might be able to lift himself up enough to use his weight to snap the wood. And with the dowel broken in half, he could possibly manage to slip the cable tie over the bottom of the chair leg. There was a problem here. Firstly, Declan had no idea where the radiator was in relation to him, and secondly, he wasn't sure that he could get there without falling over again. He sat quietly for a few moments and then tried to move himself and his chair in a scuttling movement: lift and drag, lift and drag. In this way, he only used his tiptoes, calf muscles and ankles and not his thighs. He had moved what he thought must be about a foot when he heard the door go again and he froze. The twenty minutes were obviously up and Declan lifted his head to indicate a sign of life and consciousness. The balaclava didn't enter the room, but did an about turn and slammed the door shut immediately behind him and slid the deadbolt in place.

Just a few minutes later, Declan felt his leg touch the wall and he began to edge his way along it to find the radiator. His chair jammed on something hard and it occurred to Declan suddenly that he might not be alone in the room. What if there was someone there in the room with him watching him trying to break the chair. Or what if there was a CCTV camera in the room? He froze to listen for someone else's breathing but his own breathing had become so loud and wheezy that he decided he couldn't really be certain. If the other person was breathing in unison with him, then he would not hear a thing. Declan changed the pace and depth of his breathing, beginning to hold his breath for varying amounts of time in order to catch the other guy out but heard nothing whatsoever.

Then he panicked. He heard footsteps coming towards the door and he was no longer in the same place near the middle of the room. He had to get back but had a mere second or two. He began to push with his feet in a reverse movement to the way in which he had worked his way to the wall and radiator, but discovered that although he could pull the chair with his weight on it, he could not push it against the lino. As he heard the bolt being slid across, he pushed as hard as he could with his feet, trying to tip his chair over for a second time and he braced himself for the agonising pain he knew he was about to endure. A moment later he heard the door open, he hit the floor and screamed out in agony. He didn't hear the footsteps approach him.

'Tu es bête, mec,' said the voice. 'Pourquoi tu te fais ça?' *You're stupid, man. Why do you do that to yourself?*

He did not feel stupid, his plan had worked; the man, Big Boy, grabbing his chair again to stand him swiftly upright once more, had no notion that Declan had been moving around the room.

'I like you screaming like that, Olivier,' said Big Boy. 'The dry-drown is boring on its own 'cause you can't hear the suffering. With boiling water, you can choose exactly where to hurt a man; feet are good, surprisingly, arms, head, balls too, but eyes are the best, 'cause you can watch 'em poach like eggs and the guy can't even fucking cry.' The door slammed shut again and the bolt was slid across.

If they were watching him on camera, they would not have to keep coming in to check on him, he deduced. He heard no one else breathing in the room with him. He had to get out. He edged his way to the radiator and was pleased that he found it straight away.

He rocked forward and angled his chair to hook the dowel over the pipe-fitting and gently lowered himself down to check he was straddling the pipe with the dowel at the right height. He was sitting on quite a tilt, so this plan could work. In absolute desperation, he raised himself up as high as he could, while leaning against the wall and radiator to help keep his balance. Then he thrust himself down with all the strength he could muster and tried to cause his body to fall like deadweight. The dowel did not give, but he heard it crack and so he repeated the sequence again and hearing the wood splinter, he found himself sitting bolt upright. His plan so far had worked and what is more, it had taken him barely five minutes. He shuffled around quickly and began to work on the other side of the chair. Within two minutes, both reinforcing spindles were broken. He made another mental time check – another ten minutes before his next visit.

He tried to stand up slowly, still leaning against the wall and found his left ankle sliding almost free of the chair leg, but it was just catching on something. He pushed as hard as he could and felt the cable tie flip over the bottom of the left chair leg; his trousers had been riding up his calf muscle and as his foot pulled free, he could feel his trouser leg drop again to around his shoe. His right leg, however, would not follow. The wooden dowel must have split in the middle and was still preventing the cable tie from sliding over the chair to free his right leg. Then he heard the footsteps again and as quickly as he possibly could, he crabbed-walked his chair back to what he estimated would be the middle of the room and adjusted his position to face the direction from where the footsteps came. His movements were far more rapid now with one leg free and the adrenalin rushing through his body, although he was not conscious of it, was numbing the edge off the worst of his pain. The bolt was slid across, the door opened and Declan looked up, still hooded, in the direction of the door. He assumed it was Big Boy. The same routine; an about-turn, the door slammed, bolt across, a few steps, and silence. He was on his own again.

The problem he now faced was that the second dowel had broken in the middle and he would not be able to free his other leg. Immediately, sensing fear and urgency, Declan began to move again in the direction of the radiator and was really pleased with his speed until he caught the corner of the back right leg of his chair on the edge of the mattress. He keeled over in a heap fighting as hard as he could not to scream out again. The mattress had cushioned the blow, but he could not work out how to get himself upright again. He began to twist his neck lifting his head to push the hood up.

Although it had only been about two minutes since Big Boy had left the room, he had to move quickly now, for he could not allow himself to be caught in this predicament: he had to get out of there.

With his hood raised, he could now see his right flank and part of the chair leg. He had been right; the spindle of wood had snapped in the middle. He also noticed his hand was tied to the leg beneath the seat so he could reach down and pull at the splintered spindle. He gripped it tightly and began to pull. It surprised him just how easily it came out and he was then able to reach right down as if touching his toes and slip his wrist over the bottom of the rear chair leg. He felt a surge of excitement rush through him: left leg free, right arm free, and he very quickly gripped the front part of the broken dowel and yanked it backwards and forwards until it too, came out. Gritting his teeth, he then slipped his burnt leg over the end of the right chair leg and quite literally rolled off the mattress and stood up slowly. His left arm was still attached to the chair and he pulled off the hood as gently as he could to inspect the problem. The cable tie was attached above the seat and not below as the other wrist had been. He looked around the room, saw a small kitchen area and walked carefully and silently, lifting the chair with him so as not to drag it. In a unit of fitted drawers next to a cooker, he searched for a knife. Immediately his eyes fixed on a long pair of scissors and he deftly cut through the last of the ties. He was free.

Quickly he picked up any evidence of splintered wood near the radiator, took a tea towel which he found draped over the tap, and on hands and one knee, he began to rub at the black marks he could see on the lino where his shoes had scuffed the floor as he had shuffled along in the chair. Satisfied, he pushed the mattress straight with his foot where a small vent in the skirting had been uncovered. He replaced the chair to the middle of the room, sat down on it and replaced his hood: in all his excitement he had forgotten to keep a mental note of the minutes passing by.

As he sat in his chair, he listened and thought about what he could do next. He thought about waiting behind the door and ambushing Big Boy with the scissors, but couldn't really see himself launching such an attack. These men were probably trained killers and didn't have a near-crippling burn to contend with. What would happen if the two of them walked in, Big Boy and Cosh Balaclava? Or worse still, Boss Balaclava returned with them. Declan estimated that he must have been there an hour and a half already; four check-ups from Big Boy, so about two and a half hours before Boss Balaclava would be back, and maybe five minutes before the next check-up from Big Boy. He was exhausted, and surprisingly, he wanted to close his eyes and sleep. He couldn't of course. He had to think, be alert and raise his head when Big Boy walked in.

Declan thought about what he could do to escape these brutes. He thought about going over to the wall and listening to hear exactly what they were saying behind it, but he couldn't really see the point. There was no information to be gleaned from those two half-wits outside; they knew nothing: it was Boss Balaclava who was pulling the strings. Who had Boss Balaclava been referring to when he said, "We know that, Olivier,"? So maybe he wasn't pulling the strings after all. Perhaps he worked for someone else. And what else had he said? Something like, "Somebody must have told him something" – a family secret, his grandparents. Was that it? "Was the old cow right?". Who was the old cow? An old cow interested in his grandparents. He suddenly remembered Sister O'Donnal from the detox clinic near Limerick asking peculiar questions about his grandmother. And then, out loud to himself, Declan said,

'Oh, God.'

Sat in O'Donnal's office, more than ten years ago, on a day towards the end of his detox cure, he had seen on her desk, a small Chinese-style bowl with odd trinkets in it. Beads from a broken rosary, a pretty turquoise stone on a pendant, some foreign stamps torn from the corner of a postcard, a necklace of coloured paper clips, a ladybird pencil sharpener and a man's watch: an antique Smiths Deluxe watch with an ivory face in silver. What was a nun doing with a man's watch? It could have been her father's, but then she surely would have kept it in a safer place. If she didn't care too much for her father, then probably she wouldn't have kept it at all. The watch had seemed very out of place then. Now he could see a possible link between these people who appeared to take an interest in his grandparents on his mother's side. If it involved the passing on of a family secret, it must be an interest in his grandmother more precisely because he had never met his grandfather on his mother's side: Olivier Jean Le Dour had died two years before Declan was born. This was absolutely ludicrous. What family secret had Mamie Le Dour passed on to Declan that these psychopaths were prepared to torture and kill for? The only thing he could think of was a silly wooden chest that he had once seen Mamie remove from the bread oven. She hadn't even told him the secret if that's what it was. She said it was nothing in fact. Well, that could be a way out of here. He could just fob them off with that. Tell them about the chest in the old bread oven – the key in the jar under the sink. Tell them they'd have to break down the plasterboard partition that now covered the hole in the wall and Bob's your uncle, he could walk.

The footsteps again and with it, a dose of reality: he was never going to get out of here like that: not alive. The deadbolt slid across, the door swung open and the footsteps walked into the room. Declan had not planned for what happened next. Big Boy was supposed to walk in, do an about turn and walk out. Who was this now and what did he want? Declan was petrified. He listened as best he could to exactly what was going on in his prison cell, and readied himself to launch some sort of surprise and violent attack should this person discover he was in fact no longer strapped in. Then he heard the kettle switch again. Then it was switched off straight away and he heard it being removed from its plastic cradle. The footsteps walked across the room, stopped quite close to Declan, turned and walked away again towards the door. This was agonising suspense. What the hell was going on? Then he heard a new noise, but he couldn't work out what it was – a single and very faint clicking sound. The footsteps continued back the way they had come, crossed the kitchen and headed for the corner of the room to the sink. He heard the kettle lid being flipped up and a tap was turned on.

'Oh God, no,' cried Declan. 'Please not again, I'll talk.'

'Ha-ha-ha, putain, mon pauvre. Ça t'a réveillé hein?' mocked Big Boy. *That woke you up didn't it, sucker.* Then he mocked some more. 'I've turned the light on for you, so you can see better. How's that? Ha-ha. I'm making coffee for me and my colleague, but don't worry: there'll be plenty of hot water for you later, Olivier. Ha-ha-ha.'

That had been the faint click he had heard: the light was on. Declan realised that he had had his eyes closed in order to listen better. Now that he opened them under his hood, he could make out the change in luminosity in the room. That must mean that it was getting dark outside and that Boss Balaclava would be back in about two hours. The coffee was made and Big Boy set off towards the door but then stopped. Declan kept his eyes wide open and readied himself for an attack. Keeping his feet jammed tightly to the chair legs and his arms down behind him as if he was still restrained, he watched the shadow approach and heard the footsteps stop just in front of him.

'Do you want coffee, Olivier? Here try this.' Declan felt a scolding splash on his shoulder and he yelled out again, but despite the violent stinging pain, he stopped mid cry: he did not want to attract Bag Balaclava back into the room for the fun. Big Boy just laughed out loud. He didn't hear the light switch go off, but he heard the door shut and the bolt sliding to.

He stood up, took off his hood, walked to the drawer, opened it, took out the scissors, unplugged the kettle and cut the electric cable clean through: they would not do that to him again. He stood there in the half-light feeling both very stupid and suddenly petrified. Cutting through the cable meant now he was committed to putting a plan into action. He felt stupid too because next to the electric kettle was a gas cooker with a small aluminium saucepan perched on the hob: they could boil all the water they wanted. Almost in desperation, he looked up. Above his head was a skylight and he stared at it for an instant, slightly hopeful. It was at the top of an elongated, truncated pyramid, a sort of tunnel. Not only was it too high for him to reach up to, but just to quash any hopes he might have been kindling, there were bars on it. The light was dimming and there were no other windows in the room. Using the scissors, Declan removed the remaining cable ties from his legs. He had no idea what to do next.

He began to think of ways his schoolboy storybook heroes had escaped from similar situations. He thought of flooding out the room by sealing up the door and floating up to the skylight. But this was all ridiculous: one of the walls wouldn't even hold back the water. The end wall, through which he had heard the men talking, was of similar construction to the new wall in Mamie's kitchen, which now hid the bread oven; plasterboard screwed onto a metal frame. In a flash of madness, he thought of a plan. The idea came to him from John Buchan's novel, The Thirty-nine Steps, in which his schoolboy hero, Richard Hannay, had blown his way out of trouble. He looked all around the room, opened up two cupboard doors to look inside, opened up the oven, glanced quickly up at the light bulb, walked over to the mattress, lifted it up to reveal a small air vent and let out a sigh of relief: he was leaving here alive.

6
Agent Yaouank - 2006

Agent Yaouank, was aptly named. The word "yaouank" means young in the Breton language and agent Yaouank was young. He had removed his embroidered yellow on blue, gendarme insignia badge from his uniform just six months earlier and in turn, his tearfully proud mother had spent the afternoon sewing on his new badges. The new badge was white on blue and had an additional upward-pointing v-stripe. Yaouank was no longer "élève gendarme", but "gendarme sous contrat". Not a student at school any more, but a police officer under contract. Eighteen months to go and Yaouank's career would officially begin. Aged just 19, agent Yaouank was excited. It had been by no means easy. He had understood that life as a gendarme-mobile, was a world apart from what was taught in police school, but his first encounters with difficult people had been with peers and not the general public.

Agent Fornier, his supervising tutor, was not an easy man. One evening he asked Yaouank to go into an alleyway at the back of a hotel in a small town called Plouézec not far from Paimpol.

'Don't be scared, Yaouank,' Fornier had told him. 'They see your uniform and they'll shit their pants. Trust me. You say you're with me, Thierry, and they'll hand over the goods.'

Yaouank was scared. He couldn't understand why Fornier couldn't just come in with him. This was a drugs bust right? Why did he want to sit in the car and wait?

'You're armed. They're not. It's that simple. Don't be scared, just go in there and get the stuff: you'll be fine. Trust me,' assured Fornier. 'You've got to do this, boy. You got any bloody idea how many times you're gonna be in scary situations in your career? You wanna wear that badge, you gotta earn it. Now get on in there and kick arse.'

Yaouank made his move. The alley was not in darkness but it was dim, and he wished his eyes had had more time to adjust. Second door on the right, "Privé": this was the one. Yaouank pushed on the latch, eased the door open and walked through into what looked and smelled like the back yard of a hotel kitchen. Big dustbins lined one wall. An extractor fan was still whirring and the smell of chip-fat was heavy in the air. Somebody inside moved, casting a shadow across a frosted-glass window. Yaouank's heart leapt and he immediately reached for his SIG Sauer Pro SP '22 sidearm. A back door opened and two men walked out: a hairy one in dark clothes and a fat one wearing a white apron. Yaouank said nothing, desperate to calm his breathing and scared that no words would come out. The hairy man lit a cigarette and offered a silvery looking case to the fat man. Both men stood there smoking for nearly a minute and Agent Yaouank felt more like a peeping tom than an officer of the law.

'Dammit, this is good shit,' blurted the fat man.

'That's the mix, man,' replied the hairy one. 'That's bloody good shit with pure snow, man,' he boasted.

'Jeez, my head's spinnin' but my veins is burnin', man,' wheezed the fat one.

'Put your hands up. This is the gendarmerie. I repeat, put your hands up,' pleaded Yaouank in tremolo. Realising how unconvincing he sounded, he unclipped his gun from his holster and pointed at a spot somewhere between both men and shouted,

'Hands up. Now.'

'Hey, kid, calm down, okay. You here with Thierrs?' asked the fat one.

'Thierry, you mean?' asked Yaouank.

'Yeah, man.' said the fat one and immediately turned to the hairball and said, 'This guy's gotta be Mister Agent Fornier's new recruit, man, relax.'

'Yeah, dude, put the fucking gun away, man,' sputtered Hairball, coughing. 'Give him his cut.'

The fat man took a plastic sachet out of his pocket and tossed it towards Yaouank,

'Here, catch.'

Agent Yaouank tried to snatch out into the half-darkness to catch the plastic sachet and remembered he was still pointing his sidearm. The sachet hit the floor and one of the men screamed out:

'It better not be split, man.'

'You better be talkin' 'bout the fucking sachet, man and not the merchandise inside, 'cause that coke ain't bloody split, man. It's as pure as it comes,' said the hairy one.

The sealed plastic sachet of pure white powder was about the size of a glove in length and width. Yaouank picked it up and put his gun back in its holster, buttoned the clip holding its restraining strap and eased away slowly towards the door leading back into the alleyway. He was confused and felt he couldn't cope with the situation on his own, so he would have to get backup from his colleague. Still shaking, Yaouank returned to the car and to the passenger seat where he had been sitting, but his supervisor was sitting in his seat.

'You're driving, Yaouank,' ordered Fornier.

Yaouank handed the plastic sachet over to his supervisor through the half-open window and set off around the vehicle to the driver's side.

'What the hell is going on?' insisted Yaouank, as he settled down in the driver's seat and began putting on his seatbelt.

'Shit me, this snow's pure,' said Fornier. As Yaouank looked across to his colleague in the light of the street lamp, he saw that he had put a large pinch of the white powder up to his nose and snorted it deep down into his lungs.

'Is that a good idea?' he dared to ask. 'You've opened up the sachet. I mean that's evidence isn't it?'

'Drive,' said Fornier.

Yaouank pressed the start button, fired up the engine of the blue Renault Laguna and pulled out slowly and carefully onto a one-way street. As he arrived at the main road, his colleague told him to turn left, so he did.

'What are we going to do?' asked Yaouank, innocently. 'We have to report this now. Radio it in to the station and arrest those men. Get some backup.' Yaouank then reached for the radio.

'When you get up to the traffic lights here, pull over,' explained agent Fornier, snorting back more of what Yaouank considered to be evidence.

'What are you doing? What the hell is going on?' asked Yaouank once more. 'You're tampering with evidence. I will have to report this to the adjudant-chef immediately.' He arrived at the lights and pulled over. It happened so quickly that Yaouank didn't fully comprehend what was going on. The passenger side door opened, Thierry Fornier climbed out of the car and another man sat in his place. Yaouank had never seen this man before, but with the car door still open, Fornier leaned in and said to Yaouank,

'This guy's undercover. He's from Interpol in Belgium. He's takin' over the case from here, so just do what he says, okay?' Turning to the man from Interpol, Fornier lowered his tone and said,

'The kid here wants to report the bust to the station, so I think you'd better explain a few things to him.'

Agent Yaouank's new passenger and colleague ordered him to drive off quickly and told him they were heading for the D7 in the direction of Saint Brieuc.

'Faster!' yelled the passenger.

As the Laguna came off the slip road at 45km/h leading up to join the D7, Yaoaunk was just summoning up the courage to ask who this man was, when he felt something pulling on his side. He took his eyes off the road for a second and saw his passenger's hand moving away from the clasp of the driver's side seat belt. He felt the belt and its buckle begin to slide across his own stomach and chest. Instead of returning his gaze immediately back to the road, agent Yaouank, out of utter shock and lack of comprehension, looked across in that moment at his passenger:

'What the hell are you doing, that's my seat belt?'

An instant later he saw the man reach across the car and grab hold of the steering wheel, jerking it down and to the right. The car veered off the road and headed straight for the concrete pillar of a four-lane fly-over. When the Laguna hit the concrete mass, Yaouank took off diagonally sideways from his seat and his upper torso hit the expanding airbag. The left-hand side of his head smashed against the car's front pillar on the driver's side as the car almost flipped over. The young gendarme was thrown clean through the windscreen, lacerating his face, neck and shoulders as the glass-sheet laminate tore away from the upright pillar and his body continued its trajectory into the grass bank beside the bridge.

The telephone rang on Adjudant-chef Mahé's desk. He didn't recognise the number, but he picked up the receiver abruptly – something was wrong – he just felt it.

'Oui, allo? Adjudant-Chef Mahé here. How can I help?'

'Hello. I'm awfully sorry to be the bearer of such dreadful news, Mr Mahé, but a young gendarme has just been brought into my hospital in St. Brieuc in an ambulance. And, and... er, well, I have to report that he was dead on arrival. I understand that you were his section leader. It doesn't look good and I think you should come as quickly as possible. Before the family is informed.'

'Who are you?' asked Mahé.

'I need you to get here quickly, Mr Mahé. When you arrive, ask for the acting head physician – I will be waiting here. And please drive carefully.'

Within half an hour, Mahé arrived at the hospital in St. Brieuc in an unmarked car. The delayed reaction of other motorists on seeing his Adjudant-Chef's yellow striped epaulettes with their fine red beading usually amused him. The fastening of seatbelts, the lowering of a mobile phone, a change of hand position on the steering wheel, a touching of the brakes, little telltale signs that all gendarmes looked out for. Today, nothing was going to amuse him. The doctor had warned him that this was ugly.

'I'm Doctor Khadir, Mr Mahé,' explained a man in a clean, white, half-fastened lab coat. 'Thank you for getting here so quickly.'

Adjudant-Chef Mahé guessed that the doctor was of Algerian origin and he held out his hand in greeting to the man.

'Thank you for calling me immediately,' replied Mahé.

'I am going to be as frank as I can with you, Mr Mahé,' began Dr Khadir. 'This young man would probably have survived the accident had he been wearing a seatbelt. Now how can I best say this?' the doctor paused. 'I have seen victims from enough road traffic accidents not to be surprised by most things, but I cannot imagine a young officer not putting on his seatbelt.' The doctor frowned and added, 'It just seems so stupid, I'm sorry – out of character should I say.'

Mahé had a feeling the doctor had not called him all the way to the hospital just to tell him one of his boys hadn't been wearing a seatbelt.

'Go on,' said Mahé.

'I consulted with the doctor from the SAMU, who had accompanied the ambulance,' Dr Khadir paused again, this time for longer. 'The boy's neck was broken the moment the car hit the bridge. He was reported "dead on arrival" I'm afraid. There was absolutely nothing we could have done. I'm sorry.' Mahé was no newcomer to his job and there was something this doctor still wasn't telling him.

'Please go on, Doctor,' said Mahé, resisting a glance at his watch.

'It was an off duty fireman who first arrived at the scene. He found the passenger door of the gendarme's Laguna wide open when he arrived at the accident, yet your agent had been at the wheel. The way the fireman figured it,' continued the doctor, 'is, either somebody got to the scene of the accident before he did, opened the passenger door and then fled or someone got out of there alive. In any case, it struck me as strange that the accident was called in by the fireman and not by the person we know to have opened the door before the fireman got there.'

'That is odd,' admitted Mahé, but resisted the temptation to elaborate. Ordinarily, Yaouank should have been with Fornier, so where the hell was Fornier? He thanked the doctor profusely and asked to see the body of the young gendarme before he left.

'He's in the morgue, but of course, I'll ask someone to accompany you,' said Doctor Khadir. His own place was above ground with the living and not downstairs in the morgue.

Yaouank's face was a mess: the young skin had lost all its colour. Above his mouth, around his nose and right cheek it was shredded and bloody. Part of his scalp had been cut through so deeply around his forehead that it hung limp revealing an area of the skull the size of the palm of his hand. An eye was missing as were several teeth and Mahé, not for the first time in his career, had to turn away holding his hand over his mouth. Dreading the duty he knew he had to face of informing the boy's poor mother, Mahé returned to the unmarked white Audi and made a call back to the gendarmerie in Paimpol. Agent Le Du picked up the phone and Mahé cut him off straight away:

'Mahé here. Where's Fornier?' There was no hiding his edginess. If Fornier wasn't back at base, safe, then he might be walking-wounded. Mahé couldn't otherwise understand why

Fornier would have left his colleague like that without at least radioing for help.

'He phoned in, sir,' explained Le Du. 'Asked Yaouank to drop him off at home and told him to come back to the station. He's laid up sick as a dog he reckons. Squits, sir. That's what he told me. Why what's up?'

Mahé had already rung off. His next call was going to be a little awkward. Major Gilles Cario had been at school with Mahé and yet was a rank above him. The call was going to be awkward not because Mahé cared about the difference in rank, but because Cario seemed to think he should. Mahé hadn't always considered promotion as a positive thing in his line of work and knew that he had probably already got as far as he was going in his career: something frankly that just didn't bother him. As briefly as he could, he outlined his concerns and requested very simply, that the Laguna be impounded immediately.

'I want to check for prints.'

'It doesn't look good within the force, as you well know,' said the major. 'It will only create a bad feeling among his colleagues. Nobody's under suspicion are they, Mahé?'

'Not one of ours, sir, no,' agreed Mahé.

'Well then?' said Cario, 'What's the worst? Somebody witnessed the accident, pulled over, opened the police car door, found a dead officer had been ejected from the car and then drove off? Imagine the guy had had a drink or two; you wouldn't honestly expect him to wait around while we turn up to question him, would you? Maybe that person drove off to call 112, who knows?'

'It's a gut feeling I have, sir,' pleaded Mahé. 'Come on, Gilles, please. At least until I've been able to crosscheck other 112 calls.'

'Oh, bloody hell, Mahé,' he sighed, and Mahé allowed himself the tiniest of smiles as he anticipated his senior relenting. 'I'll do the necessary paperwork,' he agreed, 'under one condition: you supervise the fingerprinting yourself. You better be bloody right, Mahé!' Major Cario put the phone down without saying goodbye.

Mahé took one look through a side window of the Laguna and cursed; there was the tiniest spatter of blood near the middle of the eggshell white, now deflated airbag on the passenger-side door. A nosebleed perhaps? Someone had been sat next to the young gendarme when the accident took place and they had survived. Shit, this was going to be awkward. He immediately phoned through to forensics to arrange prints to be taken. Someone had closed the car door, probably the fireman he surmised. But the prints of the person who opened the door from the inside, in other words, Yaouank's passenger's prints, should still be intact. He just hoped to God they weren't Fornier's; that would lead to a really messy internal inquiry.

7

The Escape

Declan, as quietly as possible, moved the table to a position underneath the skylight. He opened the right-hand cupboard door to the left of the cooker and took out a large, deep saucepan – the lower part of a pressure cooker – there was no matching lid. He also took out an aluminium funnel and placed both saucepan and funnel on the floor next to the wall from where he had removed the mattress. Then he opened the oven, removed two large baking trays, laid them out on the table and began to cut into the tea towel he had found by the sink. Soon he had two small squares of cloth, neither much bigger than a postage stamp, and he laid those down on the end of the mattress about two inches apart. In the second drawer, beneath the scissor draw, he had seen a roll of duct tape – he didn't care to think what that had been used for. Taking his chair to the table in order to climb onto it more easily, he picked up the first of the baking trays, the roll of duct tape and the scissors. He cut two one foot lengths of duct tape and fixed the baking tray to the ceiling at the base of the truncated pyramid. The tray held, but only just and so he used more tape to be certain it would stay in place. Now he could see next to nothing. He knelt down on the table, manoeuvred himself around carefully so that he was sitting on his bottom with his legs hanging down off the table, and gently, so as not to hurt his leg, he lowered himself over the edge until his feet touched the lino - his burn was still excruciatingly painful and getting worse. He estimated that he had about fifteen minutes left. He walked slowly in the direction of the door and was pleased to find it immediately. Sliding his hand up and down slowly, he felt the light switch and gently put it on. The room lit up and now he had to act very, very quickly.

He walked first over to the table to pick up the remaining metal tray. Then to the mattress where he recovered the saucepan, the funnel and the two square pieces of tea towel and placed them all on the lino tight up to the skirting board, before lifting the mattress to a vertical position. He turned around and walked forwards to pick up the table and placed it up against the wall. He positioned it on its side so that all four legs touched the wall at the same time forming a cage which cradled the mattress. Reaching over the now vertical table top, he pulled at the bottom of the mattress on each side in order to make it slide across the lower two of the table legs. He quickly inspected his work as he moved to the end of the tipped up table, and from there he could see a triangular entrance to his homemade blast shelter. The second tray he positioned over the mattress where he estimated his back would lie once he had crawled inside for cover. He then walked over to the open oven, and moving from one dial to the next, he turned each one full on. Gas began hissing out into the room. He moved along the units to the fridge, opened the door, found a litre carton of milk and took the scissors once more to cut off a corner to pour the milk out. He drank, leaving about half a litre in the carton. Carrying the milk and the sabotaged tea towel with him to the light switch, and with his finger on the switch, he looked up at the light; the chair directly below the bulb. He concentrated hard to place its exact position into his short term memory. He flicked the switch and the room fell into darkness. He could hear the gas escaping and he walked straight to the middle of the room, holding the scissors in his right hand. As he reached the chair, he lowered himself enough to place the milk carton and tea towel on to the lino next to the chair, reached up with his left hand, just touched the still hot bulb with the tips of his fingers, closed his eyes and then swung at it with the scissors. It smashed first time.

Recovering the milk and the tea towel, he carefully made his way back to the table and lowering himself to the ground, sat with his right leg straight out in front of him. Placing the tea towel over his right foreleg, he emptied the milk carton over the burn. He had taken the decision not to use water in case the pressure in the pipes made give-away noises. Although it stung like hell, he felt some relief after just a few seconds and lay down to begin half crawling, half sliding, his way into the triangular-shaped, homemade blast shelter until he could feel the air vent in front of his face. Next, he reached above his shoulders to feel for the two square pieces of cloth which he twisted round to form earplugs, before pushing them into place – one in each ear. He reached for the aluminium funnel, crushed the wide end slightly to elongate it, forming an ellipse and placed the wide, now oval end, over the grill of the vent. Positioning his mouth over the narrow end of the funnel, he tried breathing. His tongue hurt like hell, but it seemed to have stopped bleeding. Breathing through the funnel was fine. Lastly, reaching once more over his head, Declan recovered the pressure cooker pan and pulled it over his head until the handle reached the back of his neck and the lip on the opposite side sat just in front of his nose and rested on the shank of the aluminium funnel. Carefully, he wriggled both hands in underneath the pressure cooker and used his thumbs to hold the makeshift earplugs in place, three fingers of each hand to cover his eyelids and his two little fingers to pinch his nostrils.

As he lay there, he began to wonder what would happen now if the men came into the room and the gas had not hissed out enough to create an immediately explosive mix. They might be there now watching, laughing for all he knew, for he could see and hear nothing at all. He began to think of the plasterboard wall in Mamie Le Dour's Kitchen and thought how easy it would be to break down and access the bread oven. He had no guarantee that the chest was still there. He could simply take a hammer and knock a hole straight through, but then he remembered watching his father cut through sheets of the stuff using an ordinary wood saw. Desperately, he hoped this escape plan would work, because the idea of these men discovering him curled up under a mattress wearing a pressure cooker on his head with a funnel sticking out of his mouth made him cringe. For some absurd reason at that moment, he worried almost as much about the personal humiliation as the torture and death that would inevitably follow. He began to feel himself drifting off to sleep and tried desperately to fight it, but he was totally exhausted. He tried not to think of the consequences of his plan failing and, little by little, as he began to drift into a troubled sleep, his thoughts returned to the wooden chest and the bread oven.

Once the hole in the plasterboard was big enough, he could just step through and see the opening to the oven. He imagined himself being in the room and peering through the dusty gap into darkness. He felt his body relaxing and his breathing slowing down, and unconsciously, he stopped fighting sleep.

He reached inside knowing full well that he had no change of clothes and would be covered in soot, but it didn't bother him, he was too excited. The chest was right by the entrance and he didn't need the long wooden lollipop he had seen Mamie using. There was no key. Surely he could just force the lock somehow, but then suddenly he saw a little envelope pinned to the side and he quickly tore it open. Inside was a note that read: "The key is in the water itself." This had been left for Declan for he and he alone knew exactly where to find the key. He ran as fast as he could to the fountain and peered in. At first, he couldn't see it, but then he saw the reflection of the bird of prey carving which appears to fly right over the source. The bird was not holding a key, but a picture of a key in its beak and Olivier removed it. It read:

"À table, at dark heights." This too was a clue, but Olivier knew exactly what it meant. His grandmother was not stupid. "À table" simply meant it was dinner time and "dark heights" was a reference to the "Black Mountain" or "Menez Du" in Breton. The mountain wasn't really black at all. It was as green as the rest of Brittany but was formed from black slate rock. He used to walk up to the top with Mamie and at the very top, a local mason, Jean-Noël or, "Jean-Mollet" as he had been nicknamed, had built a stone table. Jean-Mollet, which translates to "Calf-muscle-John", was said to have cycled up to the top carrying all the stones, the sand, the lime and the water – hence the big calf muscles. It was at this table that he and Mamie used to picnic: the highest point in the whole county, a glorious and panoramic view over what seemed to Declan, at that young age, to be the most important place in the whole world.

'It once was,' Mamie Le Dour had told him.

Declan quickly ran up the lane and then turned east up to the track leading to the summit. He was so exhausted that he had to stop running for a moment and catch his breath. As he stood there, half-supporting himself on a hazel sapling, he noticed the dark haired woman walking along the path. She too seemed to be going in the direction of the summit and he plucked up the courage to ask her if she would mind if he walked with her. She nodded, and they walked together at an identical pace, and although they didn't talk, not one word, he felt very at ease in her company. After about four or five minutes, she reached out her hand for his and he held it. He felt so happy, he could even feel tears welling up in his eyes – she was so beautiful. Together they reached the steeper incline and had to scramble a little way. As they reached the top they looked out over what once again seemed to him to be the most important place in the world.

There was a noise in the background and Declan recognised it immediately. Mamie had always hated it, saying that it spoiled the peace she felt up there, but not Olivier: he loved it. French Air Force jets during training exercises used to fly over this spot, sometimes as often as ten times a week, and sometimes they came in really low. Once, he had been so surprised by how low one jet had passed over, that he ran and hid under Jean-Mollet's table for safety. He looked up into the sky and could see one of the still tiny, black forms just coming in over the horizon and Olivier watched it approach. The noise got louder and then suddenly he heard a high pitched scream and he looked around immediately to comfort the dark-haired woman and tell her it was okay. But as he looked around she had gone. Instead, he could see his sister, Isabelle, screaming under Jean-Mollet's stone table and he rushed to comfort *her* instead. He put his arm around her and she was shaking as the noise got louder. Olivier was trying to tell her not to be afraid of the noise, that it was only an aeroplane, but she couldn't hear him. There was something not normal about this one. The second jet fighter seemed to be coming in way too low and as Olivier looked up, he could see it was heading straight for the table. An instant later, he heard the engines right above his head: so loud were they, he felt his entire body vibrate. Then the fuselage of the plane seemed to scrape across the tabletop almost smashing it to pieces and he felt the power of an impact so destructive that he had no idea if he or Isabelle were even going to survive it.

As Big Boy opened the door, he automatically reached up for the lightswitch. He thought he could hear some hissing but didn't react quickly enough, and it wasn't until he had already rocked the button downwards, that his brain registered the repugnant odour of methyl mercaptan: the additive in natural gas.

The gas content of the air mix in the room had reached about 14 ½ percent, and as Big Boy flicked on the light, the smashed incandescent light bulb received its nominal 220volts and momentarily lit up to its full 70watts. The temperature of the filament rose almost instantly to over 2450° Celsius, and the gas around it ignited instantaneously. The door was smashed closed so fast by the initial subsonic blast, that Big Boy's trachea was crushed in by his own arm, and the shaft of the door handle itself came away and travelled straight through his shirt, punched through his skin and lodged itself in his liver. Three one hundredth's of a second later, the first of Declan's baking trays broke away from its duct-tape-moorings and began to travel up the skylight shaft. As it reached the bars at the top, it buckled and stopped. Just six one hundredth's of a second after this, the blast overpressure or BOP in the room peaked to 26 kiloPascals or 4psi and the speed of the expanding gas molecules increased to supersonic speed as the deflagrated explosion turned to detonation. The stud wall set off in its entirety in the direction of Bag Balaclava who hadn't quite had time to turn his head in the direction of the sound. As pieces of the partition wall, now breaking up into its component parts, began to hit him at speeds in excess of 135 miles per hour, Bag Balaclava was thrown the short distance of 14 inches or 35cm that separated him from the old oak desk at which he was sitting. His body travelled straight towards the desk in the direction of the glass-fronted vitrine and stayed together in one piece right up until the ornately moulded edge of the desk crushed through his spine. His legs and upper torso were launched separately towards the now shattering shop front.

The glass front that Declan had heard vibrate, vibrated again. Just under one second after Big Boy had flipped the light switch, the glass frontage of what was, in fact, the sub-office of an undertaker's reception, started to bulge out. In just a fraction of a second, it shattered into hundreds of thousands of shards of glass that were thrown across an area of over seven thousand square metres. A cloud of plasterboard dust, as well as a whole host of other more dangerous projectiles, followed straight out behind the explosion of glass confetti and it was without any doubt, this sudden and massive release of pressure in the back room where Declan lay, that ultimately saved his life.

As the blast pressure dissipated, it was followed by an almost total vacuum that began to suck air, dust and debris back into the explosion zone. A shard of glass no bigger than a matchbox rushed back into the kitchen where Declan was lying, and as it began to lose momentum it dropped a little and headed for the triangular opening of the makeshift blast shelter. It hit his foot and travelled much of the way through the heel of his left shoe before stopping. An even smaller piece of debris, the head of a plasterboard screw, also hit him. It travelled in through the space formed between Declan's feet and the mattress and wedged into his elbow with a sharp thud.

Olivier could smell burning, and smoke filled the air. He reached around feeling for Isabelle, but she was not there. He grappled in the darkness and began to cough. The aircraft must have crash-landed on the summit of Menez Du; the whole place was up in smoke. He felt a burning pain in his elbow and he realised that he must be on fire. Keeping his head low to the ground so as to avoid smoke inhalation, Olivier tried to scramble out from under Jean-Mollet's table, but he must have damaged his leg somehow because it too felt burning hot. It could be kerosene from the fuel tanks that had caught fire. On hands and knees, Olivier clambered across the burning heather-covered hilltop and began to descend from the summit. The hill was not as steep as he had remembered, but the gorse that grew in and amongst the heather was pricking viciously into his knees. He hit an obstacle of some sort and he was stopped dead as his arms collapsed beneath him. Then he realised what the obstacle was. Declan was not on the mountain, he was straddling what remained of the torso of a man. There was thick dust in the air and raising himself from the remains of this man's body in the failing light, his eyes fell on the Smiths Deluxe watch on this victim's wrist. So this was Bag Balaclava. He surprised himself then as he blurted,

'Time's up, sucker,' and he even sniggered to himself as a little boy might.

A bright light flashed through the darkness and lit up Declan's face. He dropped to the ground instantly and froze. What he had seen at that moment, however, confused Declan even more. Bag Balaclava's face had also been lit up by the searchlight. He recognised this man, they had met before.

8
Carl Grady - 2015

Carl leaned over the kitchen table in Isabelle's downstairs flat, picked up his mug of tea and finished it off. Placing the empty mug on the drainer next to the sink, he turned around, crouched down in front of her wheelchair and reached for her hands, cupping them in his own.

'I'll not be gone long,' he said reassuringly. 'I've some business to sort out for a colleague over in Dublin and I'll be back by mid-week I expect. If not I'll call you, my darling, I promise.'

'Don't worry about me,' said Isabelle. 'I'll be fine. And there's Mo next door should I really run into trouble on my own.' She smiled looking down into his face. 'You know, if I should fall out of my wheelchair going crazy on the dance floor in some nightclub, or something.'

Carl laughed and leaning on the arms of her chair, he moved forward to kiss her goodbye.

'Listen, Carl,' she said, almost in a whisper, 'don't you be worrying yourself about me being here on my own, I've plenty enough to keep me busy with my translation work at the moment.' Then raising her voice slightly, she added, 'Just you look after yourself in Dublin; I've enough to worry about already with me big brother goin' off the rails in the outbacks of Brittany, now, haven't I? I love you, now drive carefully, won't you? That's my biggest worry.'

'I'll see you Wednesday or Thursday latest,' he said and was off.

'Sure you've forgotten nothing?' cried Isabelle after him.

'Everything is in the boot of the trusty Saab,' Carl replied, poking his head back around the door.

Carl Grady worked in real-estate. His profession required him to drive a car a man can trust. So he bought himself a Saab. The "wheels" were his pride and joy and when he had first bought the car from new in 2010, he insisted that Declan come over to "check her out".

'In my line of work, Declan, image is all important. No detail is too small to ignore. You notice the choice of colour? Blue, Declan, sends out a message of honesty. Red, for example, shows that you're passionate about your product. You see, red's no good for me because I don't have a product as such. I deliver a service. The product is not mine to sell. That's the thing about real-estate. We're there to help you make the right decision about what will undoubtedly be the most expensive item you will ever purchase in your life. Now, how important is it we get that just right?'

'Oh Jesus,' thought Declan.

'Blue inspires trust in people. Clients see my car and they know, without even realising why, that's the clever part, that they can trust me.'

'Remind me never to buy a property off you,' thought Declan.

'What do you think of the plates? Not bad, huh?'

'Limerick plates,' replied Declan. 'This year's.'

'I can't believe you can't see it,' said Carl. And then he went on to spell it out: '10-L-595.'

'Yeah, and?'

'I for Isabelle, O' – then L for Leary – S-95; Saab 9-5. Not bad huh?'

'Great. Nice one. A real stroke of luck,' said Declan.

'Not luck, Declan. I reserved it. Cost me nearly two grand.'

Carl sat in his Saab 95 and tapped in his password for the sat nav, looked up towards the bay window, waved and blew a kiss to Isabelle and with a quick glance over his shoulder, pulled away without indicating. He turned left at the end of the road and began to type some details into the sat nav's screen and continued to drive for a minute or so. The screen displayed:

"calculating route."

'In fifty metres, turn right,' said the woman's voice.

'In three hundred metres, turn left,' the woman's voice said again.

'In one hundred and fifty metres, turn right,' mimicked Carl in a falsetto voice.

'In one hundred and thirty metres, go around the round-about,' she corrected.

'That's called splitting hairs, darling,' said Carl.

'At the roundabout, take the second exit onto the N24.'

Carl checked through some CD's quickly and then opted for a pirated one marked, "Michel Thomas". Picking up his cell phone, Carl touched the screen to access the directory. He then scanned down to F and touched the first name.

'Yeah, hi, Flynn, Carl here. Listen you've got to learn to pick up your phone, man. I've just left Isabelle's and I've told her I'll be in Dublin staying at yours till Thursday, so don't let me down. And call me back when you get this message, Okay?'

There was the tooting of a car horn and Carl realised he had drifted over slightly onto the side of oncoming traffic.

'Alright, alright, keep your hair on,' said Carl as he reached forward to beep his horn back at the driver who had already passed.

'In six hundred metres, go around the round-about,' announced the girl's voice over the sound of the CD.

'At the roundabout, take the third exit onto the R513 direction Cork and the M8.'

As he pulled out onto the R513 from the roundabout, Carl put his foot down gently on the Saab's accelerator until she reached eighty-four km/h. He had it on good authority that speed cameras would not flash until the speed limit plus five had been exceeded. So to be on the safe side, Carl programmed his cruise control to the national speed limit plus five and minus one – his own safety margin – equals eighty-four and set it.

Carl's ferry left at four o'clock, 16 hundred hours today, 16 August 2015 from Cork. That left him nearly three hours for a one hour and thirty-four-minute journey. He needed to be there for boarding three-quarter's of an hour before departure. Okay for time then, but he couldn't hang about.

9

A Mysterious Light

The light shone again and Declan kept his head tucked down behind Bag Balaclava's torso. Again the searchlight came and Declan couldn't work out how to get away without being lit up like a Christmas tree and being seen by his enemies. Then he thought of something; he could crawl in the opposite direction to the searchlight and each time they flashed it in his direction, he would freeze until he could get behind the building out of their view. Then he'd run or hobble as fast as he could away from them.

As he lay there, he waited for the next flash of the searchlight before making a painful dash on hands and knees towards the side of the building. The light flashed again and he dropped and waited and thought. Richard Hannay would not have done this. No. He would have assumed that that's exactly what his enemy would expect him to do and would, therefore, have gone in the opposite direction to foil them. Declan would do the same. He waited and counted and moved in the direction of the light. Again he waited and counted and moved. This must have gone on for a good four minutes before Declan began to come to his senses. He reckoned he must have travelled about 250 metres. The duration of the actual searchlight sweeps themselves was just four seconds. He knew this because it enabled him to sing to himself the first line of his father's favourite Breton song, "Tri Martolod Yaouank" – three young sailors. At the moment one could decide or not to exaggerate the pronunciation of the letter "k", the light would disappear and he could continue to move towards his enemy: but for just four seconds. Thereafter, he would have to freeze again to repeat the first line. The absence of searchlight was also completely regular: he could get to the last beat just before the first word of the beginning of the second verse and the light would come back. At first, Declan thought he was being clever, he sang the song from the beginning in his head and as soon as the searchlight disappeared he moved on hands and knees till the beginning of the first verse and froze again. He lay there thinking about this searchlight when it occurred to him he had not been that clever after all. A searchlight would have shone across and then swung back to cover a different area in its second sweep. This one covered the same ground again and again and it didn't swing back it went around and around.

This was no searchlight, this was a lighthouse. Declan knew this for absolute certain. He not only knew it to be a lighthouse, but of all the lighthouses dotted all over the Breton coastline, he knew exactly which one this was. Le Phare de la Croix – "The Lighthouse of the Cross", located just off the north Breton coast and not far from where his father had met his mother, had a white light, showed two flashes of four seconds followed by a long occultation. Seen by day, it was constructed of two towers side by side. "Those two towers, that's me and your mum that is, son."

Declan remembered his father saying to him one day, he had memorised all of the lighthouses off this coastline; their colours, their flashes, their frequencies, the duration of each pause, which was called an occultation, as well as the chart positions of the lot of them.

"You can never know too much when you're out at sea in a storm," he had said.

Of all of them, this one had been his father's favourite. He knew when he was out at sea and he passed just north of l'Île Verte, the "Green Island", going west he would shortly line up this lighthouse with the glow of lights on the mainland and somewhere in that town was the house in which the love of his life awaited his return. This was his island, Dad had said, his green isle, his Breton Ireland. Declan's father had told him about several lighthouses that had special meanings to him. One was the, "partridge lighthouse" on the south coast at the entrance to the port of Pont l'Abbé. Le Phare de la Perdrix, so called because partridges used to settle there at low tide, was supposed to be painted one-half green, but they were not allowed to by some international waterway regulations authority. Declan's father, Bryn O'Leary, reckoned that being half green would have made it Declan's lighthouse – the idea being that Declan was half green or half Irish. He did not feel half Irish or half anything else for that matter and in the end, the lighthouse was painted black and white check and Declan was glad to hear when it was finally put out of action and flashed no more.

Still, knowing where he was now was no coincidence, it was genuinely thanks to his father's passed on wisdom. He stood up, looked up at the beautifully clear sky, thanked his Dad and set off walking at a very slow pace towards the light and therefore the north coast to be absolutely certain of his bearings and his position. Declan limped no more than two metres and stopped to crouch down, kneel and finally rock sideways onto his bottom so as to avoid hurting his burnt leg. Something had got stuck to his heel and he began to pull off his shoe to find out what it was. As he crouched, his heel held in front of his face, waiting for the flash of the lighthouse to come back around, he had a terrible thought. The light flashed to reveal a quite wide shard of glass about half the length of his forefinger which had somehow embedded itself into the rubber. It was impossible to remove it with bare hands, so he swung his shoe against a small rock not a foot from him in order to fragment the glass shard so that it no longer hindered his walking. Then as he stood up, desperate to avoid tearing more skin from his thigh, he looked up once more at the clear sky. What he saw, he refused to accept. He carried on walking, still following the light, and in less than fifty metres he reached a stony shoreline. *How was that possible when he hadn't even heard the lapping of waves?*

Declan looked up again, identified the star constellation of Ursa Major – also known by such names as "the great bear", "the saucepan" or "the plough" – followed up the right-hand side of the saucepan to locate the pole star and almost collapsed in shock. According to the stars, instead of following the lighthouse north to the coastline, he had followed it west. The problem, for anyone who knows the coastline here at all, was simple; he was not on the mainland but on an island. Which one, he had no idea.

'Oh please, Dad, help.'

As he stood there at the water's edge, he began to rack his brains. He was trapped on an island. So his kidnappers had taken him on a boat after knocking him unconscious. From the centre of Brittany to its north coast in the Côtes d'Armor, was at least an hour by car. Plus the van journey on the island; Declan was no nearer to working out even where he was, let alone how to get away. He looked up at the stars again, located the pole star and, turning as he did so, he stuck his right arm out north and his left arm out to point to the Phare de La Croix. The hands of his human compass told him it was about eight o'clock. His feet told him that his left shoe was leaking.

He stood there for quite some time with both his arms still pointing straight out: due north – right arm, and lighthouse – left arm. Eight o'clock. With the exception of the two periodic flashes, he stood there in virtual darkness and just stared. Boss Balaclava had said he would be back in four hours and Declan guessed that he had probably taken a boat back to the mainland. Also, he thought, the island must be pretty small, which would explain why there had been no police sirens when the explosion had happened. He allowed himself a little smile and thought:

'Sod you, you bastards with your plastic bag and your bloody boiling water.'

It occurred to him then that he had come off remarkably unscathed considering he had been in the same room where the explosion had happened. The only residual effect he could feel from the blast was the ringing in his ears, which also impaired his hearing quite considerably. Since he felt no pain, he hoped this would pass and his hearing would return. He stopped pointing north with his right arm and using his index finger, he moved to scratch his right ear. There was a delayed reaction during which Declan started asking himself aloud:

'What the hell...?' as he realised that the square pieces of cloth were still stuck in his ears. He pulled them both out almost simultaneously, heard that he was actually shouting quite loudly and then he shut up. He listened. There was still a slight ringing, but he could hear perfectly well. Staring north, he noticed another light off to the right at about two o'clock. It looked like a boat or a buoy out at sea. Holding an almost closed fist up to his eye, mimicking a telescope, he focused on the new light. White, red and green.

It was not moving along, nor was it moving up or down, so it wasn't a boat and it wasn't a buoy. Could it be another lighthouse, he wondered?

"...first past the Peacock and then on to my Green Isle," that was how it went. The Peacock was, in fact, another lighthouse. Its real name was Le Phare du Paon or Peacock Lighthouse to Declan's dad. So named, according to his father, because of its colours. It showed white, red and green lights permanently and never flashed at all – its bright feathers permanently on display. Whether this was true or not he had no idea, nor did he care. He was now certain where he was. He'd been here once on a school trip and even seen the lighthouse, but it had been day time so it had not been lit up. Other than that, he could remember almost nothing about the island except that it was very flat and it was called the Isle of Bréhat: not more than a mile and a half off the mainland. Too far to swim – for Declan at least. He did consider swimming, thinking that the salt water would help his wounds, but unknown waters are not at all enticing in the dark and although quite a good swimmer over short distances, he could never honestly hope to have that kind of stamina. He wondered how the hell he would have got even this far if it had not been for the periodic lighthouse flashes to break the complete darkness and guide him. As he stared out to sea, he imagined the two towers together on that outcrop of rock and instead of thinking of his mother and father he thought of him and the dark-haired woman.

Declan dropped to his knees. There was a noise; somebody was close by.

10
The Passenger

Two days after the death of Agent Yaouank, there was a knock on Adjudant Chef Mahé's office door and Brigitte, a gendarme in her mid-thirties, pushed it open gently and peered into the room. Mahé's door was, in principle at least, always open.

Agent Brigitte Le Bars had been with the force for just five years. Her late entry was explained by a combination of motherhood on the one hand and then, just a few years later, the loss of her only child to a hit and run drink-driver. Applications into the Gendarmerie Nationale after such personal trauma were always frowned upon. Such motivation was known to lead to poor judgement and to reactions inappropriate for an officer of the law, but Brigitte had been persistent and passed all the necessary psychological and physical tests. Mahé had asked her to bring any related paperwork to him as soon as it arrived; he knew he could count on her for her sensitivity in this situation. Confirmation for impounding the Laguna; a preliminary mechanical report on the vehicle – zero mechanical failure; a copy of the death certificate; the coroner's report confirming a broken neck as cause of death. These were the beginnings of a file, but what Brigitte had just brought in was what really interested him: the fingerprint findings. Mahé opened the envelope marked Dactylographic Report. There were notes about ridge endings, forkings, dots, short ridges and enclosures or islands. Reference was made to a fingerprint card - second from last page of the report. Mahé skipped to the last page: the AFIS or Automated Fingerprint Identification System result. He felt a sense of relief as the report revealed that the prints did not belong to another gendarme. His sense of relief was immediately replaced by anger when it dawned on him that he still knew nothing about the passenger in the car. And then suddenly, sheer terror struck him; what the report was exposing was a murder.

The person in the passenger seat next to Yaouank had not only grabbed hold of the steering wheel but had also left a print on the release buckle of Yaouank's seatbelt. The murderer had undone the boy's seatbelt and steered the vehicle into a bridge. Under French law, that made it murder in the second degree at least, reasoned Mahé. He picked up his phone and dialled the direct line through to Major Cario's Office.

'Bonjour, Major, Mahé here,' he said introducing himself. 'I've got some preliminary findings for that case involving the death of the young gendarme, Yaouank,' he waited for confirmation to continue.

'Bad news I take it then, Mahé?' asked the Major.

'Murder, sir. No doubt about it. First or second degree,' Adjudant-Chef Mahé outlined his findings and waited for the major to comment.

'Good God, that's atrocious,' winced the major. 'For me, with no id on the guy, you can't argue first degree: it could have been intent to injure, not to kill.' Major Cario then let out some sort of grunting sound indicating that he had reached another conclusion, then added:

'If you can find out who the guy is and prove that his identity was known to Yaouank, then I would say that that's as good as first degree.'

Both men knew that the difference between second and first degree murder meant the difference between eighteen months and fifteen years. Mahé followed the major's logic: if the perpetrator had the intention of injuring the police officer in order to gain time to escape, one could assume that this person was unknown to the law. If on the other hand, the perpetrator's identity was known to the young officer, then it would have been unlikely that gaining time to escape by causing an accident was his sole intention.

'The vehicle was travelling in excess of 45km/h on impact, sir. Meaning, that whoever steered the car into the bridge, probably knew about the Laguna's safety reputation in front-on collisions; knew that wearing his seatbelt, he himself would have had an extremely good chance of coming out without any serious damage at that speed,' said Mahé. 'The passenger must have nerves of steel.'

'It got five stars in road safety tests. It was in the car magazine, Auto Express. In fact, it was all over the press; anybody could know that,' argued the major. 'No. What we know about this guy is that he's never requested an id card or passport or we'd have his prints. He therefore probably doesn't have a driver's licence.'

'He could be under sixteen,' suggested Mahé.

'Or foreign,' concluded the major.

'I'll find him, sir,' promised a very determined Mahé.

Dr Khadir heard the phone being picked up at the other end of the line and immediately asked to speak to Adjudant-Chef Mahé.

'Hello, Doctor, Mahé here.'

'It's none of my business I know, Mr Mahé but I've heard your young policeman's funeral is tomorrow morning.'

'You'd be more than welcome to attend,' said Mahé.

'I cannot, I'm afraid to say,' answered Dr Khadir, apologetically, 'I really am unable to get away. I wondered if it would be possible for you to arrange to have a wreath placed on his grave for me.'

'That's very kind, Doctor. What sort of wreath had you got in mind?'

'I have already ordered it, it's at the florist's in the entrance to the hospital here in St. Brieuc,' said the doctor.

'I'll come and pick it up personally,' said Mahé.

'I'll tell you something, Mr Mahé, something quite surprising. It is a fact that last century, as many people died in road traffic accidents as were killed by the Black Death in more than three times that period. Some people call that progress, but we in the medical profession see things a little differently.'

Mahé *was* surprised. He was currently reading a novella called "Book of Pestilence" in which the figure of 50 million had been cited as the estimated total number of deaths in Europe over that period. He had decided just a few evenings ago, to check that figure, for it was a shock for him that such suffering could have occurred on roadways yet remain relatively unreported by the press. The numbers were staggering. He wondered if the doctor had read the same book.

'Your officer didn't deserve to die.'

'No, Doctor, he was a good man and so young,' Mahé continued, 'I just wanted to say thank you for calling me and sharing your suspicions.' Mahé then briefly explained what he suspected had happened to Yaouank, but was careful to leave out any details of the findings of his inquiries to date.

'This, however, was no traffic accident, Doctor. The boy was murdered.'

'Have you managed to catch the culprit?'

'Not yet, but I will.'

11

The Green Island

Crouching down silently at the water's edge, Declan heard the noise again, almost the same, but not quite; a loud but hollow scraping. Then a wave lapped straight over both his feet and he felt its crest roll right under the seat of his pants sending a cold shiver up his spine. He took the plunge and sat down, carefully stretching his right leg out straight in front of him. The cold salt water stung his burn and he was unable to prevent himself from vocalising his suffering. Then the scraping again. He got down as low as he could in the water and tried to look about him in all directions to see if he could spot his enemy before his enemy spotted him. This time, not scraping but a thud. Declan swung round, still keeping low: this time he was able to detect the exact direction from where the sound was coming. He felt underneath the water and picked up two rocks; a flat, axe-shaped one in his right hand and a round tennis ball size one in his left. Without thinking clearly at all, Declan stood up and screamed out in fury:

'Come on then. Come on out and show yourself now you're on your own, you bloody coward.'

Short of the lapping of waves on the shoreline, there wasn't a sound and Declan, armed as a caveman might have been, adrenalin surging through his veins, shook with a mixture of frustration, terror and rage. There was nobody there. He paddled over in the direction of the noise of scraping and the thump he had heard and had to steady himself as he stepped on the occasional slippery, seaweed-covered rock. The little boy of five or six years would no doubt have loved his day out on this island, but not the man; this was a nightmare, pure torture and frightening – so, so frightening.

Declan walked into something hard and dropping the tennisball-rock, he grabbed out at whatever it was with his left hand and raised his right arm, wielding his axe-hand high in the air. The light flashed on again. This time the four seconds seemed really short-lived, but he was able to make out the form of a small dinghy in front of him. As he leaned forward to steady himself, the dinghy wheeled down in the now knee-high water and he heard the scraping, this time slightly damped, followed by the thud, the hull of the dinghy on the pebbly shoreline: the tide was coming in. He remembered his teacher telling them in French that this island doubled in size twice a day with the falling tides. Olivier, the boy, hadn't the faintest idea what the teacher was talking about: Declan, the man, understood only too well. He remembered his father telling him about a deep channel they had to follow into shore because the water between all these islands was so shallow you could almost walk it at low tide. If the tide was coming in, it would ultimately carry him in the direction of the mainland. The worst that could happen would be that he run aground and if that happened, he would get out and paddle. That was it, another flash; two rowlocks; two oars; untie the knotted rope from the chain and push off to sea. Out at sea, Le Phare de la Croix would be Declan's guide now as it had once been his father's.

He watched again for the first of the two flashes and set off paddling in the direction of the lighthouse. As the paddling turned into wading, he hoped his father had been right. He grasped the sides of the dinghy firmly with both hands to steady it in the crotch-high water, manoeuvred his weight over the side, and rolled in. He fell hard against the upper side of his right leg and screamed out again. He couldn't simply lie there though, so he forced himself to sit up on the thwart and began to slide the oars into their rowlocks. He used his right oar to turn the dinghy so his back was facing the Phare de la Croix and began to row. Declan had never rowed any distance before, but had sat in a boat as his father had struggled against choppy waters, howling winds and falling tides. It seemed to him now, there wasn't really much to it and he thanked the water for being on the way back inland and the wind for being calm. Periodically, he flipped his head around quickly to catch the second flash of light and make certain he was still heading in the right direction. As he rowed and sang Tri Martolod, turning on every third or fourth flash to check his bearings, the time quickly passed, but it must have been a good half an hour before he could definitely confirm the lights of the Peacock were now further away than they had been when he had first seen them from the shoreline. As he continued to row, Declan wondered how long it would be before he got to the rocky outcrop on which the lighthouse stood, for he was exhausted. He wondered how deep the water was where he was rowing and decided to take an oar to measure it. As he removed the oar from the rowlock, however, his question was answered; the hull of his dinghy crashed onto some rocks just below the surface of the water, and he could hear the telltale, rolling gush of breakers on rocks all around him. Waiting again for the lighthouse flash, he readied himself to focus on his nautical position and found that he had been washed up on a small island. He smiled to himself thinking how ironic it would be if this was Dad's Breton Ireland he had found. One thing was for sure, he had escaped his enemy's immediate grasp and that made him smile some more. He would have to get out, however, and paddle or wade his way into deeper water.

Declan climbed out of the boat, a little clumsily, but he managed without hurting his leg any more. The water was freezing and the salt stung like mad. He didn't care too much to think what his leg must look like underneath his trousers and instead turned his attentions to the lighthouse again as he pushed the dinghy round this tiny shoreline, back once more into the navigable waterway. About twenty minutes later, aboard and rowing once again, he, noticed there was water swishing around by his ankles. It took him no time at all to understand what had happened as he had run aground, and to realise he was sinking. The dinghy began to take on water fast, and before he had rowed another ten minutes, the water level had already reached the thwart on which he was sat. Climbing out of the dinghy, he turned around again to see that he wasn't more than a hundred yards from the lighthouse. As each double flash washed over him and his sinking dinghy, he took the plunge. The water was too deep to wade through and Declan estimated that the tide must have come in quite some way. His clothes were wet and heavy and he was tired. His progress in the direction of the Phare de la Croix seemed negligible; on the contrary, he seemed to be drifting further away. Suddenly, he felt something touch his leg and instantly he drew his legs up as high as he could to avoid becoming shark bait. He looked up again as the lighthouse flashed and saw that he was no more than ten metres from the outcrop, so he swam as hard as he could towards it. A current was dragging him back and he had to wait in order to paddle between waves. The sea here was not the same, he could feel its power and was absolutely desperate when he was finally thrown up onto the rocks. He had to cling on tightly so as not to be dragged back down into the swell.

With the tide still rising, Declan could not wait there, he had to move. He scrambled up the rock as quickly as he could, being careful not to scrape his leg on the barnacle-covered surface, and finally made it up onto a flat concrete platform. Another flash and he saw stone steps leading up to a round base on which the two towers had been built. He climbed the steps and half staggered over to the smaller of the two. She, the dark-haired woman, had guided him in his moment of darkness and now they were together and he felt safe – the towers were him and her. And then he realised something that shattered these romantic thoughts. The face of the man he had seen before – Bag Balaclava – he had been the blind man at the church. She, the dark-haired woman had been helping him. What did this mean: she was on their side helping them? He felt almost uncontrollable anger towards her. He stopped leaning against the smaller of the two towers and began to search for a way inside and out of the cold. He was dripping wet and there was a wind picking up. There was no entrance to the smaller tower and so he continued his search. As he circled the lighthouse, he discovered the two towers were in fact adjoined. He found a door but it was padlocked, and so he searched around during the flashes for a sizeable rock with which to smash it open. He found one quickly, swung at the lock, but grazed his hand quite badly as it sliced out of his hands. This angered him even more and the second blow smashed the padlock clean off, hurtling it to the ground. Declan turned the handle and walked in; one hand feeling in front of his face as he searched in complete darkness for some sort of light switch. He found a niche in the wall on the left and in it a cylinder quite waxy to touch and next to it a plastic bag. He groped at the bag and found what felt and sounded like a box of matches. He removed the box from the bag and opened it, being careful to make sure it was not upside down. He could just imagine himself emptying the matches over the floor and then dripping sea water everywhere destroying them. He struck a match and saw immediately that the waxy cylinder wasn't a candle but a distress flare. Light the flare and someone would come and rescue him.

He stepped out again onto the round base and followed the wall to the south side facing the coast. It was then he realised that he had no idea how to light a flare, so he returned to the shelter of the big tower again. Once inside, he lit another match and began to read the pictograms. On any other day, he hated pictograms, but, right at this moment, in the twelve seconds it took the match to burn the tips of his finger and thumb, he had changed his mind. He unscrewed the cap off the handheld flare, struck it over the now bared end and watched for a few seconds as a fluorescent smoulder began to burn strongly and then spit bright red fire into the air for a distance of about two feet. In a flash of reason, he thrust the flare down into the waves at the bottom of the platform and saw it disappear into the water. There was a vessel crossing over to the island from the mainland and he had just seen the strobe and port lights when he realised who was likely to be on board. He began to panic now, wondering what would happen if Boss Balaclava had seen him, and as he watched the boat continue its course unaltered, he wished he still had a flare in his inventory.

As the boat neared the island of Bréhat, the wind picked up and he sought shelter in the lighthouse once again. Picking up the box of matches, he lit one and began to investigate. He discovered the smaller of the two towers was home to a set of stone steps leading to the upper floors of the main tower. He felt his way up and around following the outer wall to the first floor. He stood at the top of the first flight of stairs looking into a circular room with a stone window ledge. In the middle of the room were a table and two chairs. Two quite tatty looking mariner's charts hung on the wall and using up another match, he recognised them as illustrating the very coastline to which these men had taken him. Another turn of steps in the small tower took him into what had clearly been sleeping quarters: a bunk, a cupboard, a chest of drawers and a small bedside table. The final set of steps in the smaller tower inevitably led him to the top floor and although the room was empty but for a quite modern looking metal cabinet against one wall, there was evidence in the form of large bolts and some remaining angle iron, of large machinery in the centre of the small circular room. He guessed that this would once have housed something mechanical and heavier than the present automated sequencing apparatus for the light and prisms which were housed on the roof of the lighthouse. Each floor had a window looking out to sea, and it was a strange feeling of accomplishment he experienced looking out of this top one, for instead of seeing a point of light flash at him for a fixed four seconds, he could look out now and follow its long sweeping beam as far across the bay as the window permitted.

Looking back later that day, Declan would be able to see the error of his ways, but right now, as this brilliant idea began to develop, there was only one way off this rocky outcrop. The modern looking cupboard against the wall on the top floor of the lighthouse sat opposite the window. He was running very low on matches and reaching in the near-dark, found two door handles. The cupboard was not locked and as he opened up both doors, dim lights came on automatically inside, revealing an extensive electrical cabinet. In one corner was a CO_2 bottle suspended on a thin metal plate within a cage. This was a modern automated fire extinguishing system for electrical cabinets with which Declan was quite familiar. There was a plastic pocket stuck to the inside of the left-hand door and in it some folded wiring diagrams. Declan didn't need them. The busbar; row after row of mould case circuit breaker (MCCB's); beautifully tidy red, blue and yellow wiring; solenoids; overload relays; timers; two high-load contactors; a selector switch showing "MAINS", "GENERATOR" and "OFF".

'That would do,' he thought.

He turned the selector switch to 'OFF' and cut all power to the components of the cabinet. The beam of the lighthouse went out. Declan struck one of the last matches and headed for the stairs and to the sleeping quarters. He lay down on the bunk, which was remarkably comfortable and waited, eyes closed, but unable to fall asleep. A lighthouse with no light would surely attract urgent attention and the coastguard or someone of authority would come out almost immediately. Of this, he was certain.

Yannick Le Borgne from the Direction des Affaires Maritimes (la DAM) heard the alarm first and immediately picked up the radio.

'Marcel Le Gall, here, Maritime Security, Over', this was internal, he could speak French.

'Marcel, c'est Yannick de la DAM. Nous avons un gros problème avec La Croix ; il s'est éteint. Over.' *We've got a big problem with La Croix Lighthouse, it's switched off.*

'Salut, Yannick, la merde. Le tableau signale quoi? Over.' *Shit, what does the control board say?*

'Rien, il est mort. Coupure totale. Over.' *Nothing, no signal.*

'Putain, merde. Je m'en occupe, Yannick, t'inquiète! Over.' *Damn. I'm on to it. Don't worry.*

'D'accord, Marcel, et tu me tiens au courant. J'appelle Le CROSS? Over.' *Keep me updated.*

Le C.R.O.S.S., the Centre Régional Opérationnel de Surveillance et de Sauvetage comprises fifteen stations all over France covering coastal surveillance including the coastguard.

'Non, non, c'est pas la peine, Yannick, t'auras assez à faire. Over and Out,' confirmed Marcel Le Gall. *Leave it, you'll have enough to do.*

Yannick Le Borgne made three further calls: the first to alert the international search and rescue (SAR) coordination centre; the second to the International Maritime Organisation (IMO) and the third to the Maritime Rescue Coordination Centre (MRCC). All procedures correctly followed, Yannick Le Borgne sat and waited at his desk for news from Marcel. The two men had worked and sometimes even trained together for over twenty-five years, but nothing like this had ever happened before. Smuggling was small business in these waters, but Marcel Le Gall, on the phone to Thomas Guyader took the decision to inform the Douanes (French Customs and Excise): his next call.

Thomas Guyader, from the centre for Sauvetage en Mer – Lifeguard - would captain the boat out to the lighthouse and he very quickly alerted his team, three men; Mikael, Christian and

Guillaume. Marcel Le Gall cut off the phone without replacing the receiver and got Yannick Le Borgne on VHF Naval channel 67 on 156,375 MHz.

'Marcel Le Gall, Sécurité Maritime, do you read me? Over.'

Yannick snatched the receiver from its cradle:

'Salut, Marcel et alors quoi de neuf? Over.' *Any news?*

Marcel explained that Thomas Guyader would be heading out to the lighthouse on search and rescue in the next ten or twelve minutes with his team from Paimpol and also informed Yannick that he had decided to engage the services of the Douanes. They would be listening to the radio and were sending out a surveillance helicopter immediately, but no boat for now.

'No, that makes sense, they'll keep an eye on things, but they won't want to get in the way at the moment. Excellent work, Marcel. Over and out.' Yannick hung up leaning forward on his desk with his face in the palm of his hands: what the hell was going on?

Lying down on the bunk, Declan wondered how long it would take someone to realise the lighthouse wasn't working and then come to rescue him. He began to accustom himself to the noises of the sea and counted to see if he could pick up any rhythms in the waves crashing against the rocks. That's what Papillon had done to escape from his island imprisonnement. A light beam seemed to flash across the ceiling briefly and at first, Declan thought he had imagined it, but then there it was again. He couldn't have been there even half an hour and already they had sent somebody, what efficiency.

12
Viscount de La Villemarqué - 1839

T he rain drummed incessantly against the imperial roof of the horse-drawn carriage as it slowed down and pulled to a stop. The road was a quagmire, damping the usual trip-trapping of hooves on cobble. Théodore-Claude-Henri Hersart de La Villemarqué felt the leather thorough-braced-suspension lean as the coachman stepped down. Gaitered feet squelched beside the carriage; a cane tapped on the window and a lantern was held up to the glass confirming de La Villemarqué's suspicions: it was dusk and the lanterns had to be lit. Claude de La Villemarqué peered across at his scribe who was pulling with his teeth at a ragged piece of skin on his thumb. They were both nervous and exhausted. And they were late.

The two men and their coachman had been travelling for three days already. De La Villemarqué and his scribe had been checking through the texts over and over all through the night prior to setting off from Pontivy in central Brittany. All the previous day and some of the evening, the two men had listened to the bard's daughter, herself already seventy-eight years of age. There had been breaks, of course, the old woman's voice was failing and she got tired quickly, but she had sung well. She was the daughter of a musician, long since dead, who had taught her the song. If the dates tied in and the academy accepted them, then the provenance of the song would pass the inspection. The song was factual and accurate. It enabled Claude de La Villemarqué to trace back in time to an eyewitness account of some atrocious suffering through Plague outbreaks that had taken place in medieval Brittany. The bard's daughter, herself born in the spring of 1760, had learnt the song from her father, a musician by profession, himself having learnt the song from his grandfather who in turn had been born in central Brittany in around 1640.

De La Villemarqué and his scribe were to attend a meeting in Paris at the end of the week with an elected member of the Académie Française, known, especially to themselves, as the "immortals". To the viscount, the man was nothing but a jumped up inspector from Paris whose principal aim was to protect the French language and history. In order for the viscount's work, "Barzaz Breiz", a collection of medieval Breton folk songs, to be published as a legitimate contribution to French history, provenance, authenticity and accuracy had to be verified. Why these bloody Parisians should assume any say in what concerned Breton history as told in the Breton language, frustrated Claude beyond even his own Breton words. Surely what was important was not to lose the thread. So what if he had had to change one or two stanzas to accommodate the inspector? If he couldn't get this in print before the old lady died, it would be lost forever.

Claude de La Villemarqué took finger and thumb and pulled on his trim beard drawing it into its neat point. He had tried to negotiate with the academy, tried to find a meet somewhere halfway between Pontivy and Paris. Deadlines were deadlines and the inspector wasn't interested in weather conditions, but this wind and rain had been relentless for weeks. The messenger bringing back the inspector's stubborn news, had taken nearly three days longer than planned to get back from Paris. And he was on horseback, not in a carriage.

The scribe looked up at his employer; he was paid a handsome wage for what he did, but it was the hours that he objected to on this latest task. De La Villemarqué would just sit and listen to this old crone whining away in some strange dialect he himself could barely understand. He got the gist, that much was clear, but de La Villemarqué's Breton was far from perfect and what he had been learning wasn't the same dialect. This was the Breton dialect from the southern, central part of Brittany around Vannes, whereas de

La Villemarqué was learning the Breton from North of Quimperlé. The scribe was to act as witness to the crone's sworn oath, listen to the song and write down in proper French exactly what de La Villemarqué translated and sign each page at the bottom. The scribe watched his employer stroke his goat-like beard to a point. This was a telltale sign: de La Villemarqué had made a decision.

'Next stop is about ten kilometres from here,' de La Villemarqué announced to his scribe. 'We have to stop, eat and rest the horses.'

The scribe did not reply but nodded: this was just an observation, but he knew when his employer's mind was made up. A decision had been made, possibly to abandon the journey, hopefully, at least. They had two days left to get to Paris but would have needed three even with the weather conditions on their side.

An hour and a half later, the coach turned off the road and drew up outside a tavern. De La Villemarqué didn't wait for the coachman to lower the step and open the door, but stepped out himself and jumped onto the firm but muddy ground.

A dim light shone out from front windows as well as from lanterns hanging either side of the front door. He could see the form of his old friend Jean-Baptiste, the owner of the tavern standing by the oak barrels from where he generally served his second-rate red wine. Cane in hand, de La Villemarqué shouldered open the front door of the tavern and, without waiting for the scribe who was still being helped by the coachman to descend the step, he walked in. Jean-Baptiste was not expecting visitors; he was stripped to the waist, had half a face full of soap suds and held a cut-throat razor in his right hand.

'Good God, Claude, what brings you to this neck of the woods?' cried Jean-Baptiste, showering de La Villemarqué with shaving suds. 'Give me two minutes,' he said slightly more calmly now, 'and I'll make myself decent.'

'I'm here with an official scribe and my coachman,' confessed de La Villemarqué. 'I'll explain later.'

'Listen, Claude, sit yourselves down by the fire and I'll be right back. Make yourselves at home.'

The scribe walked into the tavern followed closely behind by the coachman. De La Villemarqué turned swiftly, offered to take their coats and then beckoned his coachman to sit beside the fire. The coachman took off his gauntlets, placing them on the side of the hearth, removed his overcoat, which he gratefully handed to his master, sat down with his back to the fire and began to peel off his glove linings; his clothes were drenched through to the skin and he was freezing cold.

They sat together, the scribe and de La Villemarqué facing the hearth and looking at the coachman in the dim light of the tavern.

'I've got some bad news, gentlemen,' he announced. He was silent for some time, obviously struggling to find the right words to convey this news.

'We will eat here at Alençon this evening, but we cannot stay the night,' he explained, matter-of-factly. 'We will have to travel through the night, George, I'm very sorry. You and I, sir,' he said, looking at the scribe, 'will have to try to sleep as best we can in the coach. We've got blankets, but it will be by no means comfortable.'

The coachman suddenly felt quite depressed. The viscount almost never called him by his first name; an honour that cheered him up, however briefly, and made him realise that the man really saw no other alternative.

'I expect to arrive in Mortagne au Perche by early morning. There, we can rest a few hours before having breakfast,' he continued. 'In order to make Paris in two days from there, you and I will have to continue on horseback,' he said, looking straight at the scribe. 'You, George,' now turning his head to face the coachman, 'can stay on at the inn there for a few days before we return.'

George, his back to the fire, was now beginning to warm through. Under normal circumstances he would never advise the viscount without first having been asked to do so directly. Under normal circumstances, he obeyed his employer's orders. He had wanted to mention the speed on the new roads, for he thought they could stay the night here at Jean-Baptiste's and still make Paris on time for the meeting. As the scribe offered his own advice on the subject, the immediate and visible relief on the coachman's face turned out to be ill placed.

'You want to stop at Mortagne tomorrow morning?' asked the scribe, glancing up quickly to see Jean-Baptiste come back into the room announcing quietly, but purposefully, that food would be ready shortly. 'But the road network for the Malle Poste to Paris from here is so good now that you could easily make up the time we lost getting to Rennes.'

Jean-Baptiste too perked up, adding:

'You eat here with me this evening, set off with the horses dried off, rested and fed, you could double that distance, even travelling through the night. You would be in Verneuil au Perche for eight or nine tomorrow morning. The Malle Poste claim to cover Brest – Paris in sixty odd hours. They're not far behind the English Mail Coaches for speed. That's less than three days.'

Once again de La Villmarqué stroked the beard: a decision.

'Less than three days maybe, but they don't have to cross to Rennes from Quimper and then Pontivy on waterlogged tracks littered with fallen trees. How many times did we have to unharness the horses to drag trees off the road, George?' George answered by nodding in agreement.

No, no,' exclaimed Jean-Baptiste. 'All that's done for you these days; roads are cleared, drained…, everyone keeps to the right side of the road so you meet nothing head-on. They've even got men guarding the routes in some places… well, the thing is now, that you don't hear of many highwaymen trying their luck – not on those roads, not these days.'

'How do you feel about that, George?' enquired the viscount.

The coachman's honest answer would have been inappropriate and he liked his job and his master, but he coughed slowly just enough to clear his throat and replied.

'If it can be done, I'll do it. I have to go and see to the horses now though.'

Jean-Baptiste replied by signalling a sort of woahing action with both hands while he found his words.

'Don't do that on your own, George. My boy will do that while you warm up and have something to eat.'

'I'd be glad of some help, but there are things I need to do myself,' and with that, George stood up to step out into the night, leaving his huge overcoat to dry by the fire. His jacket and shirt were light and would dry off again quickly enough, but a warm overcoat would see him through the night.

'My boy's a fine hand with the horses,' added Jean-Baptiste after him.

'What's his name?'

'Edouard.'

'Fine,' replied George, 'send him out then.'

There were three things that the coachman really wanted to do himself and the first one was to take a pee. He then wanted to recover the bound manuscript from under his seat and make safe his arms. Only two things bothered George on the roads: big puddles and highwaymen. Both were unpredictable and potentially very dangerous. George was always alert in case he came across either. Rain brought the puddles, while fair weather brought the highwaymen. Big puddles, if you saw them coming that is, had to be dealt with as slowly as possible. With highwaymen, it was the opposite. He had been confronted with the problem only twice

while in service to the viscount and never in Brittany proper –
Breton speaking Brittany. Highwaymen spoke French, and there was
always a spokesman. On both occasions George had put a crossbow
bolt through their heads before they even got to the end of their
introductory sentence. Snatching at his already cocked pistol, having
laid down his preferred arm, he had asked the other highwaymen
calmly if anyone else wanted to die that day? The crossbow had
something brutally cold about it and for George, this lay in its whole
trajectory. The sound it made when it left the bow prod. The thud
made when it hit its target. But mostly, George thought, it was the
silence that ensued, that struck terror into the hearts of onlookers,
for it was during this split second of silence that the human brain
registered what had just happened, where it had come from, and
that it was too late. The silence was inevitably interrupted by the
sound of a body hitting the ground, hard. Tangible, brutal and cold.
With his left hand still tight on the reigns, he had raised them up
and forwards to move the horses on, still pointing the pistol at the
would-be attackers. On neither occasion had he advised or asked for
advice from the viscount before acting: these had not been "normal"
circumstances.

He went out to remove the bolt from his crossbow, to take the
tension out of the bow prod and make safe his pistol. The pistol
and the bolt, he locked in the compartment under his seat while
removing the manuscript for the viscount. Edouard appeared from a
side entrance to the tavern and nodded respectfully to George.

'Here, Edouard,' George waited just an instant to see the boy's
eyes make contact with his. Then he tossed a silver half-franc towards
him. Edouard caught it with both hands in the dim light and
couldn't hide his delight, but before he could thank the coachman,
George began:

'Two big handfuls of oats for each horse, and no more. As much hay as they can eat in a half hour and no icy water. Make sure you dry both mares thoroughly.'

'Yes, sir,' said Edouard.

George turned and headed for the tavern door again, key in one hand and manuscript in the other. This was not going to work, the solid oak door was heavy and had swelled with the rain. On arriving at the tavern, it had been his master that had reached the door before him, so George slipped the key safely into his trouser pocket, clutched the manuscript tightly against his chest and shouldered the door inwards and away from the storm. Once inside, he shouldered it closed again behind him and headed back to the warmth of the now blazing fire.

Four places had been set on a solid oak table near the window and George saw his overcoat had been draped across the back of two chairs and placed near, but at a safe distance from the fire. Steam rose off the shoulders in swirls up to the aged oak beams where smoked sausages hung on brown twine from old pegs along with a number of dried hams and a lean-looking silverside of beef. Jean-Baptiste reached up above the table and took down a large sausage, about the size of a man's forearm, all strung and bulging from its net-formed skin. He laid the sausage on the table and asked the three men if they had a preference for ham or salt beef, but grabbed both before anyone had time to answer.

'There's thick broth before this to help you warm through,' he explained. 'You'll have to put your own salt on the butter; they don't mix it in after churning in these parts'.

An enormous, round and crusty-looking wholemeal leavened bread sat on a well-hacked walnut plank in the centre of the table. A full butter dish was set next to the plank with a plain looking brown glazed pot next to that.

'That's sea salt in the pot there. I've taken the lid off to dry it out a bit. It's picked up the moisture in the air,' said Jean-Baptiste, as he placed a sabre-like knife on the table next to the loaf. Disappearing briefly behind the barrels into the kitchen again, Jean-Baptist fetched a pitcher of wine and laid a copper saucepan on the table. The scribe, having slid along the bench to make room for George, still fire-side of the table, stood up to reach above his head for a ladle he had spotted hanging on a hook from a beam. He began serving the viscount first. De La Villemarqué acknowledged the gesture and nodded his appreciation.

The host half-filled four goblets with the finest cask wine he had. An open cask would keep for some time if covered in a cool place in the dark. But a month or two from now, Jean-Baptist knew he would be serving it to customers less discerning.

> 'Help yourselves to all you want and please ask for more if you need it,' said Jean-Baptist raising his goblet. 'A toast to the success of your mission, gentlemen.'

'Yec'hed mat,' they said together. *Cheers*.

Five minutes must have passed without a word being spoken when George, thinking of his master and the highwaymen, broke the silence:

'Are there guards on these Malle Poste diligence coaches?'

'Their coachmen are armed and word has it they're good,' Jean-Baptiste confirmed. 'Hey, there's an idea. You two get to Verneuil-au-Perche tomorrow morning with George here... well, you could pick up the diligence coach to Paris from there. They've got six to eight places on those lines and nobody will be travelling in this weather,' he slurped back some red and added, 'You'd gain time for sure. You'd get to Paris a day before your meeting. That's what I'd do if I were you.'

'It makes a lot of sense. A whole lot of sense,' the viscount agreed. 'Then that is exactly what we shall do. George, we'll leave here in about an hour, and once in Verneuil, you can have three days to yourself before we get back. How do you feel about that?' asked de La Villemarqué, addressing himself this time to the scribe.

'Much more civilised and safer,' replied the scribe who had not liked the idea of travelling without George or someone else to protect them.

'That settles the matter then, gentlemen,' concluded the Viscount de La Villemarqué, stroking his beard to a point.

13
Help On The Way

As Thomas Guyader approached the lighthouse, he signalled to Guillaume to circle so as to approach lee side of the rocky outcrop either side of the jetty. Mikael prepared to run up alongside the jetty, but Thomas signalled to wait; he had seen something that bothered him. The incoming tide was taking them back on shore and Thomas had to make a decision. Guillaume, who couldn't understand the skipper's reluctance to moor up immediately, couldn't ever really get his head around the idea that when on shore there wasn't a moment to lose, but out at sea it was always "safety first". Guillaume circumnavigated the lighthouse to come around to where they had been before. The moment his skipper signalled the all clear, he nosed the bow out slightly using the rudder, while Christian and Mikael lowered the fenders over the starboard side. The engine began to chug as the stern swung into the jetty and the air filled with the smell of diesel exhaust mixed with sea spray. The trough of a large swell swept around the rocks as the lifeboat touched the old granite wall of the landing jetty. The boat rolled towards the jetty and its starboard gunwale began to drag on the barnacle-covered granite wall of the wharf. As the swell began to rise once more, the trough that had formed on the lee side of the jetty rose in an instant. The yaw of the hull allowed the stern to swing out and the lifeboat pitched violently before the bow levelled up once more in a scraping, jerking movement. Thomas glanced around quickly assessing the situation to make sure his crew was all safe when suddenly Christian yelled out:

'Man overboard!'

Who the hell was it? Oh God, Mikael wasn't there.

There is no mechanism in the human body able to reabsorb adrenalin at the same speed at which it produces and releases it.

'It's alright, guys,' shouted Mikael. He had been trying to grab a metal rung of the ladder, running up the jetty wall, when the deck dropped away from him. Mikael was not alright. The rolling of the lifeboat had not given him enough time to grab the iron rung with both hands and as a result, still holding onto the mooring rope with his free hand, his foot had slipped down behind the rung and finally jammed him against the granite wall. Worse still, as the boat had been thrust back up by the rising crest of the swell, the bow had caught his left ankle which was hanging free and he had felt it snap.

Christian clipped his search and rescue line onto his harness and moved along the starboard gunwale to the iron rung ladder. Waiting just an instant, he grabbed out at the ladder gripping a single U-shaped rung firmly with both hands. As he felt his fists close tightly around the iron, he pushed off from the boat with both feet and landed with them firmly on a lower rung. It was a delicate and challenging feat he had accomplished, for just a rung above him, still clinging on to the ladder, was Mikael. In the light from the SAR vessel, Christian could see that he was injured – his face was contorted with pain and he was not responding appropriately to the predicament they were in. As carefully as he could, Christian pulled himself up the iron rungs, leaning as far away from the ladder as he could to keep an arched back. In this way, he could avoid pushing Mikael off. Reaching with one hand, Christian clipped his safety line into a free carabineer on the front of Mikael's harness and relieved him of the mooring line before continuing up onto the flat concrete jetty.

La Croix lighthouse had no mooring posts, but solid forged iron rings and Christian, in the poor light, decided to drop to his knees to locate the one nearest the stern. Having tied a bowline around the mooring ring, he returned his attention to Mikael. Climbing back down the ladder he clipped himself to a rung, freeing both hands to tie a munter hitch around the carabineer on Mikael's harness before saying to his colleague and friend,

'If I can haul you up, mate, could you free your foot?'

Mikael nodded and almost smiled, but added,

'Sorry about this, Chris, really.'

From the second floor window of the lighthouse, Declan assessed the situation and decided that these guys from the national coastguard, "Sauvetage en Mer" would not be part of the balaclava brutes. They looked to have everything in hand and he decided to wait on the bunk till they found him.

Christian pulled as hard as he could, but Mikael, who was still freeing his foot, did not move. Suddenly the line went slack and for a second Christian thought he'd lost his man. Then he felt a tug on the line and began hand over hand to take the strain. Mikael was unbelievably slow; something was wrong. It must have been almost five minutes before he reached the top of the jetty and Christian quickly understood what the problem was as he hauled his buddy away from the edge of the wharf; Mikael's foot was not facing the right way. Christian unhooked his colleague's walkie-talkie and pressed down on talk.

'Thomas, this is Christian. Over.' Christian watched as Thomas snatched up his walkie-talkie.

'Thomas here, I read you, Chris. How's Mikael? Over.'

'Compound fracture, left tibia I think. Throw me the headfast and I'll secure the bow. I've set up a belay system using a munter hitch and he reckons he can make it on deck from the wharf. Over.' Christian watched as Thomas signalled to Guillaume to throw him the mooring line. Once tied off, Christian heard his walkie-talkie crackle into action again. He picked up.

'Thomas here, don't go into the lighthouse on your own, do you copy? Over.'

'Chris here, what's the problem? I'll wait. Over.'

'There's someone inside. Now help get Mikael down here and I'm coming up. Over and out.'

The two walkie-talkies can't have been more than nine or ten metres apart, but with the offshore wind, the breakers on the rocks and the engine noise, the men had no choice but to communicate in this way.

Perched on the edge of the concrete wharf, and secured by a belay system, Mikael was helped down to the deck slowly controlling the descent himself all the way. It wasn't far, but the boat was rising and falling in the swell. On deck, Thomas and Guillaume reached up together to assist Mikael's landing and to avoid any knocks. He was in obvious pain, but in very good spirits and Guillaume covered his colleague with a blanket and placed a spare buoyancy device under his head for a pillow. Thomas stepped from the starboard gunwale to the iron ladder and climbed up. Christian reached down and offered Thomas his hand and the two men stood close together as Thomas gripped Christian's arm to talk into his ear.

'There's someone inside,' he said, motioning with his head towards the white painted front door of the lighthouse. Christian turned and looked to see that the door was ajar.

'I think I saw a guy's face at the window,' added Thomas.

'Might be a ghost!' said Christian mockingly.

The mission was not going well and Thomas had little time for humour at that moment. Pointing to a strobe in the sky not six hundred metres away, he said:

'That helicopter up there is Customs and Excise and they're not out here because of ghosts, Chris.'

Their brief from Marcel Le Gall at Maritime Security was simple: one, establish why La Croix had failed to function; and two, fix it if you can. That was it. Nothing about search and rescue. Yet someone was here.

Declan lay on the bunk in the dark and waited. As Thomas and Christian headed up the stone steps, he saw their flashlights flick up and down the walls of the stairwell and briefly through the open door. He wasn't quite sure how much to tell them and he began to get very nervous, even excited as they passed his doorway. He was surprised initially that they hadn't walked straight in, for he was sure that one of the men on the boat had seen his face at the window. He had even shone his torch in Declan's eyes. But the men carried on up the round stone stairwell to the top floor. At first this annoyed Declan, but then he began to get worried. He sat up carefully and limped towards the doorway that led out into the stairwell. The pain Declan felt from the burn had become once again virtually unbearable. The cooling, soothing effect of the sea water was wearing off and, as the water evaporated away, it left a stinging salt residue and with it, a new and deeper burning sensation. Declan stood in the open doorway, shivering and had to close his mouth tightly to stop his teeth from chattering. Everything in the lighthouse seemed to echo and that made it difficult to hear what the lifeguards were saying. So he concentrated as best he could, craning his neck up and towards the open doorway above him.

'Qu'est-ce qu'il y a, alors?' asked Thomas as Christian opened up the cabinet doors. *What's up then?*

'Franchement, je ne sais pas, chef,' replied Christian. *Honestly, I don't know, boss.* Unfortunately the electrician in the team had just broken his leg.

'Est-ce que ça a disjoncté?' asked Thomas again, desperate to be able to relay some message to Le Gall. *Could it just have tripped?*

Hearing this, Declan wondered if he shouldn't head up the stairs and turn the power back on for the two rescue men.

'Non, non, je crois pas,' Christian answered, looking along row after row of MCCB's - their blue plastic levers still pointing upwards. 'Non, c'est pas ça,' and then he saw it.

'Eh, ben, tiens, "OFF" c'est bien "éteint" en anglais, non?' reaching across for the selector switch, Christian turned it to the "ON" position and hoped. There was a clunking sound, a few low volume clicks and suddenly the lighthouse beam whirred into action once more.

'Ben, voilà,' he concluded trying desperately to hide his surprised relief. Someone had simply turned the lighthouse off.

'Thank Christ you understand these spaghetti cupboards,' concluded Thomas relieved.

Christian closed both doors to the cabinet and the men headed back down the circular stone steps.

'J'ai vu le gars au deuxième étage,' said Thomas. 'Pour moi, c'est lui qui l'a éteint.' *I saw the guy on the second floor, I think he turned it off.*

'Putain, le mec, il va se trouver dans la merde!' *Jeez, he's gonna find himself in deep shit.*

As Declan listened, he realised that these two men were more concerned about who had turned off the lighthouse than helping him off this retched rock and saving him from his tortuous ordeal. So much for "sauvetage en mer". It was a shock to Declan to hear that he might be in trouble with the authorities. He quickly moved away from the doorway and headed back into the room. A light shone in Declan's face and he raised a hand to shade his eyes. One of the men asked him something.

'Qu'est ce que vous faites là, monsieur?' *What are you doing there, sir?*

Declan, who was sitting once again on the side of the bunk, now with his burnt leg outstretched, took a decision to play the ignorant fool while he weighed up his odds. He shrugged, completely noncommittal.

'You speak English, monsieur?'

'Yes,' replied Declan, allowing his teeth to chatter and putting a little tremelo in his voice.

'You came here with boat, yes?' one of the men asked.

'I hit some rocks, my boat sank.'

'Demande lui s'il est tout seul,' ordered one of the two men.

'You are on your own, monsieur?'

Declan nodded. 'On my own.'

'Have you injury?' the same man asked.

Declan responded by pointing to his burnt leg, but as he inspected it himself in the poor light, he could not see much blood, just dirt. So he elaborated using his finger to point at his trousers where the burn was and, still masquerading as a non-French speaker, he said:

'Burnt.'

One of the men swung a canvass pack off his back and pulled a substantial looking first aid kit from it.

'Il faut qu'il s'allonge,' said Thomas.

'You must to lie down on the bed, monsieur,' Christian translated.

'Je ne sais pas ce qu'il a eu comme brûlure,' Christian added. 'Thermique – chaude ou froide, chimique – alcalin, acide... radiation – j'ai aucune idée, chef. Je pourrais faire plus de mal que de bien.' *Without knowing what caused the burn I could do more harm than good.*

Declan was in a dilemma: speak in French and annoy these men by letting on that he had wasted their time; or don't speak French and don't get treated for the burn.

'Not acid,' he said, 'hot water.'

The medic of the two men, the English speaker, ripped open the Velcro on what looked like a canvass tool-roll and picked out a pair of blunt-nosed scissors. He then began to cut at the leg of Declan's trousers below the burn, but above the knee and then he stopped and looked Declan straight in the eye.

'I have to do this,' he said. 'If you have uh..., merde, comment dire l'ischémie musculaire ou nécrose en Anglais?' the man paused for a moment and added, 'Maybe when you have bad artères, you get gangrène.'

'Thank you,' mouthed Declan, having understood full well what he had just been told.

Christian continued to cut around the trouser and finally slipped the free leg over Declan's knee before beginning the same process above the burn area.

'You have burn all over the femur?' the man indicated by tracing an imaginary ark with his index finger right around the circumference of Declan's upper thigh.

'Some burns,' Declan confirmed.

'When have you get burn?' the medic asked.

'Two or three hours ago I think,' he answered, although he was no longer absolutely sure.

'Then after, your boat have sink, monsieur?'

'Yes, that's right, then afterwards my boat sank.'

'You are very lucky man, monsieur, cold water 'ave help you – I think you get no gangrène.'

First of all the medic took a pair of plastic disposable tweezers and began to pull gently at the cloth - all that remained of Declan's trousers. He then took out a tube marked "hydrogel" and squeezed a clear substance from the nozzle practically using it all up. Declan's leg looked a mess. The areas where the medic had managed to remove the cloth from his skin looked a mixture of bright red, blistered skin and bleeding sores. The worst damage was in a strip about three inches long on the upper central part of his thigh, where the cloth had stuck and the skin had torn while he had been strapped to the chair. The whole burn was then sprayed with a clear looking liquid that seemed to fizz up when it touched the skin. The medic then put a dressing over the wound and bandaged it to keep everything protected.

'Tu crois qu'il pourra marcher?' enquired Thomas. *Do you think he could walk?* And as Declan began to rise to his feet, Christian added:

'On dirait qu'il t'a compris.' *You'd think he understood.* Both coastguards laughed.

Once on the wharf, Guillaume threw up a line and harness to Thomas and together they strapped Declan in. Attached by a line, he was lowered to the deck and Guillaume assisted him to a seat where he also clipped Declan's harness onto a shorter line. As Thomas climbed down the wrought iron rungs of the ladder and stepped across to the deck, Christian untied the bowline from the mooring ring, but let the rope run through the ring while he cast off the bow. He held the two mooring ropes in one hand while each, bow and stern, ran through the iron mooring rings. As he climbed down the ladder he quickly glanced behind him towards the boat, checked his height from the deck and jumped the two feet back over the starboard gunwale. He dropped onto his knees to the deck, all with an agility the skipper couldn't help but admire, clipped his safety line onto his harness and released both mooring lines simultaneously. Guillaume angled his rudder and opened the throttle to pull the stern back out to sea from the jetty. Christian hauled in the mooring ropes and coiled them neatly and quickly.

As the boat left the concrete wharf of the lighthouse, the man at the helm gently swung the stern around so the towers were behind them and steered a course for the mainland.

Captain Thomas Guyader radioed through to Marcel Le Gall from Maritime Security; confirmed that the lighthouse was functioning correctly once more; explained that one of his crew, Mikael, had broken his ankle; and relayed the fact that they had rescued a marooned mariner from the lighthouse and treated him for burns. Le Gall wanted the details before he radioed through to Yannick Le Borgne from la D.A.M.

'Un très bon résultat, Thomas, mais ton gars, ça va? Over.' *A very good result, Thomas, but is your man okay?*

'Oui, oui, ça va, mais il nous faut une ambulance, même deux, direct au port,' replied Thomas. 'L'autre est bien brulé. Over.' *Yeah fine, but we'll need an ambulance, two even, at the port. The other guy is badly burnt.*

'Et l'autre, qu'est-ce qu'il foutait là? Over,' insisted Marcel. *What the hell was the other man doing there?*

'On sait même pas. Il ne parle pas le français,' explained Thomas. 'Je crois qu'il est Anglais. Over.' *Not sure, he can't speak French. I think he's English.*

'Et Le Phare de la Croix, qu'est-ce qu'il y avait? Over,' probed Marcel. *And the lighthouse, what was it?*

Before replying to this question, Thomas glanced up at Declan who had his eyes closed and had been wrapped up in a blanket by Guillaume. Then he continued:

'Mon avis, c'est l'Anglais qui a coupé le jus au phare. Pour nous faire venir. Over.' *In my opinion it was the Englishman who switched off the lighthouse in order to get us out here.*

'Mais quel con!' replied Marcel. So the Englishman had shut down the lighthouse by switching off the electric in order to be rescued. 'J'appel les gendarmes à Paimpol, tu as compris, mais putain, quel égoïste, quel con. Over and out.' *I'm calling the police at Paimpol, what a selfish fool.*

'Ecoutez les gars,' announced the skipper, 'Il y aura des flics à Paimpol à cause du brûlé là, puis une ambulance pour toi, Mikael.' *There will be police waiting at the port for the Englishman.*

'Les flics?' blurted Guillaume. 'Pourquoi, qu'est-ce qu'il a fait?' *Police? Why, what's he done?*

'C'est lui qui a éteint le phare,' explained Christian. 'Peux-tu imaginer les conséquences? Putain, le pauvre con, il est vraiment dans la merde. Et il ne sait même pas!' *It's him that turned off the lighthouse, silly fool, Can you imagine the consequences? He's really in the shit now and he doesn't even know it.*

Declan, who had been listening intently since the moment the skipper had mentioned on the radio that he thought the Englishman had turned off the electric in the lighthouse, had understood all too well. So there would be police waiting for him in Paimpol harbour.

On VHS channel 9, Captain Guyader asked for Jean-Luc Le Bars, the harbourmaster at Paimpol. The harbourmaster was the sort of man whose facial expressions enabled him to switch between comedian and executioner in a split second. People instantly knew if he liked them or if he did not. He was a rotund fellow, a gentleman or a thug. In uniform his two moods were just as flagrant: he was the old sea dog in the corner of the bar with a pipe in his mouth, yet with his hat on and back straight, there wasn't a rank above him.

Jean-Luc had already been informed of everything, but was just toying a little with the gendarmerie choosing to make a point about territorial rank in *his* port. He knew full well the police needed search warrants to search a boat, and that he, as harbour master, did not. This gendarme was a young adjudant and great fun to bicker with. The harbour master, who had already lost his licence twice for drink driving, had it in for the police. Pulling rank like this, as well he knew, would never get him anywhere, for they could always talk to Customs, the Douanes, and override him if it was an important issue, but he could never resist the temptation to aggravate them; he simply didn't like them. The adjudant pointed out that until the vessel was actually in his harbour, he had no jurisdiction whatsoever.

'Wrong, sir,' he informed him. 'They've just stated their intention to land here and they're mine, legally. And out there,' he added, pointing a finger about six hundred metres offshore at the boat showing green, white and red lights, 'they're certainly not yours, unless you have a warrant.' The harbourmaster allowed himself a broad smile. 'The law states, however, that the harbourmaster, that's me and not you, has legal powers to detain, caution or even arrest persons committing an offence within his or her designated port and or its tidal range responsibilities, sir. In this case that includes six hundred metres off-shore,' Jean-Luc continued. 'No, sir, I shall open the gates for you and your men, when I'm good and ready,' he concluded, putting on the most pompous voice he could muster up. What a wonderfully entertaining evening this was turning out to be.

'Now listen up, Mr. Harbourmaster...' began the adjudant.

'Very well, but you'll have to be quick then,' interrupted the harbourmaster, pointing a finger once again at the approaching boat, 'for shortly I shall be a very busy man. I have a possible criminal act to investigate. In *my* port, sir,' he grinned. 'So now you listen up, Mr Officer, I'm expecting two ambulances to come through here any moment now, so I shall have to ask you to move away from the gate while I let them through. Don't go too far just in case I should decide to make an arrest. At such point I shan't hesitate to inform you, should I request your assistance.' He gave all three gendarmes another toothy grin, a cheeky wink, turned his back on them and walked away.

As the skipper navigated his SAR vessel back into port, he could see the lights inside the pyramid-shaped bay window attached to the gable end of the harbourmaster's building. Thomas Guyader knew Jean-Luc Le Bars and had done for years. Jean-Luc was old school, them and us, land and sea. He was not a man to cross.

No more than two minutes later in a very short burst, the sound of a siren could be heard approaching the port. Onboard the boat, Declan too had heard the siren and he sat up to watch as the flashing blue lights disappeared behind a building with a frontage in the form of a pyramid-shaped modern veranda. Hearing the siren, the skipper looked up as well, and then turned to catch Declan staring in the direction of the commotion.

The adjudant had evidently decided it would be more sensible to cooperate with this old fool of a harbourmaster for the time it took him to get bored of his games. He had ordered one of his men to reverse the car to a small gravelly parking space away and to the right of the barrier in order to let the ambulances through. The gates were unlocked and the old fool swung one of them open to let the two vehicles through. Immediately afterwards, the Renault Clio from the gendarmerie, pulled out from its spot and followed directly behind the second ambulance. The adjudant had walked through and stood at the open end of the gate in order to prevent the harbourmaster from closing it quickly behind him.

'I take it you won't be charging us with trespassing!' snapped the policeman as the Clio drove on through to the landing pier.

The harbourmaster didn't answer but started to swing the gate closed, forcing the adjudant to move out of the way quickly to avoid being hurt.

Fifty metres away at the landing pier, the SAR vessel began to manoeuvre alongside its mooring. The harbourmaster, having decided not to bother locking the stable door after the horse had bolted, left the gate open. Instead, he headed directly to the quay in order to save time and avoid being the last man there: this was still his investigation.

'Bonsoir, c'est bien vous le capitaine?' began the adjudant, looking at Christian. *Are you the captain?*

'Ben, non, c'est lui,' he answered, pointing to Thomas. *Er, no it's him.*

'C'est vous le capitaine, monsieur?' the inquiry continued.

'Oui, monsieur,' confirmed Thomas.

'Vous cachez un "sans papier" à bord, Capitaine?' asked the adjudant accusingly. *Are you hiding an illegal stowaway, Captain?*

'Bonsoir, Capitaine Guyader,' interrupted the harbourmaster. 'Take no notice of my "friend" the adjudant from the brigade of Paimpol; for the moment, this is still my inquiry. Now I understand you have rescued a shipwrecked mariner?'

Listening intently, Declan preferred being called a "shipwrecked mariner" to an "illegal stowaway".

'Oui, un Anglais,' confirmed Thomas, glancing quickly at Declan. *An Englishman.*

'And in your opinion, would he need hospitalisation?' continued the harbourmaster.

'Ben, oui, d'après Christian, il s'est bien brûlé.' Er, y*es he's quite badly burnt.*

'Il n'a pas les neuf pourcent de la surface de la peau brûlés, mais ce sont quand même, des brûlures de deuxième voire troisième degré. Ça pourrait devenir critique. Mon avis professionnel: il vaut mieux qu'il voie un médecin.' said the medic. *Second or third degree burns. It could be critical. He ought to see a doctor.*

The harbourmaster, returning his attentions to the adjudant, said,

'Et, ben, voilà: votre investigation va continuer à l'hôpital.' *Your investigation will have to continue at the hospital.* 'Dans le monde de marins professionnels, nous ne parlons plus de "sans-papiers", mais "d'étrangers en situation irrégulières"', bellowed the harbourmaster in a voice so loud that it echoed around the small port. *In the world of professional mariners we don't talk about "illegal stowaways" any more, but of "foreigners in an irregular situation".* 'Et ici, au Port de Paimpol, chez moi, on est encore innocent avant d'être condamné! Est-ce que j'ai été assez clair?' he concluded glaring at the three policemen. *And in my port, people are still innocent until proven guilty – do I make myself clear?*

'Nous allons en reparler.' retaliated the gendarme, desperate to have the last word and with that he turned around and said to his two men,

'On va suivre l'ambulance.' *We'll follow the ambulance.*

Declan was able to walk pretty much on his own to the ambulance that awaited him, but for Mikael, a stretcher was lowered down to the deck of the search and rescue vessel and Christian helped the two ambulance men manoeuvre the stretcher up onto the wharf and into the awaiting ambulance. Declan did not see the second ambulance follow behind. The adjudant glared at Declan the whole time and made him feel extremely uncomfortable. What he couldn't get his head round was the fact that he had been kidnapped and tortured and was now wanted by the police. He hadn't done anything wrong. As Declan lay there on a stretcher in the back of the now moving ambulance, he began to see things in a very different light. He could see that turning off a lighthouse in such treacherous waters was perhaps not the cleverest thing to have done, but under the circumstances... Shit! Under the circumstances? His captors and torturers they might have been, but he had just killed two men. He had just murdered two people. In self-defence. Premeditated self-defence; did that exist?

'Votre nom, monsieur?' asked the medic in the back of the ambulance. Declan tried to sit up to see if the police really were following.

'Your name, monsieur?'

They were; he saw the Clio with its flashing lights right out of the back windows.

'O'Leary,' said Declan.

What the hell was he supposed to have done, broken free from his chair and then asked the balaclava boys to let him go? He imagined himself trying to negotiate his release:

'I mean come on, guys, I've got this far, you could let me go now, it's a fair cop don't you think?' The whole thing was ludicrous. He should be praised for his bravery, compensated for his suffering. They bloody tortured him. He should be hailed a hero, not find himself on the run like a fugitive.

'Prénom, monsieur?' continued the medic.

'Declan.'

'Oh, so you are Irishman?' suggested the medic. 'They 'ave said you was English.'

It occurred to Declan then, in a moment of clarity, that in order to be a fugitive on the run, he would first have to be on the run. Richard Hannay had been a fugitive. He had been able to turn to a friend, someone high up in the Foreign Office.

'I 'ave been to Ireland on 'oliday last year, eez beauty-ful,' ranted the medic.

The only friend Declan had to turn to was a mechanic. The hospital was not far and Declan's stretcher was wheeled down from the back of the ambulance where he was transferred to a hospital stretcher and wheeled into accident and emergency.

'Aux Urgences.'

Once in A&E, he lay there in the middle of a corridor, thinking about how there seemed to be little consideration for one's dignity, how anyone could just walk by, when two people did: two of the gendarmes he had seen at the port. A nurse arrived and explained to Declan that a doctor would be along to see him as soon as possible and that then he would be transferred to somewhere more private. He pretended not to understand a word. One of the two policemen, the adjudant he presumed, informed the nurse they had an arrest warrant for this man and would need to speak to the doctor first.

'J'ai un mandat d'arrêt pour cet homme, mademoiselle, et il est impératif que je parle au médecin.'

'Ça se peut,' she replied – *that may well be*. She wasn't interested.

Declan knew him to be lying, for they were unable to present such a document to the harbourmaster or they would have done so, fervently. Furthermore, they had not been anywhere since, except right behind the ambulance. What happened next struck Declan as really bizarre. The adjudant pulled out his radio as soon as the nurse had walked around the corner. He signalled to his colleague to check around the corner after her, and then came right up close to the head of the stretcher-bed, leaned into the wall of the corridor and talked into his radio in such a low voice that at first, Declan thought he was talking to him.

'Oui, écoute, j'ai le gars – là avec moi.' *Yes listen, I've got the guy here with me now.* 'Oui, un Anglais, c'est ça.' *An Englishman, that's right.*

There was quite a long pause and Declan had to resist the temptation to look up to see if the man was still there, but then he heard his quiet voice again;

'Je ne sais pas, je vais regarder. Attends.' *I don't know. Hang on, I'll look.*

Next, the adjudant walked over to the side of the stretcher-bed and pinching an edge of the sheet between thumb and forefinger, he lifted it up as if to inspect Declan's dressing.

'En haut de sa jambe, côté droit. Ah, ben, oui, c'est ça, une brûlure je pense.' *On the upper thigh, there's a dressing. A burn I think.*

'Psst, quelqu'un arrive,' the other policeman called out as he began to approach his colleague and Declan. *Psst, someone's coming.*

'... s'il était sur l'île de Bréhat? Je ne sais pas. Il y a quelqu'un qui arrive... oui, d'accord. Salut.' *On the island? There's someone coming. Okay. Bye.*

So the police were beginning to make the possible link between him and the explosion on the Isle of Bréhat. They knew more than the coast guard. That must mean, thought Declan, someone realised the dinghy was missing, reported it and the police were now putting two and two together.

The adjudant had stopped the person who Declan presumed was the doctor before he got to the stretcher-bed. All Declan could hear was the doctor replying that without any paperwork it was impossible to be sure they had the right man. The doctor too was quite short with the gendarmes.

'Look,' he said, 'I don't care one way or the other, who he is or what he's done. You sort out your arrest warrant and you take him away.' Then the doctor came over to Declan and spoke in perfect English.

'They tell me you speak English, young man,' stated the doctor.

'I do.'

Strolling to the end of the stretcher-bed, the doctor picked up a clipboard and read:

'O'Leary, Declan. Is that you?'

'Yes.' With this, the doctor turned around to address both gendarmes and said:

'Celui-ci n'est pas votre Olivier', Messieurs. Et maintenant vous allez me laisser m'occuper de mon patient.' *This man is not your Olivier. Now I would be grateful if you would allow me to treat my patient.*

The doctor looked at Declan and smiled before he started to push the stretcher bed down the corridor.

'On the night shift,' explained the doctor, 'we are often understaffed and even the doctors have to be stretcher bearers. I'm Doctor Khadir.'

The doctor found a free room and swivelled the stretcher-bed around to go through the door backwards. Declan raised his head slightly to see if the gendarmes were still down the corridor, but they were actually following the stretcher.

Once in the privacy of the hospital room, Dr Khadir lifted back the sheet and carefully removed the dressing from Declan's burnt thigh.

'The police will not follow you in here: you can relax for the time being,' said the doctor.

'You're a lucky man, from what I understand. These burns could have been much worse.'

'I sure as hell don't feel lucky,' said Declan.

'I can see that,' replied Dr Khadir. 'This is a scald from boiling water, am I right?'

'Yes,' confirmed Declan.

'You are lucky, because in the case of circumferential burns like these, we sometimes encounter muscular ischemia, which is where the damage to the blood vessels is grave enough to prevent any, or sufficient circulation at least, to the skin. In this case, we would have to graft. In the very worst cases, amputation is the only option, Mr O'Leary. You must have spent a lot of time in the water after you burnt your leg. They told me your boat sank at sea.'

Using a cotton wool bud and surgical tweezers, Dr Khadir gently and meticulously removed little particles of dirt and sand from the open parts of Declan's wound as he continued to talk.

'What you have are second-degree burns or more precisely, partial thickness, second-degree burns. It was the time you spent in the sea that prevented any further deterioration. I think you should heal up quite well within three to four weeks and have minimal scarring in the longer term.'

Dr Khadir paused, glanced up at Declan's left elbow and then continued to smear a clear looking fluid over the entire surface of the burn before putting a dressing over the leg.

'Let me see that elbow,' insisted the doctor. Dr Khadir pushed back on his swivel chair and removed a swab, a bottle of iodine and a pair of finely pointed stainless steel tweezers from the top drawer of one of the white melamine units behind him. He then soaked the swab with iodine, took Declan's arm in his left hand, applied a good dose of iodine to the wound using the swab and, looking through the tiniest lower portion of his bifocals, he gripped hold of something in the wound with the tweezers and pulled. Declan felt it grate, metal on metal, as he tried to control his breathing to ease the pain. His curiosity was aroused as he heard the dampened, "chink" sound of a small piece of wet metal being dropped into a stainless steel kidney-shaped bowl.

'The name Khadir signifies green in Arabic, Mr O'Leary, but not in the sense that you westerners understand it. What I mean is that I was not born yesterday, Declan.' The doctor's voice had tones of disapproval in it, nothing nasty, but not as friendly as it had been. 'Khadir is derived from a mysterious holy man or prophet, who guides travellers. Khadir is a master of rivers and waterways and that is what saved you this night. Water takes many lives, Mr O'Leary, but it saves many more.' The gentleness was back in his voice again and Declan hadn't really noticed until it disappeared for a second time as Doctor Khadir spoke again.

'There are a lot of things I do not know, Mr. O'Leary, such as who you really are; or how you got the head of a screw stuck in your elbow; or why when you burnt your leg you were sat down, but didn't get up. But I do know you can understand French.'

'How do you know?'

'When I spoke with the gendarmes, your heart rate raced: had you not understood what was being said, that would not have been the case. Simple.'

'Je m'appelle Olivier Declan O'Leary, ils m'ont attaché à une chaise avant de me brûler,' confessed Declan.

'Who tied you to a chair, the police? Who burnt you? Who's they?' quizzed the doctor.

'Je ne sais pas,' whispered Declan, frightened.

'Wait here for me a moment, I'll be right back,' said Dr Khadir, and he walked out of the room closing the door firmly behind him.

In less than a minute, the doctor walked back in, a plastic carrier bag in hand.

'These are from lost and found: some dry clothing, socks and a pair of shoes your size – size 44. There's a pair of clean trousers here. I don't know if they'll fit you properly, but they are better than the half-mast pair you have. And look what we have here, a coat. It looks like it'll be a bit big for you, but take it, it'll keep you warm.'

Declan felt himself begin to break down, tears welled up in his eyes. He wanted to tell this doctor everything, but he had just killed two men not eight hours ago. Plotted to kill and killed. He couldn't talk to anybody, he had to get away.

'My given name is Farouk,' said the doctor. 'Farouk means able to tell good from evil. I can't help you against your enemy, Declan, this is *your* battle. But when you walk out of here, the police are waiting for you. I think they are not the people that burnt you, but you must be careful who you trust.' Farouk pulled a card out of the breast pocket of his white lab coat, scribbled something on it and handed it to Declan. 'I've added my mobile number to the card; call me if you there's anything I can help you with. Now listen carefully. We are on the ground floor here, that window will open enough for you to climb out of it should you choose to do so. I will tell the gendarmes that you are just getting dressed if you want a five-minute start on them. Whatever you decide to do my friend, be careful. And good luck.'

The door closed and Declan found himself on his own. Sometimes, while asleep, during periods of rapid eye movement or REM, the only thing that distinguishes a dream from a nightmare is the ability of the hero to react as required. It might be screaming out for help, running as fast as you can or punching out at the right person at the right time. So maybe Descartes was wrong with his, "I think therefore I am", Declan figured. He was sure he wasn't dreaming, but he couldn't find the courage to slide open the window, climb out and run: he couldn't think, therefore react.

There was a hard rap on the door. Declan listened.

'J'étais nul en Anglais à l'école,' said what sounded like the younger of the two policemen.' *I was rubbish in English at school.*

'Tant pis, on parle pas, mais on lui fout des menottes.' *It doesn't matter, we'll just cuff him.*

'En fait, est-ce qu'on a un mandat d'arrêt ou pas?' asked the youngster again. *Have we actually got an arrest warrant?*

'En fait, non!' replied the adjudant. *No actually, we haven't!*

'Ben, nous n'avons pas le droit de lui mettre des menottes.' *So we're not supposed to cuff him.*

'Mais qu'est-ce que j'en ai à foutre. Ouvre la porte, là!' *Bloody well do it anyway, now open the door!*

They had just confirmed what Declan suspected: no arrest warrant. They were only taking him in for questioning and weren't supposed to be putting handcuffs on him at all. This was crazy. The two gendarmes intended to put handcuffs on him for the simple reason that they couldn't speak English well enough to explain that he was being taken in for questioning. He should have run: they had nothing on him, no id. He looked up at the window at the exact same time as the door swung open. The two gendarmes walked in, cuffs in hand.

Declan was actually impressed by their speed. Within six seconds of entering the room, they had placed handcuffs around his wrists. Quite how it had happened he wasn't sure. He reflected on the speed with which the now dead balaclavas had cuffed him using cable ties and wondered if they too could have been gendarmes. Surely not?

He was marched down the corridor towards the hospital entrance, straight past reception. The occasional glance up, but no one really bothered. No one questioned the police. Once outside, the older of the two policemen raised a hand in the air and Declan saw the Clio set off immediately from its parking spot about thirty metres away. It drew up just in front of them and the younger policeman opened a rear door, while the adjudant manhandled Declan into the back exactly like in the movies; hand on head under the top of the door seal. To his surprise, Declan kept cool. They hadn't got anything on him and all he had to do was stick to his story.

As they sped away, he thought about what they might ask him at the station. He would have to deny having taken the boat from the island for starters. He couldn't afford to have them make that link or they would find out about the two dead bodies and then he really would be in trouble. This would have to be quick. What boat could he say he had been on? All the boats he'd ever seen had numbers on their hulls. They'd be able to double check anything he said and find out he was lying. Windsurfer then. Where had he set off from? Where would he tell them he left his passport? Jesus, this was going to be tougher than he thought. Windsurfing in normal clothing instead of a neoprene suit; passport fell out of his pocket along with a flask of scalding hot coffee which he always kept on board with him just in case he got thirsty, and so on and so forth and, oh no, he was really in trouble.

Suddenly Declan realised something he had previously overlooked – a small detail which awoke him out of his reverie. There had been no link to the boat on the island. The adjudant had spoken to somebody on the radio and that person had asked him to confirm if there was a burn on his upper right leg. It was only after that, he had mentioned the Island of Bréhat. The only people apart from Declan himself that could associate the burn on his upper right leg with the Isle of Bréhat were the three black-balaclava men – two of whom were now dead. It had been Boss Balaclava on the line talking to the adjutant. Oh God, thought Declan. He was in a trap. Now he had to find the courage to think and therefore react.

As the car set off along the road, he noticed there was a surprising number of people milling about near the hospital entrance. The new day had already begun and it was just beginning to get light. The police car turned down a lane and Declan saw a road sign marked something "Guyader", like the captain of the rescue boat. Then at the next junction he saw, "rue Jean-Moulin" – a resistance fighter. They'd only been on the road about two minutes when Declan, who was surprised by the crowds of people in the car park of Carrefour supermarket next to a roundabout, spotted the sign for the Gendarmerie Nationale. It wasn't that in itself that surprised him, however, it was the fact that the gendarme at the wheel didn't go straight ahead at the roundabout following the sign. Instead he turned immediately right. It seemed they weren't taking him to the station at all. Declan became suddenly very scared. Who were these men? Their journey took them down a slight hill on quite a busy road for about two minutes. Declan's pulse was racing. The gendarmes were not even talking to one another. He could glean nothing. The car pulled over to the left, just outside a café, and one of the gendarmes, the adjutant in the passenger seat directly in front of Declan, was getting out. He opened the door a fraction and turned around to ask the gendarme next to Declan if he too wanted cigarettes:

'...des clopes?'

'Gauloises blondes,' said the gendarme next to Declan and the adjutant spun his head to the front again and swung the door open.

The next thing Declan saw was a flash of white – a van passing his window. The driver had not even had time to brake. The Clio door was ripped off its hinges and sent flying down the road with a deafening, metal-bending crunch, followed by:

'Putain!' screamed at the top of the adjudant's voice. He was very badly shaken and unable to disguise the fact, but he took charge of the situation incredibly quickly ordering his two colleagues out of the Clio after the van driver. The van had skidded to a stop and as far as Declan could judge, the policeman was in the wrong. For a short time, Declan just watched as the three policemen began gesticulating what appeared to be a blatantly biased assessment of the accident. Then he looked across at the crowd of people beginning to gather outside the café. He saw the open door of the Clio next to the pavement across the rear seat from where he sat and he made his move.

14
Erwan Le Roux, Philologist - 1840

E rwan Le Roux sat at his desk looking through the manuscripts. There was a problem. Something didn't quite tie in. He couldn't put his finger on it, but something was wrong. Le Roux was a historian and a fanatic. He called out to his wife, Eleanor, asking for more sustenance – cider, crêpes and salted butter. Eleanor was not Breton by birth, but she had soon adopted her husband's homeland and quickly picked up the language.

'Chistr 'zo mat met gwin eo an tad,' she said to him as she put the silver tray down on the corner of his desk where he had cleared a small space for just that purpose. 'Cider is fine, but wine is the father of all drinks,' she repeated, this time in French. Erwan Le Roux beamed a big smile at his wife – he loved this woman more now than he had when they were first married forty years earlier.

'Too early for wine for me, darling. Can I trouble you again, Ellie?' asked Erwan hopefully. He knew the answer already and launched into his query.

'I've got a problem with the provenance of a song that de La Villemarqué published last year. I don't want to make waves, but I think he's wrong,' he suggested.

'He's a much-respected man, darling, you must be absolutely certain if you are going to challenge him,' said Eleanor.

'Well, tell me what you think.' And Erwan began to weight down the corners of three separate manuscripts which he proceeded to arrange in what appeared to him to be a very specific order. 'My problem is here,' he mumbled, biting off a mouthful of crêpe at least as tasty as his late mother's had been, 'this is the song from Elliant in the south that de La Villemarqué had published last year; this one,' Erwan continued, placing the fingertips of an open hand on the second manuscript, 'from Plouescat on the north coast, is one I collected myself; and this one, originally collected by a scolar named Jacques Derrien, comes from Langonnet on the river Ellé. Three songs, three regions,' he concluded. Eleanor couldn't see a problem there and said so.

'They're the same song,' said Erwan, frowning. He looked up at his wife, two fingers lying gently over his mouth and his thumb under his chin. Eleanor walked around her husband's desk and glanced quickly at all three manuscripts.

'What dialect is that one written in?'

'They were all sung in the dialect that comes from Vannes, the "Vannetais",' he replied, looking a bit puzzled, 'Why?'

'Because I can read them all and I shouldn't be able to, should I?' she concluded a little bit smugly, but hopeful she wasn't making a fool of herself.

'Good Lord,' he replied. 'You've got it. That's it.'

There were many problems with de La Villemarqué's published text, but this was the key that made sense instantly to Erwan. The place names and therefore the geography didn't fit correctly even with the version of the song 'The Plague of Plouescat' that he himself had transcribed. The dialect was all wrong, although the songwriter could have been a travelling bard. As for de La Villemarqué's version, it had been deliberately altered; of that much, Erwan was certain.

Such tampering annoyed Le Roux more than he could rationally explain. Serious historians, as far as he was concerned, had a responsibility to report findings and conclude, where they could, based uniquely on factual evidence. Where there were gaps, reasoning had to be justified but never should evidence be tampered with. At this time, in the mid part of the 19th century, the arduous task of unravelling many centuries of historical and sometimes intriguing events, could not be made easier when other people were tampering with evidence to suit their own desired interpretations.

The technique practised by most, involved cross-referencing eye witness accounts passed down through song, with church records, other written records and knowledge of local geography. This presented many challenges: differing interpretations of Latin texts did not help; written records were often incomplete or biased, and variation in dialect and incorrect notes meant that songs could change and place names too. Such changes in dialect, usually in songs passed down with no written record, were predictable and also happened to be

Erwan's particular field of expertise. He could quickly spot a word out of place or a fault in the rhythm of a song, and in this particular one, there were many.

'Well, what I'm going to do,' he concluded, a little undecidedly, 'is,' he paused, 'make detailed notes of all the inconsistencies and send a copy to my friend, François Luzel for a second opinion: just see what he says.'

'Could it not just be he's made some errors?' suggested Eleanor. 'After all, from what I understand, he hasn't been speaking Breton that long himself, has he?'

'No, no, it's not that,' contested Erwan. 'No, no, this is deliberate. What you get with these songs, you see, are layers. Layers of language; layers of time and error; and layers of "meddling", I call it.' Eleanor sat herself down on a chair by the big bay window behind her husband as he explained as briefly as he could how he carried out his work – his personal method.

'Everybody works slightly differently, Ellie, but this is my way. Time never changes the rhythm of a song in the same way as meddling would, for example. If, say, I can't remember the words to a song that my parents sang to me when I was a child, I might decide to make up some other words to fill in the gaps. Depending on my musical talents, I might improve the song or I might alter the rhythm if the words I try to slot in are too long or too short,' he continued.

'All of those kinds of changes are random, yet oddly enough they are predictable, when one understands two things: firstly, how these people lived their lives at any given time enables one to understand how the use of words actually changes from one époque to another; and secondly, parental errors spread and become family errors and sometimes regional ones.' Eleanor gazed at Erwan admiringly: he always took the time to explain his work and she felt that he respected her for it. She felt honoured to be involved.

'Am I talking too much?' he asked. 'I usually do.' Eleanor did not reply, but smiled and shook her head and so Erwan continued.

'Where was I? Oh yes, in other words, the more families that sing an erroneous or "modified" version of a song or "history lesson", the more likely it is to become regional and regional means the use of dialect which means predictability.' Clasping the bolée with both hands so as to avoid any chance of spilling the liquid over his display of papers, Erwan took another sip of cider to wash down the remains of his crêpe.

'Wow, the cider is good this year isn't it?' he remarked, quickly sipping again at his bolée. 'Am I making any sense?'

'About the cider or the predictability of dialect?' Eleanor retorted, smiling. Her husband smiled back.

'You not only know what words someone would likely have used at the time the song was changed, but you can often work out what they should have been singing based on the vocabulary used at the time the bulk of the song had been "written", so to speak. Well to be more accurate, "sung". Just imagine, Eleanor, imagine there's some really important historical event during someone's life. Something so important that they decide to add a verse to talk about that occurrence too: thus adding that incident to the history lesson for future generations. We must remember that these people, generally speaking, of course, could not read or write. These I consider as "historical-event layers".'

The sun had moved across the sky enough to alter the light being cast over the desk and Erwan, taking another bite into a crêpe, picked up the bolée of cider in his left hand and turned around to face the bay window. He reached up with one hand to open the left, green-embroidered drape to its full, while Eleanor, standing up, with both hands, pulled the right-hand one so the room and desktop lit up almost instantly. Erwan tilted his cider bolée up to his mouth and drained it. Eleanor glanced across at her husband and saw the three initials on the base of the cider bowl: p c c. The bowl had been in the house when she moved in with Erwan after their wedding and had been one of a set. Now there was only one cup left and Eleanor had no idea what the three letters stood for, but always thought to herself: 'Pour le Cidre à Chéri' – *for my darling's cider*.

'Now that brings me to the layers added by what I call meddlers,' continued Erwan. 'You see here, the use of Latin means that the church added some lines: enormous quantities of it in this case. So much of it in fact, it appears they were trying to change the entire meaning of the song, thus influencing the history lesson. Now it wouldn't be the first time that's happened. Assimilation of pagan beliefs into the dogma of the Catholic Church towards the end of the Roman Empire is certainly the best researched. Are there any more of those crêpes, darling?' asked Erwan, negating any suggestion of greed by adding: 'I've hardly touched the butter.'

'I'll fetch some more,' said Eleanor. 'I suppose you'll be wanting to wash them down with something as well?' she added, smiling. 'I'll be right back.'

When his wife walked back into the drawing room just a moment later, he picked up where he had left off.

'Where was I now? Ah yes. In this case, the alterations carried out by the church are not only historically fascinating in their own right, but they are also relatively easy to spot and therefore just as easy to remove, in order to see the history lesson as intended by the songwriter – the eye witness.'

'That makes sense,' agreed Eleanor. 'But what about de La Villemarqué's alterations?'

'Well, take this one for example: he's taken the word "perchenn", which means pole, and changed it to "dervenn", which means oak tree. In itself, the change is not enormous: pole... oak tree... oak branch, what's in it, one could ask? The problem is when you put it into context. He also changed the word "dilhat" – and I'm sure it's him that's done it – meaning garment or surplice, to "liñsel" meaning bed sheet. A bed sheet tied around an oak tree has a certain imagery about it, but it bears absolutely no resemblance to the image conjured up in the original wording of the song.'

'Which is?' prompted Eleanor.

'Which is, if you take the other two versions of the song, a priest was seen administering what was known as "extreme unction" to his parishioners. Extreme unction was essentially a name given to the sacrament for the anointment of the sick and dying. The question is this: does one remove the text believing it to be added by the Church or was it part of the original lyrics of the song?'

'Does it really make that much difference to the "history lesson"?' asked Eleanor.

'I understand the question,' Erwan said, hesitantly. 'Things start to get a little more complicated here, you see. If we take de La Villemarqué's "oak tree" version, we can choose to accept it as a true eyewitness account, but then we would be tempted to dismiss, as a church corruption of the song, the part referring to a priest or holy man called Rasian, in a town called Langolen who claimed to heal everyone, because this would obviously make the Church look good if everyone was singing about this heroic priest.' In full flow, Erwan skipped the crêpes, but quickly took a small sip of the cider from his now full bolée.

'If the original word, "dilhat", meaning the linen vestment normally worn by men of the cloth over a cassock, is left unaltered, then the image is completely different you see?' Erwan recognised the blank expression on his wife's face: he wasn't doing a very good job of explaining this dilemma.

'Let me put it like this,' he paused, without touching his bolée. 'A priest, who gives a holy sacrament to his dying parishioners using a garment attached to a long pole, does not create images of a heroic priest, but of a non-believing coward.'

'I see exactly what you're saying,' confirmed Eleanor. 'So the lyrics are original and almost certainly not added by the Church?'

'Exactly,' beamed Erwan. Reaching out for another crêpe, he leant over his desk, vaguely gesturing at other stanzas common to the three texts. 'What that means in the bigger picture is even more exciting. If that part of the history lesson is true, then we can start not only to ascertain which related parts of the texts are certain to be genuine, but we can remove parts that have revealed themselves to be false.'

'I'm getting a little confused again,' said Eleanor. 'Can you give me an example?'

'Of course. If we can assume that this priest or holyman, Father Rasian, really existed, then the three texts each have their version of where he was preaching. According to all versions of the song, the holy man was in Langolen near Ar Faouët. A village where so many souls had already succumbed to the Pest. A village, according to the song, so underpopulated, that the grass in the market square was high enough to have cut a crop of hay. The next piece in the puzzle is a geographical one,' he continued, sitting down now and adjusting his position over the papers to focus on the relevant part. 'Langolen is not near "Ar" or Le Faouët at all and Plouescat is even further. The only place that fits the bill here is Langonnet. An easy enough error to make in a song. So I went there. Jolly good crêpes, but they don't have a market square and never have had.'

'So where could it have been then?' asked Eleanor, frowning.

'Well, when I asked at the Abbey of Langonnet, they told me of a small village called La Trinité de Langonnet, for there, is the church of St. Bever and the old market square,' Erwan stood up abruptly. 'And that's when I realised it must have been there in that little village. In his song, the musician sings about the sufferance of the people he meets on his journey, the atrocities he witnessed of human suffering. He told them to come to a specific fountain and drink from it if they were thirsty. The musician's name was Olivier. He wanted to lead the people to clean water: the highest source of spring water in the area. That spring emanates from the foot of the highest hill visible from the banks of the river Ellé in the diocese of Vannes. That's the river which forms the natural geographical boundary where the dialects change. The water trickles out of a fountain just a hundred or so metres from the church. At some point, according to this version of the song, Rasian saw Olivier in the village and began ringing the church bells to announce his imminent hanging. Olivier had to run and hide.'

'Why on earth would the Church want a bard hanged?' asked Eleanor, alarmed. 'It makes no sense.'

'It does if the bard has more followers than the priest. Parishioners pay good money in collections and they were falling in number, and those that had survived, were rapidly losing faith. Olivier promised to lead them to clean water – for free.'

'Yes, I see, when you put it like that, it's obvious,' Eleanor agreed.

'When you spotted the link just now with the dialects, it all became clear to me. One song, one dialect, three corrupted versions. Had the song originally come from Plouescat or Elliant, it would have been sung in the Léonard dialect or the Cornouaillais dialect respectively, but it was not. The song was sung in Vannetais, which reached as far as Langonnet along the river Ellé.' Erwan reached again for the cider.

'This requires a toast,' he proclaimed.

15

The Fugitive

Declan stepped out, feet together onto the pavement and stood up. His hands still cuffed in front of him, he walked towards the crowd by the café and sidled in behind them. Nobody was watching him. He carried on along the pavement for about fifteen metres, heard someone shout, but resisted the temptation to look back. They were not shouting to him, so he just carried on walking and had opened up a distance of about fifty metres when he noticed he was crossing a tiny bridge with metal railings right next to the pavement. He stopped, looked over the railings to see a short drop of about two and a half metres on to a grass bank. At the bottom of the channel was a little brook no wider than a metre in total. From either side of the brook, two rows of houses backed on to grass banks bounding the water channel before it all disappeared under the road. It was August and Declan could see that this channel, running straight through the middle of the town, had been built to take a great deal more water than was currently trickling down it. Surreptitiously, he turned his head slowly back in the direction of the crowd. Still nobody had noticed his disappearance and flicking his head round in all directions, he quickly clasped the railings with his cuffed hands and vaulted over the side.

Declan's landing was a great deal harder than he had expected. With his hands cuffed together, he had almost no control over his fall and he rolled down the bank nearly into the water. There was a dusty, single file track on the opposite side of the brook and from his crouched position, his eyes followed it through the tunnel leading under the road. Quickly, he stood up and took a running jump diagonally across the water and prepared, as best he could, for a landing roll in the faded light under the cover of the tunnel. He got onto his knees as fast as he could and stood up. Getting his bearings for a second, and despite the searing pain from his burn, he began to run along the tunnel. As the tunnel got darker and darker, he had to move more slowly. The light he could see at the end of the tunnel now appeared more clearly and as he stopped to look back, he estimated that both ends of the tunnel looked about the same size so he must have been approximately halfway through. He stopped to walk for a short distance, but he wasn't entirely sure why – he wasn't out of breath. Declan had become a fugitive of the law.

He considered his situation carefully and realised he was in an enormous amount of trouble. The most immediate problem, he felt, was the handcuffs. That was not only a physical handicap, but it further prevented him from blending in with the general public. With handcuffs on, there's no going into a supermarket to buy food. He hadn't eaten since the day before. He also had no money and no plastic and he must have left his phone at Mamie's. In his mind, he knew he was frightened of coming out of the other end of the tunnel, because he had no idea what he would see. He also knew that he had to open up the greatest possible distance between him and his pursuers before they found out he had gone. They quite probably already had found out. If they were to jump down over the railings now and look under the tunnel, they would certainly see him, so he had to keep moving. But then he didn't want to surface at the other end of the tunnel, blatantly out of breath, because that would attract attention and he was wearing handcuffs. Albert would be able to get these cuffs off him. Albert would listen to him, feed him, hide him and give him time to think. That was what he had to do; he had to get to Albert's.

As Declan approached the end of the tunnel he slowed right down to assess what was awaiting him. He couldn't see up onto the street, but nobody was looking over the barrier down at him either. He decided to continue along the miniature towpath for no other reason than he didn't know what else to do. This side of the tunnel was different: unkempt and dirty. Somebody's dumping ground and an old building roofed in what looked like asbestos. Most of the windows, although too high to reach up to, had been broken, presumably by stones. He saw piles of empty bottles, beer and wine. The flora had changed too: these banks were neglected and full of weeds; some pleasant smelling; others foul. Some distance further on, the wall disappeared on the opposite side and was replaced by galvanized wire fencing. There, he thought was a possible way out. He took a leap as he had earlier in the entrance to the tunnel; this time to cross back over. Behind the fencing, which was rusty and broken down in parts, there appeared to be a railway yard. There were piles of sleepers, old wagons on clearly disused sections of railway line. The name of the café the police had parked in front of was "Café de la Gare"; that made sense now. Declan hadn't noticed a railway station at the time, but then he hadn't really looked. He approached a big old, coal-stained brick-red building with its corrugated roof. Ducking carefully behind enormous piles of gravel ballast, he began to approach it. He listened, treading carefully here, because it too had become a dumping ground. Heaps of rubbish bags of different colours, grey, green, yellow but mostly black – a lot had been ripped open by vermin. There was even a fridge and an old big-screen tube television. Someone had also dumped one of those garden pergolas: canvass torn and the white pole framework just thrown down on top of it.

Declan could hear the traffic behind this old railway building, but otherwise, there seemed to be no commotion at all and he thought how he would have loved to have been able to be a fly on the wall watching the gendarmes' reaction right at that moment.

Richard Hannay had boarded a train, but he had money and he wasn't handcuffed and he wasn't a fugitive from the French police at the time he boarded his train. There had been a French guy in one of Declan's mother's favourite films, "La Vache et Le Prisonnier" starring that actor, Fernandel. As a P.O.W. he had got on a train to escape the Nazis. He'd got through German lines dressed as a peasant walking his cow on a rope – so innocent that no one questioned him. But they hadn't been looking specifically for him either. The assassination attempt on De Gaulle by Frederick Forsyth's character, "The Jackal": he had walked straight through the French police line. Handicapped he had been, his gun hidden in his crutches: who would suspect a handicapped old man? Now that was clever. But unlike Declan, the Jackal didn't have any bloody handcuffs on. He would have to walk along innocently, just minding his own business with his hands cuffed together in front of him. How dare they put them on him? They had no right and what's more, they knew it. Then an image came to Declan's mind of an innocent-looking man that no one would ever have suspected. And he walked along exactly like that with his hands together in front of him; the blind man at the church with his white stick. That virtuous-looking bastard pretending to be blind that wanted to suffocate him not twelve hours ago with a plastic bag.

'Yeah,' thought Declan, 'I might be in a tight spot right now, but at least I'm still alive.'

He needed a white stick. A white pole from the pergola frame. Declan walked over to the heap of rubbish and began to play that game, Mikado, where you have to remove a stick without moving any others or you're out. Quietly, Declan selected a pole, a bit too short, but he removed a plastic foot from another one to make it look more realistic and then a white plastic elbow caught his eye and he slotted that over the other end for a handle. No dark sunglasses, he'd have to gaze into space: always in the wrong direction, always seeing nothing. He remembered what Dr Khadir had said about his pulse racing noticeably. He would have to control his every emotion if he was going to pull this off.

Declan practised walking as he had seen the blind man do. Tap, tap, tap. First to one side then to the other. It was not as easy as it looked. The angle of the white stick had to be just right so as to touch the ground as he moved forward but not catch on it. That meant that the tapping had to be more rhythmic, so Declan began to move the stick with greater flexibility and he could feel his walking become less rigid. Just around the corner, behind the huge brick-red building, there was a tremendously loud noise. A blast of a horn. A train. No ordinary train; this was an old steam train and Declan found himself looking up as a cloud of steam rose above the roofline.

'No good,' he thought to himself. 'That was no good.' He had to learn to move his head in the direction of the sound, but not focus his eyes on things that moved. A pigeon flew into view and again, Declan looked up, *damn*! He closed his eyes, carried on tapping and walking and then he realised something else; the stick was only going to help him avoid obstacles on the ground. He knew that there was nothing in front of him because he had just seen for himself, but strangely he felt his face was very vulnerable. For a blind person, any obstacle sticking out from, say, a wall, like one of those plastic telephone hoods that offered no privacy whatsoever, would be a nightmare: a blind person could walk straight into it. Then Declan smiled at the idea that a blind person, victim to such misfortune, might have cuts and bruises on his face as a result; no makeup required there then, for he had plenty. He also liked the feeling of smiling, it seemed to fit the optimism of his new character, his new identity. A blind person would be unaware of the effect of his or her facial expressions on others around. He would have to react more readily to the surrounding sounds, as he had when they put that hood on him. And in just fifty metres, Declan felt he had made tremendous progress in his acting ability. As he walked around the corner, he saw the steam train, the platform, the tourists. He saw a clock in the distance at the end of the platform, tap, tap, tap... nine thirty-five in the morning – look, don't see.

Tap, tap, tap. Declan walked across the yard in the direction of the platform. He planned to miss the gate where he could see a sign for ticket reservations. He had no money, there was no point, so he walked straight past, along a wall and saw in the corner of his eye a sign for a toilet. As he immersed himself deeper and deeper into his role, he saw a policeman run across the road by the building where it said "Billets et Réservations" and underneath this, just "Tickets". He stopped walking and tapping and raised his head trying to smell the toilets: they stank. He followed the smell, tapping once more and took a decision. He deliberately walked into the toilets marked "Femmes", tapping his stick against the wall and back again the whole time. Finding a cubicle, he eased inside and relieved himself.

He had locked the door behind him, so he knew that no one could be watching, but nevertheless, he felt at the wall for a flushing system as a blind man might, before "discovering" the pull-up handle. Walking out of the ladies' toilets, he passed or rather was passed, by a woman hurrying in. Tap, tap, tap...

'Ici c'est marqué "Femmes", monsieur.' He heard her say, and then immediately, 'Oh, pardon, excusez-moi, je n'ai pas fait gaffe, monsieur, je n'ai pas vu. Excusez-moi!' *This is the ladies' toilet, sir! Oh excuse me, I didn't realise.* And she disappeared into a cubicle herself as quickly as possible.

Declan walked out of the ladies' toilets, tap, tap, tap... and along the path to the platform. Up ahead of him was a small wooden barrier and he headed straight for it. As he tap-tapped his way along the platform, he noticed how the other passengers, or rather tourists, for this was no ordinary train, would step quickly out of his way as he approached. Occasionally he paused and lifted his head, tilting it slightly for effect, to listen to the sounds in his immediate environment, but never once did he focus his eyes. Then his white stick hit the barrier and he stepped slightly to one side and began again with the tapping. Now he was headed directly for the edge of the platform and as he approached the drop he wondered if anyone would come and save him from this imminent fall, but nobody did. His stick tapped thin air where the platform dropped down to the tracks and Declan tapped again trying to feel his way as if he saw nothing. He stroked his stick backwards and forwards quickly along the concrete edging of the platform and adjusted his entire body to line himself up in a straight line with the track down below, before setting off again: tap, tap, tap…

About fifteen metres away, Declan saw a ticket controller dressed in period costume.

'Bonjour, monsieur, bonjour, madame, your tickets please,' he kept repeating: 'Merci.'

Declan had no ticket. But he had a plan. Just before the ticket control was a big sign fixed to the wall, 'Le Vapeur du Trieux'. Tap, tap, tap and Declan's white stick told him that the platform in front of him was clear, then suddenly, "whack". The blind man hadn't seen the board. It was in a stupid place anyway – an accident waiting to happen. The policeman who had been running across the road was now searching the platform and began his desperate manhunt. Declan saw him just in the corner of his eye and buried his face in his hands; he must have been there for ten seconds unable to move on. He saw blood on his hands and from the stinging sensation he guessed he must have cut his forehead. Then came a voice that he recognised. A woman:

'Ah, mon Dieu.' He could hear her footsteps approaching quickly from behind. The woman from the toilets.

'Ça va, monsieur?' she enquired, hand on his shoulder.

Declan had to think fast. He was bent over double, his cuffed hands still holding his white stick, but also covering his face. The woman was asking him to let her look.

'Laissez-moi regarder, monsieur.'

But if he lowered his hands revealing his face and stood up straight, then the gendarme might recognise him. Declan switched into his role pretending he could see nothing.

'Je saigne, madame?' Declan asked. *Am I bleeding?*

'Oui, un peu, monsieur. Attendez, je dois avoir un Kleenex,' and Declan waited, while she rummaged through her handbag. Her disposable hanky was a wad of hand towels she had just removed from the ladies' toilets not five minutes ago – the same cheap, recycled paper and slowly he lifted his head.

The woman began to dab at his forehead but decided to hold it there and in doing so she shielded his face at the moment the gendarme walked past. This gendarme had been the driver, luckily for Declan, for he had not had as good a look at him as the other two and neither had he had a chance to look at Declan's new clothes. The policeman walked straight past the blind man with the woman and carried on towards the end of the station, searching frantically.

'Ce n'est pas la première fois, madame,' Declan said. *Not the first time I've banged my head.*

'Je vois ça, monsieur. Vous avez énormément de courage. Je ne sais pas comment vous tenez le coup, franchement,' she praised him. *I see that, you're very brave.*

'Vous devez peut-être monter dans le train, monsieur?' the woman enquired. *Are you boarding the train?*

'Oui, mais...' Declan hesitated; he had no ticket. 'Je ne trouve plus mon billet de train,' he lied. *Yes, but I can't find my ticket.*

'Ne vous inquiétez pas pour ça, monsieur,' she reassured him. 'Venez avec moi.' *Don't worry about that, you come with me.*

Linking her left arm in Declan's right, she held the paper towels firmly to his forehead and guided him along the platform. Declan walked, head slightly down, eyes almost closed, the woman's right hand covering much of his face and his cuffed hands clasping the white stick pointing at, but not touching the ground just in front of him. The coat was far too big for Declan and the sleeves which were thankfully too long, easily covered his hands and cuffs.

'On y va?' she asked cheerfully. *Shall we go?*

'Mais je ne trouve pas mon billet,' Declan insisted, suddenly remembering that due to the handcuffs, he wasn't even able to make a token search through his pockets.

'Et moi je vous ai dit, monsieur, de ne pas vous inquiétez pour cela,' she insisted. *And I told you, sir that you don't have to worry about that.* On arriving at the ticket gate, she greeted the guard.

'Salut, Georges,' she said. 'I'm not going to give you a kiss,' she explained, nodding by way of explanation at Declan, her blind and clearly wounded, companion. 'Plus tard,' she added, flirtatiously. *Later.*

'Salut, Sarah,' Georges replied.

'Pourras-tu prendre ma veste?'she asked. *Could you take my coat?*

Georges, the ticket inspector, was evidently delighted to help her undress, and standing there now without her lightweight summer coat on, she was very clearly dressed in period costume from the 1920's: Sarah was a stewardess on the tourist train.

'Faut dire quelque chose par rapport à ce panneau-là,' she added, pointing a little way down the platform at the sign that Declan had deliberately walked into. 'Le monsieur vient de se cogner la tête. C'est vachement mal foutu.' *We should say something about that panel, it's badly placed; this man just banged his head.*

The gendarme came tearing down the platform again as the whistle of the steam train sounded once more, announcing its imminent departure.

'Il est déjà neuf heures quarante: dépêche-toi,' Georges insisted. 'C'est l'heure du départ.' *Hurry, it's already nine forty, the train's about to leave.*

The gendarme stopped right in front of the ticket controller, not a metre away from Declan, and glanced back up the platform as Sarah, the stewardess, explained quickly in French to her blind passenger that they would have to hurry. Declan's pulse did not race. He set off with his guide and nurse for the nearest carriage. The policeman hadn't noticed a thing.

'Sarah,' Georges called out behind them, and Declan very nearly turned around to look. 'À tout à l'heure.' *See you later.*

The train, Le Vapeur du Trieux, pulled away sluggishly but proudly from the station. The drawn-out double blast from the whistle and the billowing clouds of coal-smoke mixed with steam began to arouse excitement among the passengers. Sarah, having seated Declan by a window, left him with the makeshift-compress, assured herself that he was okay and carried on with her job with the promise that she would be back shortly.

Declan sat in the safety of the carriage considering what a luxury it was to be able to sit and rest, knowing that the police were no longer right on his tail. The next problem he faced was how to get the handcuffs off and in order to do that he needed to get to Albert's. Albert would just get his angle grinder out and cut straight through the chain. As he sat and thought about the metal bracelets hidden just under the sleeves of this ridiculously oversized, brown-check coat, he thought of the risk of the sleeves catching fire from the glowing red-white sparks spitting from the grinding wheel. Logically, he thought, trying to picture Albert at work setting him free, that would dictate the order in which Albert would have to make his cuts. Chain link first, at least that way he could whip the coat off if it did get too hot and start to smoulder – he'd already been burnt enough without inflicting any more on himself. The next part would be harder still, because the metal was touching his skin and would inevitably heat up, even glow red hot, as Albert pushed the grinding wheel through the cuffs. As Declan, eyes closed, pictured Albert, he remembered the action he had made with his hands as he explained how someone must have cut through his brake pipe. He racked his brains for the name of the tool he had shown him. That was it, "une pince-monseigneur" in French or bolt cropper. In using a bolt cropper, the coat wouldn't be at risk of catching fire. That, he imagined, was exactly how Albert would do it. If only he had a bolt cropper, then he could just snip through them himself and have done with it.

As the train pulled into Pontrieux, Declan tried to get a glimpse of the platform to see if there were any police there waiting for him. He was hoping as well that Sarah would return to his seat before he had to get off the train. Not only would Sarah help him through the ticket control but in terms of his personal confidence, she had become a vital part of his disguise getting past the gendarme just before boarding the train. He decided to close his eyes in order to hear more clearly and immediately he could hear her voice. He wasn't sure if she had been silent before, or whether he could hear better with his eyes closed, but he kept them shut for two or three minutes nevertheless. Then he heard her say:

'J'arrive, monsieur. Nous allons descendre du train ensemble, monsieur.' Declan felt a hand on his shoulder and he raised his head slightly without looking.

'Vous dormiez, là, monsieur?' *Were you asleep?* It was Sarah and Declan, relieved, smiled into thin air.

Sarah helped him down the short wooden steps onto the platform, and having inspected his forehead, she linked his arm as she had before and they set off together down the platform and straight past the ticket inspector.

'Salut, Jean-Pierre,' he heard her say, 'Ça va?'

'Salut, Sarah,' replied the voice.

Sarah walked Declan to the end of the platform and out into the car park where there was a horse-drawn carriage waiting to transport the tourists into the town centre. He desperately wanted to separate himself from the crowd, but then Sarah became quite insistant the journey into town, although only ten minutes on foot, was quite treacherous if you didn't know the route. He tried to convince her he would be just fine walking, but Sarah would have none of it and she explained to the coachman that the blind man had lost his train ticket and he jumped down off his seat to help Declan up onto the carriage. Then Declan heard a voice call out:

'Dad, that man's got handcuffs on him.'

It was a child's voice in English and Declan suddenly wished Sarah would go away and mind her own business. He felt guilty for having used her at the same time as being grateful to her for having saved him from the police, but right now she was getting on his nerves. As she turned around to take a last look at the carriage before leaving, she waved and Declan, who had been watching her walk away, raised his white stick in a sort of salute. She saw him look and wave his stick and the expression on Sarah's face was one of astonishment and he could see a deep furrow of bewilderment, then hurt forming on her face as her waving hand froze: had she been the police, he would just have blown his cover. He felt an enormous sense of guilt, of betrayal towards her kindness and wished things could have been different.

The horse-drawn carriage pulled away out of the station onto the main road and Sarah was gone. As the horses pulled and the carriage juddered on behind it, he heard that child's voice again.

'Mum, look, Dad doesn't believe me. That man there with the white stick has got handcuffs on. You look.' A young Scottish boy, delighted with himself for his discovery.

'Sean, be quiet,' said his embarrassed and now clearly frightened mother.

So the mother had seen the handcuffs too. Declan looked down at his wrists and saw that both bracelets and the chain had slipped down and were clearly visible. The only way to hide them now was to raise his hands to let them slide down his wrists again, or push them up one at a time. Either way, it would be in clear view of everyone on the carriage. Out of the question; he had to react.

He couldn't stand it anymore and as the carriage almost drew to a standstill at a roundabout, he leapt off and ducked behind a half-glazed bus shelter and turned his back on the tourists willing them to keep shtum. The horses pulled away slowly and jerkily and it took an age to create any distance between him and the tourists. He hoped that nobody on the carriage had really comprehended the situation as well as the young boy and his mother clearly had done. Declan began to get quite angry and realised immediately it was through frustration. He wanted his hands free, at least the chain cut through so he could walk normally and not with his bloody hands clamped together in front of him. He was beginning to get very hungry and it didn't help seeing a sign for a supermarket for he had no money and no plastic on him. He wasn't prepared to get caught shoplifting, he would have to do without. The sign for the supermarket showed a roundabout and indicated to drivers to take the last exit. From where he was stood he could see the other roundabout with its green road signs and decided to set off in that direction in order to get his bearings, pick up the main road away from the coast and head back inland to Albert's.

Tap, tap, tap... undercover once again, he approached the second roundabout and saw there was a whole collection of different stores and business leading off to a commercial zone where the supermarket was situated, and just beyond that he saw a DIY store. He would walk in, he didn't have to buy anything, he'd look for a bolt cropper, cut through his chain and walk out: borrow it so to speak. Declan could feel himself accelerating as if approaching a finish line, adrenaline rushing, and had to remind himself constantly to slow down to a blind man's pace.

About five hundred metres further up the road, he found himself trying to catch his breath, as he stood at the entrance to the store. And he tap-tapped his way inside. He was nervous. On the one hand, he had to stay undercover as the blind man in order not to look stupid with his hands permanently together in front of him, but at the same time, he dreaded the helpful service his handicap might attract. Still tap-tapping, he headed in the direction of the aisle marked "OUTILLAGE". Playing the role of a blind man meant that he could not simply scour the shelves for the required tool. What could he do, drop the act? As he turned the corner, he saw a man looking up and down at a whole selection of drill bits and other accessories and a plan came to his rescue.

'Excusez-moi, monsieur,' he began, 'Vous travaillez ici?' *Do you work here?*

'Non, monsieur, mais je peux peut-être vous aider?' replied the DIY man helpfully. *No, sir, but I might be able to help you.*

'Je cherche un cadeau pour mon neveu, il souhaiterait une pince-monseigneur,' replied Declan, controlling his breathing well, but certain he had guilt written all over his face. *I'm looking for a present for my nephew, he wants a bolt cropper.*

The man beckoned Declan with his hand to follow him, but he wasn't falling for that one again, so he just stood there, head cocked, listening. The man clearly felt a bit silly and he quickly spat out:

'Il y en a ici, monsieur.' *Over here, sir.*

Declan followed the man's voice down the aisle, tap, tap, tap... There was a choice of two and the man who had led him there obviously didn't want to get any more involved than he already had.

'Vous avez le choix, monsieur, 'y a une grande ou une petite,' then he added: 'Elles sont juste devant vous,' and then he was gone. *There's big or small, sir, just in front of you.*

The truth was that Declan was glad to see the back of him for he could not hide his disappointment when he saw the packaging;

fashioned such that they could not be used without tearing open the seal. He did not want to get caught or accused of shoplifting. As he walked, tap-tapping to the end of the aisle, he saw, to his delight, a whole collection of reels of chains and cables of varying sizes and thicknesses. There was a tape measure fixed to one of the sides of the shelf and much more importantly, a bolt cropper fixed to the end of a piece of chain. He thought how ironic it was to fix a bolt cropper in such a way, when it would be so easy just to cut straight through it. Then he saw the sign saying, "Veuillez demander l'assistance d'un technician". Customers were not supposed to use the bolt croppers themselves but ask for assistance. Declan had no time for this and he bent down to pick them up, laying down his white stick. He quickly gripped them in such a way as to allow them to open, delicately placing the chain between the jaws. He found he didn't have sufficient leverage to be able to close them down firmly enough to get through the chain and quickly lifted his left knee up placing his foot on to a bar between two reels of chain. Leaning over, pushing with both hands on one of the handles and pushing the other handle against his upper left thigh, he forced as hard as he could.

'Qu'est-ce que vous faites là, monsieur?' came a voice.

'Shit, why now?' thought Declan. 'These shop assistants were just like policemen, never there when you need one.'

Thwack. And to Declan's relief, he felt the metal link give under the force of the bolt cropper's jaws.

'J'ai perdu ma canne.' *I lost my stick.* Declan explained and the man bent down to pick up his stick for him.

Declan watched the man examine his white cane before returning it to him and it was evident he found the stick more than a little odd. This little distraction enabled Declan to see that a middle link had only been cut through on one side and maddening as this was, he decided to take his leave as quickly as possible. He wasn't sure if the shop assistant had seen his cuffs or not, but he was not prepared to hang around to find out. He turned the corner, tap-tapping and sped up towards the entrance of the shop and walked straight out at a pace faster than any blind man he'd ever seen.

As he left the shop he looked over his shoulder and staring at him through the glass shop front, standing by the tills, was the shop assistant – he had seen Declan looking back. He had to get out of there in case the man alerted the police. He started to walk briskly across the car park when suddenly it began to rain. Not just a light drizzle, but a torrential downpour and anyone and everyone in the huge car park began to run for shelter. Declan, also desperate to find shelter, could not return to the cover of the shops, he had to keep moving and put some distance between him and the DIY store in case the assistant had made the call. Besides the shops, there was no cover except for a petrol station. He recollected having passed it on the way down from the roundabout. Taking cover under there would be too obvious: he'd stand out like a sore thumb if the police did turn up. He dived under the cover of a shopping trolley park and as he stared at the collection of bright blue crossbars, chains, cages and wheels, he thought for the second time that day what a useful tool a bolt cropper would be – a man, hands together, pushing a trolley around a shop. But no coins meant no trolley. As he followed the skyline along the road up beyond the petrol station he noticed a dark archway in the bank below the road-line. It was only just visible because the tree growth was thinner there. He thought it must be some service access road, because he could recall no road leading back that way from the roundabout. The rain eased off for a moment and he could see sunshine trying to push through just behind a thin looking layer of white clouds. As he began to work out how to get to what appeared to be a tunnel under the main road he saw thick black clouds cutting out the Sun once again. This was going to be a downpour far worse than the first and he began to run.

He reached the outer curb of the car park and crossed over a small grassed area before coming to an earth bank dotted with the odd silver birch. Seeing that the bank was going to be slippery from the last downpour, he took a run at it and made it to the top without sliding back down. A quick look over his shoulder – nobody there. The car park was now empty of shoppers and it was just as well for at that moment a hail storm swept across the whole commercial centre in his direction. He had heard that one of the worst places to be during a storm is under a tree, so he ran down the other side of the bank where he could see a narrow gravel track. The track ran parallel to the bank of trees before turning into and under the main road through a low concrete tunnel. At the bottom of the bank he slipped up and landed on his backside. The trousers Dr Khadir had given him, were covered in mud all over the seat area where he had slid down the last part of the slope. As he was pushing himself up onto his feet, his cuffed-hands in front of him, he felt an agonising stretching sensation from the burn on his leg. This pain was followed by the first sting of hail on the back of his head. He bent down to pick up his stick, and before he had time to half run, half limp his way across the short patch of grass between him and the tunnel, the track and the grass had turned white with balls of hail. He ran like mad as best he could for the cover of the concrete underpass.

There was a flash of lightning some distance off and Declan decided to count the number of seconds between the flash and the boom. Only three, not even. That meant that the lightning had struck between two and three kilometres away. Another flash and he counted less than two seconds. So the electric storm was moving nearer and fast. He was grateful for the coat the doctor had given him, not only because it hid the cuffs for him on the train, but it was now getting cold. The other advantage was that the coat was long enough to hide the seat of his pants, now covered in mud from slipping on the bank. Another flash, this one seemed longer and

Declan reckoned there was less than a second before the deafening boom rumbled and crashed in the monstrous black sky above. The air felt so charged that Declan wondered whether he was safe standing where he was with metal handcuffs around his wrists. He looked outside and could see that everything was covered in hailstones, some as big as hazelnuts, and in a panic, he threw down his white metal stick and crouched down low into a foetal position with his back to the wall. He wanted to wrap his arms around his knees and put his hands tight under his arms, but the handcuffs prevented even that. A second later, there was an almighty crashing sound and he had the impression it was right at the entrance to the underpass.

He hadn't seen the flash, but there was no point in counting the seconds: the lightning had struck one of the birch trees on the bank where he had slipped up. Looking up in the direction of the ear-splitting explosion, he saw the tree, a good four inches in diameter, keel over and land on the car park side of the bank. He wasn't sure if it was the wetness of the ground that had prevented there being any smoke or fire, but the tree just seemed to blow apart, leaving a scraggy splintered stump. The storm was right above his head. It was so dark in the tunnel by this time, Declan could barely see his hands and had to squint to make out the chain securing the two metal bracelets that formed the handcuffs. As his eyes adjusted to the dim light, he could see the link in the middle with its one side snipped through and he tried to force the link open by jerking his hands apart. It was no good; the split link would not budge. He wrapped his arms around his knees and began to use his legs as well as his arms to force against the link and he thought he felt it bend open a little. He looked down and raised his wrists to see if the gap had widened enough to pass a neighbouring link through it. It had not. He felt very despondent: *why the hell did that shop assistant have to turn up at that very moment?*

The sky seemed to be clearing slowly and Declan stood up from his foetal crouch and headed towards the opposite end of the tunnel. Partly he wanted to see where the track led to, but more urgently to assertain in better light if the link really had opened up. The track was short and led up to a set of gates with a steep grass bank with shrubs on one side and a roadside crash barrier on the other. He returned to his cuffs and saw that any widening of the link was so negligible that it might even be his imagination. Leaning against a corner wall of the concrete tunnel, he noticed how often it had been hit or scraped by vehicles passing through and cutting the corner on the way. The tunnel itself was easily wide enough to drive through and Declan was surprised to see that kind of damage, thinking to himself that a driver would have to be drunk to hit the tunnel wall. As he stared at the collision and scrape damage, he noticed just above his head, a short piece of rod-like metal sticking out of the wall. It was evidently part of the concrete's steel reinforcing and he wondered if it would help to prise open the link for it really didn't need much. He raised both hands above his head and tried to hook the half-cut link over the rod of bent metal protruding from the damaged wall. He managed it although it was quite a tight fit and then he pulled down on the handcuffs as hard as he could with his whole body. The rod did not move and this time he felt the chain link give. He shook his wrists, the now wide open chain link only hanging on through bloody-mindedness: it fell and his hands were freed. Halfway through a celebratory jig, hands held high and punching the air, he heard a car coming.

He quickly glanced around the corner of the exit side of the tunnel leading up to the gates and confirmed that the car was not coming down from the main road. Judging by the speed of the vehicle, he would not have enough time to cross over the track to hide in the undergrowth before the car appeared at the entrance to the tunnel on the shop-side from where he had just come. On the side he was at the moment, there was nowhere to hide. He decided to run for cover anyway and taking the risk he dashed across to the other side of the track in full view of the car. Declan was now confused for there was no car, no noise, no nothing. Looking into the tunnel again, he spotted his white stick and unsure really why he wanted to keep it, set off under the road again to fetch it. As he reached his stick, about halfway through the tunnel he heard a voice and he could just see the bonnet of a light blue car – stopped – engine off. There was a man on a mobile phone reporting, from what Declan could hear, that the only visible damage was a fallen tree. Very close to electric lines but nothing touched. Quickly, he made his way back to the exit of the tunnel and readied himself to hide in the undergrowth on the right.

He heard the car start up again, but instead of coming through the tunnel, it began a three-point turn to head back in the direction from where it had come. Declan removed his oversized check-coat and held it over an arm while he slid the bracelets of the handcuffs as high up his arms as they would go. Not half an hour ago, Declan would have thrown this ridiculous-looking coat away – glad to be rid of it, but now it hid his cuffs, hid the mud on the seat of his trousers and kept him warm and dry. He put the coat back on, fastened it, and set off up towards the gates accessing the main road at the top of this short track. As he neared the top, where he could see the gates were locked with a chain and padlock, he kept his head just below the level of the crash barrier and the vegetation that grew up and around it. There was little traffic on the road compared to just before the storm and Declan, moving as close as possible to the barrier in order to see the road signs, finally spotted the exit for his immediate destination. He was heading for Guingamp on the D787.

16

The Blind Hitchhiker

Having waited for a gap in the traffic, Declan climbed over the crash barrier and instantly switched to blind mode. He tap-tapped his way along the road in the direction of another roundabout further up ahead and within about three or four minutes he had reached it. Standing by the side of the road, about fifty metres from the roundabout exit for Guingamp, he waited. His hands now triumphantly apart; his left one holding the white stick, and his right one holding out the hitchhiker's thumb.

This road, not half a mile out of town, was now quite busy and Declan was just in the middle of assessing the effect of the white stick on his chances of being picked up by a passing car, when he spotted his worst nightmare. Driving along the road to the main roundabout where he stood, coming from the direction of Pontrieux and the DIY store, he saw a police car – tardis blue, Gendarmerie written in white on the side and their big sets of blue and orange roof-lights displayed as war-medals on the chests of veterans. Declan couldn't hide, it was too late; if they hadn't spotted him already they'd soon see him if he ran. He thought of Dr Khadir and tried to control his breathing and his heart rate, but it wasn't easy. Logically, he thought to himself, *I'm blind and I can't see them.* He began to concentrate as best he could on how a blind man would act and react. Don't look, for starters, just listen he thought, so he closed his eyes for a moment. Should they stop, why then he'd simply ask them for a lift. As he rehearsed his moves, he heard a car pull up onto the gravelly part of the hard shoulder where he was stood. So, eyes slightly opened, but looking upwards, Declan very slowly took a step back; melting hail crunching under his feet. It was the police. They rolled on and came what he considered would have been frighteningly close for someone who really was blind. He controlled his breathing and desperately tried to control his heart rate. The car stopped and he smiled into thin air. Both gendarmes got out at the same time.

'Vous allez où, monsieur?' asked one of them. *Where are you going?* Avoiding a direct answer, Declan replied:

'C'est gentil de votre part de vous arrêter, monsieur.' *Thanks for stopping.* Declan heard one door slam.

'Vous allez où, monsieur?' the voice repeated. The second door slammed.

'Vous êtes à plusieurs, vous n'allez pas me faire du mal, messieurs?' Declan began an artificial plea: *there are several of you; you're not going to hurt me?* In the hope of throwing them off the sent he added:

'Je n'ai jamais d'argent sur moi, messieurs.' *I never carry cash.*

'Gendarmerie Nationale, monsieur. Je répète: vous allez où, monsieur?'

Trying to appear relieved, Declan replied:

'À Guingamp, monsieur.'

A second car pulled up and Declan began to get seriously worried. He cocked his head in the direction of the other vehicle but refused to allow himself to focus on it. In a flash, all of his questions were answered:

'Bonjour, Robert,' said a voice turning then to the policeman, and saying; 'He's my patient. His name is Robert Le Boulch. My name is Dr Khadir, Here's my id card. Left my surgery yet again without his prescription. Now I've told you time and time again, Robert, if you're leaving town, take public transport, it's safer. Remember what happened to you last time?' Dr Khadir continued. 'I'll take care of him, officers, I'll drop him off at his home.'

'Attendez, Docteur, un instant.' *Just hold on there, Doctor.* One of the policemen was on the radio evidently checking the id of a wanted person.

'Ben, non. Il est Français, non il est là avec son toubib. Ben, non, Le Boulch. C'est ça qu'il dit. Non il n'a pas de menottes. Ben, en fait, ben, écoute il est aveugle.'

Tail between his legs, the gendarme on the radio excused himself and they drove off very quickly.

The man they were looking for was not French but English; he was on his own and not with his doctor; he was wearing handcuffs, and he wasn't blind – wrong man.

'Jump in, Olivier.' said Dr Khadir. 'Where are you going? I'll take you there if I have time.'

'I'm heading for my friend's garage just south of Carhaix in the county of Morbihan,' said Declan. 'It's just on the border in fact. Can I ask you what you were doing right there, right at that moment at the roundabout? I mean what, I mean how come you arrived when you did?'

'A long story, Olivier, but I'll tell you,' answered Dr Khadir. 'What happened to your handcuffs?'

Declan held up his hands so the sleeves of his coat dropped revealing the two bracelet parts of the cuffs still firmly in place.

'Hey, just a minute. How did you know they had handcuffed me?' asked Declan, suddenly suspicious.

'A long story and I did promise I would tell you. Clever of you to have cut through that chain. How did you manage that?' Dr Khadir asked.

'A long story, Farouk, but I'll tell you,' replied Declan, smiling.

'Then I'll begin, shall I?' suggested Dr Khadir. 'I followed the police car out of the hospital... no, it began before that. I left you to get changed and I immediately phoned through to the police station; it's only two minutes away from the hospital. I told them that I had finished with my patient and they could come and get him. They had no idea what I was talking about, so I became quite insistent. I told them I understood there had been an arrest warrant issued for a man that fitted your description, but they had never heard of you. You see, for the police to take you in for questioning they don't need an arrest warrant, so those two policemen told an unnecessary lie.' Dr Khadir yawned. 'Then, as I said, I followed the police car to the gendarmerie and they drove straight past it. So I turned down in the direction of the supermarket and followed them into town. What were they stopping for, cigarettes?'

Declan nodded quickly in agreement and Farouk continued:

'You see, smoking is not good for one's health. Anyhow, I saw the accident and stopped on the other side of the road. As I got out I saw you on the pavement, you were walking away.'

'Why didn't you help me then?' asked Declan. 'I don't mean to complain, I just mean, well, what prevented you from helping me at that moment?'

'As I crossed the road, I saw you stop at the railings by the little brook, "Le Quinic", it's called, that brook. The next thing I knew you'd jumped over the railings. I could hardly have come after you, no one else saw you jump and me following you would have caused a commotion and drawn all the attention back to you.' The doctor opened his window slightly and suggested Declan do the same if he was too hot.

'From where I was stood, I guessed you had turned back under the road and I was right. And the next bit was pure genius,' said the doctor, letting out a long almost uncontrollable laugh. 'You see, Olivier, if you were back in my country, they would have called you Khadir as well, for it was the brook you followed, the little waterway, that's what saved you from the police. And then you boarded a steam train – steam is water. It was the power of water that took you on your next step to safety. Disguised as a blind man, that was ingenious – I was only able to pick you out in the crowd thanks to that coat. Now, you see I know where that train goes. I returned to the hospital, quickly finished some paperwork and as soon as I could, within minutes, I left to come and look for you in Pontrieux. My bit was easy really. Now, what about filling in some gaps for me, Olivier?'

Declan explained about the handcuffs and reiterated how he had escaped along the brook. He explained about the disguise as a blind man and the ladies' toilets. About how he had felt guilty using Sarah. And then how it all went wrong with the horse and cart and about how he managed to cut through one half of the chain link, then running out of the shop and about the storm. He told the doctor how exhilarating it felt as he was able to free his hands finally. Then he explained how he had decided to keep the oversized coat because it covered the mud on his backside. At this point in Declan's story the doctor began to laugh so much, he almost had to pull over.

'You nearly threw away my gift of a coat to you, but you decided to keep it because of slipping down the wet bank. You slipped up because of the water and I only recognised you at the roundabout because of that coat. There aren't two coats as big and as silly looking as that one, and you kept it. Saved yet again by the water. You are also a Khadir, my friend: a master of waterways.'

Doctor Farouk Khadir turned off the D3 following signs for La Trinité Langonnet. As they drove through winding country lanes, Declan began trying to work out what he was going to say to Albert.

'Why do you think the police behaved like that? I mean where were they going to take me?' asked Declan.

'I can't answer that,' replied Farouk. 'I haven't the faintest idea. It makes no sense at all to me. Why did they lie about an arrest warrant?'

Declan wanted to avoid telling Farouk about the gas explosion and the two bodies on the island, so he decided to drop the subject and just shrugged.

They had been driving for almost an hour and Declan, having talked a bit about his life, the use of his two given names, his parents' car crash and about Isabelle's handicap, drifted in and out of sleep bites. When Farouk next spoke, Declan seemed to come out of a trance, for he could barely remember anything the doctor had said, but realised that it was obviously of some importance, at least to the doctor.

'I'm sorry,' said Declan, 'but I was concentrating on something else and not really listening. Would you mind repeating that again?'

'Not at all. I was just chatting, to be honest with you: just passing the time. I thought you had fallen asleep is the truth. What I was saying was, you know the problem with what we call the west and their "modern" pagan movement, is that the true link was broken many centuries ago. You see,' he continued, 'there are fundamental points that westerners seem to fail to understand. When you think about earth, wind, fire and water, there was an actual order to these elements traditionally. First comes fire. I suppose a modern day interpretation could be the Big Bang theory creating dust and debris which gradually form into bigger and bigger parts, such as stars and planets like our Sun and earth. Closer to home it would be, say, an exploding volcano. The volcano being the fire that creates land or earth: the second element. Land or earth on its own has no sense because life cannot exist without water, element number three. But without wind, the fourth and final element, water could never be carried from one place to fall on to land in another place in the form of rain: thus renewing and completing this cleansing cycle. Each and every single tiny raindrop ever formed contains a particle of earth or dust at its very centre: without earth, there can be no water. Without fire, there can be no earth and without earth and water, there can be no wind.'

'Wow,' replied Declan. 'You make it sound so obvious and logical, it makes me wonder how the Christian Church could ever have converted the pagans to believe in Christ the son of God and the Virgin Mary and all that.'

'That is something completely different, Declan. That was manipulation through dictatorial re-education and of course the menace of the Knights Templar, the Spanish Inquisition etc. By fear really. No, I'm talking about Empedocles, the Greek philosopher who first described the four basic elements – all many centuries before the Catholic Church even existed. One should not forget that the Catholic Church was exceedingly wealthy and, at that time at least, also extremely powerful. Some people believe that the writings of a monk named Martin Luther and the subsequent founding of the protestant church began the events that finally put an end to the power the Catholic Church wielded. A force to be reckoned with right across Europe until several centuries beyond the Middle Ages and into more modern times. Personally, I would say there must have been something else even more powerful than the Church and all its money.'

Declan felt he had missed the point of much of what the doctor was talking about, but decided to say nothing for he knew he had been asleep during a part of the journey. Presently, they approached the church at La Trinité Langonnet and Farouk began to slow down as he drove through the village.

'It's a bit further on. Albert's house is just the other side of the garage past the cemetery. There, look, you can see his roof from here.'

Farouk drew up the car beside a neo-Breton style house with a large hangar next to it, signalled left and pulled up into a forecourt full of disused cars in various stages of decay. A dog came out from somewhere, began barking and was followed fairly swiftly by a man in mechanic's overalls. Declan jumped out of the car as quickly as he could, excited by the idea of seeing Albert again after his egregious ordeal. He had forgotten how much his leg still cramped his movements, and the shock of touchdown on the tarmac forecourt sent a searing pain across his upper right leg and he quickly reverted to his limping.

'Who's this?' asked Albert nodding almost inconspicuously at Farouk.

'He's on our side,' replied Declan. 'Doctor Khadir, please meet my very good childhood friend, Albert. Albert, this is Farouk, a doctor who has become a good friend in a very short time.'

'*Friend*, is good for me,' replied Albert, offering the doctor his hand in greeting. Farouk took Albert's hand and momentarily lowered his head in a kind of bow. Albert suddenly noticed the bright cuffs on Declan's wrists and pointing vaguely at them with a limp finger, suggested that maybe they should come off.

Farouk explained he had to head straight back to Paimpol, and despite Albert's insistence, declined the offer of a cup of coffee. He shook both men's hands and double-checking that Declan still had his hospital card with his mobile phone number, the doctor handed Declan a small bag:

'Painkillers for the burn on your leg – paracetamol – I meant to give them to you in the hospital and forgot when I went to fetch those clothes.' Farouk got back into his car, reversed a little, and set off back out from the garage forecourt onto the D109, to Carhaix.

17

Tractor and Trailer

'Od am I glad to see you alive and well,' cried Albert with exasperation. 'I came round in the morning to the old mill to pick you up, but you'd gone – no sign of you.'

'It's a bloody long story,' began Declan. 'Both bloody and long.'

Albert beckoned Declan into the hangar and in an instant, laid his hands on a pair of bolt croppers. Just seconds later, both hoops were off and each made a satisfying clanging noise as it hit the concrete floor of the garage. Declan rubbed both wrists with the palm of the opposite hand and felt an inexplicable sense of elation. Albert looked up, having picked up the pieces of incriminating evidence from the garage floor and smiled.

'I bet that feels better,' he said, winking at Declan. 'I was telling you what happened when I came round to the mill in the morning to pick you up. I saw what I thought was your blood on the kitchen table. Then I saw the bench tipped up, and when I saw your phone on the floor, I knew something was wrong. I guessed there'd been a struggle. I looked at the drive and saw tyre tracks but I knew you'd gone on foot. When I phoned the police, they told me to wait forty-eight hours. And if you weren't back in that time, they'd start a search.'

'They started that alright.'

'When I told them your car had been involved in an accident, they suggested I contact Carhaix, since the accident took place outside their jurisdiction.' Albert paused and scratched his head. 'Am I talking too quickly, Olivier?'

'No, no, not at all, please go on.'

'Well, when I explained that your car had been sabotaged, they insinuated that you might have done it yourself to claim the

152

insurance.' Albert breathed out hard, shaking his head as he did so. 'I told the police that you were not just any old client, but an old friend of mine and that you were not the sort of person to commit insurance fraud. And then the guy, I could barely believe it, he asked me if you were struggling to meet the payments on the car. Asked if you were experiencing any financial difficulties: "Could it be that he's recently lost his job?" the guy suggested – "it does happen", I couldn't believe it, so I thanked him and put the phone down. Anyway,' continued Albert getting his breath back, 'the long and short of it is, my intuition told me to sort your car out and worry about the police afterwards. I've taken some pictures of the sabotaged brake line, but I went ahead anyway and fixed up your car, sorry. Also managed to polish out those little scratches, so she's as good as new. Trouble is, Olivier when you get the insurance expert out and all the paperwork together, it can take weeks. This lot cost me forty euros in parts and two hours' work.'

Monique came out of the house and offered Declan a bite to eat saying that he looked exhausted and hungry. Declan must have given off signs that only the desperate can, for immediately Monique began to order Albert into the house to sort out some spare clothing, before organising a towel for Declan to take a shower and then she set about preparing a bite to eat. Above all, Declan was hungry, but he also needed the bathroom.

Washed and shaven, Declan began to explain to a horrified Albert and Monique, exactly what had happened to him – the torture, the escape, the boat, the lighthouse, the police. Albert and his wife sat there, both mesmerised and appalled.

'Quelle horreur!' said Monique.

After a generous meal of honey-roast pork in cider, Albert showed Declan to his bedroom and told him he'd wake him the next day:

'Just sleep,' said Albert. Declan slept.

The following day, well rested and feeling much more his normal self, he joined Albert in his kitchen for café and croissants.

'Today, Albert, I'm going to run the Audi up to Carhaix, check she's good and ready, so to speak,' but then it occurred to him what he was implying and tried to cover his tracks. 'Not that I'm casting any aspersions about your mechanical know-how, but if you've re-done her brakes, then I'll take it steady until I've got used to any changes – noises or anything.' Once again, Albert changed his tune completely.

'You *are* doubting my mechanical expertise, Olivier. That is exactly what you're doing. I told you she's good: I fixed her. And I'll tell you something else as well; you'll not be taking her anywhere.' If ever there was a perfect silence for effect, this was it.

'Here are your keys.'Albert tossed over a set of old-looking keys on a faded, gold-leaf-embossed, leather key-ring.

'It's your replacement vehicle while we try to discover just who is trying to kill you. Your car stays under wraps here in my garage until then.'

'What car is this then? I don't know if my ego could handle the shock of downsizing from an as-new TT to an old Peugeot,' he said, trying to make light of the situation.

'It's a Someca,' said Albert, dryly.

'That's a bloody make of tractor, Albert, come off it.'

'You get use of the tractor, the trailer and there's a cord of firewood free of charge,' explained Albert matter-of-factly. 'but the wood, I want back.'

'You are joking, right?'

'No, I bloody well am not. 'That cord of wood is three cubic metres of finely seasoned oak firewood, and it's worth 180 euros if not more.'

'I don't mean that at all. I mean about the tractor. You are joking right?'

'Listen here,' said Albert in a conspiratorial tone, 'I'm being realistic. Somebody deliberately cut through your brake line, possibly in order to kill you. And when that didn't work, they kidnapped you, tortured you and now you tell me the police are probably looking for you in connection with a double murder. At least one of those guys in his balaclava is still out there, Olivier. Now, if you want to be able to move freely around central Brittany at this time of year without drawing any attention to yourself or raising any eyebrows, then travel by tractor loaded with seasoned firewood. The rest of the time you can get away with it being freshly cut, green firewood.' Declan looked despondent, but he could very clearly see that Albert was right.

'Put these on as well.' continued Albert, throwing over a pair of faded blue dungarees, and as Declan caught them, Albert also frisbeed over a French peasant's flat cap adding: 'and put this on your head too.'

Half an hour later, Declan had had his first lesson on how to drive a tractor.

'The only real difference between this and what you're used to,' explained Albert, summing up, 'apart from the obvious speed and comfort, is that your throttle is a lever on the steering column as well as a foot pedal. So don't forget to throttle down when you stop at a junction. Oh,' he added, sniggering, 'and the brakes work on this.'

Declan smiled a broad smile at his friend and in an odd sort of way, he began to look forward to his new adventure – Carhaix on tractor – it was time to go and see the notary.

'Here,' Albert said, handing a small white envelope to Declan, 'there are two hundred euros in there, and I put this on charge – you left a phone cable in your car. Call me should you need anything. I'll see you this evening.'

Flat cap in place, Declan gently revved the 1965 Someca 4-eleven's forty-one horsepower engine, slipped into gear and brought the clutch up almost gently enough. He just had time to see Albert roll his eyes mockingly before the whole procession of tractor, man and wood-laden trailer jerked into movement forcing him to concentrate on turning the steering wheel firmly so as to point in the direction of the short concrete slipway leading off the garage forecourt out onto the road. Declan narrowly missed the breeze block wall.

Heading north on the D109, Declan drove the tractor past the bar and a couple of hands went up in the air in a salute of recognition. They must have thought it was Albert, so he just raised an arm to wave back. About a mile up the road looking up at the near perfect dome of Minez Du, he passed another tractor transporting wood. This one was red, while Declan's was orange, but what Albert had said about being inconspicuous, really hit home in that instant. Both men raised an arm in salute as they passed and continued on their respective ways. After about five or six miles, ten minutes up the road and a third of the way to Carhaix, he began to feel more at ease with gear changing and sat proud as any man at the helm. He turned off the road where he had seen the dark haired woman and where he had come off the road twice and felt an enormous sense of pride having survived what he had. He wondered if he would ever see her again. He began to feel comfortable enough to take his eyes off the road a little and started to enjoy the view that the top of the Black Mountain ridge offered. Soon he saw Carhaix and the church tower away in the distance. He had to be a good half-way there now.

Off to his right, Declan caught a glimpse of two enormous birds of prey soaring high up in the sky. One so high up it was not much more than a dot, while in just a few seconds the other had dropped out of the sky to tree-top level. They were magnificent. He knew what they were: Mamie had watched them for hours with him while they sat picnicking at the stone table on Minez Du. The weather was perfect for thermals and the second of the two red kites soon reached heights that made it difficult to focus on again. The only clouds in the sky were thin and sparse stratus ones some twenty odd miles away over the next mountain range, the Mont d'Arrée. Declan kept his cap on despite the sun's heat and remembered what Albert had said about travelling inconspicuously.

A while later, pulling away from a junction, by now only a mile from Carhaix's centre, Declan turned sharp left towards a roundabout and saw, in the corner of his eye, some logs on the road on the opposite side. In a double-take reaction, he realised that the logs had not been there when he pulled out from the junction – they had fallen off his trailer, and quickly he pulled over in order to load them back on. Into neutral, clutch out again, throttle closed a bit more, hand brake on, foot off the brake, okay. He jumped down and ran across the road almost scooping up the logs as he passed them. He stowed three of the logs under his left arm and quickly assessed that the fourth and last one to have fallen, would not present a danger to an oncoming car, so he waited. Declan's focus moved from the log by the central reservation to the oncoming car as his brain registered that the car was slowing. A bloody gendarme.

'Why now of all times?' he thought.

The car, with two gendarmes aboard, stopped. The driver indicated to Declan to fetch his remaining lost log. Declan, keeping his cap low over his eyes, waved a thank you with his right hand and scurried across the road to scoop up the fourth and final piece of flotsam.

'Relax. Control your breathing,' he said to himself.

The driver of the police car lowered his window, thanked Declan and wished him a "bonne journée" before continuing on his way. Quickly he threw the logs onto the trailer; checked that no others were about to fall, and jumped back into the seat of the Someca. What an amazing disguise:

'Thank you, Albert,' he mouthed.

Driving with the throttle using only the foot pedal now in town, he trundled his way up Carhaix's high street and parked in the biggest car park he could find – the idea of manoeuvring the tractor around in tight spaces with the trailer attached, he found a bit daunting. He parked the tractor in such a way as to be able to pull out forwards; he did not really feel confident about reversing either. Into neutral, clutch out again, throttle closed, hand brake on, foot off the brake and okay.

He walked out of the car park and crossed the narrow side road before cutting through a short pedestrian walkway onto the high street. Turning left towards the notary's office, he walked past two banks; Crédit Agricole and Caisse d'Epargne. On the opposite side of the road was a café with a small terrace – empty but for one smoker. Along from the café were two clothes shops and a closed down shoe shop. There were windows above each building, but all looked empty – window frames in serious need of paint, dirty, worn and torn curtains and telltale cobwebs on the panes. He walked past a news-agent's and an estate agent, a crêperie-pizzeria and finally came to another side road: this one was cobbled. He stopped to cross the road, but although no cars were coming, he hesitated for a moment: he hadn't made an appointment to see the notary on this occasion and it suddenly occurred to him that while his attire looked perfect on the tractor, it was completely out of place for the task in hand. To hell with it, thought Declan, and was just about to step out into the road, when he saw something that nearly made his heart stop. The heavy glass door of the notary's office swung open and the dark-haired woman stepped briskly out. She descended the granite steps and began walking along the pavement in the direction of the two high-street banks. He froze, unable to decide how to react.

Clearly she hadn't recognised him: in fact, she hadn't even looked at him. Declan's brain was racing. Partly he was excited to see her but hated to admit this to himself, for she had conspired with a man who had tortured him: the now deceased Smiths Watch Bag Balaclava. As long as she didn't recognise him, his whereabouts were still unknown to the enemy and therefore he was safe: at least for the moment. Finally, although only a few seconds had passed, Declan, without crossing the road, began following her. She carried an A4 size manila envelope under her right arm. Her hair was kept back away from her face with a green headband. The green matched her shoes – elegant suede shoes but without much heel: shoes his mother would have called sensible. He watched her heavy jet-black hair swinging from side to side as she walked and then he caught a glimpse of the outline of her slim waist through her pale cream blouse as she passed rays of bright sunlight reflecting off a window of the pizzeria. His eyes lowered to her legs. She was wearing dark trousers, quite narrow at the bottom, beautifully creased and well-fitting at the top. Declan watched her hips swaying gently and then found himself staring at her perfectly pear-shaped bottom. Why did he have to feel aroused by her of all people?

He had to snap out of this trance suddenly as the woman stopped and opened the door of the estate agents. She walked straight in. Another minus point if she, like Carl Grady, worked in real estate. As he crossed the road, still following, he began wondering just how many minus points she would have to accumulate before he could stop fancying her and decided that real estate was probably a perfectly respectable profession.

Slowly, he continued along the pavement and approached the estate agent's window. As surreptitiously as he could, he began looking at the photos of properties for sale in the window, when out of the blue came the woman's voice:

'Are you following me?' she asked.

Declan was so taken aback by her abruptness that he could barely answer her.

'Yes,' he replied, suddenly. 'I am.'

He was pleased with himself for an instant, for now, it was the woman that seemed to be stuck for words. She looked older than he had remembered - late twenties, maybe early thirties. A beautiful oval-shaped face. Her lips were full and quite red, her complexion, slightly olive. She smiled – beautiful pearl-white teeth and he found himself staring at her mouth.

'Why?' she asked him.

He tried to think of something cool to say but quickly decided that this wasn't the movies and whatever else he had been thinking about, she owed him an explanation – at least for the company she kept.

'I saw you come out of the notary's,' he began, 'and we've met before.' Now that did sound stupid, thought Declan. 'I need to talk to you,' he added quickly, 'about something extremely serious.'

The woman looked unconvinced, even puzzled, and Declan decided to cut to the chase.

'Some friends of yours tried to kill me and I want to know why. Is that serious enough for you?' Recollecting the excruciating pain inflicted on him by his torturers, and the fear of facing death, he could suddenly see himself able to stop fancying this woman a lot more quickly than he had imagined. The hurt he saw in her eyes a second later, captured his heart again firmly; she seemed so fragile and he just wanted to hold her. She appeared to have no notion of what he was talking about.

'I'm not making much sense, I know,' added Declan, calmly, 'but I do need to ask you some questions.'

'How did you know that I work at the notary's?' she asked him, naïvely.

Declan was surprised by her question, not just because it was he who was supposed to be asking the questions, but because he hadn't the slightest idea it was there that she worked.

'I didn't know you worked there. I was going to the notary's anyway. I just presumed you worked here,' he added, pointing an open palmed hand to the estate agent's front window.

She didn't look very convinced.

'My name's Olivier Declan O'Leary,' he said, 'and your office is handling the sale of my late grandmother's estate.'

'Madame Le Dour. So you're the Irishman it took us so long to find?' she said, looking seriously relieved. 'I'm off for lunch in about ten minutes, would you like to join me? I'm just going to grab a sandwich and eat it on the terrace there,' she said, pointing in the direction of where Declan had seen the lone smoker.

'I don't normally dress like this,' Declan confessed, suddenly embarrassed by his appearance. 'It's a long story.'

'I've got to get back to the office first,' she explained, 'and then we can have some lunch. Why don't you wait for me there?' she suggested, again pointing to the terrace a short way up the road.

'Okay,' replied Declan, pulse now racing. 'I'll see you in a few minutes.'

They parted company and while the woman set off back to the notary's office, Declan headed towards the café with the terrace. Suddenly, paranoia kicked in. Declan hadn't even asked the woman her name and she hadn't volunteered it when he had told her his. She knew all about him, yet he knew nothing about her.

18

The Silver Watch

Instead of heading for the café, Declan decided to wait in the entrance of a bank to keep a lookout. For the next ten or so minutes, he carefully scrutinised each and every passer-by, but shortly the streets were too busy to allow him to check everyone. Then he saw her. She was already sat down on the terrace ordering something from a bar-tender. On the table in front of her were what looked like two paper-wrapped sandwiches – was one for him or was she expecting someone else? Declan waited another moment or two, but she looked up and down the street constantly and he guessed it was safe to join her.

As he approached the terrace, he saw his reflection in the window of the bar, the faded dungarees, the cap. Despite the immediate temptation to remove the silly looking flat cap, he left it on: if he was going to look stupid on their first date, why not go the whole hog. As he looked across the terrace to the table where she sat, he saw her looking up, waving. Waving and smiling. Could it be that she liked him?

'I got you a *casse-croûte* as well,' she said, pointing to a sandwich as Declan joined her at the table. 'and by the way, my name's Candice, Candice Gautier.'

'Enchanté,' replied Declan. 'I'm Declan in Ireland and Olivier in France – don't ask me why, it's always been like that.'

'Maybe it was just easier for you as a child in Ireland not to have a French name.' Declan felt himself blush. 'You've gone all red; I didn't mean to embarrass you.'

'No, no you didn't embarr—'

'I'm stuck with Candice, because my middle name is Penelope.'

'What's wrong with that, it's a beautiful name?'

'But then I learnt at school in English you say Penny.'

'Penny's pretty too.'

'Yes except when you want to spend one.'

'How's that, spend one?'

'I don't want to be called by a name which, when you abbreviate it, can also mean "going to the toilet".'

'Ah, yes, *spend a penny*, I see what you mean.'

A part of him wanted to enjoy this time with Candice and talk niceties for an hour, but deep down, he knew he had to broach the subject of Smiths Watch Bag Balaclava and that, fairly swiftly. What was he going to tell Albert this evening if he didn't?

Hi, Albert, thanks for the loan of the tractor – I went on a date with a lovely woman.

Declan half coughed to clear his throat, before beginning his questioning.

'Oh,' said Candice smiling across the round blue metal table at Declan. 'so this is where it gets serious, right?'

'I said that we had met before,' began Declan. 'and that was...'

'By the church in La Trinité Langonnet and,' she paused for a second, 'by the road when you nearly crashed your car.' Declan was taken aback – she had remembered him.

'Nearly crashing my car was careless: I wasn't concentrating and I was actually very lucky not to have done any damage,' he said, 'but I had another accident in almost exactly the same place the next day.' He watched her face very intently, but he could see no suspicious reaction. On the contrary, Candice gently bit her bottom lip and gave Declan a look of genuine concern.

'Straight after I left the church where I saw you for the second time,' he explained, trying to establish a link between the two events, 'somebody cut clean through my hydraulic brake line while my car was parked by the church. Whoever did that to my brakes, caused the accident and could have killed me.'

'Oh my God,' said Candice. 'That's awful.' She was either a very good actor or she really knew nothing about it, he decided.

'The problem I have,' said Declan, this time quite accusingly, 'is that the only people I saw at the church during the time that I was parked there, was you and your friend the blind man.' Then Declan thought he saw a hint of anger in her eyes and he quickly tried to backtrack, adding: 'and I just wondered if you saw anything suspicious.'

'The blind man is not my friend,' said Candice, emphatically.

'*Was* not your friend,' corrected Declan, trying to sound like the tough guy. 'He's dead.'

'Dead?' asked Candice. And Declan quickly added:

'I think so,' for he had no intentions of telling Candice the whole story right now – it was simply too much for anyone to take in – Declan the murderer; the Irish bomber.

'I wanted to go to the church, I just love the stained glass windows and the wooden carvings: it's my favourite church,' explained Candice. 'When I got out of my car, there was this man on the ground trying to get up, so I went over to help him.'

'He was just lying on the ground?'

'Yes. Just lying on the tarmac. I asked him if he needed help and he told me had fallen over. He said he couldn't find his stick.'

'He'd lost a stick?'

'Well,' said Candice, pausing for just an instant, 'I asked him what it looked like because I assumed he meant a walking stick and he said it was white. Well, I thought if his stick was white, then he must be blind, right?'

'So where was his stick then?'

'On the roof of the car next to mine.'

'Hang on a minute. He couldn't see to walk, but he could drive?'

'It wasn't his car, stupid. He told me that he had placed it there while he tied his shoelace and then forgotten where he had put it. Then he fell over. I remember the conversation clearly.'

Declan decided to change his line of questioning a little and asked:

'When you said you helped him up, Candice, did you take the man's arm?'

'Yes of course. I'm not going to pull him up by his hair, am I? Why?'

'Did you notice anything on his wrist?' In order not to prompt the response he was hoping for, he quickly added:

'A bracelet or anything?'

'No,' replied Candice and then she closed her eyes as if trying to remember back. 'Yes,' she corrected, 'I did actually: his sleeve slipped down as I helped him to his feet and I saw a pretty looking watch – silver I think.'

'That's exactly right,' said Declan, rejoicing, and now he prepared his next question with a triumphant pride:

'What use do you think a blind man has for a watch?' he asked, cocking his head slightly to one side and raising his eyebrows a little comically.

Candice looked completely blank for a second and then she stared straight back at Declan – eyes acknowledging and mouth falling open as she realised what Declan was implying and she said, barely uttering her words:

'How can a blind man see the face of a watch?'

'Exactly,' beamed Declan.

'He was lying on the ground next to your car. That's where I saw him.' Candice added, suddenly. 'So you think he must have cut through your brakes?'

Declan now faced a conundrum: he now knew with absolute certainty that Smiths Watch Bag Balaclava had cut through his brake line. He had to decide either to stop there or tell Candice everything, for with the culprit now dead, there were no further leads to follow.

'Can I see you again after today?' Declan blurted.

'You will have to if you want to sign for your grandmother's house sale.' Candice replied, coolly.

'I meant for lunch or something?' he asked. Then Declan found himself checking her fingers quickly for any rings.

'Are you checking my fingers for rings to see if I'm married?' mocked Candice. 'What is this, Mister O'Leary? Are you asking me out on a date?'

'No, not at all,' he lied. 'I didn't mean it like that...'

'I'd love to,' she said flashing him a broad smile and her beautiful dark brown eyes gleamed.

Declan was not smiling back but frowning and he saw Candice's confidence disappear instantly.

'I'm very sorry,' Candice continued quietly. 'That was rude and very presumptuous of me.'

'No. No. Please,' said Declan. 'It's not that at all.' He didn't know where to begin. That blind man, Bag Balaclava was dead. Declan had bloody well killed him, and his bastard mate, Big Boy.

'There are some things I think you should know about me first – something I have to tell you,' Declan confessed. 'Very serious things.'

'Do I really need to know?' asked Candice with a saddened look in her eyes.

'I need you to know,' he answered, desperate to start making sense.

'Please, could I see you this evening?' he continued, vaguely embarrassed to find himself begging.

'I'll meet you by the Church in La Trinité after work, say six? Is that okay?' she asked glancing quickly at her watch.

'I'll be there,' replied Declan, relieved.

'I have to get back to work,' she explained and getting up to leave, she pointed at his sandwich and added: 'You haven't touched your lunch.'

As she walked away down the street, Declan sat watching her, admiring her. He imagined holding her and kissing her; her lips, her neck. The relief he had felt when he believed that she had had nothing to do with Bag Balaclava and the cutting of his brake line was overwhelming. It was only when Declan forced himself to look back at the table, that he saw Candice had left some money there to cover their drinks and he felt slightly ashamed. It had crossed his mind to follow her back up the road to make sure she really did return to the notary's office, but that thought too had made him feel even more ashamed. He wasn't hungry. He looked down the street again trying to catch sight of Candice, couldn't and decided to be on his way. Picking up his sandwich, he stood up and walked away from the table. He stepped off the terrace and headed along the high street in the opposite direction to Candice and turned down the short pedestrian walkway back in the direction of the car park and to the tractor. Declan's mobile started ringing and it startled him. He was wondering who it might be when he saw the name Isabelle flash up on the screen. He quickly answered.

'Hi, Is, how are tricks?'

'Good,' she said, 'I'm not phoning up for any particular reason. Just having a break from my translating work. How are you? Have you been into Mamie's house?'

Once again Declan didn't know where to begin, and very quickly decided to say nothing about his ordeal over the phone – why worry her – she couldn't help him anyway. He stepped out of the walkway and onto the pavement by the road opposite the car park, still walking as he talked.

'I did go in briefly,' he explained, 'but I haven't signed anything at the notary's yet. What about you what have you been up to?' He stopped for a second to check for traffic before stepping out to cross the road.

'A bit bored really; Carl's away in Dublin until Thursday – something to do with work. So I'm on my own. Maureen's been round every day and we've been out a couple of times to the park.'

'I'm sorry,' Declan interrupted, 'What did you just say? Carl's in Dublin?'

'Yes, until Thursday...' Declan cut her off abruptly. 'Listen, Isabelle. I'm really sorry. I'll call you back as soon as I can. I've got to go – don't mean to be so blunt. I'll explain later. Call you tonight. Bye.' He hung up.

He scoured the car park as quickly as he could and stepped back a couple of paces taking cover in the pedestrian walkway. What he had just seen worried him, and at that moment he could make no sense of it at all: parked just in front of him in the car park, was an Irish registered, shiny blue Saab-95 with the plate number, IO-L-595.

Declan's return journey under cover as a wood delivery man, was a lot less stressful than the journey out and when he finally arrived back on Albert's forecourt, he swung the Someca around in a smooth circle, reversed her into the space by the entrance to the hangar, swiftly followed the stopping procedures and switched off the engine. Albert, who had been watching from the entrance to his garage, began his applause. He had been racking his brains to try to understand why Carl Grady's Saab had been parked in Carhaix. He had lied to Isabelle, telling her he was in Dublin. What the hell was going on? Could Carl have been behind the plot to kill him; the torture, then the kidnapping? In the whodunit stories, detectives always look for a motive, he thought. He and Carl might not get on brilliantly, but what on earth would Carl have to gain by having him bumped off? Murdered? And then Declan realised something that disturbed him deeply. Surely not? It couldn't be! What had just dawned on him was that if he was out of the way, Isabelle would stand to inherit the old mill for herself. Carl Grady, working in real estate, would know that of course.

Declan changed from his disguise into something more casual – black jeans and smart blue shirt. A little later, as he sat at the table eating an omelette with Albert and picking at some chips, he had explained to his friend about his future brother in-law's car being parked in Carhaix. Albert had agreed that it was possible that the man might have wanted Declan dead.

'People have done worse for less.'

'Something else cropped up today as well,' Declan began sheepishly; he hadn't told Albert about Candice nor about meeting up with her by the church in just ten minutes from now. 'There's something I have to sort out this evening,' he confessed quickly. 'I've got to see someone at six o'clock.'

'So that's why you wanted to eat early. Sounds to me more like you've found yourself a lady friend,' said Albert mockingly. 'The problem is, you've got no lights on the tractor.'

'We're meeting by the church.'

'So I was right then? It is a girl you're going off to meet?'

'Well sort of,' admitted Declan, once his friend's laughter had calmed, 'but it's not quite what you think. It's to do with the sabotaged brake lines. I'll tell you all about it later.'

'I hope so,' replied Albert.

Declan grinned at Albert, slid his chair back away from the table and stood up grabbing at his slightly worn black leather jacket which hung over the back of the chair. He felt silly. He was so excited to be going to meet Candice he found himself doing a grown-up version of skipping as he headed up the road. He felt so silly in fact, he actually looked over both shoulders to make sure that nobody had witnessed his nervous and childlike walk. The walk turned into a fool-in-love's casual, not-a-care-in-the-world stroll and he knew he looked at least as silly as skipping and he didn't care. The words of Farouk came to him and he began to relax by concentrating on his breathing. Finally, his breathing normalised, his pulse rate lowered and his walk settled into something more casual and controlled as he turned the corner of the building opposite the church. He noticed what he thought was her car and in a flash, he recognised her swishing dark hair from behind as she walked leisurely through the tidy, but modest church gardens. Candice looked relaxed.

Declan glanced up at the church clock and then – a distant childhood memory – that faint, almost intangible leaden sounding "click" just before the bells started their sequence. He was smack on time. Ding, ding, ding... as the church began chiming six.

He headed in the direction of the entrance to the gardens, saw that Candice had changed, and instantly found himself admiring the firm cheeks of her beautifully rounded bottom. She was wearing cream slacks which enhanced her shapeliness and Declan began feeling that deep hollow yearning that accompanies unsated love. He wanted to hold her, to smell her hair and feel the softness of her body against his.

The bells stopped their tolling and Candice turned around delicately as she scanned the area around the church. She saw Declan and instantly smiled, waving both hands above her head.

As Declan reached her, for just a fraction of a second, they both found themselves unfamiliarly close to one another and this closeness created a slightly awkward moment. Declan, face to face with Candice, had suddenly recoiled. He had recoiled partly because etiquette dictates that you don't say hello twice, therefore no kiss or handshake upon their second meeting that day, but much more, because deep down, he would have felt a sense of rejection had it been Candice that recoiled first. God this bloody French social etiquette didn't half complicate matters, he thought.

'Hi,' she said, 'you made it then.'

Declan thought, but didn't dare say out loud:

'I wouldn't have missed it for the world.'

'Yes,' he confirmed and then added, 'Listen, do you think it would be possible to go for a walk somewhere? What I have to talk to you about, well I just don't really feel comfortable here, what with the bar being just opposite?'

'Sure,' she agreed, 'Where to? Minez Du?'

'...Minez Du?' Declan suggested, uttering the place name at exactly the same time as Candice.

'You get a wish for that where I come from,' said Declan.

Candice looked confused.

'When two people say the same thing at the same time, you get a wish,' he explained.

'I think I've heard that before,' she said, 'but I think it's American. You have to say, "Chips". I was just surprised when you said it because I thought you were from here; Brittany.'

Declan smiled. His origins were in Brittany, but he tended to forget and considered himself more Irish than Breton. His sister, Isabelle, was a different story. She was very definitely both Irish and Breton: as well as speaking English and French, she could read and speak Gaelic and Breton fluently. Spanish, Italian and German too, for that matter. She was clever, thought Declan to himself, and despite her handicap, she had found a niche through her knowledge of the two minority languages that brought in plenty of translation work she could do from home. He'd have to phone her that evening he thought. He must not forget.

'What place did you drift off to then?' asked Candice, 'You seemed to be in a world of your own for a minute there.'

'I was just thinking about my sister,' Declan explained and nearly added: "I think she'd like you". He stopped himself from saying it for it sounded a bit presumptuous in the sense that his sister might "approve" of his choice. So for want of something else to add, he asked:

'Do you speak Breton, Candice?'

'No. It became sort of trendy and began a comeback after I left school, so I was too late,' and then she said something odd that surprised Declan; 'Your grandmother spoke Breton, didn't she?'

'That's right, how do you know?'

'I had a look through your file this afternoon and found something a bit bizarre. If we are going for a walk up Minez Du,' she paused, 'well, you've got things you want to tell me and I'll tell you what I found today. Shall we take my car to the foot of the hill?'

'Yeh. Great.'

Candice parked her blue Renault Megane at the end of the track leading up to the Minez Du, and she and Declan climbed out. Candice locked up and there was a sort of nervous moment of anticipation between them as they looked across at one another and smiled.

'Ready then?' she asked.

'I am,' Declan confirmed and they set off together up the gravelly track, sheltered from the wind by the tree-lined hedgerow.

As they set off walking, bar the crunching of gravel under their feet, there was silence. Neither said a word. Over a minute must have passed and finally, he decided that it was up to him to begin. He eventually thought that the best tactic would be to start from the beginning. He told Candice about the discovery with Albert of the snipped brake line. The going for one too many drinks and waking up on his own at the old mill. He described his fear during the kidnapping, the torture and then he explained to her how he got away from the island.

'But how did you actually get out of the room away from the three men?' asked Candice, as fascinated as if he was reading to her from a book.

He told her what he had done: the light bulb, the gas, the baking trays, the duct tape and how he had made himself a makeshift blast shelter. Declan swallowed hard, there was a lump in his throat and he felt all the emotions of the nightmare coming back to him. He told her about the sinking of the boat and the lighthouse and then described his escape and Doctor Khadir.

'Are you crying?' Candice asked him. 'Oh you poor thing,' and she reached out her hand for his and he held it. He felt so happy, that he could feel tears welling up in his eyes – she was beautiful. Declan began to laugh lightly.

'What's so funny?' asked Candice.

'Just a déjà vu,' confessed Declan, 'I'll tell you about it one day,' he said. 'The worst thing is I don't really know what they wanted from me. And now you see why I wanted to talk to you. You were the only link I had to the man with the watch.'

'I really can't help you with that, I'm sorry, but as I said, I just don't...' Candice paused, 'didn't know the man.'

Slightly embarrassed, covering her mouth with her hand, Candice began laughing.

'So what's funny?'

'I'm sorry, but it's just your name for him, "Smiths Watch Bag Balaclava". It's not funny I know, I'm sorry.'

Declan knew full well that sometimes people in shock tend to laugh. He himself only minutes after surviving the explosion, had fallen on top of the torso and still found the nerve to utter the words: "Times up, sucker!" Maybe a bit too early to share that one with Candice, he decided.

'I've told you what happened to me and now it's your turn,' Declan said.

'How do you mean?'

'You said you had found something bizarre today. In my file.'

'Oh yes. Sorry. Well after your story, it just doesn't seem very important, that's all.'

'What was it?'

'Well, when we first put a dossier together, say the death of someone in the family or just a house sale, it's usually me that prepares it for the notary. And, well,' she hesitated, 'your grandmother's had a really curious thing in it. On its own was a small brown envelope with, "Pour Olivier, mon petit fils", written on it. Well I have to confess,' whispered Candice, 'I felt the envelope like a child might a Christmas present, trying to work out what was in it.'

'So there's something in the envelope?'

'No, there isn't, but there was. It felt like a key. Look,' she continued, pulling the now folded envelope out of her beige coloured leather Chloé handbag she wore over her shoulder. 'A corner has been torn open and there's nothing inside.'

'How come?' frowned Declan. 'You're telling me that that envelope was in your office for safe-keeping and now a key has been removed from it, while it's been in your possession?'

'Not mine personally,' said Candice.

'No. Sorry. I didn't mean it like that.' And then he looked at Candice for a second and at the envelope in her hand. 'So that's addressed to me, right?' he asked, rhetorically. 'So I could open it, right?'

'Of course,' agreed Candice, handing the envelope over to him.

He looked at the corner where it had clearly been torn open, felt the envelope and ripped it open completely. The A5 size sheet he found inside was extremely crumpled and Declan had the impression that the piece of paper had already been pulled out through the hole, read and put back in. The paper had just two handwritten lines on it and Declan tried to understand it. It read as follows:

"An alc'hwez-mañ a zigor ar voest hag a vo kavet e-barzh peadra da gavout da Oliere hent betek an eil alc'hwez ha betek an teñzor meur."

Declan, although able to understand some simple expressions in Breton, was completely at a loss when it came to the written language. He quickly handed the paper back to Candice asking her if she could fathom anything at all from it.

'It's Breton,' she said, 'but I have no idea what it means. I'm sorry.'

'My sister, Isabelle would know. And I'm supposed to call her tonight.'

'This might sound stupid,' began Candice, 'but it might be better if I kept the envelope until you come into the notary's office, because that way we can say that the key was still in there before you saw it. Does that make any sense?'

'I'm not sure quite what you mean. You mean the notary might have removed the key?'

'I don't know.'

'Fine,' said Declan, pulling out his iPhone. 'I'll take a picture of it and send it to Isabelle. That'll be a lot easier than me trying to read it to her over the phone.

Soon they reached the steeper part of the mound leading to Jean-Mollet's stone table. Declan, having scanned the horizon and taken in the magnificent panoramic view, looked across at the now wind-blown Candice. He held up an outstretched arm to her, beckoned her to his side. Candice moved towards him, slid under his arm and as Declan's hand lowered over her shoulder, she snuggled her head against his neck and chest. Declan lowered his face to her head to breathe in the fragrance of her hair and smiled - ecstatically happy, as he stared out over the view from what for him, was once again the most important place in the world.

'I've made an appointment for you to sign for the mandate for the house sale first thing tomorrow morning. A bit pushy, I know.' There was a pause - silence but for the wind in their ears. 'There was a free window so I made you an appointment with the boss. Is that okay?'

'Perfect,' said Declan.

'This feels really strange,' said Candice. 'We've only just met, but I feel like I've known you for years.'

'Strange? Is that positive or nega...?'

'Wonderful,' she said. 'My turn now. Can I see you again at the weekend? After the appointment: let's not mix business with pleasure.'

'Great,' replied Declan. 'Where? What ti...?' and suddenly Candice reached her mouth quickly up to find Declan's and kissed him on the lips.

'That was nice.'

'Only nice?'

'Really nice. Really, really nice. Is there any more where that came from?' he asked.

'Are you free at the weekend?'

'All weekend. And the following week. And the week after that...' Declan stopped. Candice didn't know he'd just lost his job.

She dropped him off by the church and reminded him that she had made an appointment for him to see the notary first thing in the morning.

'Well,' she corrected, 'a quarter past nine to be precise. Is that okay?'

Declan pictured himself travelling all that way again by tractor and was just about to share this dread with Candice, when she suggested coming by to pick him up first thing in the morning.

'That'll save you having to put your tractor costume on again for me.'

They kissed goodbye and Candice turned her Mégane around and set off, leaving Declan by the church.

Declan related very little of his romantic sortie to Albert. Firstly he was embarrassed by his own emotions, which all seemed childishly hasty, and secondly he didn't want Monique asking too many questions about Candice.

'She had nothing to do with the brakes, Albert,' Declan had confirmed. 'She works at the notary's and she's coming to pick me up in the morning for the appointment with her boss.'

'Bit beyond the call of duty that, isn't it?' Albert said, smiling with a raised eyebrow.

'What's her name?' asked Monique.

'I didn't ask,' said Declan. 'Why?'

'Just wondered if I knew her, that's all.'

'Didn't ask, mon cul!' *my arse!* Albert muttered. 'Still, your business is your business. You'll tell me when you're good and ready I suppose.'

'After what you've done for me Albert,' he said, again trying to make light of the situation, 'you'll be the first to know. You can be my best man.'

Declan excused himself and went outside the front door to send a text message to Isabelle using his iPhone and attached the photo of the message in the envelope.

'Can U help me on this 1 plz, Is?' and he waited.

'Have 2 work out cost! ;)'

'Btw it's weird where dyu getit? IS'

'Mamie. N V lope @ notary. Y? D.'

'can transl8 but cant understand! Is.W8 a sec'

'Herc goes – good luck. IS: "The key opens the chest in which Olivier will find all he needs to lead him to the second key, the real treasure,"'

'Gonna call U now Is, that Ok? D.'

'yes ☺.'

'Hi. Thanks for picking up so quickly. You okay?' asked Declan.

'I am. Are You? You sound really troubled. What's up, Declan?'

'God, Isabelle. I don't even know where to start.'

'You're crying, Declan. What's up? What on earth is the matter?' asked Isabelle.

Declan started at the beginning. Isabelle was absolutely horrified.

'Why didn't you call me?' she said. 'I could have called Carl. He could have come over to help you. I could have come with him. Oh, Declan.'

He did not know how best to break the news to his sister. She clearly had no idea at all that Carl was already here in Brittany. No idea that Carl was even a possible suspect as far as Declan was concerned.

'Listen, Isabelle,' he said as calmly as he could. 'You remember this afternoon when you called, I said I had to go?'

'Yes. I do. Why, what else haven't you told me? Is there more? Does it get worse?'

'I don't know yet,' he said, stalling. 'Carl's car was in the car park near the notary's.' There was silence on the other end of the phone. 'He told you he was in Dublin, right?' the silence continued. Declan didn't know what else to say. Isabelle was clearly shocked.

'You could have told me that on the phone this afternoon, but you didn't, why?' Declan was dreading this reaction. 'Do you think he might have had something to do with what happened to you? Is that it?' Declan became suddenly very angry.

'He bloody well lied to you about where he was going. How do you expect me to react?'

'Not like that. I know you're traumatised, but your reaction is not rational. I know you think he can be a bit of a prick sometimes and you're right, but seriously, Declan... Carl's my boyfriend, my fiancé. I don't know what to say to you. I'm going to call him now. And you make sure you answer the phone when I call you back in two minutes.' Isabelle yelled down the phone.

So that was it, thought Declan: you screw my sister and you think you can screw me too. Carl had got another thing coming. And how the hell did his sister hope to convey – in less than two minutes – to Mr Carl Bloody Grady what had happened to him in the last forty-eight hours? And all that, with any real conviction? Unless Carl already knew. Oh holy shit, thought Declan: Isabelle knew as well. They must have planned it together.

19
The Rendezvous

Declan's phone rang. It was Carl's number. He stared at the tactile screen – frozen – unable to react. Quickly and suddenly, he pressed the green button to accept the call, put the cell-phone to his ear, but said nothing.

'Declan?'

'What?'

'It's me, Carl. I think we should talk.'

'Just what the hell are you doing here in Brittany, Carl? Why did you tell Isabelle you were going to Dublin?'

'Stupid. That's what that was – is, I mean. I think we should meet up. Like soon. Like what are you doing now – tonight? I owe you an explanation, Declan. I'm sorry. Isabelle told me about your car being sabotaged.'

'Yeah, well,' said Declan with a tip-of-the-iceberg nonchalance.

'If you've got no transport, I could come and pick you up and we could go somewhere for a drink and a talk.'

That would be a bit easy for him wouldn't it now, Declan thought. A sitting duck.

And then he had an idea.

'Okay,' he suggested, thinking "home territory" advantage. 'How about at the entrance to the church in La Trinité-Langonnet in about half an hour?' That way, Declan reasoned, he could see Carl arrive and jump him.

'Fine,' said Carl. 'I have the address on my satnav for La Trinité and I guess I'll find the church easily enough. Half an hour then?'

'Fine.'

Declan had no intention of meeting Carl at the entrance to the church, and he rushed back into the house to share his suspicions with Albert to put a plan into place as quickly as possible.

'He's coming here. Carl Grady,' Albert looked confused. 'Isabelle's boyfriend. Fiancé. The real-estate man.'

'Here? Why is he coming here? You shouldn't have told him where you are. You're a fool.'

'No! Not here, here. Not your house. By the church. In half an hour.'

'You want me to get the bolt croppers ready for his car?' asked Albert, smirking. 'Come on then, Olivier. I've got a plan.'

'What plan?'

'A very clever plan,' said Albert. 'One that involves having a drink in the bar up the road, now that can't be bad, hey?'

'We can't go out drinking tonight, Albert. Get serious.'

'Oh yes, of course. You've that meeting tomorrow. The one that isn't a date haven't you? With that girl that doesn't particularly interest you either, haven't you?'

'For God's sake, Albert, my life's at stake here and you're sat there poking fun at me and proposing we go down the pub.'

'Planning an ambush, Olivier, is what I am doing,' replied Albert, in his defence.

'What's the plan?'

'You told this Carl fellow to meet you at the entrance to the church, right?'

'Right.'

'You hide behind one of the yew trees where you can see the pub window and the entrance to the church. When your man turns up, you watch and wait. And, by the way, so will I, but from the bar.'

'See you've allocated yourself the hardest task.'

'Meanwhile, I tell the guys in the pub there may be a punch-up and get them all ready and psyched-up, while you stay lurking in the shadows of the yew tree and signal to me using this,' Albert passed a small cardboard box with black writing on it to Declan.

'A rape siren? Do you think my sister's boyfriend wants to rape me?'

'It comes from the States, that one. I carry it with me all the time. Anything goes wrong in the workshop and I let this off, Monique calls emergency services. This is loud, Olivier. I mean loud.'

Declan began to like the sound of Albert's plan.

'Now,' continued Albert, 'I hear nothing for five minutes, you come into the pub with this Carl bloke for a casual drink, but knowing full well that me and the boys are all ready and waiting. If you don't come in the pub, I'll assume there's a problem and me and a few guys will come out for a smoke or something. Casually, you know.'

'So far, so good,' said Declan, 'and when do I let the siren off?'

'If you are attacked or surprised, or just this guy doesn't turn up on his own and you feel worried: pop goes the weasel whistle.'

'The what?' asked Declan.

'You set off the rape alarm and me and the boys pile out the pub and kick arse.'

'Yeah, but why the whistle? It's an old rhyme and it's weasel? It doesn't mean whistle. Where did you get that shit from anyway, Albert?'

'London-man in pub last week. In Londres, weasel-word rhymes with coat. So you hit the rape alarm and we pile out the pub with the sleeves off, gloves up, pulling no punches, innit?' said Albert, almost in English.

'You mean: roll your sleeves up, gloves off. Stick to the French, Albert, just for tonight, please.' Albert pulled a heavily laden key ring out of his pocket and began to scrutinise it.

'We go in the... , Peugeot.'

'I'm walking,' said Declan.

'You might be seen. Put this cap on, I'll back up by the wall of the church and you jump out when you see the coast is clear,' said Albert, and they left together and at once.

About twenty minutes later, Declan, squatting beneath the only low hanging branch of the old yew where it stretched over the wall of the churchyard, began to readjust his legs: stiffness was setting in and the skin under the dressing was taut and stinging. He heard a car and decided to sit on the ground, injured leg outstretched and upper torso leaning on the yew. He was still well hidden.

Carl's car stopped by the bar and then, having overshot the turn, manoeuvred awkwardly towards the car park next to the church. Declan watched as Carl, apparently alone, swung his Saab around and parked up. He got out and looked around. Declan presumed he was looking for him. He waited three or four minutes to make sure no one else was coming and that Carl really was on his own, then quietly moved his way along the branch and over the church wall. The wall was not high on the church side, but the drop must have been almost shoulder height on the other side. Declan slipped down the wall as quietly as he could and placing his feet delicately on the ground as he walked, he approached the entrance to the church just twenty metres away in almost complete silence.

At about ten paces from Carl, Declan identified himself. His left hand in his pocket clutching the rape alarm – a black slightly oversized key ring, with two flat, round buttons on one side.

'Evening, Carl,' said Declan coolly, index finger ready to let out 130dB at the slightest sign of trouble.

Albert had seen the car pull up, figured that it must be the foreigner because of the awkward way in which he approached the car park, and stood at the end of the bar watching – hawk-like. Everyone in the bar was waiting on Albert's signal to exit through the front door and launch a counter-attack.

'Declan. Hi,' said Carl.

'You wanted to talk. To explain yourself, wasn't it?'

'Now hang on a minute,' Carl began. 'I owe you no explanation whatsoever. To your sister maybe, but not to you.'

Declan almost lost his temper in that instant. He wanted to swear and insult Carl but could not work out how to justify it. What could he say? What had Carl actually done?

'So what the hell are you doing here then? What business have you got that's so important that you have to lie to my sister?' asked Declan, just beginning to feel really stupid.

'Business,' said Carl.

'Yeah, business. What business? Whose business?'

'Real estate of course. My business. We are thinking of operating as an agent selling property in France from Ireland. It's a new market for us – a chance to increase sales. Isabelle would do the French side of things. Micky Flynn and I run the Irish side from Dublin and Limerick. Your sister wants to spend more time here. I'm hopin' to make that possible. It was gonna be a surprise.'

Declan stared blankly at Carl – no idea what to say next. Best policy was usually honesty.

'I've been a total jerk, Carl,' said Declan. 'I've no idea what to say next.'

The pub door opened and Declan heard a voice:

'Ya un problème, Olivier?' *Is there a problem, Olivier?*

Suddenly Declan was going to end up with an awful lot more to explain if he did not react quickly enough.

'On arrive, là,' yelled Declan in the direction of the bar, and grabbing Carl's arm said, 'We can go for that drink in here, Carl, c'mon. I can see there's a whole shit load I've got to tell you.'

Declan, as quickly and as briefly as he could, explained the misunderstanding to Albert, ordered "une tournée générale" which he estimated, given the number of men in the bar would set him back about forty euros, sat down with Carl in as quiet a corner as he could find and began to tell his story to his future brother-in-law. Carl was speechless. Horrified.

'My God, man. I'm so sorry. I had no idea. If I'd told you I was here you could have called me and I'd have come for you. Of course I would,' Carl insisted.

Declan looked at Carl and smiled. Although relieved by his genuine concern, he could not help thinking that with no phone on him, imprisoned on an island and then stranded at sea, there would have been little or nothing Carl could have done to help.

'It wasn't your fault, Carl. You couldn't have known.'

Declan had decided not to say anything about his suspicions about Carl having been involved in the kidnapping. Luckily, Isabelle had not mentioned a thing.

'Micky Flynn? The Micky Flynn?'

'The one and only, why? You seem surprised; he's bloody good at it I can tell you that.'

'Bloody good programmer he was, why'd he give it up?'

'Not really sure he has. I do know he was advised to cool it a bit.'

'I warned him he'd get caught in the end.' Declan shook his head. 'What's the news from Isabelle then, she coming over?'

'She's flyin' over tomorrow and I'm going to pick her up,' Carl said, trying to brighten up the mood.

'Great,' said Declan. 'Where's she landing?'

'Paris.'

'Paris? You'd better not drink too much tonight then, Carl: it's nearly six hours to De Gaulle airport from here by car. That's a twelve-hour drive there and back. What time does she land?'

'No. She's catchin' the VGT – Very Grand Train – from Paris and she'll be in Lorient for about four o'clock tomorrow afternoon. I've worked it out, that's about an hour's drive to get down there from here.

Declan hesitated and then decided first of all not to bother correcting Carl's French concerning the TGV and secondly he decided not to volunteer to accompany him to Lorient. Carl had got his trusty satnav and Declan was going to see Candice, hopefully.

'An hour's about right,' he said, instead.

Albert wandered over to their table, deciding it was probably time for introductions. The three men drank one more beer before heading back to Albert's, where Carl too, had been offered a room for the night.

A few minutes before they set off from the bar, Declan stepped outside leaving Carl to practise his French with Albert. He pulled a card out of his pocket and texted the mobile number on the back,

'Here's my mobile number, are you free to talk? Declan O'Leary.'

Declan's phone rang almost instantly and he answered.

'Declan? Are you alright? Is everything okay?'

'Hi, Farouk. I hope I'm not disturbing you. I know it's late, but I just wanted to say thank you for your help.' He told him briefly about the undercover tractor trip to Carhaix, the fire-wood and the meeting with Candice, but it took a minute or so before he was able to pluck up the courage to confess to having master-minded the explosion on the island of Bréhat. Farouk seemed unsurprised by Declan's confession replying,

'Life can sometimes confront a man with choices he doesn't always wish to make.'

Declan felt almost absolved; he had not been the one who'd started the trouble, but he had certainly put a stop to it, at least for the time being.

20
Adjudant-Chef Mahé – 2015

Behind the reception desk at the hospital in St-Brieuc, a woman in her fifties was on the phone. Mahé, having seen as he approached, that she was occupied, slowed down his pace a little before he reached the desk. Her hair was nearly white all over, a few remaining traces of dark: a record of the jet black hair of her youth. She wore a hands-free headset and elegant, metal-rimmed glasses. Mahé marvelled at the apparent ease with which she appeared to pass off these necessary tools of her trade as finery – as bijouterie.

The receptionist placed a contemplative index finger on her pursed lips, glanced up at Mahé and held out the very same finger towards him in a gesture as if to say:

'Just one moment please'.

He stopped a good metre from the desk and felt as if she had just blown him a kiss.

'D'accord. On fait comme ça. Merci. Au revoir.'

A button was pressed and the receptionist gave Mahé her full attention.

'Good morning, sir, how can I help you?'

'Good morning, madame. You have, or had a physician here called Khadir.' began Mahé.

The look on her face told him she was listening and he realised he hadn't actually said anything that prompted a response.

'This is going back a few years to 2006 to be precise,' he continued, being everything but precise. Mahé decided to try again. 'I need to speak to a Dr Farouk Khadir concerning some recent developments in an inquiry that dates back to the year 2006.' Mahé produced his id card and placed it on the desk in front of her.

'The doctor still works here,' she confirmed. 'but not all the time. Dr Khadir is a neurosurgeon and he is regularly called out to Rennes, Brest, Paris – sometimes even further afield. If you can wait a second I should be able to tell you where he is today, sir.'

Judging by the continual pressing of buttons, Mahé deduced that more calls were coming in constantly.

'He's not here today,' she said. 'He's in Paimpol. That's where he usually is when he's not out on call.'

'That's great. Thank you. Would it be possible for you to call through and leave Dr Khadir a message that Adjudant-Chef Mahé would like to speak with him?'

'I can try of course, but I can't guarantee the message will get through.'

'That's fine. I shall go there straight away.'

'Paimpol isn't that far from here: about half an hour's drive, that's all,' she said, helpfully.

'I imagine it would take a little longer than that, were one to respect the national speed limits,' replied Mahé, dryly.

The receptionist blushed, smiled a coy smile and returned her attentions to her panel of buttons and her next caller.

21

The Open Door

Declan walked into the notary's office exactly fifteen minutes after Candice. It was 9:15 am. Candice stood over the desk in the entrance-hall-cum-reception area holding the receiver of a telephone to her right ear.

'I'll put you through, one moment please.' She looked up at Declan and said by way of explanation, 'Our receptionist is off today and it's mayhem. I'll just go and tell the notary that you're here. Hold on a second.'

She disappeared through a granite archway lined with a highly polished oak frame. There must have been a door there once, thought Declan and he walked over towards it casually glancing at each side, checking for telltale scars of once-were hinges. He looked down the corridor to see Candice disappear through an end door on the left. The door closed firmly behind her. There were four other openings leading off the corridor: three doors and an opening that appeared, from where Declan was stood, to lead to a stairwell. One of the doors was marked "toilettes". Of the other two doors on opposite sides of the corridor to each other, one was slightly ajar and he wondered which, if any, led to Candice's own office. As he began to imagine what her office would look like from the inside, he heard the voice of a man and he suddenly froze; the hairs on the back of his neck stiffened with terror. The voice came from the open door. It was him, Boss Balaclava.

22

An Ongoing Inquiry

Mahé arrived at the hospital in Paimpol approximately forty minutes later, walked into the entrance hall and across to the desk marked, "Acceuil". He was disappointed to find the desk deserted. No charming woman. No nobody. Just as he turned around to see if anyone was on their way, he recognised the man he had first met nine years earlier, walking towards him in a fastened white lab coat – stethoscope around his neck.

'Dr Khadir, thank you for coming to meet me. I have some questions I need to ask you.'

Farouk looked confused.

'I am not here to meet you. I had no idea that you were coming, let alone that you were coming to see me. To what do I owe this pleasure? It's Mr Mahé or Adjudant-Chef Mahé, am I right? Although I imagine you've since been promoted?'

Mahé had not and didn't answer the question.

'I tried to get a message through to you to let you know I was coming,' Mahé explained.

Reaching over the desk, Farouk picked up a piece of paper with his name scribbled on it and got his answer: "Adjudant-Chef Mahé on his way to see Dr Khadir, please inform."

'Ah. There we have it. Adjudant-Chef Mahé, how can I help you?'

'As I said, I have a few questions I need to ask you.'

'Your timing could not have been better in that case, for I have about an hour on my hands right now. If we need to go somewhere I should get changed, but,' he continued, unfastening his lab coat and coiling his stethoscope into one of its front pockets, 'if the hospital canteen suits you, we can go there now: it will be quiet at this time.'

'We need quiet,' replied Mahé.

In the canteen, Farouk offered Mahé a coffee which he declined and so to gain time, rather than have a coffee himself, he filled a plastic beaker from a cold water fountain and ushered the gendarme to a quiet table by the long run of windows overlooking the hospital car park. Mahé began at once:

'Over the weekend you treated a patient here for burns. His name was Olivier Declan O'Leary.'

'Was?' asked Farouk. 'Has something happened to him?'

'I have no idea,' replied the gendarme. 'I need you to tell me what you can about him. What happened, what he said, where did he go afterwards? Anything and everything.'

'Why?' asked Farouk. 'What's he done?'

'I shouldn't have to point out to you that during an inquiry, withholding information from the police is a crime, Doctor Khadir.'

'No. I will tell you of course, but it is human nature to ask questions.' Farouk suddenly remembered a detail that might encourage Mahé to divulge at least something – a trade-off.

'I treated him and turned him over to your men. They had an arrest warrant for him and they took him away. He must have escaped police custody.' Mahé looked totally bewildered by this news.

'What?'

'He was taken away in a police car by three of your officers.'

'A police car? Are you sure it was a police car?'

'Yes, I saw it.'

'So, after you treated O'Leary for burns, you walked out of the hospital and into the car park to see in which car your patient was driven away?' Mahé asked. 'Is that normal procedure would you say, Doctor? Do you see all your patients off in this manner?'

Had any such arrest warrant been issued and a suspect apprehended by his officers, Mahé would have known about it. Of that, there was absolutely no question.

'What I am trying to say, Dr Khadir, is this: how do you know it was a police car?'

'I saw the officers leave to go to their car.'

Mahé was confused. His suspicions were simple: following a violent explosion on the Island of Bréhat just days ago, the bodies of two known criminals had been found in the rubble. Preliminary forensic reports indicated that two other men may have managed to get out alive. Something was amiss in this whole affair and what Mahé believed was, that O'Leary must have been "collected" from the hospital by men masquerading as officers of the law. It would not be the first time. If, however, the doctor had seen the car, that could change matters completely, for it would be a stunt many times riskier for any gang of criminals to pull off.

'Are you sure you saw their car, Doctor?'

'It was a Renault Clio bearing the word "GENDARMERIE". It had all the flashing lights.'

This brought Mahé back to his earlier question.

'So, once again, Dr Khadir, I'm going to ask you the question: is it normal procedure would you say, to treat your patient and then proceed to follow him or her out into the car park to determine in which vehicle they are being driven away? Were you checking up on my men, Doctor? Did you doubt them?' he added, probing.

'My patient was terrified of your men. He had been tortured. I could see that.' admitted Farouk. 'So, to answer your question, no. Obviously, it is not normal procedure.'

'So, when you saw the men,' Mahé pulled out a notepad quickly and clicked on the button of his ballpoint pen he had clipped to the side of the pad. 'Three gendarmes you say?' he began writing. 'What did they look like? Could you describe them to me, Doctor?'

'Listen. What is all this? Two of your officers came into the hospital and their faces should be captured on the C.C.T.V. camera in the foyer.'

'Thank you for that Doctor. I'll send someone round to take a look at that as soon as possible. I imagine the images are stored here for later viewing? Who would I have to speak to about that?'

'I have no idea, but I imagine the director of the hospital would be able to put you in touch with someone from security. Did you ever find the man that killed your young policeman? The one who died in the car accident? Yaouank I think was his name.'

Mahé looked around the hospital canteen and bit down gently on his bottom lip for several seconds.

'Did you treat anyone else that night, Dr Khadir? I mean specifically in relation to the events I have mentioned from that evening – the O'Leary incident?'

'No. There was another man, a coastguard. But he had an extremely complex fracture, from what I could gather from the medic, and rather than waste time here waiting for x-ray confirmation, I had him sent straight to Rennes in a helicopter from the port.'

'I know about that,' said Mahé. Next, Mahé did something he had never done before and swore he would never do again; he revealed some details of the case to someone outside the inquiry.

'What I say next, Dr Khadir, must go no further?' Mahé stopped, silent and staring, still waiting for the doctor to acknowledge what he had just said. Farouk nodded.

'Four sets of fingerprints were found at the location of the gas explosion that occurred on the Island of Bréhat on the night Mr O'Leary was treated. Two of the sets of prints match those of the two bodies found at the site. A further set matches Mr O'Leary's. He applied for a French id card here in Brittany nine years ago. The fourth set, well...' Mahé paused for a moment. 'To say we have no match is not true. We don't know the identity of the person, but his or her prints, well I'm certain it's a man. The prints match up with those found in the car with Agent Yaouank's following the collision in which the young officer was killed.'

'Langonnet,' said Farouk plainly.

Mahé glared at Farouk across the table. The doctor had just revealed the village in which O'Leary's id application had been filed. But O'Leary had never signed for his card nor had he been in to collect it. The doctor could therefore not possibly have known that, unless the man himself had told him.

'What do you mean, Langonnet? How do you know that?' snapped Mahé.

'That's where I dropped him off,' replied Farouk, meeting the policeman's gaze fully.

'Why didn't you tell me any of this?' said Mahé, seriously annoyed. 'You're wasting my time and hindering my inquiry, Dr Khadir. You're an educated man. You understand the gravity of this, surely?'

Farouk lowered his voice – a technique he had learned to get people to listen: a technique far more effective than shouting.

'Two of your officers, and I am certain they were your officers, came into my hospital to arrest a patient of mine on the pretext that they had an arrest warrant for him. An arrest warrant, which incidentally, they were unable to produce. Further to this, they were unable to confirm not only the identity of the injured man in my care but also unable to confirm the identity of the man they said they were looking for. The two officers didn't even know the man's name! Nor did they know for certain what nationality he was.' Mahé looked very confused. 'Strange, I thought. What would you have thought, Mr Mahé?' asked Farouk, '*Before you preach to me.*'

Mahé shook his head.

'What did you do next?'

'It had been a very calm night until then, so I followed the Clio.'

'Where did you follow it to? Where did it go? Wh... where did they go?'

'To the tobacconist-café opposite the train station from where that tourist train leaves.'

'Le Train à Vapeur. Right. Okay,' continued Mahé.

'I watched him board the train and I went to pick him up from the next station, Trieux,' confessed Farouk to the chief warrant officer.

'Had you arranged that with him? I don't understand. How did you know he would get off at Trieux?' asked Mahé.

'There was an accident at the café involving the police car; the Clio. A white delivery van. A bakery van. Declan escaped. I watched him go,' said Farouk.

'Good Lord, so that's what all that was about.' Now Mahé was intent on listening to absolutely every single word the doctor said. Mahé had seen the accident report and knew the three officers involved. Their stories seemed to tie-in a bit too well for Mahé's liking. A dictation more than the recounting of factual events.

'Had you arranged to meet this Declan man, what's he called? Oh, okay: Olivier Declan O'Leary. That's the man's full name. I've got it.'

'By the way,' continued Farouk, 'I forgot to tell you that as I followed the police car, I, they... well, we arrived at a roundabout right next to the Gendarmerie. Your officers did not exit the roundabout for the Gendarmerie but turned off towards town. I wondered where exactly they were going with their captive. That's when I followed them to the train station.'

'That in itself is not so significant,' said Mahé, dismissively. 'International warrants are always Rennes, Nantes; it depends a bit on jurisdiction as well.'

'At Trieux, I found him. By chance more than anything really. He was trying to hitch-hike back to see his friend at the garage in Langonnet. So... well... I gave him a lift.'

'Can you tell me exactly where he is now, or where you dropped him off?' asked Mahé.

'He's a good man this, Declan Olivier fellow. I don't know as I am prepared to betray him,' declared Farouk earnestly. 'What I mean to say, Mr Mahé is, I think you might have the wrong man.'

'Don't get me wrong, Dr Khadir,' Mahé protested. 'Mr. O'Leary is not a suspect. On the contrary, I believe him to be in great danger. I need to find him before someone else does.'

23
The Killer's Voice

Declan would never forget that voice. Turning on his heel, placing his feet gently and silently, but at the same time as quickly as he possibly could on the black and white chequered floor tiling, he headed straight for the exit of the notary's. There were footsteps behind him and without looking back, he let the door swing shut, opened the second glass door onto the street, jumped down the granite steps to the pavement and seeing there was no traffic, ran diagonally across the road towards a cobbled side-street.

Candice walked into the reception area saying,

'Maître Le Goff will be with you in a few ...' she stopped. Declan had gone. For a moment Candice thought that he must be using the toilet, but her mind registered having heard the door shut and she began walking towards the exit herself when her colleague, Monsieur Dupont, called after her.

'Candice, I was looking through your schedule for today and I see that you've squeezed in a slot for the Le Dour property in Langonnet with a man,' he paused, seemingly for effect,

'O'Leary.'

Eric Dupont considered himself suave, even flash. In his late forties, Dupont still looked good. He played tennis and tanned well. The occasional rinse kept his hair naturally dark and he wore money. Watch, cufflinks, shades, tie-clip, two rings – his jewellery alone was worth over eighty thousand euros. His Gucci suit, one of many, fitted as if personally tailored for him and his leather soled shoes were handcrafted in Italy. In his career, Monsieur Dupont, Eric, was not in charge. As a man, he felt very much at the top. His hierarchical superior was a notary: a fool. It was true, there was money to be made in real estate, but not by filling in paperwork, rubberstamping this or that and wasting time with other matters such as divorce settlements, inheritance law or percentage based small-fry property sales. Where his employer, the notary, Maître Charles Le Goff, would pick up a check of around seven to eight thousand a month, Dupont would sometimes pay that out in wages in a single weekend. The real money was not in low sales with silly mark-ups, but in enormously high sales with a ludicrously high mark-up. Dupont did not sell dream houses to dreamers, he sold dreamers their dreams – lots of them – in small affordable packets.

Once, just a few years earlier, Dupont had had a traitor in his midst. A salesman and user. Owing Dupont forty two and a half thousand euros in total accumulated street value of lost sales through personal use and foolishness, this man had fled to Ireland and landed up in a clinic after being picked up by the Garda, the Irish police, for theft. Dupont had his overheads too, somebody had to pay. Somebody always had to pay. Dupont sent a man out there to find him. He had found him alright. He had paid. In Dupont's line of work, not his cover at the notary's but his real line of work, two things counted and two things made a man – your reputation to pay and your reputation if you didn't get paid. Be both reliable and ruthless. Dupont employed men to undertake work he couldn't do himself. He knew that. But that didn't make him any less a man. Dupont understood the mechanics of life. He had seen men torture other men and enjoy it. Dupont had felt sick. If a man had to die, reasoned Dupont, it had to be quick. The young policeman had died quickly. A self-righteous little prick with a big mouth.

'How the fuck did he ever think he was gonna earn a decent wage doin' that kinda shit?' he had asked the fat guy Fornier.

Fornier had defended the youngster, saying,

'He's just a bloody kid, what d'you expect. Give 'im a chance. I'll teach 'im the trade.'

Dupont could never have taken the risk of letting the boy blab. He had even thought of dispatching Fornier when he had ended up doing the job himself. That useless piece of shit. Fornier owed Dupont. He owed him big time. That was back in 2005 or 2006. A long time ago.

The first time Dupont had understood the value of real estate was back in the nineties. An agent, a representative, a middleman from the Ukraine, was looking to make an investment for a Russian client and had promised to make it worthwhile for Dupont. Eric the Envoy, they had called him. Their messenger. Their operative in France. Dupont was Belgian and in his early twenties at the time, had boasted an ability to be able to operate freely anywhere in Europe, especially France. Something he believed had impressed them.

His first assignment had been to assure the sale of an abandoned chateau in Brittany to a Russian businessman. An easy enough job. Nobody else wanted to invest that kind of money in an old listed ruin and Le Goff's predecessor, Maître Lucas, had been impressed by his young clerk. The sale of several other similar properties had followed in quick succession and by the time the world was celebrating the arrival of the new millennium, Dupont had, outside of France of course and thanks to backhanders, banked his first million. On rare occasions, he had been invited to these magnificently renovated architectural treasures whose sale he had assured – sometimes through cunning and sometimes through trickery. It was these "clients" from the east that had asked Dupont if he could "shift" their products. And Dupont had begun to build up his network of thugs. There were ex-con thugs; thugs in uniform as he called the police and street corner child-lookouts: thugs in the making. These kids could earn more in a fortnight than their daddies, had they been in work at all, could have earned in a month. Why go to school? He even threw in their mobile phones for free.

Candice couldn't stand Dupont. He had asked her out on dates again and again and indeed still did, though not so regularly anymore. Once he had made a joke implying that she only said no because she was afraid he'd "slip" a Rohypnol in her drink when she wasn't looking. Candice had had no idea what that was, but when he explained and made a play on words saying "Rapeynol", the thought had made her retch. He was smug, conceited and vulgar and Candice hated him.

'Have you seen him?' she replied, quickly deducing that he probably had not seen Declan or he would not have asked her the question. 'Is he here already?'

Candice objected to her colleague's interest in anything she did professionally, but her involvement with Declan was now personal. She was being innocently obtuse with Dupont: giving nothing away but without seeming to be too objectionable.

'No, no I haven't,' he replied, looking at Candice a little awkwardly. 'Listen up will you, I think I may have a client from the east interested in that property – increasing its value quite considerably compared to your value-estimate of course. I would be inclined to consider it a

heritage property, so if you haven't signed anything with this O'Leary man as yet, I think I'll talk to the boss about taking over the sale.'

'Quel bâtard!' thought Candice, but said nothing.

Dupont checked his watch slowly. Nine-twenty.

'My man's late,' and as he continued talking, he stared at the face of his Piaget watch, admiring the smooth movement of the second hand as he gave the crown a few gentle turns for good measure. 'If you're "manning" the desk, so to speak, today,' he said, 'I trust you'll let me know when he gets here.' Dupont wiped the face of his timepiece with a soft cloth he used for the lenses of his Versace shades. He would never wear a Rolex: fakes were all too common and the majority of people simply would not be able to see the difference. Piaget sounded classier. 'If you're making coffee, I'd love one,' he concluded.

Candice reached over the reception desk for a manila envelope she had seen lying there earlier, picked it up and replied:

'Sure. I'll let you know when he arrives. You'll have to make your own coffee though: I'm just going up the road. I'll be five minutes.' Candice walked out of the building and onto the street in search of Declan.

She stopped on the pavement outside the notary's, looking around frantically for him. There was no sign. Why had he left like that? There must be a reason.

'Candice,' she heard him call from across the road, but couldn't see him. A car passed and she heard his voice again:

'Candice, chuis là.' *I'm here.*

She had been looking for his face, but he had called her with his back to her. He was facing a shop window on the corner of a narrow cobbled street opposite her office. She crossed the road to join him.

'Why did you go? Why did you walk out like that?'

'It's him,' Declan said. 'It's his voice.'

'Whose?' asked Candice. 'Whose voice?'

'The man in the corridor,' said Declan. 'I have to go; I can't stay here.' And Declan began to walk away briskly.

'Wait,' she called after him, but Declan did not stop. Candice began to run after him and as she turned the corner bearing right at the end of the cobbled street, Declan jumped out and grabbed her. She let out a scream.

'Sorry,' said Declan and a woman passing by said,

'They always say that kid, but they never mean it.'

'Boss Balaclava. It was his voice. I know it was him. I swear.'

Quickly, Candice began to put the pieces together. There were only two men in the building: the notary, Le Goff; and her colleague, the clerk, the arsehole, Dupont. Declan could not have heard the voice of the notary, for the door was closed when he had spoken to her.

'Tell him I'll be through in just an instant,' the notary had said to her.

'Boss Balaclava, Eric Dupont. Oh dear,' said Candice. 'We have a problem.'

'Yeah, we've got to go, got to keep moving.'

'Boss Balaclava…' Candice couldn't believe what she'd just said, 'His name is Eric Dupont. He was just on his way into the notary's office when I left the building. He went to tell Maître Le Goff that he would be taking over your house sale.'

'He can forget that,' objected Declan. 'I'm not signing anything for him. He wants me dead.'

'Calm down,' pleaded Candice. 'The problem is more immediate than that. I told Boss… Dupont that I hadn't seen you, yet I've just told the notary that you're in reception waiting for him. Dupont could be out here any second.'

'Like I said - we've gotta keep moving.'

'We have to go to the police,' said Candice.

'I can't,' replied Declan. 'They're in on all of this. We've got to go back to Albert's. He'll know what to do.'

Candice turned the corner of the cobbled street to face the main high street when she saw Dupont looking frantically up and down the road.

'We have to walk around behind the supermarket to double back and pick up my car,' said Candice.

'No,' said Declan pointing just a bit further along the road. 'We take the bus, it's there now and it'll probably be leaving in just a few minutes. He'll be looking for your car, but he won't check the bus.'

'Two singles to Gourin please, sir,' said Declan as they climbed aboard the coach.

'Je pars dans une demi-heure,' replied the driver.

'You leave in half an hour?' and as Declan began to think of an appropriate insult in French, the corner of his eye registered the roof light of a taxi approaching from the bottom of the hill by the roundabout. Declan leapt off the bus, hurtling in front of it and got there easily in time to hail his taxi. As the taxi slowed to a halt, the driver, his window already lowered due to the heat of the summer, said,

'Where to?'

'Just down the road,' said Declan putting three fifty euro notes into the man's hand and signalling to Candice to hurry up.

The taxi driver didn't bother to switch the meter on, but as both his newly acquired passengers settled in the back and belted up, he asked,

'Just down the road where, sir?'

'Left at the roundabout and along the bye-pass towards McDonald's please,' said Declan, intending to direct the driver as and when he needed to know without giving him the final destination straight away.

An annoyed look from the driver in the rear view mirror told Declan that he was not comfortable with the arrangement. Rather than succumb to this pressure, Declan assured the driver that they were about fifteen minutes away and he handed over another fifty euro note between the two front seats. The driver took the note without saying thank you, and waited for further instructions.

24
Doctor's Orders

D r Farouk Khadir stood up at the table in the hospital canteen, reached into the front right pocket of his white lab coat to retrieve his coiled stethoscope and stepped sideways to allow him the space to replace his chair. Stethoscope around his neck, he began fastening his lab coat.

'Mr Mahé, you need to visit a man called Albert in the village of La Trinité-Langonnet. Tell him I sent you and that you are a friend of Olivier's. In France the man you're looking for calls himself Olivier, but in Ireland he's Declan. Needless to say, Albert calls him Olivier.'

'Who is this Declan Olivier man? Why all the attention?'

Pulling a visiting card from his breast pocket, Farouk invited Mahé to call him in the event that he should encounter problems trying to convince Albert.

'Listen,' said Farouk, 'Tell Albert that you know about the tractor and the cord-of-wood "disguise" to get into Carhaix town centre.'

'What on earth is that?' asked Mahé, suspiciously.

'You don't need to know, Mr Mahé. Albert needs to believe that you do.'

'Surely if I knew, it would be more convincing?' argued Mahé. 'It is, after all, only human nature to ask questions, Doctor.'

'Very well,' Farouk conceded. 'Olivier, or, Declan, was kidnapped and tortured.' He paused for a moment, not wanting to incriminate Declan as the perpetrator of the explosion on Bréhat. 'The people that did this to him are still at large and as you have almost certainly gathered, there is police involvement. Involvement of which you have been, until now at least, unaware. Now that does not look good.'

Mahé did not appreciate this comment one bit.

'Now just a moment, Dr Khadir. I don't know what you're insinuating here, but I intend to get to the bottom of this myself.' he snapped.

'When I say, "it doesn't look good", I mean from Mr O'Leary's point of view. What I mean to say is that Olivier has made the assumption that there is, how should I say this, a degree of police corruption in this matter.'

Mahé was angry.

'Now you look here—'

'What you or I think,' said Farouk, interrupting him, 'or for that matter, what the press thinks about any police involvement here, has little bearing on whether or not Olivier is going to trust you. Now you told me you need to find him before somebody else does, Mr Mahé. If you can gain Albert's trust, he will be able to help you find Olivier. I am merely trying to save you time.'

'Where can I find this Albert man then?' asked a disgruntled Mahé.

'He has the garage just outside the village on the D109. Show him my card.' reminded Farouk.

'And Olivier drove into Carhaix on a tractor, right? Disguised?'

'Transporting a cord of firewood.'

'And a cord of wood,' Mahé confirmed. He too stood up, shook the doctor's hand, thanked him and walked out of the hospital canteen.

In different circumstances, Mahé would have called through to a Gendarmerie Brigade more local and arranged for a pick-up, but he knew today he had to handle this one himself.

25
The Car Chase

D upont was no fool. He tried to remember her exact words. Candice had not denied having seen O'Leary. He had not, in fact, asked her if she had seen him. No, Candice had deliberately given the impression that she had not seen O'Leary by asking him, Dupont, if *he* had seen him. The clever bitch! She *had* seen him though. And told the notary. A bitch, but nevertheless, not that clever. Dupont headed for the street and looked around for Candice. There was no sign.

A man of Dupont's stature did not run unless he was on the court returning a volley. Better men played golf. Can't pick up single women easily on a golf course. A brisk walk took him to the turn-off leading to the car park where Candice always left her car. He knew she would go there. Her car was still there. *Shit*. Candice had just walked out of the office. There was no receptionist: nobody to answer the phone. If it rang out now, the notary would become aware that something was amiss. He returned to the office and within a few minutes had transferred the phone at reception to the one in his office and from there he transferred calls to his Blackberry. Anyone calling would know their call had been transferred, but they would not know that Dupont would be deliberately ignoring them depending on caller id. He popped into the boss's office to inform Le Goff, that he would be taking a look at the property in Langonnet himself and walked out once again. Candice's problem if she'd left work without informing the boss of her whereabouts.

Dupont fired up the flat six-cylinder engine of his black Porche Cayman 718 and knocked her gently into reverse. Candice's car was still parked up. Headlights on full for a brief moment, Dupont, now in first, ignored the one-way sign which only applied to a short, thirty-metre stretch of road. This "shortcut" would save him having to negotiate the narrow streets and "priorité à droite" of the main highstreet. He arrived at the by-pass and chose to cut across country – less speed controls there than on the main road and he would thus be able to save himself a good eight minutes. The engine now racing, the clock read 120km/h as he could see the bridge over the canal by the lock gates at the bottom of the valley. Suddenly a horrible thought struck Dupont: what if Candice had no idea what was going on? What if the boss had misunderstood what she had said and the Irishman really was late? What if Candice had delivered her envelope, returned to the office and the Irishman walked in for his appointment? Her car had still been there after all. The Irishman had reeked of drink the day they took him at the mill. He probably was late. Dupont glanced down quickly at the speedometer to see 130km/h and found himself unable to decide whether or not he should return to the office.

Dupont heard his cell-phone, glanced at the screen, recognised the number as being one of his girlfriends' and ignored the call. She could wait. He was thinking of dumping her anyhow. Too demanding. Twenty-six. Wanted kids and all that. Instead of returning the phone to his pocket, he tossed it gently onto the passenger seat next to him. He slowed a little as he neared the narrow stone-built bridge: the road ahead leading up the opposite side of the valley was straight and he could see that nothing was coming. The clock read 115km/h. He quickly reasoned that even if his first suspicions were correct and Candice had somehow headed to Langonnet with the Irishman, what was he going to do there on his own anyway? The best thing would be to turn around, head back to the office and make some calls. Start making other arrangements. About eight hundred metres after the canal, there was a mini-roundabout and he would turn around there and head back.

Dupont had been up since six that morning. He had had a cereal bar for breakfast and washed it down with an espresso with a half sugar lump, well stirred. By nine forty-five, at the time when Dupont's prefrontal lobe received the message from his hippocampus concerning the short-term memory record of exactly what Candice had said about the Irishman, glucose levels were already dropping. The liver had stepped in to produce ketone bodies from stored fatty acids to appease the frontal lobe and, for now at least, everything seemed just fine. In the time it had taken him to reason that his first suspicions could be correct and that even if they were not, it still made sense to be back in his office to start making other arrangements, Dupont had travelled just six and a half metres. By the time he had deduced that Candice may have been telling the truth, that the Irishman-drinker might, by now, be there with her and established that he was driving at 130km/h, he had travelled a further eighty-six metres. Dupont's cerebral metabolic rate of glucose consumption (CMRglu) was still at its midmorning high. His phone rang, reach for phone, she can wait, 92 metres further down the road towards the canal. Narrow bridge ahead. Nothing coming – slow up a little – 74 metres.

As Dupont reached his conclusion to turn around and head back to the office he put his foot down once again to cover the eight hundred metres to the mini-roundabout as quickly as he could.

Moving along the canal perpendicular to the road was an ornate and brightly painted turn-of-the-century canal barge. A young Dutch family, who had been cycling along the towpath, had stopped by the lock for a picnic-breakfast, while the water levels rose for the fluvial step-up. The first of the three children, having decided that the bridge would make a good vantage point, dumped his bike on the edge of the road and ran to sit on the wall, his feet dangling.

'Kom snel en kijk!' the boy said. *Come quickly and look!*

His parents, looking up, saw him on the wall of the bridge and the boy's mother shouted,

'Let op, Luuk. Kom hier! Nu!' *Careful, Luke. Come here! Now!*

His father had heard the approaching engine and screamed out to his son,

'Nee. Blijf daar, Luuk!' *No. Stay there, Luke!*

Dupont had not seen the bike on the edge of the road. By the time his brain registered the obstacle, he had almost reached the bridge and as he began to move his foot off the accelerator to hit the brakes, he was already upon it.

Taxi to Albert's

The taxi had been travelling a few minutes, when Declan gave the next instruction:

'Next exit to Paule, please.' The driver began to indicate and slowed down to turn southwards.

'What do you think Albert will say?' asked Candice. 'I mean what do you think he will suggest we do?'

'Thing I love about Albert is you never know. But it's usually right. I mean he often has really good ideas. Well, they're more plans than ideas. I don't know, I mean he's sound that's all.'

At the crossroads, Declan told the driver to carry straight on, and six minutes later they were just passing the church at La Trinité-Langonnet.

'You can drop us here,' said Declan. 'Anywhere here.'

'Here, by the church?' asked the driver.

'Here's fine,' he confirmed.

The driver halted his cab just twenty metres from the bar and preoccupied himself with the meter that had not been activated. Both Declan and Candice got out of the cab and began to walk the short distance to Albert's garage.

Mahé vs. Albert

Mahé arrived at the village of La Trinité-Langonnet on the D109 and followed Dr Khadir's instructions: past the church to a garage on your left. The village centre was lifeless but for a couple walking hand in hand in the same direction of travel as he. He slowed a little as he approached them, because just there, on a bend, the road narrowed and he could see a taxi approaching in the opposite direction. The taxi passed and Mahé pulled out to overtake the couple. Once around the corner, as he was about to speed up, he spotted the garage – if you could call it that. He indicated left, looked in his rear-view mirror to see the road behind was clear and turned up a ramp to a garage forecourt that looked more like a mid-eighties film set. In the open doorway of a hangar stood a man in grimy overalls.

Mahé parked up where he could find space, stepped out of the unmarked Audi and began to walk towards the hangar doors. The man had gone.

Albert shuffled quickly to each of the two corrugated iron doors and began, as best he could with a steel toe capped boot, to clear any debris from the groove in which the lower door runners were designed to slide. He began to heave both doors closed. As the second door reached the first to form a relatively narrow opening, he stepped through the gap giving one last helping tug so the second door clanged against the first.

'How can I help you?' said Albert.

What precision, thought Mahé, and what perfect timing.

'I'm looking for a man called Albert.'

Albert did not answer, forcing the visitor to elaborate while revealing nothing of his own identity.

'Does the name mean anything to you?'

Albert shrugged:

'What name?'

'Is your name Albert?'

'Who wants to know?'

'I do.'

'And you might be...?'

Mahé was used to this sort of waste of time standoff, but was reluctant to produce any id. He had been warned by the doctor that he would have to gain this man's confidence if he wanted his cooperation. Instead, he produced the doctor's card and handed it over to Albert.

'What brings you here? I didn't call for a doctor,' said Albert, knowing full well that this was not Dr Khadir.

Declan and Candice turned the corner, but Albert had not seen them. He had seen a taxi make a U-turn on his forecourt just moments earlier and that is what had drawn him out of his hangar, but he had not seen Declan walking with the young woman as they approached his garage.

'Dr. Khadir is a friend of mine and he told me to come and speak to you.'

'To me? How's that, to me?' asked Albert.

'You are Albert are you not?'

'Like I said, who wants to know?'

Should he show his id or not, wondered Mahé, but doubted it would produce the desired effect. This man had almost certainly heard the allegations of corrupt police involvement.

'I bet there aren't two Alberts running garages in this village,' said Mahé smugly. No answer. This nut was a tough one to crack.

'The doctor told me if I told Albert about Olivier having travelled incognito to Carhaix on a tractor, then he'd believe I was on his side,' said Mahé.

Albert shrugged.

'Oh come on man. Albert, you are obstructing the course of justice by withholding information from...'

Albert stopped him.

'You had better identify yourself properly,' he said. He had suspected the visitor was a gendarme from the moment he set eyes on him. 'You could be anybody for all I know.' And then he saw Declan. Somehow he had to signal to him, not to walk up to the garage. He had to do it without being seen by this policeman.

Albert began shouting.

'Listen here, alright. You *police* turning up here, think you own the place. Well, you *police* don't even have a search warrant. Show me some *police* id then if you can Mr *Policeman.*'

Declan looked towards the garage forecourt to see Albert waving his arms in the air and shouting at a man. Then he heard Albert shout out the word, police. Declan stopped.

As he produced his id, Mahé added calmly,

'And he transported a cord of firewood with the tractor.'

Albert stood staring at the man, silent for a moment. *Why would he suddenly add that?*

It was this abrupt silence that made Mahé wonder if this man in overalls, who was certainly the Albert he was looking for, had not been shouting in an attempt to be heard. To warn someone nearby perhaps. This O'Leary chap?

'Albert,' said Mahé, 'is Mr Olivier O'Leary in your hangar? Is that why you closed the doors? Open them up for me please.'

Albert obliged, pushing the right door open enough for a man to pass through.

'So you *are* called Albert then?' said Mahé, just about to step through into the hangar when he stopped, urging Albert to go in first.

At that moment, Mahé saw Albert's arm come quickly down to his side, but his reactions were not fast enough and the man's eyes were still focusing on something over the policeman's shoulder.

Mahé turned around and saw the young couple no longer holding hands. He turned in a flash, and looking Albert straight in the eye, he said,

'If that is Olivier over there,' his arm outstretched pointing across the road, 'I need to talk to him before somebody else finds him. You and I both know that his life is in danger. What do you think we should do, Albert?'

Albert, eyes staring at the ground and chin on chest, nodded a naughty schoolboy confession. If the doctor had given him his card, and told him about the trip to Carhaix with the wood, then he must have trusted this man: it was such a ridiculous sounding story. Declan had said the doctor was a friend.

'What do you want him for?'

'To talk. Ask him some questions. I believe he may be able to help me with my inquiries.'

Mahé realised that sounded like a synonym for an arrest and added, 'He may have vital information about a man I have been looking for since 2006. A murderer,' and for good measure, Mahé added, 'Olivier is not under arrest, Albert, you can trust me.'

Albert waved an arm, beckoning Declan towards the forecourt. Mahé watched the couple take each other's hands once again and begin crossing the road to the garage. Albert did not trust this man entirely, but saw no way of escaping his persistence.

As Declan and Candice approached the two men on the forecourt, Mahé spoke first.

'Mr O'Leary,' he began. 'My name is Mahé and I am here to help you.'

Declan looked at Albert for confirmation. Albert gave none, but shrugged.

'How do you intend to do that?' asked Declan.

'He wants to ask you some questions,' said Albert.

'Are you a policeman?' asked Candice innocently.

Mahé decided, without giving away any details of the case, that he would have to divulge something significant if he were to convince these people.

'I believe, Mr O'Leary, one of the men you saw on the Island of Bréhat a few days ago, one of the men that tortured you,' he saw their faces change, 'to be a murderer. A ruthless killer. A man I have been trying to find for many years. I need your help.'

'Boss Balaclava?' blurted Declan looking at Candice.

'Eric Dupont,' said Candice.

The officer's expression was one of total disbelief. The search was over. He had not expected it to be this straightforward.

'I work with him at the notary's office in Carhaix,' she said.

28

Man and Boy

I t is said that accidents happen in slow motion. The truth is, everything is relative. Memory retrieval of events leading up to the moment of collision, combines with a heightened self-awareness through anticipation and fear. An adrenalin-induced alertness through sheer terror of the inevitable – there was nothing slow about this accident. At 140km/h there would be no memories of events for Dupont. None before and none after. The Porsche hit the boy's bike with such impetus and at such high speed, that coupled with the downwards momentum towards the valley floor, there was no perceptible slowing of the 1.6 tonnes combined load. The car, man and bike travelled in a straight line across the bridge, causing a noise so loud, that the boy's shock reaction as he turned, thrust him off the wall and into the water. Dupont's reaction time was relatively quick and in the 0.38th's of a second it took him to cross the bridge, he had already clasped the wheel more firmly and begun to place his right foot over the brake pedal. As he applied the vented twin disk, power-assisted ABS-fitted brakes, his front offside tyre held the road superbly well. The nearside one, however, had been jammed hard against the boy's bike which in turn had buckled up under the wheel arch as it slid the length of the narrow curb. As a result, the tyre of the nearside wheel was barely touching the road. Although the vehicle's left side slowed considerably, the right side slowed only negligibly and the Porsche began to turn sideways. As the car neared a full broadside some 60 metres or 1.4 seconds beyond the bridge, it jolted, flipping up into a series of midair spins. Landing roof first, it bounced and began to veer off its straight-line trajectory. Its next bounce, on the front bumper, took it down a short, but steep wooded bank. Three fair-sized birches, trunks as thick as a man's thigh, had been ripped through at about a metre off the ground before Dupont's car stopped; its front end embedded deep into the waterlogged escarpment. Less than ten seconds later, a Dutch mum and dad began to scramble down the bank to where a trembling and frightened young Dutch boy, Luuk, was swimming through dirty pond weed to safety.

29

Taking Statements

M ahé folded his notepad before slipping it into a jacket pocket. 'I will, of course, need you to accompany me to the station at some point,' he explained. 'For a statement,' and looking at Candice, he added, 'And you say you have worked with this man, Dupont for some time?'

'Four years,' said Candice, nodding her head.

'It may be that a statement from you would also be helpful,' said Mahé. 'The sooner the better to be honest with you. We can then get started with the arrest of this man and get this mess cleared up. Forensics might want to check out his office for comparative fingerprints or find out what else he's been up to, but the best thing you can do now is go back to work and pretend that nothing has happened. Try to act normally.'

'I'm not going back there with him on the loose,' said Candice.

'In that case,' said Mahé, 'I'll have to get a warrant as soon as possible: I don't want him covering up his tracks or running.'

'Can't we give our statements now?' asked Declan, hoping to get this man, Boss Balaclava, whatever he was called – Dupont, locked up as quickly as possible.

'Can you get to the Gendarmerie in Carhaix after lunch, say, about two o'clock?' asked Mahé. 'That'll give me time to arrange a room there for us. I can't take the statement from you myself, it must be taken by an officer of the Gendarmerie Départmentale.'

'We've got no transport,' said Candice. 'I left my car in Carhaix: Dupont was following us. I think. Anyway, we decided not to take my car. We took a taxi instead.'

'My car's here isn't it, Albert?' asked Declan. Albert looked over his shoulder to see who Declan could have been addressing.

'Who's Albert?' he said winking at the policeman. 'Your car was sabotaged and you can have it back when I'm finished with it,' said Albert, this time looking at Declan. 'If you have to go to Carhaix from here under your own steam, it's by tractor. That clear?' Another wink. 'Need any firewood delivering to the brigade, Officer Mahé?' Mahé shook his head at Albert.

'You've got your car in Carhaix?' asked Mahé, seeing Candice nodding her head. Very well,' he continued, 'you can come up to the station with me now and we'll try to get this thing sorted this morning. Why wait?'

This was music to Declan's ears.

Mahé walked over to the unmarked Audi and leaned in to pick up the radio to make contact with the "Réseau Radio Gendarmerie". *Police Radio Network.*

'TEN-ZERO, TEN-ZERO, Adjudant-Chef Mahé Gendarmerie mobile, in need of assistance.' *Crackle.*

'TEN-TWO: Control Centre. Go ahead.'

'Request contact with Brigade in Carhaix.' *Crackle.* Mahé waited a moment.

'TEN-FOUR. Carhaix here. Okay, received. Go ahead.'

'TEN-TWO Adjudant-Chef Mahé – Gendarmerie mobile, St Brieuc. Two witness statements to take. Requesting a room and an officer to take statements.'

'Gendarmerie Départmentale, Adjudant-Chef Poulichet speaking.' A woman's voice. A woman the same rank as Mahé. Her insignia would be white, indicating county based where his was yellow – mobile. 'Have the witnesses been cautioned?'

'Not necessary,' said Mahé. 'They have important contributions to make towards an ongoing inquiry.'

'TEN-TWENTY-THREE. We're waiting.'

10-23, meant simply, "turn up".

'We're good to go,' said Mahé, turning to Declan and Candice.

Declan was just having serious second thoughts about this whole arrangement when his iPhone signalled that he had received a text message. A message from Farouk:

'You should trust policeman named Mahé – your enemy is also his enemy – have sent him to find you, Farouk,' message from one hour ago.

'Bloody signal,' thought Declan.

Declan and Candice chose to sit in the rear of the car so that they could be together. Mahé drove north from the garage forecourt in the direction of Carhaix on the D109. As he drove, he left the police radio on. Just six minutes into the journey Mahé and his two passengers heard a police report of a road accident involving a single vehicle. A high-speed car accident on the "route de Pont Daoulaz" the message said. Officers just arriving on the scene had found no vehicle as yet. A 112 call reported a black sports car travelling at high speed losing control on the bridge over the Nantes-Brest canal south of Carhaix.

30
Back At The Mill

Declan parked his Audi TT down a narrow lane about a quarter of a mile from the mill, making sure he was far enough over on the verge to let any farm vehicles pass. He had not been followed, of that he was certain. He stepped out of the car and onto the hard gravelly ground of the track and turned to head for the rear of the car. Opening up the boot, he grabbed both handles of his holdall in his right hand, pulled it up onto his shoulder and swung the boot shut. Pressing the close button on the key, Declan waited for the telltale clunk and then watched the rear hazard lights run through their triple – we're-just-locking-up – flash sequence.

Satisfied, and just about to turn heel, he heard the noise of a twig snapping. He froze. Nothing. Then he saw a small dog, spaniel-like, nose its way out of the lower undergrowth of the hedge opposite not twenty metres away. The dog stopped, right front paw raised and stared at Declan for several seconds. It had evidently decided that he was okay and allowed to be there for it just carried on along the track. Not ten seconds later he saw the animal drop to the floor. Declan walked towards the spaniel slowly, thinking perhaps it was hurt, but as he approached he heard a half-squawk immediately followed by a manic flapping of wings. As he looked up following the sound, he recognised the magnificent bright colours of the cock pheasant's plumage taking off over the hedge-row and he continued to watch it as it disappeared across a meadow and towards a small distant coppice. The spaniel had gone. For a brief moment, Declan reflected on how much he loved this countryside.

Setting off once more in the direction away from the road, he walked carefully. He was pleased with his progress – thanks to Monique and regular changes of the dressing, the burn on his leg was beginning to heal quite well. He followed the track to its dead-end, where he knew he would be able to find the bank running adjacent to the feeder stream of the mill pond. The ground was boggy and Declan saw that the stream was silted up and overgrown; barely recognisable as the crystal clear brook he remembered from childhood. His shoes sank deep into the sodden turf and his undercover approach to the old mill became more of a "here I am" marker-buoy-style stroll across the grass as he left the cover of the waterlogged undergrowth for the dryer middle-ground of the field. He reached the swing gate, which to his surprise still swung, and stepped tentatively onto the narrow planks of the footbridge where the now rotten water wheel was still mounted. Manoeuvring surreptitiously along the top of the old millrace wall, which thankfully now had a concrete skim-covering over its upper stones, he approached the back door to the mill.

31
A Man, his Dog and a Riddle

Lilian Bouvier was a local historian, hunter and heretic. He had the reputation of a man who knew his stuff. He knew that foreign registered Audis didn't usually park down quiet farm tracks on Sunday mornings in mid-September in the heart of rural Brittany. And that hikers don't usually carry bloody great big holdalls over their shoulders. This guy was up to no good. As he crouched down low, unseen beside the hedge to watch the man, he cursed himself under his breath; he hadn't spotted the dry twig and it snapped with a deafening crack that would have alerted even the most ignorant passer-by. It did. Lily didn't move, but he could see from the man's reaction he had heard the crack loud and clear. He had been right about this man: he was obviously on his guard. A moment later, Filou saved the day. Filou was a little Breton spaniel with no pedigree at all – a damn good gundog as it turned out. Lily had seen Filou while out hunting four years earlier – the little spaniel had apparently got lost and followed him all afternoon and then jumped into his car. There was no collar, no tattoo, no microchip and no one to answer the posters he had put up in the local bars and bakeries. Lily and Filou had been together ever since.

Lily had heard the cock pheasant and then seen it take off over the hedgerow. He wished this foreigner had parked somewhere else that morning, for he had missed seeing Filou's reaction to a fine-looking game bird on his pre-open season sortie. Still, the hunting season had not officially started and Lily, while taking his dog out for a trial run, had been very careful not to have a single cartridge case anywhere in his possession in case he was controlled by the guard.

If he wasn't mistaken, this man was making his way over to the old Le Dour watermill from the rear. That meant that this guy had been tipped off because not everyone knew that way through to the mill. What was it he wanted? The old lady had been dead about a year and evidently, there was no next of kin interested in the place. A notary from Carhaix had put a "For Sale" sign up but there had been no interest. That hadn't really surprised him since the building was a little dilapidated. Sadly, the old lady had had no sons to help out with basic maintenance and the only daughter had married abroad. He struggled to remember her name, for the daughter, although a bit younger than him, had attended the same school – that'd put her in her late fifties, early sixties now.

The name Le Dour was well known in the area and particularly in La Trinité-Langonnet by those that knew about its church. Lilian Bouvier had researched the church's history for many, many years, but had been unable to conclude. His professor at Rennes had insisted he base his thesis on something more substantial, something concrete, and he had finally chosen what he considered to be the dull, already exhausted and regurgitated history of the Dukes of Brittany. He'd got his masters degree forty years ago back in 1975, and immediately continued with his personal and preferred research subject: Paganism and The Reformation. This had always been his working title, and his professor, Professor Rok, had just laughed. The fool couldn't even speak Breton, let alone read it. In Breton, "rok" meant arrogant or arrogantly and Lily thought this fitted the old professor pretty well. Professor "Arrogant" had been patronising in his attitude to Lily's choice of subject-matter, mocking about his native language and finally, he had been damned rude about his late family.

More than forty years later, however, Lily was a much calmer man than his hot-headed student counterpart had been, and some years earlier he had begun to understand that historical research had to have hard evidence on which to base its hypotheses. His research had been inconclusive because the paper trail had dried up. How ironic was that? A paper trail, just like a water source, can only "dry up" so to speak, because there was paper there to begin with.

Lifting the gate just slightly to make certain that it would not squeak, he swung it open slowly. Dipping his head down low under the overgrown and overhanging hedge, he peered across the yard along the mill race to see if he could spot the intruder without being seen himself. From this vantage point, he heard the sound of a door slamming shut and as he watched, he could just about focus on the speckled image of the man's upper torso as it crossed in front of the old single-glazed window. The window reflected moving leaves in its upper panes and rippling water in its lower ones. He had to make a decision: creep up ambush-style and have the advantage of surprise, or walk up boldly, matter-of-factly and stand his ground. He finally opted for the physically less strenuous of the two and closing the breach of his shotgun, crossed the footbridge and walked along the cemented millrace wall, past the old waterwheel and straight up to the back door of the old mill. Filou, right behind his master, was, of course, alert and ready.

Leaning under the small wedge-shaped slate roof of the porch which covered the back door, Lily carefully crouched down before scanning the inside of the room through a lower pane. The holdall had been dumped on the floor in the middle of the room and whoever this man was, he was here on a very purposeful mission. The zipper had been left open and tools had been removed. He could see a handsaw on the table and the foreigner, his back to the door, was holding a crowbar in one hand and a hammer in the other. Quickly the man turned around as if confirming that he was still alone. Lily did not flinch; a good hunter knows that the eye will not see a stationary object as easily as a moving one and this man noticed nothing untoward.

There was a thud as something was smashed against what sounded like a dry-line wall. He scanned the room again using only one eye, thus enabling him to keep his head sideways and as low down as possible. Two more thuds and a crack. The intruder, obviously focussed on his work, turned around and laid down both hammer and crowbar on the table and picked up a saw. This next operation was to Lily's advantage, for as the foreigner began to saw through sections of what appeared to be a plasterboard wall, his sawing action told him when he could look without being seen; the moment the sawing stopped, there was a chance the intruder could be looking back over his shoulder towards the door. After about five minutes, he had cut a hole large enough for a person to get through. Lily watched fascinated as the man disappeared behind the wall through the hole he had just cut. Whoever this man was, he was looking for something, he knew exactly where to find it and he had come equipped. What could he be looking for?

At that moment the man appeared in his plasterboard passageway and immediately set eyes on Lily who was standing just behind the door. Lily's reactions were lightning fast. The man was carrying a very old-looking wooden chest, both hands grasping a metal handle fastened to either end. The intruder moved quickly towards the table intent on laying down the chest and, so it appeared to Lily, his focus was on the crowbar. Only a fraction of a second after their eyes made contact, Lily had pushed down on the door handle with his left hand, nudged it open with his left knee, stepped into the room in a fluid movement and brought up his shotgun to aim it straight at the man's head, just a table length away. His, voice raised almost to a shout, he gave the order not to move. Declan stopped in his tracks. There was a dog barking somewhere outside and Declan looked at this man, this intruder, in all his hunting regalia, with extreme contempt.

'What in hell's name do you think you're doing here?' Declan questioned in a most patronizing and angry voice.

'I was going to ask you exactly the same thing, young man. Who the devil do you think you are coming in here, breaking down someone else's wall and stealing their valuables?' said Lily, standing his ground firmly and still aiming both barrels in the direction of Declan's face.

Lowering the shotgun to his waist, but still aiming it at Declan's midriff, he motioned him to lay the wooden chest on the table.

'All this used to be my grandmother's. She's dead, and now it's mine. It's my wooden chest, my treasure inside it, my table and my wall. All of which is in my bloody house. Now you get out before I get any angrier with you,' screamed Declan at the old man.

All of a sudden, Lily's face began to frown and then his mouth nearly fell open in disbelief.

'Can this be? Olivier?'

He quickly lowered his shotgun and then swung round to prop it up against the scullery wall and the sink unit.

'I'm so terribly sorry,' said Lilly, recoiling. 'I had no idea. Are you truly Olivier Le Dour?'

'Olivier O'Leary,' replied Declan.

'Of course,' said Lily. 'I have no right even to be here, I'm so sorry, I'm intruding. I thought *you* were the intruder. I thought someone was trying to steal from you and your family. I'm so sorry,' he said.

'There is no family anymore,' snapped Declan. 'Me and my sister, that's it. And now you know, you can leave.'

'How long have you known about that chest and its whereabouts, if you don't mind me asking? I know you might think it none of my business, but I have been searching for it for over forty years and others for over a century and a half.'

'You're right it's none of your business and I've already asked you to leave. Please leave.'

'You are mistaken, young man. I said you might think it none of my business, but I believe it is perhaps as much my business as it is yours and your sister's.'

'How can it be your business when it doesn't belong to you?' asked Declan.

'Well that's a very good question,' replied Lily, 'but can you imagine, if inside that chest was a painting like, say, the Mona Lisa. Sure enough, it could belong to you, but you would appreciate no doubt that others may have a legitimate interest in it and that you would be unwise to do anything other than take great care of her,' Lily bluffed.

'How do you know it's a painting and not gold or diamonds for example?' asked Declan.

'I didn't say it *is* a painting. That was just an example. But surely you can feel by the weight that it's not filled with gold, Olivier? You'd have been desperate to put it down due to the sheer weight of it, were it filled with stones or precious metal. Am I right, Olivier?' asked Lily, a little too smugly.

'Tell me what's in it then,' said Declan.

'I'm surprised your mother, or rather your grandmother didn't tell you, Olivier,' said Lily, again trying to raise the younger man's curiosity in order that he may decide to open the chest up in his presence. If this was what Lily thought and hoped it was, then his thesis could finally be written and a lifelong ambition fulfilled.

'Tell me what's in here and tell me the truth.'

'My name is Lilian Bouvier, or just plain Lily if you prefer. That is true. I'm a historian and writer. That also is true. I have been looking for what I think is in that chest for all of my adult life. That too is true. But I cannot tell you what is inside it for I do not know,' said Lily plainly and frankly. 'I believe that in your chest is a collection of documents, probably not all of them that old, but some as many as four or five centuries old. I believe they tell the truth about a secret almost lost in time; one that led many people in power at certain times in the past, to want to cover up that secret forever. A secret so powerful, so important to mankind that they were prepared to kill for it. A secret that links the whole of mankind back to the dawn of time and one that frightened monarchies, religious leaders, heads of state and governments to such an extent that its total destruction was their only solution,' Lily breathed in deeply and shrugged, feeling certain he'd confused this man more than he had answered his question.

'The truth, Olivier, is not always easy to see, let alone understand. Since the dawn of time, long, long before any scriptures, humans have evolved with their environment and indeed originate from it, we are one. Paganism, or anything else you might call it, in its most basic form, teaches us just that: we should be at one with our environment, with our planet, we are simply part of it, originating from and belonging to one and the same group of molecules that form this Earth. The pagan trinity is three people in one; Mother Nature; her lover – the Green Man; and their son. It might seem an odd way of expressing the idea, but it is an explanation that dates back to a time when man huddled around fires in the entrances to caves, when communication through speech was just developing and when earth, wind, fire and water, the sun and moon etcetera were all respected and feared. While man respected and feared all of these so-called "elements" he also felt respected by them; they fed him, sheltered him, kept him warm and watered him. This oneness in a sense makes pagans both worshippers and Gods all in one, Olivier. The problem with pagan beliefs in our modern world is that money has no place, no purpose and certainly no value. In a world where there is no money, there is no power either; can you see now why people in power fear paganism?' Lily asked.

'I'm not really sure what you're talking about,' confessed Declan, mildly embarrassed.

'If paganism has its enemies today, Olivier, it's not the Catholic Church as such. Those times are long since gone. The real war against paganism took place during the first centuries following the crucifixion of Jesus.'

'So the pagans were defeated by the Romans, is that what you're saying?' Declan asked.

Lily looked puzzled, and for a moment Declan thought he couldn't answer his question, but he replied:

'No, not entirely. The Roman Empire was suffering the consequences of regular uprisings from a population ready to turn to rioting. The beliefs of the workers, tradesmen and businessmen were a mix of pagan beliefs, but fundamentally one of a plurality of gods. This did not bode well with the Roman Catholic Church, the official religion of the empire at that time, which claimed there was only one God. It was not a question of live and let live, because the Church had enormous wealth, armies and therefore influence, and was passing the message, in no uncertain terms, all around Europe, that "accept our beliefs, our church, our God and we will let you live in peace." The alternatives were wars, the crusades and ultimate submission to the Knights Templar.'

'So the Romans were not really running the empire at all?'

'No. I mean, yes they were, but they were ruling a population whose beliefs were vastly different. Give me a chance to answer one question at a time, would you, Olivier?' Lily said smiling, but unable to hide his frustration. 'You just asked if the Romans defeated the pagans,' he paused again. 'I would answer to that, that to say that the pagans lost would be inaccurate. It is far more complex than that. The emperor at the time, Cornelius, called for the now famous Council of Nicaea. Some claim that this was the day when Jesus became God or immortal.' Lily looked briefly at the floor and scratched his chin, before continuing. 'Whatever way you look at it, the conclusion of the Council of Nicaea was an attempt to satisfy all parties. A bloody clever attempt I'd say,' he added. 'To claim that Jesus was, in fact, the son of God, that he was immortal and that Lord God, the Father, Jesus Christ his son and the Holy Spirit were all actually one and the same entity, appeared at the time to satisfy everybody's middle ground. The pagans had their plurality of Gods in the Holy Trinity and the bishops could confirm that these "gods" were, in reality, one and the same, but definitely only one.'

'So everybody won then?' asked Declan, naïvely.

'You really do like nutshell-answers don't you, my friend?' Lily laughed. 'You'd never have made a historian.' He stepped outside the porch, lit up his pipe and sighed a long sigh.

'I'm sorry', blurted Declan, following Lily outside, 'but it's not my field at all. It must be fascinating to know so much about where we come from.'

'We historians don't always know, we surmise,' said Lily. 'To come back to the pagan story of who won, you need to remember that a lot of pagan holy days were later adopted by the Romans to appease the citizens. Christmas Day and Easter Day were originally pagan celebrations assimilated into the Catholic calendar, and the famous Halloween became All Saints' Day. There's also the age-old "chicken and egg" question with the choice of sites for churches and yew trees. But in all honesty today, no old church looks right without a yew in its grounds.' Lily shrugged and lifting his palms to the air with arms outstretched, he raised his shoulders for effect. 'When you're sat eating an omelette, do you really care which came first, the chicken or the egg?'

'Typical French,' said Declan, mockingly.

'I'm not French, I'm Breton.'

Declan smiled.

'Touché,' he said. 'So the people just accepted these new holy days?'

'What the Council of Nicaea created that day, something of far more consequence to the human race at that time than just Jesus becoming God, was a carte blanche as far as the Church was concerned to gain political power, wealth and influence. The Church became more powerful than the state and had power over monarchies right across Europe. Later, with this power, came a reign of terror during the crusades and the inquisitions to rid the world of so-called non-believers and it was no longer led by a church based on the teachings of Jesus, but by a new, state authorised, official Church doctrine that kept consecutive Popes in their positions of wealth and power for a long time after the Roman Empire fell.'

'How long did this reign last – I mean we've still got popes today, but they can't declare wars... can they?' asked Declan.

Lily placed his pipe carefully on its side on the almost flat surface of the window ledge and with his now free right hand, he indicated to Declan that they should go back into the mill, but Declan didn't respond.

'For the popes and their Catholic Church, some say that this monopoly of power continued until the sixteenth century when it was undermined by the Reformation of Martin Luther, the German Augustinian monk who laid the cornerstone of the modern protestant church, but I don't agree.'

'I've heard of him,' said Declan. 'I thought he was an anti-Semite. Why not, why don't you agree?' asked Declan.

'Now listen here,' Lily insisted in a somewhat patronising voice. 'What is in that chest is what interests me, Olivier. Not because I want to keep what's inside, but because I don't ever want it to be lost.' Lily reached again for his pipe and puffed delicately on it once more, withheld the smoke for some time before exhaling and then continued. 'What I believe finally brought the papal dictatorship to its knees is best explained by what's in that chest. Now it's my turn to ask you some questions if you don't mind, Olivier.'

'Fire away. Figuratively, that is.'

'You have no idea what is in the chest do you?' asked Lily.

'No,' answered Declan honestly, 'but it is mine.'

'Yours and your sister's,' corrected Lily. 'but I don't accept that either. If I am right about what's in there, you will understand when you've opened it: one, that it has no great monetary value; and two, that on your own it will mean nothing to you. Did your grandmother ever refer to you as a pagan prince, Olivier?' asked Lily out of the blue.

'How do you know that?' asked Declan frowning. 'I mean how do you know that what's in the chest will mean nothing to me? You told me you surmised, but that you didn't know,' he added quickly, thinking at first that it sounded clever. And then, Declan simply said, 'I know where the key is to open it.' He couldn't explain why he spoke openly like this to Lily. It was a mixture of growing trust in the man opposite him, personal resignation and above all, pure curiosity.

'Now you're surmising,' said Lily.

Declan looked bewildered.

'I do,' he said, 'I know where the key is. I'll show you.' And he stepped around Lily and his pipe back into the house and walked towards the window where he bent down under the sink, picked up a jar with a gold plastic screw-top lid and held it up to the window for a second or two. Lily, laying down his pipe, followed him inside. Declan then unscrewed the lid in a flash and emptied the contents of the jar onto the chestnut-planked tabletop. There, among what seemed like a dusty array of sad and worthless belongings of a life gone by, was a small brass key. Picking it up, he swivelled the chest around to face him, placed the key in the lock and turned.

'I wasn't surmising about the key,' he said. 'I knew.'

Lily carefully removed a folded transparent plastic bag containing an envelope from an inside jacket pocket and held it up to show Declan.

'This contains a letter from my great-great grandfather to my grandfather,' said Lily, proudly. And he slipped the paper from its protective envelope within the bag in a sort of magic-show, theatrical flurry, straightened it out and read aloud:

'...mais ce sont les contenus du casque qui vont te montrer la vraie clé, mon cher ami. Meilleures salutations, Grand-père.' -

'It's the contents of the chest that will reveal the real key? So there are two keys then?' asked Declan. 'What else does that letter say? Are you part of my family? Who are you?'

'No, no, nothing like that. You can relax, we're unrelated,' said Lily, smiling. 'My great-great grandfather was a renowned philologist of the nineteenth century. He was the Viscount de La Villemarqué. He was responsible for some of the documentation that I'm hoping you will find in that treasure chest of yours. He was famous for his collection of traditional Breton folk songs, the "Barzaz Breiz", first published in 1839.'

'Well if it's been published, even in 1839, surely then it's not lost forever.'

'There was much dispute about, how can I say this, the exactitude of his work at the time? There was one man, Le Roux, a critic of my great-great grandfather's work, who made a link between one particular song and the end of the Black Death as we understand it today.'

'That sounds ridiculous. Forgive me for saying so, but it does.'

'At first, yes,' agreed Lily. 'Le Roux's problem with de La Villemarqué's published text, which in later versions was modified to some extent due to pressure from other critics such as Luzel, who appears to have changed his mind at some point, was, as I mentioned, its exactitude.'

'Okay,' said Declan, following only some of what Lily was saying, 'but you're losing me a bit there.'

'Sorry. You're right. I do that. I ramble. Le Roux was a philologist and a pedant. He deciphered very precise history lessons from song or verse. He believed that stories passed down through song from essentially illiterate generation to illiterate generation over many centuries, even millennia, if properly interpreted, could tell the most accurate eyewitness accounts of any given historical event. Often more accurate, he believed, than the written word.'

'More, even, than the Bible itself?'

'Sometimes more accurate than many of the Church's own accounts,' said Lily, cautiously.

'Okay,' said Declan again. 'and the Black Death?' Declan's expression looked suddenly enlightened. 'Lilian Bouvier did you say? Did you say your name was Lilian Bouvier?'

'I did. Why?'

'You've written a book about the Black Death – my sister's got a copy of it. The Book of the Pest... or something. And I remember seeing your name on the front. Is that you?'

'Book of Pestilence,' said Lily. 'Have you read it?'

'No, but I will now that I've met you,' said Declan, wishing that he had just been able to say, yes I have.

Lily had heard that before. His book didn't have a large readership, but he thought it would be fun to meet Declan's sister – someone possibly interested in his work.

'Ah well, I'll see if I can't dig you out a copy. Where was I? Ah yes, you asked me about the Black Death. It came to France on an Italian trade ship in the year of 1347. Most people believe it only lasted a short time, but in fact it continued for another 350 years. Well the thing is it's a bit of a mystery as to why it stopped – there was no cure – there were no vaccines, no antibiotics,' Lily paused. 'I was telling you about a link between a Breton song and the end of the Plague.'

'Sorry, I interrupted you. Please go on.'

'Well. From a song titled, "The Pest of Elliant", this philologist, Le Roux, claimed to have identified not only the correct village with its church, but also the whereabouts of the exact spring from which the song-writer's medieval followers were advised to drink if they wanted to live.'

'And where was that spring then?'

'I'm hoping the contents of that chest will enunciate just that,' said Lily.

'We'll soon see,' said Declan. And he lifted the lid carefully to reveal a faded, brown leather-bound book-like folder.

'That, my friend, is treasure,' exclaimed Lily, gazing, mouth open, into the chest. 'Gently does it now, may I?' he asked, reaching carefully into the chest with both hands.

'Go ahead,' replied Declan, backing off slightly to offer Lily more room for manoeuvre. 'There's still something I don't understand, Mr Bouvier. How is it that you just happened to be here when I found the chest and you just so happen to know so much about it?' he then added, becoming suddenly very suspicious of the man again as he formulated his question.

'I can see what you might be thinking,' explained Lily, in a near whisper, 'but I beg you to believe me when I say that this is the most serendipitous moment of my entire life. This letter comes with me everywhere and has done for nearly thirty years. And please, please call me Lily.'

'Okay, Lily. So how come you know so much about my so-called family secret then?'

'Dare I ask you to allow me to explain as we begin to look through some of these manuscripts, Olivier, I'm unbelievably excited to see what you've found?'

'Sure,' confirmed Declan nodding his head.

Lily unfastened two worn leather straps holding the brown book bindings together, and opening them out slowly and with extreme care, he revealed the first page of a quite large collection of papers. Documents that varied in thickness from parchment to a delicate film of paper so thin it was almost transparent. The edges were mostly tatty and generally quite rough and their colours varied as autumn leaves; yellows, beiges, marmalade oranges and dusty browns of all shades. The whole pile, Declan estimated, must have been about eight inches thick and probably contained over a thousand sheets.

'This one's got a stamp on,' Declan blurted out excitedly. Lily took the tracing-paper thin folded envelope very gently from Declan's fingers and held it up to the light coming through the window.

'That will have a date on it won't it?' asked Declan.

'It's called a "pli". It should have a date on it, but let's hope it's legible,' replied Lily as he placed the folded envelope on the kitchen table and delved into another jacket pocket searching purposefully for something. He retrieved a small shiny object from his pocket and Declan recognised what it was not from its initial shape, but from the gesture Lily made as he swung open the casing to reveal a small hand lens. Picking up the folded paper again and holding it to the light, Lily examined the document only an inch or so from his eye.

'I can make out the date,' he said, as Declan stood there, now less excited about his treasure he felt was turning out to be a bit of an anti-climax in comparison to what he had expected to find, 'sixty-nine it says.'

'That corresponds roughly to your forty years search for the chest,' said Declan

'No, Declan. The date here is 1869. That's not forty-odd years ago, but over a hundred and forty years ago.'

'What does it say?'

Lily carefully unfolded the pli and held it out in front of him in such a way as both men could read it together.

'It says:'

"*Mon cher petitfils, My dear grandson,*
I made a little sketch for you this morning while waiting for the Post Office to open.Who knows, perhaps this kind of picture on a pli could one day become popular. Can you solve this riddle?

I have a mouth, but I do not talk, I murmur
I have a bed, but I never sleep,
I have no legs, but I always run.
Guess who I am and from where I come,
And you will already be on the right path.

Kindest regards
your Grandpère
Claude Hersart de la Villemarqué"

Declan thought about the riddle and decided he must have heard it before, because the answer came to him in an instant.

'It's a river,' Declan said, 'That's the answer, it's a river.'

'That's the first part of the riddle,' said Lily, 'but which one?'

'Oh,' replied Declan, realising that his stroke of genius left them no clues. 'How can we know which river?'

'The clues are there for the trained eye, Olivier,' Lily continued, 'And like I said, that treasure won't mean much to you on your own. I'm not going to tease you. Look here. Not all of the postmark, or the obliteration mark as they used to be called, is legible. The town name is too blurred and that would have been a great clue, but the number 2612 can be seen clearly. For someone who knows the old French post office numbering system of the mid to late nineteenth century, that number is enough.'

'Couldn't we just ask at La Poste?'

'No need,' said Lily. '2612 is Quimperlé. I recognise the town from the sketch as well. It doesn't look like that anymore, but the river hasn't changed much. There used to be an abattoir there once, a long time ago, and de La Villemarqué must have sketched this from that side of the river.'

'You know which river it is then?'

'The bridge in the sketch became quite famous at the end of the nineteenth century thanks to a Norwegian impressionist painter. The "Washerwomen in the morning in Quimperlé". Fritz Thaulow was his name. Same bridge, different view,' confirmed Lily, 'Pont Fleuri.'

'And the river?'

'There are two converging rivers at Quimperlé which is where the town gets its name from. Kemper means confluent in Breton and the Breton name for the town is Kemperle which translates to mean the confluent of the Ellé with the other smaller river, the Isole. But this one in the picture is the Ellé. You "Guess who I am and from where I come, And you will already be on the right path." Easy when you know how.'

'So we need to follow the river Ellé to its source? Where's that?' asked Declan.

'Not ten minutes from here in a car,' replied Lily, 'but that's not where the author of the riddle wanted his grandson, my grandfather, to go.'

'But the riddle is about a river and what else could the phrase, "... and from where I come", mean if it doesn't mean the source?' Declan reasoned.

'The letter goes on to say, "And you will already be on the right path". This letter was written, and very deliberately, in such a way as to ensure that nobody, without much more information, could have fully understood the riddle. That is your family secret, Olivier.'

'I still don't understand it,' said Declan.

'You have to put yourself in the shoes of the person to whom this enigma refers, rather than the shoes of the person who wrote it or for whom it was written.'

'This is getting worse,' said Declan, now convinced that it would have been far more exciting to have found gold or diamonds rather than a bundle of someone's old paperwork. 'I too have a note – from my late grandmother,' proudly, Declan went to retrieve the note written in Breton from his pocket but it was no longer there – he must have left it in the guest-room at Albert's.

'I don't have it with me, but I can remember what it said,' explained Declan. 'It said: "the contents of the chest will lead Olivier", that's me, "to the second key and the real treasure". So what did all that mean?'

'It is a riddle about just that. And the clue is in one of the songs that the author of this letter published in his collection of songs, the Barzaz Breiz.'

I'm still not getting this, thought Declan. Lily could see the blank expression on Declan's face.

'I never said this would be easy,' he said and then added: 'I told you it won't mean anything to you on your own.' Lily paused for a moment, trying to readjust his hat, but quickly gave up and placed it on the table. There are times when a hat is simply no longer comfortable and it must come off. He combed back his hair with his fingers.

'This letter,' said Lily, holding up the pli from Quimperlé, 'is addressed to a Mr Bouvier, in Chalon sur Saône. Monsieur Bouvier was my grandfather. So what this tells me is that my great-great grandfather, Claude Hersart de La Villemarqué, must have known about the second key. He wanted his grandson, my grandfather, to find it too, but he didn't make it easy for him – hence the riddle. The fact that this pli has found its way into that treasure chest of yours, tells me that my grandfather must have solved the riddle and made his way from Chalon sur Saône here to La Trinité-Langonnet,' Lily explained.

'So our two families must have met at some point then,' said Declan. 'I mean before you and me? Our grandparents, maybe?'

'There's one thing for sure, that note from your grandmother is telling you that clues to help you find the treasure are in that chest,' said Lily, pointing to the open chest, 'Or more specifically, in its contents,' now gesturing towards the leather-bound collection of papers. 'You, or we, if you would allow me to assist, have to decipher what all that means. And so far, the clues are pointing to the treasure being near "une fontaine" or a spring. Now that isn't necessarily the river's source.'

'Oh,' said Declan, 'I see the difference,' then he started to frown. 'But a river at its source is very small and is ultimately joined by dozens of tiny tributaries, brooks or streams before it becomes a river. There could be hundreds or even thousands, not dozens of tiny springs that flow into it somewhere along its banks. It'd be like looking for a needle in a haystack. I mean where do you start?'

'You put yourself in the shoes of the person to whom this riddle refers rather than the shoes of the person who wrote it,' repeated Lily. 'The song tells of a man called Olivier, not you, just the same name, who led people to a fountain or spring.'

'Okay, right,' said Declan. 'Big deal. Or rather, honestly, where is the big deal? So this guy, Olivier, buried some treasure somewhere close to a spring not too far from here.'

'There is much more to it than—'

'So if we get ourselves a good metal detector together with some sturdy walking boots and a few spare years, we could strike lucky.'

Lily raised his voice in an attempt to calm the younger man.

'You knew the whereabouts of the first key. I know the whereabouts of the spring. I know which spring it is.'

'Why didn't you just say so straight off? Why all this bloody history lesson? And how come, if you know roughly where the treasure is buried, you didn't just go and dig it up yourself?'

'I didn't know there was any treasure there,' and in that instant, Lily realised how careless his answer had been.

Declan stared, a split-second stare of disbelief, as the significance of Lily's confession dawned on him. Thanks to Declan himself, Lily had not only learned of the existence of the treasure, but now he, and he alone, also knew where to find it. Declan on the other hand, had no idea where it was.

'Oh, brilliant. That's just brilliant,' said Declan feeling suddenly really stupid.

'It's the fountain here in the village of La Trinité Langonnet,' blurted Lily, trying to ease the situation as quickly as possible by sharing with Declan what he knew. Then he added, staring at Declan:

'I don't know for certain, I'm just very sure. I hunt pheasant, Olivier, not treasure. I do possess a metal detector though and you're welcome to borrow it.'

'I've got to tell Isabelle straight away.'

There was a beeping sound from Declan's phone and he snatched it out of his pocket. A text from Isabelle. She was already there.

'Hi, with Carl in Lorient wil b in trinity in bout 1hr, Is. ☺'

'Talk of the devil,' said Declan. 'That was my sister. She says she'll be here in about an hour. No hang on, she sent the message forty five minutes ago. The signal's rubbish here isn't it?'

'Never owned one of those things. Don't have the slightest idea how they work,' said Lily looking disdainfully at Declan's phone.

'My sister will be in La Trinité in about ten minutes. Why don't we meet at the fountain?' suggested Declan.

'We should take the wooden chest with us.'

'Do you think you would be able to find the treasure?' asked Declan. 'if we went there?'

'I don't know about that,' said Lily. 'but I believe that is where we are being instructed to go.'

'Hey. Less of the "we". It's not your treasure,' Declan reminded Lily. 'You can do what you want with the paperwork afterwards, but the treasure belongs to me and my sister. We agree on that at least, don't we?'

'I'm not talking about the treasure, I'm talking about the song,' argued Lily. 'The song tells everybody to go to the fountain. Not just you and your sister, but everybody. That includes me. Like I said, put yourself in the shoes of the person...'

'Yeah, yeah, I know – "...the person to whom the riddle refers,' said Declan texting his sister.

'Landmarks were not the same then. There would not have been the roads that there are today let alone the signposts. You follow the river upstream past the Abby of Langonnet and what you see first as you approach the source of the river Ellé, back then at least, would have been the spire of the church in La Trinité-Langonnet and behind it, the summit of the Minez Du. If you're looking for clean water, you'd be well advised to head for a spring at the foot of such a geological outcrop don't you agree? The church spire would lead you the rest of the way. Important landmarks they were at the time, certainly for land navigation. Their spires and towers would have been not only visible for miles around, but audible as well.

'Meet @ fountain asap. somthin 2 show U :D'

'How can a church tower be audible?' asked Declan facetiously.

'Bells,' Lily explained, but he could see that Declan was not listening.

> 'Right we have to leave,' confirmed Declan, gently gathering up the papers and the chest. 'Very useful things these,' he added, unable to resist waving his cell-phone at Lily.

'Shall I take that chest?' offered Lily. 'You've got your tools.'

'They can stay where they are. Where are you parked?'

'Miles away. I wanted to ask you if I could come with you? Filou doesn't lose much hair so he won't mess up your car.'

'Sure. My feet are already covered in mud anyway,' said Declan, but suddenly he had an uncomfortable thought. Why did this man presume that he would care about a dog being in his car? He must have seen that it was a tidy-looking sportscar and not an old banger like Albert would mostly drive around in.

'You look like you've forgotten something. What's up?' asked Lily.

Declan did not answer straight away, still unsure of what to do. He wondered if this wasn't somehow a trap. And then an idea came to him.

'Everything okay?' asked Lily, still waiting for a reply.

'Yeah, yeah.' said Declan, sounding flustered. 'Change of plan.' Placing the chest back on the table, he gestured to Lily to take it instead. 'Here, you take the chest, I've got to lock up.'

Declan calculated that it would take both hands to hold the chest for it was just a bit too big to fit under one arm. This way Lily would have to leave his gun behind. He, on the other hand, would have both hands free and could pick up one of the old shovels from the lean-to shed on the way out. At least that way, he'd be armed in case the old man tried anything.

To Declan's surprise, however, Lily seemed delighted with the new plan and said so:

'That's a good idea. If you lock up, I can leave my gun here. If that's okay with you?' he added.

This answer took Declan by surprise and he replied, he felt, a little too avidly.

'Yeah, great. Yes, I mean. No problems.'

Having locked the front door to the old mill, Declan continued with his new plan and said to Lily, this time much more casually,

'I'll grab a shovel, we may need it.'

'That's good thinking,' replied Lily.

The two men set off along the race and back to the car. Declan unlocked the car doors from a good ten metres away and had to point out to Lily that in Ireland they drove on the other side. Filou had no such problem and simply jumped in through the first door opened and raced to the back seat. Declan placed the shovel in the boot of the car and held his hands out to relieve Lily of the wooden chest.

32
Case Closed

Major Gilles Cario sat at his desk looking through a letter from one of his men requesting a transfer to the Gendarmerie Maritime. It would be sad to see him go, he was a dammed good agent, but why hold the man back? He was just deciding to make a favourable recommendation to his superior when his phone rang: Mahé – another good agent.

'Cario,' said Cario.

Mahé outlined the details of the case. He had found the young policeman's killer from the file back in 2006. His body had been found at the scene of a car accident in which no one else had been involved. Prints matched. A Belgian man, married and divorced – two kids, both studying but still with their mother. The man, Mr Eric Dupont, aged 48, had been working for a notary's office in Carhaix for a good number of years. The job was really just a cover, for assets on frozen French accounts had shown he had no need of his salary there; he was running a substantial drug ring and money was absolutely no object.

'I remember the case with Agent Yaouank,' said Cario. 'It was a good hunch you had that day to impound the car. Excellent work. That puts another unsolved case to rest, Mahé. Well done'

'Not entirely,' argued Mahé.

'How's that, not entirely?'

'I'd like to start an inquiry into what appears, from preliminary evidence, to be officer-involvement in the distribution of narcotics,' Mahé explained.

'No, no, no, no, no!' yelled Cario down the phone. 'That's a bad hunch, Mahé. This case is closed, do you understand me?'

'I have a witness statement from a—' Cario cut him off:

'I've seen the statement. I've also seen the forensics report from Bréhat. Your witness says he was held prisoner there by these men. Bound to a chair. Well, ask him... no, Mahé. Ask yourself: why were the Irishman's fingerprints found all over the scene? Hey? Mahé? Latent prints from two of the dials on the gas cooker – which, by the way, had been left on – a baking tray with charred masking tape jammed up against a skylight: more prints. Let's see, a cooking pan, drawer handles, pair of scissors... etcetera, etcetera, etcete... bloody ...ra. Forensics say your witness statement doesn't tie in: the man was not restrained, he had free run of the place. How come he got out alive? Where do you think you're going with this Mahé? Hey? You answer me that.'

There was silence on the other end of the phone.

'Good. That was the right answer,' continued the Major, more calmly. 'You've solved the crime. They'll be no trial. What more could you want? You want to gain yourself a few Brownie points here, Mahé, put in your recommendations at the end, that in future we run a check on other European databases for fingerprints. This Dupont chap's fingerprints were on record at Belgian military HQ. He had been exempted from national service for reasons given... let's see, there – full-time employment overseas. Hardly overseas, France is it? Looks like he got a job abroad to avoid national service, but I'll make no further comment on that. What I mean to say is, we could have found our man earlier. Any further questions, Mahé?'

'No, Major,' replied Mahé.

'Back to work then. What we have on Dupont concerning his contact with the Russians, I'll hand over to Drug Squad, but you keep your nose out of it. I want that report on my desk before it goes to the public prosecutor.' Cario hung up.

33
Meet At The Spring

Declan put his seat belt on, started up the engine of his Audi TT and began reversing back up the track to the road where he could turn around to join the D109.

'You need to put your seatbelt on too,' urged Declan.

'No, you're alright,' said Lily. 'I wear it if I'm on a long journey but otherwise, I find it annoying when I'm driving.'

Declan thought of saying something about most accidents happen within just a few miles of home or something like that, but couldn't remember whether it was most fatalities or just accidents or whether it was two miles or three miles.

'But you're not driving, I am,' he said finally.

'Keep your hair on, Olivier,' said Lily.

'And what I find annoying when I'm driving is that ding, ding, ding that tells me the car knows that somebody on board isn't wearing their seatbelt. It detracts from my concentration.'

'Alright, alright,' said Lily. 'Why all the fuss? We're only going down the road.'

'You'll know why, "all the fuss" when you meet my sister.'

'Is she handicapped or something?' asked Lily.

'Handicapped yes, but not *or something*,' replied Declan, angrily.

Lily decided this must be a sensitive point in Declan's life story, and began fastening his seat belt. The dinging noise in the car stopped and Lily conceded that it had been annoying.

'So I guess your sister had a car accident and wasn't wearing a seatbelt.'

'My sister was the only person in the car wearing her seatbelt and the only person that survived,' said Declan, curtly.

Lily decided to drop the subject. The two men approached the village of La Trinité-Langonnet and Declan slowed to turn off towards the fountain. Lily was pleasantly surprised to see that his driver clearly knew the way, for even following the signposts it was not that easy to find.

'Just now I was telling you we had to think about this riddle from the point of view of the person to whom it refers rather than of the person who wrote it,' said Lily. 'Imagine now that you're following the river Ellé from Quimperlé in a time when there were no roads like we have today. At some point along your journey, as you near the river's source, you will see that,' Lily pointed out the Minez Du through the windscreen of the car, 'the highest point in the county of Morbihan. Although the county's borders were not defined at that time as they are today, the river Ellé formed a physical and natural border to the North West. Still, if it's clean water you seek, you'd be tempted to stop searching wouldn't you? You wouldn't keep looking for the source itself? I know I wouldn't anyway.'

'You already told me about this,' said Declan. 'The church spires, the bells. I was listening and I agree. It makes sense. I can see that it wouldn't necessarily be the source that you would be looking for.'

Lily was again surprised that Declan had been listening, for he had had the distinct impression that he had not. A few moments later, Declan swung into a parking space in the Place du Vieux Marché, switched the engine off and opened his door.

'You can get much nearer than this,' said Lily.

'There isn't much parking down there,' Declan pointed out, 'and what there is, I'll leave for my sister: she's in a wheelchair,' he placed his right foot onto the gravelled surface.

'The road's all been banked up and you can get quite a few cars down there now,' Lily explained. 'Plus we've got to carry the shovel down there and the chest. Do you really want to walk?'

'You've got a point there,' said Declan and he closed the door, started the engine again and drove down from the old market place to the fountain.

'You know that one of my great-great grandfather's critics, a man called Le Roux, used this old market place to help him determine precisely which fountain it was. All from the lyrics of that song this medieval Olivier wrote.'

'How?' asked Declan.

'Well, the simplified version is that some of the towns they thought were identified in the song, never even had a market place. Deductive reasoning, you see,' said Lily.

As the two men approached the fountain, they could see another car already there.

'That's Carl,' said Declan. 'That's his Saab.

Declan pulled in just behind Carl and rushed out to see his sister.

'Hi, Carl,' he said, walking around the car to Isabelle's side, 'How was the traffic in Lorient?'

'Yeah, great, not too bad at all.'

Isabelle's door opened and Declan leant forward and peered in.

'Lovely to see you again, Sis,' he said, 'You're looking well. Was your trip okay?'

Lily stepped out of the Audi and Filou shot out after him. Carl opened the boot of his Saab and started to unfold the stowed wheelchair. Filou ran around the car to sniff Carl and the chair; all seemed fine. Then he ran around to Declan, saw Isabelle and cowering a little under the sill of the door, he sniffed the air next to Isabelle's leg at calf-level - all fine - and he shot off again to check the surrounding area for pheasants. Lily walked around the Audi slowly and waited for some introductions.

'I'm so glad you're here,' said Declan. 'I said I've got something to show you. But there's also someone here I want you to meet.'

'You don't look like you've been tortured, Declan, or are you back to being, Olivier, now you're here in France?'

'A bit of both. Here, look. There's somebody I'd like you to meet,' he repeated.

'I was going to say, judging by the look on your face, I'd guess you've met someone special. At first glance, you don't come across as a man who's been held hostage and tortured.'

Carl walked towards the passenger side door of the Saab to help Isabelle into her chair. Declan reached down to his sister and she placed both forearms around his neck as he eased her legs around so that they were facing out of the car. Isabelle could now turn her head properly and gave Declan an odd look as he began to introduce Lily.

'This is Lily.'

'I was expecting more of a—' Isabelle began.

'Lily, this is my sister, Isabelle.'

'Enchanté,' said Lily

'Carl, meet Lily, Lily, mon beau-frère.' *My brother-in-law*.

'Bonjour, monsieur,' Carl replied in passable French.

'What did you just say, Isabelle? More of a what?' asked Declan. 'Lily's not the surprise; we've found, I've found a treasure chest – I'll show you. We'll show you.'

'What are you on about, Declan?' said Isabelle. 'I've never heard you ramble so much.'

'He gets that from me,' confessed Lily.

Declan stood back to let Carl place the wheelchair in the correct position to help Isabelle ease into it and headed towards the boot of his car to retrieve the leather-bound collection of documents from the wooden chest.

By the time he had returned with the chest, Isabelle was sitting in her wheelchair.

'That's not your normal set of wheels, is it, Is?' asked Declan.

'No, I know. Carl got it for me – a new off-road version.'

'It's like with a mountain bike they call in French a vee-tee-tee: a "vélo tout terrain". That means literally a bike for all terrains,' Carl explained.

'He's showing off his French,' said Isabelle.

'So if you take the word for wheelchair in French, "fauteuil roulante", well, that makes a "fauteuil tout terrain" – an FTT.'

'Funny thing that,' said Declan.

'The other one is still in the boot if you really don't like it,' Carl said.

'No, Carl. It's fine,' she said. 'I'm in it now. It is very lightweight too, but it's quite a bit wider than my normal one.'

'Enough room for you to have a look through this,' said Declan, placing the collection of bound papers on his sister's lap. 'Not too heavy is it?'

'Not at all. What is it?' she enquired.

'It's a long, long story,' said Lily.

'Yeah, really long,' confirmed Declan.

'Well come on, then. I want to know,' said Isabelle impatiently.

Declan began by explaining that the documents found in a wooden chest at Mamie's were not the treasure itself. He then placed the chest on the back seat of Carl's Saab.

'That's the chest, look,' he said, pointing. 'That's the chest I found hidden at Mamie's.'

About two minutes later, Isabelle had begun to understand what the two men were trying to explain and patting the leather binding with four fingers, said,

'So the whereabouts of the treasure is revealed in these pages, these documents?'

'Exactly,' said Declan.

'You will be careful with them, Isabelle, won't you?' said Lily.

Declan was on the verge of putting Lily in his place when Isabelle answered calmly:

'I can see how delicate and valuable they are. You really don't have to worry. I will be careful.'

'So somewhere around here there is buried treasure?' asked Carl.

'Yep, and that book there has all the answers,' said Declan, pointing to the manuscripts which Isabelle had begun to leaf through.

'That one there is a postcard, that one, look,' said Declan pointing to the letter from Lily's great-great grandfather.

'It's not a postcard,' corrected Lily. 'Postcards didn't exist at that time.'

'Well anyway, Carl, that's the letter that led us to this spring. The French call them "fontaines", like fountains, but they're really freshwater springs,' he said. 'The sketch on the front is of the river Ellé in Quimperlé.'

'Very freshwater spring in the case of this one,' added Lily. 'I told you about that, Le Roux chap, who reckoned there was a link between that song and the end of the Black Death in France. This is where he made that link.'

Isabelle began carefully looking through the uppermost section of the documents held between the leather bindings, fearful of them sliding off her lap. She admired the little sketch of the river with its bridge, but like Declan, she would have been unable to recognise it. There were some pieces of paper so thin that the slightest pull in the wrong direction from clumsy fingers would have torn them. These, Isabelle decided, would have to be inspected properly, professionally: cotton gloves, tweezers and at a desk with a lens. There were texts in Latin, Breton, French of course – old French, but also English which surprised her. A birth certificate: Mum's original "livret de famille" and opening it, Isabelle saw the addition of the two last names: Declan's name; Olivier, Declan: "de sexe masculine" and hers; Isabelle, Sinead: "de sexe feminine". There were some very old photographs of megaliths. Carnac she recognised. Some huge

menhirs only one of which she knew, the big broken one. The
menhir brisé it was called. A watercolour sketch of Stonehenge with
English writing on it. And German – another surprise. The further
back she looked in the collection, the older the texts seemed to be.
Texts was not the right word, for some were photographs and others
sketches and hand-copied – more Latin; Greek or rather ancient
Greek. Some pages in Hebrew. This was beyond belief if it was
genuine, for there was also runic writing and hieroglyphs; Egyptian,
she believed and a strange form of writing that she had seen before
on a TV documentary; cuneiform perhaps? This writing, unlike the
hieroglyphs and the runes, had never been written on paper, so these
had been meticulously copied out by hand. Originally these texts
would not have been cut into stone, rather pressed into clay and then
baked in the Sun. Isabelle was going to have fun with this lot back at
home. She was on the point of closing the two leather covers, putting
her new toy away for later when a thick brown, concertina-style
parchment caught her eye. What surprised her was not the way it had
been folded, but the fact that it looked as though it had been added
to in many different handwritings. As she pulled it out and began to
unfold it, she saw that it was a family tree. It must have gone back
five centuries, maybe more, for the earliest inscription was fourteen
something. Nearly six hundred years ago. "Arbre Généalogique de
la famille LE DOUR" its title read. It was a family tree. Her
grandfather's family tree. Her family tree. She looked over to call to
Declan and could hear Lily's voice.

'Le Roux believed that the song Olivier wrote, or rather sang,
guided people to this exact spring. Of course, back in the latter part
of the Middle Ages it really would have been just that, a spring. There
would have been none of this ornately carved granite surround.'

'It's weird,' said Carl. 'It looks like it's shaped in the form of a
keyhole.'

'Yeah,' said Declan, 'I've always thought that. You can ask Isabelle. Why is that, Lily, do you know?'

'I haven't a clue,' admitted Lily, 'but it is the only one shaped like it anywhere and there are literally tens of thousands of them all over Brittany.'

'Ten thousand springs like this?' asked Carl. 'Are you sure you've got your numbers right?'

Isabelle closed the bindings, fastened the strap and with both hands, returned the collection of papers to the chest on the rear seat of Carl's Saab. Feeling for the unfamiliar hand rims of the "FTT", she reversed away from the car and began to manoeuvre across the road towards the fountain.

'Not ten thousand like this,' said Lily. 'Tens of thousands altogether, I said, and none like this.'

'You've got to be kiddin' me,' said Carl.

'I'm not kidding at all. There are over two thousand fountains in Brittany claimed to heal the sick. Some you bathe in, some you drink from. Some cure infertility, some help with skin disorders, others cure headaches or eye problems.'

'And this one?' asked Declan. 'What does this one do?'

'There is no evidence that any of them do anything but flow to the sea: it's all myth. This one here, nobody knows for sure. It was kept secret for a long time. I don't really know why,' confessed Lily. 'There was a time when people took away the carved stones for garden ornaments. Sold the stone on to collectors or dealers.'

'Like grave robbers. Well, I mean people are drawn to old artefacts. I'm not saying this was a grave,' said Carl, who looked up to see Isabelle at the edge of the road. 'Do you want a hand down?' he called over.

Declan and Carl both began to walk over towards the stone step-over and Isabelle, nodding her consent, gripped the sides of her chair. The two men lifted her easily over the foot-high granite wall and she took the *reigns* once more.

'Mind out for the ruts in the stone paving,' warned Declan, 'and some of the stones wobble a bit.'

Isabelle let out a slight sob, barely audible, but Declan heard it.

'Are you okay, Is?' he asked.

'I remember playing here as a little girl with Mum on holiday. I could walk then. I'm sorry.'

Declan reached for her hand and a tear welled up in his eye. He bent down and kissed the top of her head and squeezed her shoulder.

'I'm so sorry it's turned out like this for you, Sis,' he said.

'It's okay,' she said, 'I'll be fine. It was a bit emotional that's all. I was more missing, Mum, than missing my legs,' she said bravely. 'Go on now, don't fuss over me. I'll be fine.'

Declan knew his sister well enough to know when she wanted a moment to herself and Carl too smiled his concern and left her alone for the time being.

'Everything alright?' enquired Lily.

'Yeah, just fine. Old memories,' Declan explained.

'I was telling you about this man, Le Roux, who was convinced there was a link between the Black Death and this fountain,' Lily continued.

Carl looked across at Isabelle and she smiled, waving him off with a light finger movement as if to say, 'I'll be fine'.

'What was the link,' Declan asked. 'a cure for the Plague?'

'I hear your scepticism, but yes. That's what he believed.'

'Crazy old fool,' said Carl.

'A fool he certainly was not,' Lily objected. 'You can dismiss all the stories about sacred healing springs if you wish, but this song led people to this water source over four centuries ago. This very one, of that I'm certain. There's a date on it somewhere,' and Lily began to walk back a few steps away from the granite surround. 'And you can say it's a pure coincidence if you wish, but the date, there look – 1696, is extremely significant.'

'How's that, significant? In what way?' asked Carl.

'It put an end to three and a half centuries of incessant Plague outbreaks. That was it, the Black Death as people knew it, was over in France. And shortly after that, all over Europe too: the three and half centuries' old nightmare had ended.'

'And do you believe that?' asked Declan.

'It's not a question of believing it,' argued Lily. 'It's a fact. The question is, was it the sacred fountain that put an end to it?'

'That's just plain lunacy,' said Carl. 'Nobody can seriously believe that the Black Death came to an end because of a magic fountain.'

'That's a fair argument,' conceded Lily, 'but lunacy it is not. On the contrary, in times of sickness and this was pandemic don't forget, you'd be well advised to drink from a clean water source. You can believe what you like about the prophecies of Nostradamus for example, but fundamentally, Michel de Nostredame, that was his real name, was merely a physician or more precisely an apothecary.'

'Merely a physician? What's that supposed to mean?' asked Carl. 'I'd rather have listened to a doctor than a musician – no offence, Declan – if I thought I was at risk of catching the Plague.'

'Nostradamus was a famous physician during the time of the Black Death and oddly enough, he was continually urging people to drink clean water. He was famous for it. The same advice as this medieval musician, Olivier, was giving at that time,' said Lily.

'So Nostradamus may equally have been responsible for ending the Plague?' argued Carl.

'I'm not saying anybody ended the Plague,' Lily corrected. 'I'm merely conveying the beliefs of this philologist, Le Roux, of the nineteenth century.'

'A philolol... a what?' said Carl.

'A philologist,' said Declan, 'is someone who finds musicians more interesting than doctors'

'So this Le Roux bloke believed that a musician called Olivier, rid the continent of the Plague, is that what you're saying?' asked Carl.

'No. I'm not saying that either. What I am saying is that this scholar,' said Lily, choosing a different word than philologist for Carl's sake, 'Mr Erwan Le Roux's research led him to conclude that the Church had been, at that time, convinced that this Olivier chap, had rid the continent of the Black Death.'

'Do you believe that yourself?' asked Declan.

'No. Well not exactly. What I believe is that whatever the Church thought or didn't think four centuries ago, had absolutely no bearing on what it did or how it reacted,' explained Lily.

'Lily always has a way of explaining things so you understand less afterwards,' said Declan to Carl.

'I mean to say that the Catholic Church was on its knees at the time and so desperate, that they reacted because of what the people believed not because of what the Church itself believed: they had almost lost their entire European congregation.'

'Yeah, when you look at it like that, it's worse than the housing crisis of 2008,' said Carl. 'You'd do anything to win people's confidence back wouldn't you?'

'For people of our modern world, these would have been times of incomprehensible misery. There was a papal decree forbidding the body of a Plague victim to be left in any church overnight. Which meant you had to bury them the day they died. In many, many places there weren't even enough fit and healthy people to be digging the shallow graves. All of Europe was home to a people who had been battered again and again by as many as one hundred separate outbreaks of the Black Death over three and a half centuries. Can you imagine being so weak that you can barely hold a shovel? You know you're dying yourself. You've got a horse-drawn cart of bodies to dig holes for because the Church won't store them, and halfway through the job you realise that one of them is still alive; only just, but still alive. What do you do, wait? Or do you do the decent thing and put them out of their misery the only way you can – a shovel over the back of the head – before you bury them. What if it's your brother or your child? Some Plague victims were said to have lain down in their graves of their own volition, so desperate were they for the end to come. Many even dug their own graves.'

The two men, Carl and Declan, were silent as they tried to imagine such misery.

'This really happened. Our ancestors lived through this. There's an account in the lyrics to this man's song that tells of a woman who had to pull a body-laden cart to the cemetery single-handed – her husband unable to help her, for he had gone completely insane. The scene has become a famous painting, The Peste of Elliant, 1849, by Louis Duveau. It's now kept in the art museum at Quimper. The bodies she pulled in the cart were those of her seven children. Can you imagine such horror, such pain, such loss? You can't. One thing is for sure, you probably wouldn't bother attending mass the following Sunday.'

'That's horrific even just to think about it,' said Declan.

'You might not go to mass, but you might try to find a sacred fountain that people around you were singing about. Olivier not only described people's personal plights through his song and told his listeners exactly where to find the fountain, but he put his lyrics to a melody that everybody knew at that time – "he who thirsts come drink from the fountain".'

'Now that is clever,' admitted Carl. 'And it worked of course.'

'Now who believes?' Lily asked, mockingly. 'It is possible there were people that were helped,' he reasoned. 'After all, this spring flows from the foot of the highest hill in what is today the county of

Morbihan. If you imagine all the bodies everywhere, not just human, but those of farm animals no longer tended for. The waterways must have been riddled with pathogens causing all sorts of deseases: cholera, dysentery, typhoid to name but a few. At times, the land would have been littered with carcasses; the skies filled with flies and, of course, birds of prey,' continued Lily and pointing skywards over the peak of the Minez Du, he added, 'Look there now, you have a pair of red kites combing the landscape for food. You can hear their cry,' he paused for a moment and saw that Declan's sister too was now listening and looking up at the kites. 'Can you imagine the skies back then, the sound of so many on the wing?'

Just the thought of it made Declan shudder.

'That's revolting,' said Carl, 'and to think I used to like those birds.'

'What's interesting here,' added Lily, 'Is... well, you see how the granite carvings around the fountain are weatherworn? Just look underneath the coverstone – the ceiling if you like – and tell me what you see.'

'I've seen it before,' said Declan. 'I came here a lot with my Gran, and she showed me. It's a bird.'

'Let me see, Declan,' asked Carl.

'What kind of bird?' asked Lily. Carl looked underneath the granite-domed roof of the fountain saying,

'How do you expect us to be able to tell you what kind of...' but he stopped short. 'It could be a recent carving. I'm not suggesting it is, but that it's hardly worn. It's a bird of prey, isn't it? A kite?'

'Judging by the tail feathers,' said Lily. 'I think I'd agree with you on that one. Makes a bit of a change from your archetypal biblical-dove, wouldn't you say?'

'So if the Church was so concerned about losing its congregation, you said,' Carl butted in, 'then how come they built this keyhole shaped granite surround for the fountain?'

'This was not built by the Church, but by the people,' said Lily. 'The Church was, instead, building stone crosses and having them erected at the entrance to every single town, village and even every hamlet – no matter how small. Hundreds of thousands of them everywhere. And at what cost?'

'I've seen those,' said Carl. 'I've seen them while I've been driving around. They really are everywhere. What are they for?'

'You agree that it is an amazing undertaking? The crosses are there partly to celebrate the end of the Black Death, but also as a reminder to all, that it was thanks to the Church that it was quelled,' said Lily. 'Can you imagine trying to regain the confidence of a people after such suffering? It is said that during the early years of the Plague, during the fourteenth century, Muslims in the south were converting to Christianity in order to be saved. Well, three hundred and fifty years on with an estimated body count of over seventy-five million souls the world over, the Catholic Church was not exactly flavour of the month either.'

'If they were so worried about this fountain, why didn't they destroy it?' asked Declan. 'It would have been easier and cheaper than putting up all those crosses.'

'The Church couldn't have destroyed it; the water would still have flowed.' argued Lily. 'If they smashed down the stones, they would have upset a lot of people. What they did instead was far cleverer: they defaced it. Come closer and look at this date here and I will show you.'

Carl and Declan followed Lily right up to the front of the fountain.

'Here you are,' said Lily, 'another date. This one says 1702. It is universally accepted that the earlier of the two dates represents the date of the completion of the stonework surrounding this ancient and, you'd have to admit, mysterious spring. The later of the two dates has a more official look and as you can see, these carved numbers straddle the form of a religious cross. The newer date of 1702 and its cross are believed by many to be a Christian blessing of the fountain, but some believe it was the Church putting a claim on something that wasn't theirs to claim,' said Lily, persuasively. 'There are more inscriptions around the back. Come and see.'

Isabelle; having negotiated the granite flagstones with her new all-terrain wheelchair positioned herself to see the carving of the bird. It was, she thought, like a sort of Michelangelo ceiling but in miniature and sculpted, and, she reasoned, if you had never heard Lily's explanation, which she just had of course, you would never make any connection as to what that bird was doing there. She reached for her mobile phone to take a picture of it and leaning forward slightly she estimated the angle she would need for a bird-on-the-ceiling-selfie and clicked. Wrong angle. Isabelle tried again.

'Like you said for All Saints and Halloween?' asked Declan.

'Yes,' said Lily, 'and like churches being built on sites of worship marked by yew trees.'

'I've heard that too,' said Carl. 'Or was it the other way around?'

Suddenly Carl grabbed Declan's arm.

'What was that?' he said. 'Did you hear that?''

'Isabelle?' Declan screamed and already Lily had begun to move around to the front of the fountain in the direction of the sound.

Metal on stone and then a splash. Not followed by silence, but by panic and struggling.

Carl and Declan arrived running towards the front of the fountain simultaneously, but Carl, trying to stop too suddenly, lost his footing and slipped on the wet moss. What they saw shook them so badly that for a second, Declan, while Carl was still scrambling to his feet, stood frozen – unable to move.

'Oh my God! Oh my God! Help me get her out. We've got to get her out.'

Isabelle's front wheels had slipped into the fountain as she tried to take a picture of the bird of prey. She lay upside down, face first in the fountain. One back wheel was spinning, the other jammed hard against the granite uprights. Her paralysed legs were lifeless, but all three men saw Isabelle's arms thrashing from her shoulders.

Lily acted first, grabbing the crossbar at the rear of the seat and began to pull. Isabelle was still thrashing.

The wheelchair did not give as much as half an inch. Declan rushed to help and began to pull at a wheel. As the left wheel lifted, the right one slipped diagonally, sinking deeper into the rectangular opening of the fountain. The framework of Isabelle's wheelchair jammed even tighter. Isabelle was still flailing her arms and Declan could see her black hair floating up towards the surface of the water. He saw bubbles rising up. He was scared and panic-stricken.

'What the hell did you do that for?' yelled Carl. 'How are we gonna get 'er out now?'

'What did I do?'

'You pulled on the wrong bloody side you fool,' Carl screamed.

'And what the hell did you do?'

Isabelle was no longer moving. Lily bent down at the edge of the fountain and, with his sleeve rolled up to his elbow, reached under the water to grasp the axle of the right-hand wheel.

'Please lads,' he pleaded. 'help me to lift.'

Both men grabbed a wheel.

'Not yet,' said Lily. 'On the count of three: I'm trying to free up the chair. One, two and three... now pull.'

In sheer desperation, Declan and Carl pulled and pulled as hard as they could. Lily screamed out. The chair came flying out of the granite square. Both men fell over backwards onto the wet flagstones and Lily, whose hand had been caught between the granite wall just under the water and the central axel of the right-hand wheel, had also been struck over the head as the chair lifted suddenly and abruptly out of the water.

Carl and Declan scrambled to their feet and lunged once more towards the fountain to help Isabelle. Her body was now floating lifeless, her head down in the water. Lily was bleeding badly from his forehead.

'Give me your right hand,' yelled Declan to Carl, 'we're going to reach underneath her, underneath the water and lift her out from around her waist. You've got to help. Don't let go.'

Isabelle was light and the two men were able to lift her easily. As she came up, dripping water everywhere, she was deadweight. Declan suggested to Carl that they lie her down on the grass rather than on the flagstones and they carried her together to a grass lawn next to the keyhole-shaped stone structure. Neither man had done any first aid since school and were both at a loss as to how to react. Declan positioned Isabelle's body so that she was lying on her side in something that resembled the recovery position.

'Don't we have to get the water out of her lungs first?' asked Carl.

'I'm not sure.'

Lily, who had placed a handkerchief from his pocket over a deep cut to his forehead, was still bleeding from the wound to his knuckles.

'You need to administer mouth to mouth resuscitation,' shouted Lily to Declan and Carl.

'Put her on her back again then,' said Declan.

'You have to cover up the nose, don't you? And breathe in through her mouth,' said Carl.

Declan reached down, pinched his sister's nose and began breathing into her mouth with his lips placed over hers.

'That's good,' said Lily encouragingly, 'but you need to hold her chin down with your other hand and tilt her head gently backwards as you breathe.'

'Her chest moved,' said Carl. 'I think she's breathing.'

'Keep going,' said Lily, 'that's not her breathing, but you breathing for her. You've got to keep going.'

As Lily climbed over the stone wall surround, he knelt down next to Isabelle and began to carry out cardiac massage as he had learnt it through work, but using only his free hand – the other clutching his forehead with a handkerchief. Five pumps to the chest, let Declan breathe twice. He was certain it was something like this and he carried on.

'Don't stop breathing into her mouth,' Lily cried to Declan. 'Your sister's life depends on this.'

'I think she's already dead.' exclaimed Carl. 'We were too slow.'

'Call for an ambulance,' said Declan, panting between breaths.

'Why can't you call? I don't speak French,' Carl said.

'That's a good point he's got there,' said Lily.

'You carry on giving mouth to mouth then,' yelled Declan. 'And don't screw up – you heard what the man said.'

'I didn't screw up. You're the one that jammed her wheelchair into the fountain, not me,' said Carl.

'How bloody dare you. It's not her wheelchair anyway, it's the piece of shit you bought for her—'

'Breathe!' screamed Lily. 'You're worse than two schoolchildren.'

'Call 112,' said Lily to Declan, 'and ask for the SAMU. They're going to ask you a lot of questions so just answer them and don't hang up until they tell you to do so.'

There were lots of questions, but he answered them all as clearly as he could. The man on the other end of the phone verified Declan's number and finally told him he could end the call – they would contact him again if they needed any further information.

'They're on their way,' said Declan triumphantly. 'They are sending a doctor. She's going to be alright.' As he looked over at Lily and saw his expression, however, he realised, as if waking from a dream, that nothing was going to be alright. He walked over to Isabelle and saw her skin had turned a faded white. Her finger nails looked grey and as Carl raised his head between breaths, he saw that his sister's lips had turned a deathly blue.

Declan had no idea for exactly how long he stood there. He could remember that Lily had not stopped heart massage. He knew he had taken over from Carl, or at least he had offered to, yet he could not remember touching her cold blue lips with his own once he had made that call.

A distant siren. Blue flashing lights. Another car. An ambulance. Activity – pointless activity. Clunking doors. Velcro and zippers and clicking metal. A stretcher. Lift. Up. Into the ambulance. Somebody putting a dressing on Lily's head. A man's voice, a walkie-talkie.

'You're the man that made the call?'

'Oui.'

Siren. Blue lights. Silence...

34
So Much for Treasure

While Carl turned the Saab around to follow the ambulance, Declan sat on the stone wall, eyes to the floor, shaking his head slowly, remembering that they had all met up there at the fountain on his suggestion – to look for treasure. *What would he give now, never to have heard of the bloody treasure?* He felt sick and didn't want to drive. Instead, he gave directions to Carl. The ambulance had driven on ahead.

'Where now?' asked Carl.

'Sorry, Carl, left and then right in about a mile and a half. You'll see a sign for, Plevin.'

'Where's that?'

'P.L.E.V.I.N. It's Just the name of a village we have to go through.'

'Don't go all down in the dumps on me now, Declan. She's in good hands. Now if this had been in Ireland, you'd have reason to worry, but France has a reputation second only to the States. And even then...'

Declan suddenly wondered how Lily was. He hadn't even offered him a lift back to his own car.

'...because over the pond, while the rich get one set of services...'

He tried to remember seeing Filou. *Why was he thinking about the dog?*

'...so when you average it all out, France, for my money at least, is still...'

He checked his pocket for his keys. His pocket was empty. The flowerpot.

'...of course, Ireland and the UK don't look too good on the international league table. That's weird when you hear it said like that isn't it? An international league table of medical...'

Declan's memory was playing tricks on him.

'Can you remember if I handed my car keys to that man, Lilian Bouvier?'

'You did. Left here?' asked Carl. 'Declan, left here?'

'Plevin. Yeah. Left. No, no. Right. I said turn right. Didn't I? Sorry.'

'You haven't been listening to a single word I've said have you, Deck?' said Carl. 'Sorry. Forgot not to call you that, Declan, mate. Brother-in-law. Come on, cheer up. You'll see. We'll go in and see Is – they'll probably keep her in tonight and for the day tomorrow to monitor her, you know. Next day we'll get a metal detector and find that bloody treasure. We'll hire a JCB if we have to.'

Declan remembered: Lily would leave the Audi at the mill with the keys under the flowerpot by the window.

The hospital staff were clearly busy and communicated very little, so Declan and Carl felt more in the way than anything and finally decided to head back outside. Declan could not face Albert that evening. No, that was not fair. He did not feel he could cope with Monique's constant questions. Maybe that was unfair too. Carl was at a loss as to what to do, where to go, so Declan suggested they check into a hotel. Carl was keen to spend the night not too far from Carhaix hospital so that the two of them could go and visit Isabelle first thing in the morning. This was going to be tough on Carl, Declan thought. The term people used here, he was certain, was "in denial".

'There's the Noz Vad Hotel here in Carhaix,' Declan suggested. 'It's just around the corner from here and you can go in first thing in the morning for any news.'

'What does that mean?' asked Carl.

'Noz Vad?' Noz Vad meant "Goodnight" but Declan decided not to translate for Carl. 'I've got no idea,' he said.

'No, I mean what does that mean when you say, "*you* can go in first thing in the morning for any news?" Aren't you coming with me?' asked Carl. 'Cheer up Declan. I'm sorry about what I said earlier on. It wasn't true, you were great. Isabelle's gonna be fine you'll see.' Declan had seen her limp body being carried off on the stretcher. He had seen the helpless expressions on the faces of the doctor and the paramedics.

At the Noz Vad Hotel Declan asked for a room for two.

'We sharing a room, Carl? I don't know as I want to be on my own tonight. I'll be honest.'

'Deux lits, monsieur?'

'Excusez-moi?' asked Declan.

'Two separate beds or one big bed, monsieur?'

'Two,' said Carl.

'Voilà. This is your room key. 113. First floor, room number 13. Along the couloir on your left. Breakfast is from seven a.m. in the morning.'

'A.m. is always in the morning,' said Carl as they headed for the stairwell. 'It's as if he's learnt the language robot fashion, but can't understand what he's saying.'

'At least he speaks it, which is more than we can say about your French,' thought Declan, but again he said nothing,

Neither man slept well that night. Images of horror. Vivid scenes of Isabelle lifeless. Carl dreamt that Isabelle had spluttered up the water and sat up. Declan heard her say goodbye as she floated away. He awoke screaming. Carl was already sitting up on the edge of his bed.

'You okay, Carl?' Declan asked.

'You didn't wake me if that's what you mean,' said Carl. 'I was already awake.'

'I can hardly sleep either.'

'I've been thinking about yesterday,' said Carl. 'Thanks for translating all that stuff for me.' Carl was talking about the scene at the hospital: fiancé was not family and the doctors in A&E would give him no information, so he had to come and get Declan from the waiting room.

'What I've been thinking is,' Carl continued, 'they said they had taken her off to intensive care right? That means she's still alive, right?'

'I'm not sure,' admitted Declan. 'I can't honestly remember where the nurse told me they had taken her. I can't remember the exact word. I just said something to you. The first thing that came into my head. I think. I know I was under a lot of shock.'

'That's what I've been thinking about,' said Carl. 'I think I was under shock. I said to you by the fountain that she's dead. I knew it myself then really, I suppose. But I didn't want to face it. I still don't. I, I can't imagine a life without her. She's so small, always sat down like that. But she wasn't really, Declan. We used to make love. Normally, I mean. I know I shouldn't be talking to you about your sister like this, but I want you to know that she was always a complete woman to me.'

Declan thought about the night he heard of his parents' death and the joy he had felt when the doctor told him his sister had survived. Handicapped.

'That's really sweet, Carl. She was always a brilliant sister to me. Always so happy. That was largely thanks to you. You know that, don't you?'

'We still have to go to the hospital tomorrow morning, don't we?' asked Carl.

'Of course we do,' said Declan.

'Why? What for?'

'I don't know, Carl. We've got to go because we agreed we would.'

'She died, didn't she? By the fountain?'

Water takes many lives, but it saves many more. That's what Farouk had told him. Why hers?

'You don't want to answer,' concluded Carl. 'But I know now. I just wish deep down that I could say one last thing to her.'

'What would you say?'

'I don't know. I guess it's just an idea of something to hang on to – some hope.'

'If I could say just one more thing to her,' said Declan, 'I'd sing her a song. One hundred and fifty thousand million green bottles hanging on the wall...'

Tears streaming from his eyes, Carl looked at Declan, allowing himself just the hint of a smile,

'That's funny.'

'Try and sleep a bit if you can, Carl. I don't know as I will want any breakfast in the morning.'

'Me neither.'

'We can go down to have breakfast, or at least a cup of tea, as soon as it's light and then head for the hospital from here,' said Declan.

'It's past the first two roundabouts and halfway to the third,' said Carl, 'I checked the route on my phone late last night.'

'I thought now was still late last night,' said Declan.

'Let's try and get some sleep.'

'Yeah, you're right, Carl. Good night.'

'Or, "Noz vad" as they say in Breton,' said Carl.

The following morning, both men, having slept only bouts of a few minutes each, got up, showered and Declan headed for the self-service breakfast canteen to grab an orange juice and to wait for Carl who was having a shave. It was just seven a.m.

Carl came down to meet Declan, and together they decided to have a cup of tea before walking to the hospital. They could get there as early as eight, they had been told. These were not the visiting hours, but the time from when the front desk would be manned.

The hotel breakfast was generous, but neither man could face eating much, so instead, they opted for a pot of English breakfast tea and Declan brought back a small jug of fresh milk to the table along with a freshly baked croissant each.

At seven forty-five they paid their hotel bill and placed what little belongings they had brought with them into the boot of Carl's Saab. They began the six-minute walk to Carhaix hospital. Declan knew the way and Carl had memorised the route from Google maps. They walked in silence.

The hospital car park was surprisingly full. Staff, visitors, overnighters or people using the car park because it was convenient parking, Declan had no idea. There were two sets of sliding doors to the visitors' entrance of the hospital. They had been here the day before but had approached the desk through a series of corridors leading from A&E. The reception area seemed bigger than it had previously – just fewer people maybe.

'Can you do the talking again, Declan, please?' asked Carl.

'Of course.'

'Bonjour messieurs, qu'est-ce qu'il vous fallait?'

'Madame O'Leary, Isabelle? Elle a été admise hier soir aux urgences,' said Declan, nervously. 'On voudrait des renseignements s'il vous plaît.'

'Room 128 gentlemen.'

Both men looked at each other, staring.

'She's alive,' they said, simultaneously.

Searching around the foyer for a lift or a stairwell, they looked like a pair of clowns.

'The elevator is just along the corridor, there,' said the receptionist. 'Or you can take the stairs over there in the corner. First floor, room—'

'Twenty-eight. Yeah, we got it, thanks,' said Carl, and set off heading for the lift. He saw that Declan was opting for the stairs and turned around quickly to follow him.

'Doucement, messieurs.'

They leapt up the stairs taking three and four at a time and swinging around the metal bannister rail or pushing off the wall like excited children, before slowing to enter the corridor from the top of the stairs calmly and sedately.

A sign read, "Chambres 1-14" with an arrow left, and "Chambres 15-28" with an arrow right. Both men turned right and began walking briskly. At the end of the corridor, the last door on the right, they saw a plaque: "Ch. 28". The door was slightly ajar and they waited a second, uncertain of how to react. They could hear someone inside. Carl urged Declan to go in, by gesticulating a thin-air knock on the door with a knuckle of his right hand.

Declan tapped a "one-two-three" against the door using the back of a finger.

'Oui,' came a voice.

He pushed the door gently to let it swing open under its own weight.

'Isabelle?'

They were greeted by a woman probably in her thirties, Declan estimated. She was in the room on her own. She wore a white tunic fastened diagonally across her front from her right shoulder and there was a light blue beading all around the hem. Declan looked around the room. The woman was just finishing making up the bed as the two men walked in.

'Where's Isabelle?' asked Carl, seeing another door off to the right. This door too was slightly open. Carl eased it open a little and called out,

'Isabelle? You in there?'

Declan looked around the rest of the room quickly and saw only a cardboard box with some personal items he recognised as being his sister's; a headband lay on top of a cardigan and on top of that sat her gold wristwatch and a pair of earrings. "O'Leary", said the printed stick-on label. An empty bed. A box of personal belongings. Declan pointed to the name, his bottom lip trembling so uncontrollably that he was barely able to formulate his question.

'Madame O'Leary? Ma sœur?' he said to the woman.

'She is no longer with us,' she answered. 'Those are her things,' she added pointing to the box: 'Ses affaires personnelles. I have to prepare the room ready for another patient. Are you family? Of course, you said "your sister", I'm sorry.'

Declan looked at the box containing his sister's personal artefacts and couldn't believe the nonchalance of this supposed nurse.

'Where is she? Where is my sister? Where is Mme. O'Leary?' Declan yelled.

Neither man had heard the footsteps from behind them, so when the voice came:

'She's here,' Carl nearly fainted. Turning around to the sound of the voice, Declan just managed to stop Carl from falling and he too could not believe what he saw.

'You two look like you've just seen a ghost,' said Isabelle.

'You're alive. I can't believe it? You're walking. What have they done?' asked Carl.

'You're walking, Isabelle. How come you're walking? This isn't happening. It can't be happening.'

'I'm not walking very well,' Isabelle replied. 'I'm gonna have to get used to this all over again. I'd forgotten how hard it was.'

'She's alive, she's walking, Declan. Can I hold you?' said Carl.

'I was wondering when you were going to ask me that,' said Isabelle. 'Com' on, you can lean on me, Carl. I'll be your shoulder to cry on.'

Carl held her gently, but firmly. He was sobbing.

'What are you so unhappy about all of a sudden?' Isabelle asked. 'Thought you'd got shot of me did you?'

'I thought I'd lost you. We've been mourning you all night. You've no idea.'

'I haven't any idea, that much is true,' said Isabelle. 'There, there now.'

'So what happened?' asked Declan placing his hands on Isabelle's arms which she held around Carl's shoulders.

'I told you, I haven't a clue. The last thing I remember was trying to take a picture of that bird of prey at the fountain,' she said.

'You don't remember falling in?'

'No. The doctors here told me that I had fallen in, but I can't remember a thing.'

'So how come you're walking? What did they do to you?' asked Declan.

'I've no idea,' she said again. 'But that reminds me, there's a man here wants to speak to you. A doctor. Dr Khadir. Says he's a friend of yours. He's in the corridor behind me if you can get past this emotional wreck of a boyfr... fiancé I've got here in my arms.'

Declan eased past Carl and his sister, gently patting Carl on the shoulder and kissing Isabelle on the arm just above her elbow as he did so.

'Well done, Sis. Nice one.'

Out in the corridor, Declan recognised Farouk instantly and lunged to shake his hand.

'I've no idea how you did it, but you are a genius, Doctor,' said Declan.

'Nothing.'

'And modest with it,' added Declan.

'No, Declan. I mean I did nothing,' Farouk repeated. 'I saw your family name come up as there was talk of flying your sister to Rennes last night, but it never happened.'

'I don't understand,' said Declan.

'Neither do I,' said Farouk. 'I got here this morning about an hour ago.' Farouk was holding a clipboard in his left hand at about waist height and Declan had taken no notice of it until now. Farouk raised the clipboard up and sat it comfortably in the crook of his elbow.

'Look,' he said, 'this is the hospital report on your sister from last night.' And using the index finger of his right hand to point, Farouk talked Declan through the events of the night before. 'The ambulance team was astonished that they were able to resuscitate her en route to the hospital, but despite oxygen, she had stopped breathing again before they arrived. Once at the hospital, a team tried... it says here... there look, CPR for twenty-five minutes to reanimate your sister. They stopped and gave up at 20:25.'

'What's CPR?' asked Declan.

'Cardiopulmonary resuscitation,' said Farouk. 'Your sister was certified dead at that time – let's see, estimated time of death 19:50. Confirmed 20:35. Crossed out, and 20:40 entered as the time at which the team managed to reanimate her. A change of verdict, as it were.'

'So this is a miracle?' suggested Declan.

'No, not at all,' said Farouk, dismissively. 'Mistakes like this are extremely rare, but she had already been reanimated in the ambulance, she was very cold as well and her brain was continually supplied with oxygen. That's also thanks to you, Carl and your friend, Lilian, is it? It is possible that the team here in Carhaix succeeded in reanimating her as well without realising they had done so. All that, with a very low pulse, is possible although unlikely.'

'But how come Isabelle can walk now?'

'I'm a neurosurgeon, Declan, and although certain conditions exist which could explain what we've witnessed, I personally have not the slightest idea how this could have happened. At 3:45 this morning a nurse reported having assisted Ms O'Leary to the lavatory in room 128. Everything gets written down in hospitals. Nobody here or in the ambulance had been made aware that Isabelle would normally have been in a wheelchair. When I saw this report this morning, I had just missed the nurse, she had gone home. So I asked the doctor who had been monitoring your sister on and off all night if there could have been a mistake, because I knew your sister couldn't walk. Together, the doctor and I checked in her room. That was at 7:20 this morning and Isabelle stood putting her things into a box she had acquired from a hospital orderly.'

'So how can you explain it then?' asked Declan.

'As a surgeon, I cannot explain it. I don't know enough about your sister's particular case. I have heard of cases similar to this, but never witnessed anything quite like it myself. There exists a condition known as conversion disorder. While very rare, this condition is psychological and can affect a victim's sight, hearing, their ability to speak or even, in some cases, cause paralysis. The symptoms invariably develop as a result of some extreme emotional stress and this can include the loss of a loved one. In your sister's case, both her... well, your parents. My guess is that she must have witnessed an extremely violent accident that night. How old was she, fourteen years of age at the time?'

'The doctors in Ireland said back then, they could find no reason for her paralysis unless it was brain damage from the accident. Meddew-lar, does that make any sense?' asked Declan.

'The medulla oblongata,' suggested Farouk. 'Yes. That makes sense in as much as any damage may not have been obvious without the correct tests and that in the absence of damage to nerves, it could fall into the category of displacement disorder.'

'Can I ask you something Farouk? In all earnest?'

'Of course.'

'If, say, just saying, there was nothing physically wrong with my sister, could she have been putting this on? I mean inventing it? Pretending to be paralysed all these years?'

'Many people think of displacement disorder as a form of expression to compensate for an emotional need, but no I do not think so,' answered Farouk. 'Shell shock is an example of this disorder. A trauma so unimaginably stressful that the mind, in some cases, can convert the suffering into a physical disorder. Now also referred to as post-traumatic stress disorder. The truth is that all this theory stems from Freud and can, far too readily sometimes, be dismissed as nonsense. One should not forget either, that there are probably a lot of malingerers as well as genuine sufferers and such games can never help scientific reason.'

'So something really could have happened to her in that fountain then?'

'Oh yes, there's no question of that. Something definitely happened. The question is—'

'What?'

'I was going to say...' repeated Farouk, 'the question is, what do you want to believe?'

'I don't want to believe,' said Declan. 'I want to know.'

'Knowing everything, Declan, would be a miracle in itself.'

'Yes, but the fountain?'

'I have no idea. You're the one that led your sister there. Isabelle told me this morning, just before you arrived, that she discovered a family tree going back six centuries. Your family tree. Linking you to a man called, Olivier, also a musician, who lived from 1642 to 1715.

Making you a direct descendant of a man who, some claim, put a stop to the Black Death in Europe. That's what Isabelle believes.'

The first bit she got from Lily, Declan thought, but he hadn't known about the family tree.

'Jesus,' he exclaimed.

'Probably not,' said Farouk. 'Now I have a question I need to ask you.'

'Of course, anything, what?'

'I gave you my card with my mobile phone number on it. It's important that you keep that number safe. Do you still have it?'

'Of course. I've kept your card. Why?' asked Declan not just surprised, but flattered too.

'I've made a note of your number as well. If you change it, you absolutely must let me know.'

'Okay,' said Declan. 'Is it about my sister?'

'Your sister and much, much more. I can't explain easily, but one day soon, I may need to call you and I need to know that I can find you, quickly.'

'Of course, Farouk. I promise. And thanks again for being such a help.'

'It is I who should thank you.'

'Oh no,' said Declan. 'After all you've done for me?'

'Just the start. As I said, I may have to call you for... well, we'll talk more about all that come the day, but now I imagine you'll want to be with your sister.'

Declan checked his pocket quickly for Farouk's card, wondered for a brief moment just what day Farouk could be talking about, and turned around to face the doorway of room 128 again.

'Declan, tell her, will you. She's not coming to the fountain again with us. We're gonna find the treasure on our own – just you and me,' Carl insisted.

'Please, Carl. Don't ask me. I've been trying since she was fourteen to get her to do what she's told and I never managed it.'

'Well I'm not taking you there, and that's that,' said Carl.

'Give me the keys then. I've got my driving license. All I've got to do is try driving with foot pedals. I bet it's a lot easier than what I've had to do in my car.'

'Don't say I didn't warn you, Carl,' said Declan.

'Why do you want to go, Isabelle?' asked Carl. 'You've seen it now. We'll look for the treasure and we'll tell you where it was.'

'You'll never find it,' said Isabelle.

'How's that, we'll never find it?' Declan looked at Isabelle with a knowing look. 'You've found something in that chest haven't you? You bloody well know where the treasure is don't you?'

'Can I come then?' she asked.

'I told you, Carl – always gets what she wants.'

'Well please don't go anywhere near that water again,' said Carl.

'Yeah? Or what? What are you going to do?' asked Isabelle.

'That's called overplaying your hand, Carl,' said Declan.

'That's settled then,' said Isabelle. 'Let's go.'

Declan remembered that he had to pick up his car at the mill. Carl suggested they pass by there on the way back and offered to give his opinion on a possible sales value of their grandmother's property – based on his knowledge of what he'd learnt of the French property market of course.

Lily had been true to his word and left the keys under the flowerpot by the door. Isabelle hadn't wanted to get out of the car – she had said to Carl it would be a bit too sad to see where Grandma Le Dour had lived out her last days with no family around her and feeling guilty as she did, could not face up to that just yet.

Declan recovered the shovel from the boot of his car, and knocking off any dust or loose soil by giving it a quick tap to the ground, he placed it in the boot of Carl's Saab.

'No point in taking both cars up there, is there?' suggested Declan.

'No I suppose not. We'll be coming back here later won't we?' said Carl.

Declan got back into the Saab.

A short while later, they arrived in the village of La Trinité-Langonnet and Isabelle asked Carl to park a little distance from the fountain.

'I want to walk,' she said. 'I just want to walk.'

The three of them walked down the lane to the fountain and Carl insisted on taking Isabelle's regular wheelchair anyway, just in case she got tired.

At the fountain they stopped, and looking across towards the square pool where Isabelle had fallen in, they all stared in a moment's silence.

'We were so lucky,' said Carl. 'Not to lose you, I mean.'

'Come on then, Isabelle,' said Declan, 'Are you going to share with us what you've found in the chest?'

Carl recovered the shovel and began wielding it – the archetypal Irish navvy: 'Yeah, come on, Isabelle, tell us where to start digging.'

'I don't know,' she confessed. 'I was bluffing at the hospital.'

'What? Come off it, that's a joke right? The clues to knowing where the treasure is buried can be found in the chest. That's what the note said,' said Declan.

'If I hadn't told you something, you wouldn't have brought me here. So I made it up.'

'I might have known,' said Declan.

'Well, where is the chest then? Let's have a look,' suggested Carl. 'There must be a map or something.'

'It's still in your car,' said Declan. 'I've just seen it, it's on the back seat.'

'I'll get it,' said Carl. Just a few minutes later, Carl returned with the Saab, parked up and removed the wooden chest which he placed on Isabelle's wheelchair and positioned it a little closer to where his fiancé stood.

'One thing I meant to tell you about, Declan,' said Isabelle, 'Is our family tree. I found it in the chest. Family Le Dour it says. It goes back nearly six centuries. And guess who we're related to?'

'Don't tell me,' said Declan, 'Let me think. It's not that medieval singer-songwriter, Olivier, is it?'

'That African doctor told you, didn't he? Farouk? He's dishy.'

'Isabelle,' Carl protested.

'I'm just winding you up,' she said, 'but you're going to have to get used to other men looking at me now.'

'Men are always looking at you, Sis, you just never notice.'

'Ah, you are sweet, Declan.'

'But Farouk, the doctor, nah, he wasn't looking at you,' said Declan, teasing.

'Now you're being horrible,' she replied.

'So, hang on a minute,' said Carl, changing the subject, 'let me get this right: you two are supposedly related to that man Lily told us about – this medieval guy. The feller that sang that song that led people to this fountain? Is that right?'

'Olivier, he was called. And according to the family tree in this chest, we are direct descendants,' explained Isabelle. 'I'm going to sit down for a moment, my legs are getting tired. I'll get the family tree out and show you.'

Isabelle lifted the chest from the wheelchair, and placing it on the rear seat of the Saab, she removed the leather-bound document collection and sat down in her chair for a short rest with the documents on her lap.

'We really could do with studying this properly before we come here planning to dig,' said Carl.

'Or get a metal detector,' said Declan.

Carl began thrusting the shovel haphazardly through the turf into the soil as if expecting to strike a treasure chest.

'There's a car coming. Quick,' said Declan to Carl, 'hide the shovel. Just lay it down behind the wall or something. We're not allowed just to start our own archaeological dig around a public monument. There must be laws against it.'

Carl hid the shovel in a border behind the fountain and began an innocent visitor's tour of the monument.

The car, a white Citroën Berlingo, was approaching the fountain from the opposite direction – along a dirt track, rather than from the road – from the east rather than the west. The morning sun shone at such an angle that it was difficult to see through the windscreen; a clear view of the driver was impossible. The two men tried not to stare, but there appeared, at a casual glance, to be two people inside the vehicle. The van stopped and as the driver's door opened, a familiar dog, Filou, sprung out. A moment later Lily's head appeared above the roof of the cab. Declan turned to Carl making a gesture as if to say it was safe to recover the shovel.

'Morning, gentlemen...' Lily stopped suddenly as he walked around the front of his van and saw Isabelle. 'Good heavens. I'm... I'm so sorry. I didn't see you there.' Isabelle was sat once again in her wheelchair near the rear of the Saab, away from the road.

'I don't mean I'm sorry to see you, Isabelle, just surpr—'

'You're digging yourself a hole there, Lily,' said Carl, raising the shovel to make his pun clearer.

'You're no more surprised than anyone else here,' Isabelle admitted. 'They told me at the hospital that I was dead on arrival.'

'How come they let you out so early?' asked Lily, once again showing his surprise.

'They didn't let her out,' said Declan, 'she told 'em she was leaving.' Lily began to get the picture.

'I'm just looking through some of these documents, Lily,' said Isabelle. 'It's absolutely incredible what's in here, but I'll be honest, I'm a bit lost with it all. I can make neither head nor tail of any of it in terms of finding treasure. I haven't the faintest idea what I'm looking for.'

'Can you hold on just a moment?' asked Lily, 'I've got something in the back of the van for these two treasure hunters and then I'll come and have a look at it with you.'

Lily opened the back of his Berlingo and retrieved an object that looked a bit like a lawn strimmer.

'Olivier,' cried Lily. 'Or, Declan, whichever you prefer,' he added. 'I promised you the loan of my metal detector,' he held it up so the two men could see it.

Declan ran alongside one wall across the grass that flanked the keyhole-shaped stone surround of the spring and reached Lily in a flash.

'Oh excellent,' he said.

'It's not difficult to operate,' said Lily. 'Look, there's the on/off and you wear these on your head and when you hear buzzing and squeaking, sort of like a radio being tuned, you dig. It's a lot of trial and error really, but you soon get used to it. You can adjust the sensitivity here with this dial. It changes the depth you're searching to and the type or density of the metal you're looking for. In the beginning, you'll pick up bottle tops and all sorts, but you quickly get to know what you're likely to find from the noise and the settings. Here, try it,' he said.

Lily watched for a brief moment as Declan tried out the new toy. It became immediately apparent to him that Declan must have seen such a device being used somewhere before, for he began swinging it gently from side to side in front of him with the dish just centimetres off the grass.

Declan took off the headset to allow Carl to listen to what he had found.

'You can put yourselves on loudspeaker if you want...' suggested Lily. But they had already seen the button and the whirring-whining became audible to all.

'There's a volume control just next to that button—'

'Got it,' cried out Carl and the volume dropped to something less aggravating to onlookers.

'So you seein' this woman again then?' asked Carl out of the blue.

'I might be. Who told you anyway?'

'It's written all over your face, mate.'

'Like I said, I might be. I hope so. I'm supposed to call her tonight.'

Lily returned his attention to Isabelle and to something of a more academic approach to treasure hunting.

'So you thought I was dead, but just turned up on the off chance the lads would be here hunting for treasure anyhow?' said Isabelle, teasing. '*Business as usual*, was that it?'

'Not exactly like that, no,' said Lily, overwhelmed not just by Isabelle's evident good health, but by her cutting humour.

'I've always been a bit odd,' admitted Isabelle, 'but the inverse of "here today – gone tomorrow", has even taken me a bit by storm, I must confess.'

'I see what you mean, "here today – gone yesterday." Well I am thrilled you're still with us,' said Lily. 'Truly I am. Yesterday I believed we had lost you.'

'I was told that without you, I probably wouldn't be alive.'

'Well, I imagine that's a bit of an exaggeration,' said Lily, and then he began to explain why he had come to the fountain that morning. 'I initially went to your late grandmother's mill, but no one was there, so Filou and I began doing what we do best.'

'What's that?'

'Tracking,' said Lily. 'I saw car tracks so I knew a car had been and gone. It hadn't stayed long because the grass under the wheels where it parked, looked about the same as where it had driven in and out. I thought it might be a French left-hand drive car, because the only person to get out of the car, came from that side.'

'Yes that's right, only Declan got out, but you were wrong about the car.'

'No. Those were just my initial thoughts,' said Lily.

'So where did Filou come into all of this?' asked Isabelle, now fascinated.

'He sniffed the ground by the boot of the Audi and then ran off towards the back door of the mill. I watched Filou and went to look at the back door under the flower pot for some keys. They were gone. When I went to look at the back of Declan's car where Filou had first been, I saw footprints in the grass that I hadn't seen immediately.'

'Amazing,' said Isabelle, 'but then how did you know to come to the fountain?'

'That was easy. The shovel had been removed from the boot of the Audi so I assumed it had been taken to the other car. And probably placed in the boot. Right next to the rear of where the Saab was parked, was a small amount of clean dry soil where, I presume, Declan had tapped the spade to clean—'

'Hang on a minute,' Isabelle interrupted, 'how did you know it was a Saab and how did you know it was Declan that got out of the car? I'm confused.'

'Declan must have been the one who fetched the keys, because nobody else knew that he had asked me to leave them there, right?'

'Okay.'

'Not his car, because his car was already there,' Lily continued. 'The person who got out went straight to the flowerpot and to the boot of the Audi and nowhere else. Therefore it was not someone snooping about, an opportunist, but someone who knew exactly where to look and exactly what they were looking for.'

'Agreed,' said Isabelle, nodding. 'That's logical.'

'The shovel was missing from the Audi and had, I presumed, been put into the other vehicle. Now since it was not Declan driving, but definitely he who got out, then it must have been a right-hand drive car. The only other right-hand drive car driven by someone who Declan would have talked to about the treasure, was Carl. Therefore it was a Saab.'

'And why to the fountain?'

'To be honest with you, I was shocked that anyone could even contemplate looking for treasure, having just lost someone so close, in such a sudden and brutal manner. And I think it's fair to say that we all believed that you were – well... I'm just glad it turned out the way it did.'

'But you brought your metal detector anyway.'

'I first went home to get it. I don't live far,' explained Lily.

'Okay, Sherlock, you've passed the test.'

'You're a translator, if I'm not mistaken?' said Lily. 'It's just that after that interrogation, I think you might be in the wrong job.'

'What's your job, Lily?'

'Historian and treasure hunter.'

'I see too, that you're a modest man, Mr Bouvier. I loved your book by the way.'

'Thank you. That's very kind. I don't often meet people who have read it.'

'I was a bit unsure at the end if you were suggesting that the Plague was God-sent to defeat a corrupt Church, or whether Paganism has a miraculous at-one healing ability with the world around it.'

'I was discouraged by my editor to elaborate further on that point, for I had no conclusive evidence of any miracles. The story therefore only presents a hypothesis and I was encouraged to leave it open – obliged to change my original wording if I wanted my book in print. I suppose one could say that runs in my family.'

'You mentioned before, that the date on the fountain over there – what was it again, 1690 something?'

'1696.'

'I couldn't remember exactly. But you said it marked the last case of Black Death in France. Yet in your book you say that there was another outbreak in Marseille in 1720.'

'I didn't say it marked the last case of the Plague, rather that it put an end to three and a half centuries of incessant outbreaks.' Lily smiled a broad smile at Isabelle.

'What's tickled your fancy?'

'I'm just impressed, that's all,' said Lily.

'What about?'

'You really did read it. No, the thing with the outbreak of 1720 to 1722 was that quarantine measures were already in place and an infected cargo had been impounded. Corrupt merchants at that time, pressured and bribed state officials to relax regulations so that the infected cargo of garments was allowed to be unloaded and sold on. It was a man, a doctor named Peysonnel who alerted the authorities in Paris. Finally this outbreak, although it reached beyond the port and killed some fifty thousand plus people, it was the very first time in history that a ruling state became directly involved in order to protect the rest of the population during an epidemic – the world's first lockdown. That particular incident should never have happened and, in my book, I believe I did stress that point.'

'I see, yes you did – I remember that part as well. Didn't this doctor discover some amazing fact about corals or something?'

'Indeed he did. He discovered that these precious stones were not simply mineral deposits, but living creatures.'

'Talking of precious stones, do you think there is treasure here somewhere?' asked Isabelle.

'The kind of treasure I have spent all my adult life looking for is the paper kind, like the documents sitting in your lap. I'm not into precious metals and jewels.'

'So why are we here?' There was a cry of excitement from the two younger men.

'We've found a coin,' yelled Carl.

'It's nothing,' said Declan. 'Just an old half Franc.'

'Can you read the date on it?' asked Lily.

'No, it's too dirty and it's worn,' said Carl. 'Why? Could it be worth something?'

'Probably not,' said Lily. 'It's just that it could be silver or aluminium. If it's the latter, adjust the sensitivity of the machine and you'll only pick up more dense metals.'

'Like silver and gold?' asked Carl.

'Yes,' said Lily and then added under his breath, 'and old horseshoe iron.'

'You're toying with my brother and my fiancé, Lily. Can I ask you why?'

'They're loving it, don't you agree?'

'But you don't believe there is any treasure here, do you?'

'Oh yes I do. I'm certain there is treasure here. More certain now than I have ever been before.'

'Where is it then?'

'Do you remember that note your grandmother left you? Or left Declan to be more precise?'

'I have it here,' said Isabelle, quickly reaching in a pocket for her phone. 'Oh no. I forgot. I lost my phone. I think it must have fallen in the fountain yesterday.'

'I am sorry,' Lily blurted, 'that's the only reason I really came here. Or rather, went to the mill. I found your phone yesterday and wanted to return it to Declan. Well, to you now, as it turns out, happily.' Lily retrieved a mobile phone from his pocket and handed it to Isabelle. 'This is yours, I believe.'

'Yes it is, but I think it won't work anymore.' Lily watched, puzzled, as Isabelle deftly removed an earring and used it to open something on the side of her phone, before confirming that it was ruined. 'It doesn't matter. It was only a phone and I can remember what the note said anyway. It read:

'...gavout da Olier e hent betek an eil alc'hwez ha betek an teñzor meur,' she quoted, '...to show Olivier the way to the second key and the real treasure.'

'I am impressed,' said Lily, smiling.

'So what's the point? In Mamie's note, I mean.'

'I'm not toying. Nobody is toying. There is treasure here. In that note from your grandmother, you are not told to look for treasure, but for a second key,' said Lily.

'That's true.'

'That spring has been flowing from this hillside for hundreds if not thousands of millions of years,' he began. 'A long time before mankind was even on the planet, water flowed from here. Before any complex life form inhabited this earth, those rocks were being formed. Proterozoic, they are called – pre-life rocks – formed from sediment sinking to the bottom of shallow ocean shelves at the dawn of time. Some people, no, Isabelle, many people take me for a fool, but I believe that if life began in water, perhaps like this,' he said pointing to the fountain, 'then we need look no further for miracles. There is nothing as vital as clean water for the survival of the complex organisms we call life.'

'Oxygen perhaps?'

'There is oxygen in water. A whole lot of it,' said Lily.

'Oh yes, H_2O, of course.'

'What you mean though is air; another element of course. Oxygen is only a small percentage of air, but you don't need clues to find it, for it moves everywhere freely. Can you see how the water flows out of the square pool and into the granite channels? The channels themselves form the shape of a key and the whole key-shaped channel of flowing water has been placed in the middle of a stone surround built in the shape of a—'

'Keyhole,' said Isabelle, excitedly, 'That is the clue. The second key is the treasure. The water itself is the treasure.'

'It may sound stupid to you that it should be that simple, but I, along with some of my ancestors knew about this spring, and I believe too, so did some of yours. Yesterday, after they took you away in the ambulance, I went to wash my face in the fountain. You won't be aware of this, but your wheelchair struck me in the face as we pulled it out trying to save you. I ended up with a gash on my forehead that the ambulance driver said I should have stitched up. He put a dressing on it and I said I would see myself to the hospital.'

'So what happened? I can't see anything: no cut, no bruising.'

'I didn't go. Instead, after everyone left, I took the dressing off and washed my face in the fountain. That's when I saw your phone and fished it out.'

'So what happened to your head, it can't have been that bad after all can it, if it didn't need stitches?'

Using thumb and forefinger, Lily indicated a distance of about six centimetres across the right side of his forehead.

'All this was a deep cut, open and bleeding yesterday. And now it's gone.'

'What did Carl and my brother say?'

'They haven't even noticed. People don't always see unless they look,' Lily said.

'You think the water healed you?' asked Isabelle.

'No, I don't,' said Lily. 'I have been coming to this fountain for decades and often washed in it. Tried it, tested it, so to speak. Looking for proof of that miracle. How did it cure people of the Plague, if it did? I always believed in the miracle of the tale as told by the song, but it always failed me. I now believe the fountain healed me yesterday, because your brother led me here. I don't think it would do it again today. I know this may sound completely crazy to you, but I believe that your brother had a calling to come to the fountain in the same way as your medieval ancestor had a calling during the Black Death. I believe your brother is the key, Isabelle. I believe Declan is the treasure.'

'I don't think you're crazy at all,' said Isabelle. 'Hold this will you? I'm going to show you something.' Isabelle held out the leather-bound manuscripts to Lily. He took the documents and watched, his mouth open in astonishment, as Isabelle stood up slowly out of her wheelchair and carefully walked towards him.

'The doctors told me that my paralysis might have been psychological all along.'

'And the cut on my forehead? I think we've found our treasure, Isabelle,' he said, nodding in Declan's direction, 'he's right there.'

'But how can that be? Does he know?'

'He will do one day. Your grandmother knew and probably your mother too. It would seem, rather sadly, that they died before they were able to convey to him all that they had intended. Still, he'll find out one day. They will look for him.'

'They? Who's they?' asked Isabelle.

'They, are the other elements. They'll find him. They have to.'

Arctic-blown wave crests began to level – smooth and polished as a car roof. From deeper waters, bubbles rose and burst; sparkles of orange, white and pink reflecting an autumnal evening sun. A shadow streamed upwards from under the keel and the steady rocking of the boat altered, first stationary, then tipping. As the water's surface heaved into a dome, like the back of a giant shining spoon, frenzied krill leapt into the air. With no warning to the untrained eye, the surface broke, the water seemed to boil and a humpback whale lifted so high out of the water that it cleared the height of the boat's twelve-metre forward mast.

An eagle angled its two and a half metre wingspan to avoid the splash. The skipper had seen Aaron adjust his flight path, felt the changing movement of the boat and anticipating why, had turned her attention to the water's surface to see exactly where the whale would breach. Aaron was a white-tailed eagle that had never migrated; overwintering in Iceland, just waiting to meet the right mate. From the displacement of water caused by the whale, Cora guessed it was Varða resurfacing after her deep dive of thirty-seven minutes. She made a mental note. The whale's tail flukes were raised, displaying a unique pattern on her underside. Click, click, click; some quick shots – definitely Varða – a large female of unknown age, forty maybe, at a guess. Cora had shared today, her birthday, with Varða for the past four years. Varða's real age was her business as was Cora's her own.

Varða landed flat on her back, shooting a sea spray across the sparse open deck of the clinker-built ketch. Instead of turning her back to the wash to shield her face behind the hood of her sun-bleached, red, Henri Lloyd sail jacket, Cora faced the drenching full on, laughing; her mouth wide open until just before the freezing sea water stung her cheeks. Smiling, she drew the clinging strands of silver-blond hair from the sides of her face. She felt alive.

Her peace was disturbed, ship's radio.

'Cora?' said a man's voice, 'It's me, Farouk. Happy birthday. You still in the land of fire and ice?'

'Thank you, that's sweet. Yes, north coast of Iceland. I've had a wonderful day.'

'I have some exciting and long-awaited news.'

'No. You're serious right, you've found him?'

'I've found him – our Water Man.'

Don't miss out!

Visit the website below and you can sign up to receive emails whenever GERARD DUNMOORE publishes a new book. There's no charge and no obligation.

https://books2read.com/r/B-A-BPTJ-PYCDB

BOOKS 2 READ

Connecting independent readers to independent writers.

About the Author

Gerard Dunmoore was born in Manchester in 1965. After studying engineering at Hertfordshire he moved to Berlin where he was working and studying when the wall came down. He has an MBA from Rennes School of Business. Today he lives and teaches in Brittany, France.

He began writing short stories more than thirty years ago and contributes regularly to a poetry section in a regional monthly publication. *The Water Man Legacy* (genre: speculative fiction – 90,000 words) is the first in a series titled *Tides of Time*. The sequel, *Wind and the Willows*, will be published later this year – spoiler alert: it has little to do with waterway-wildlife camaraderie.

Set in the heart of Brittany, *The Water Man Legacy*, Gerard's debut novel, entwines surprising and fascinating nuggets of local history. It is an action thriller, pacey and full of suspense. Initial reviews describe it as:

"–an emotional rollercoaster of laughter and tears."

"–a novel not be read in a public place!"

This novel promises to take you on a journey. Enjoy it.

Milton Keynes UK
Ingram Content Group UK Ltd.
UKHW010618280723
425939UK00004B/183